PUFFIN BOOKS

TREBIZON: REBECCA'S FIRST YEAR

Rebecca Mason, frightened and alone, sets off to the West Country to start her first term at Trebizon, one of England's most famous girls' boarding schools. Caught up in the whirl of school life, however, homesickness is soon forgotten and she quickly becomes great friends with Tish Anderson and Sue Murdoch. But conflict with Elizabeth Exton, the sixth-form editor of *The Trebizon Journal*, over a poem she has written threatens her ambitions to be a success.

In Rebecca's second term at Trebizon, Tish seems determined that Sue should compete for the music scholarship and not captain the hockey team. Rebecca's loyalties are divided as she desperately tries to reconcile her friends. And in the summer term mystery surrounds the handsome new maths teacher who shows no interest in helping Rebecca with her maths, which could separate her from her friends if she doesn't do well.

The first three of these highly popular books are here together in one volume covering Rebecca's first thrilling year at Trebizon.

Anne Digby was born in Kingston upon Thames, Surrey, but has lived in the West Country for many years. As well as the Trebizon books she is the author of the popular *Me, Jill Robinson* stories.

Books by ANNE DIGBY

BOYS v. GIRLS AT JUG VALLEY JUNIORS
THE HEADMASTER'S GHOST AT JUG VALLEY JUNIORS
HANDS UP! AT JUG VALLEY JUNIORS
THE PHOTOFIT MYSTERY AT JUG VALLEY JUNIORS

The **TREBIZON** stories

FIRST TERM AT TREBIZON
SECOND TERM AT TREBIZON
SUMMER TERM AT TREBIZON
BOY TROUBLE AT TREBIZON
MORE TROUBLE AT TREBIZON
THE TENNIS TERM AT TREBIZON
SUMMER CAMP AT TREBIZON
INTO THE FOURTH AT TREBIZON
THE HOCKEY TERM AT TREBIZON
FOURTH YEAR TRIUMPHS AT TREBIZON
THE GHOSTLY TERM AT TREBIZON
FIFTH YEAR FRIENDSHIPS AT TREBIZON

JILL ROBINSON stories

ME, JILL ROBINSON AND THE TELEVISION QUIZ
ME, JILL ROBINSON AND THE SEASIDE MYSTERY
ME, JILL ROBINSON AND THE CHRISTMAS PANTOMIME
ME, JILL ROBINSON AND THE SCHOOL CAMP ADVENTURE
ME, JILL ROBINSON AND THE PERDOU PAINTING
ME, JILL ROBINSON AND THE STEPPING STONES MYSTERY

ANNE DIGBY

TREBIZON:

REBECCA'S FIRST YEAR

PUFFIN BOOKS

PUFFIN BOOKS

Published by the Penguin Group
Penguin Books Ltd, 27 Wrights Lane, London W8 5TZ, England
Penguin Books USA Inc., 375 Hudson Street, New York, New York 10014, USA
Penguin Books Australia Ltd, Ringwood, Victoria, Australia
Penguin Books Canada Ltd, 10 Alcorn Avenue, Toronto, Ontario, Canada M4V 3B2
Penguin Books (NZ) Ltd, 182–190 Wairau Road, Auckland 10, New Zealand

Penguin Books Ltd, Registered Offices: Harmondsworth, Middlesex, England

First Term at Trebizon first published by W. H. Allen 1978; *Second Term at Trebizon* and *Summer Term at Trebizon* first published by W. H. Allen 1979
Published in separate volumes in Puffin Books 1988
This three-in-one volume published in Puffin Books 1992
10 9 8 7 6 5 4 3 2 1

Printed in England by Clays Ltd, St Ives plc
Filmset in Ehrhardt

FIRST TERM AT
TREBIZON

CONTENTS

ONE

GOING AWAY TO SCHOOL

'Have a good first term, Rebecca. Try and be happy.'

'Remember, this is a wonderful chance for you. And you'll soon make new friends.'

'Yes, Mum. Yes, Dad.'

Rebecca's voice was flat. It was a Tuesday morning. Her trunk had been loaded into the luggage van. Her hand luggage was up on the rack in an empty compartment somewhere down the corridor. She had deliberately dodged the carriage reserved for new girls.

Now she was in the corridor of the train, leaning out of the window while her parents, on the platform below, kissed her goodbye.

'Off you go!'

They stepped back as the train started to move away. What a forlorn little figure their daughter looked, half-drowned in her brand new school cape, an arm reaching out of it to wave. The breeze was wrapping her fair hair round her face.

Rebecca thought how grand some of the people on the platform looked, seeing their daughters off on the train, and how small and round and homely her own parents looked in comparison.

'I hope you like it out there –' she called, her voice hoarse. She pushed her hair out of her eyes with the back of her hand, brushing away a tear at the same time.

'We'll be back in England for Christmas,' called her mother. 'We'll all be together again. Write to us!'

'And write something for that school magazine!' shouted her father.

Rebecca waved as hard as she could; the platform seemed to be sliding rapidly backwards, her parents getting smaller and smaller. It was as though all her past life were slipping away, a dreadful feeling.

'Get your head in!'

Rebecca did not hear, but just kept on waving. By leaning out as far as she could, she could still see them – little pin people – way back there on the platform. They were going, going . . . gone.

'Are you deaf?'

Somebody grabbed the back of her dark blue cape and pulled her in and then, getting their fingertips under the top metal edge of the window, slid it up and snapped it shut.

'Can't you read? You're not supposed to lean out of the window,' said the voice.

Her eyes blurred, Rebecca could not see the person properly, except that she was a girl in a checked coat. As far as Rebecca could tell she had nothing to do with either British Rail or Trebizon School. She had her back to her now as she bent down to pick up a large black bag that she had dumped down in the corridor of the train.

'Mind your own business!' said Rebecca, angry and miserable.

The girl stood up, holding the bag, and turned round to

face Rebecca. Her brown eyes had narrowed down to frightening slits. Her whole appearance was striking, indeed, overpowering. She had long black wavy hair, bony features and a rather hawk-like nose. She towered above Rebecca for she was almost grown-up and very tall and elegant. She wore her beautifully cut tweed coat open and with graceful flair. Under the coat she was wearing a blue skirt, cream blouse and striped tie, and a navy v-necked jumper. This was the winter uniform of Trebizon School, the same outfit that Rebecca herself was wearing. Sixth Formers could wear a winter coat of their own choice in place of the regulation blue cape, and this girl was a Sixth Former.

'Did you say something to me?'

Rebecca hung her head, cheeks hot with embarrassment. She felt very small and insignificant in front of this imposing figure.

'I was rude. I'm sorry.'

'What's your name?'

'Rebecca Mason.'

'Ever been away to school before?'

'No.'

'Heard of prefects?'

Rebecca's spirit sank even further.

'I'm both a prefect and school officer, if that means anything to you. My name is Elizabeth Exton. If you don't mind me saying so, you'd better learn a few manners if you want to fit in at Trebizon.'

'Elizabeth!' shouted a girl from the other end of the corridor. She, too, was tall and grown-up looking and was wearing a camel-hair coat over her school uniform. 'Come on! I've found a free table in the Buffet Car!'

Elizabeth Exton crooked her arm round the bulging black

bag, rather like a doctor's, and hugged it close to her as though its contents were very important.

'Okay, Emma. Coming!'

She moved off along the swaying corridor without looking back.

Rebecca wondered where she had heard the name Exton before, and what was in the black bag, and just what was meant by a 'school officer'. But she didn't really care. She turned and pressed her forehead against the cool glass of the corridor window and watched the railway sidings slipping past.

It seemed a bad omen, somehow, getting on the wrong side of a prefect the minute she had set foot on the train. So she would have to learn some manners if she wanted to fit in, would she? 'Rotten boarding school!' she thought savagely. She had no desire to go to Saudi Arabia with her parents, now that her father had been posted there by his firm. She knew that was impossible, anyway. But if only she could have stayed in London, at her day school, with all her friends!

'As the firm is paying, we may as well have the best,' Mr Mason had told his wife, trying to sound nonchalant, although in reality he was still rather stunned by the news of his promotion, and the fact that full boarding school fees for his daughter went with it. He had been to a very ordinary school himself. 'Trebizon is the one with the big reputation. They turn out musicians, artists, novelists – all sorts. If they've got any talent a place like that brings it out.'

'We could never afford it ourselves,' agreed Mrs Mason, though not without a pang. 'It's on the coast, too. It's the chance of a lifetime for Rebecca, and I'm sure she'll make the most of it.'

It was true that Rebecca wanted to be a writer when she grew up, and she had already won prizes in poem and essay competitions. It was also true that her new school produced a magazine each term, *The Trebizon Journal*, that was quite breathtaking to look at – a copy had been sent to her parents with the school prospectus. Not only was it thick and glossy, like a real magazine, but it had some really good stuff in it, and all the writing and art work was done by girls at the school.

'See what it says here,' her father had said, holding up the Principal's Summer Newsletter, which had been tucked in a pocket at the back of the prospectus with a lot of other bits and pieces. He quoted from the Newsletter: 'It has long been a tradition at Trebizon that the girls who rise to the position of Editor of our own *Trebizon Journal* seem to go forward to carve out for themselves a distinguished career. We are sure that the past year's Editor, Mary Green, who has been offered a post on a national newspaper, will prove no exception to this rule.'

Standing in the train's corridor, it suddenly came to Rebecca where she had heard the name Exton before. Wasn't Fred Exton a well-known business tycoon, always 'taking over' small companies? Hadn't there been something about him, in the same Newsletter, in connection with the school magazine?

'Until recently, it looked as though increases in printing and paper costs would force us to publish *The Trebizon Journal* once a year in future, instead of once a term. Thanks to the generosity of a parent, Mr Fred Exton, to whom we owe a deep debt of gratitude, the magazine is to continue on its present termly basis and a tradition that goes back fifty years thus remains unbroken.'

Rebecca remembered her father giving a chuckle.

'Freddie Exton, eh? Glad to see he's been putting his ill-gotten gains to some useful purpose.' Later, taking his daughter's hand, he had said, 'Who knows, Becky? You might become the Editor of that magazine yourself, one of these days.'

Yet none of this could make Rebecca feel enthusiastic about coming to Trebizon. As she watched the factories and housing estates of west London racing past, sombre on the grey September morning, she felt only the dull ache of homesickness.

Suddenly she heard laughter. Two girls came rushing into the corridor from the next carriage, laden with hand luggage, their blue capes flapping. They looked about Rebecca's age.

'Shove over!' said the first one, a girl with jet black curly hair, turned up nose and an enormous laughing mouth.

Rebecca shrank against the window, her back firmly turned, as first the dark girl and then her friend, who had sandy-coloured shoulder-length hair and spectacles, squeezed past her.

'Thanks!'

'Let's find a compartment, Tish,' said the sandy-haired one. 'We've shaken her off.'

'I suppose even Roberta Jones can take a hint.'

With much giggling and scuffling of feet they made their way along the corridor, peering into compartments as they went.

'I could have screamed when she walked in!' Rebecca heard the dark-haired girl called Tish say. 'Imagine having to listen to *her* voice all the way!'

'Look!' There was a whoop of joy. 'An empty one!'

The door of a compartment slid to and Rebecca sighed. The corridor was silent again now; just the sound of the train rushing over the rails. Seeing those two, obviously close, reminded her of another dreadful fact. She was being pitched into Trebizon in the Second Year. Everyone else would have been there a whole year; they would all be fixed up with friends, in twosomes and threesomes, like her and Claire and Amanda, the two friends she had left behind in London.

Rebecca felt weary. She must find her compartment, sit down, read a book or something – anything to take her mind off things. She walked down the corridor, trying to remember where she had left her hand luggage. The first three compartments were all occupied – it must have been about the fourth one along where she had left her things.

She peered into it and found herself staring directly in at the two girls who had passed her just now. They had taken over the entire compartment, sprawled out on the seats, amongst a scattering of belongings: hockey sticks, a violin case, and carrier bags that spilled out sweets, books and oranges. The black-haired girl looked up and saw her and seemed to scowl.

Her cheeks hot, Rebecca quickly turned on her heel and hurried back along the corridor the way she had come. She stood once more by the window and stared out, feeling confused. Had those two taken over her compartment? It looked like it.

'Hey!' The black-haired one had slid back the glass door and stuck out her head, calling to Rebecca. 'Thought you were somebody else. Are you lost? There's a denim bag and a hockey stick in here, up on the rack.'

Slowly, Rebecca retraced her steps and entered the compartment. She looked up and saw her bag and then sat down in the corner by the door and took a paperback book out of the deep pocket inside her cape.

'You're new aren't you? First or Second Year?'

'Second.'

'Like us. You'll be in Juniper then. I'm Ishbel Anderson. Tish for short, and this is Sue Murdoch.'

'Hallo,' said Rebecca politely, then opened her book and started to read.

'Do you have a name?' The huge grin came again. 'Or did your parents forget to give you one?'

'Rebecca Mason,' she replied, without even glancing up from her book.

TWO

ALL ABOUT THE MAGAZINE

Rebecca read her book with cool concentration. If these two thought that they had to make conversation with a new girl, just when they had escaped from this Roberta Jones person, they could think otherwise. She could look after herself perfectly well!

After one or two curious glances in her direction, the two friends settled down soon enough to a long, low buzz of conversation that seemed, to Rebecca, all set to last for hours.

'Hallo! Rebecca Mason? I've been looking for you!'

Sliding back the door, a woman put her head into the compartment. She wore chunky jewellery and a thick blue jumper with a high neck and a light grey coat; her hair was blonde, streaked with grey, and swept back off her face and she had clear blue eyes and a friendly smile.

'For me?' asked Rebecca guiltily, looking up from her book.

'Yes, I'm Miss Morgan, your House Mistress. That means –' her nose screwed up as she laughed, 'that I'm supposed to be looking after you on the train. We've got a special carriage for new girls – which makes it sound as though they're infectious, doesn't it? – so they can begin to get to know one another before they get to Trebizon. But you've managed to avoid us nicely!'

'I – I'm sorry,' began Rebecca. She rather liked this person. 'I did see them, but they seemed younger than me, and I thought –'

'Quite right, they are younger. All First Years. And you're going to be a Second Year, aren't you? Like Ishbel and Susan here. As a matter of fact you'll be in the same form as them, too, you're down for II Alpha. And naturally you'll be in Juniper together.'

Juniper House, by far the largest boarding house at Trebizon, was where all girls lived for their first two years there. Miss Morgan came further into the compartment, gripped the luggage rack to steady herself, and raised her voice above the noise of the swaying train as it rushed into a tunnel.

'This is very suitable. Ishbel, Susan, please look after Rebecca for the rest of the journey. Her parents are going to live in Saudi Arabia and she's never been to boarding school before. Rebecca – you'll be comfortable here, so I won't ask you to move.'

She went out into the corridor, leaving an awkward silence.

Rebecca couldn't stand it. She stood up and put her book in her pocket and felt for her money. It made her feel uneasy that Miss Morgan had told these two something about her. She would go for a walk down the train.

'Going somewhere?' asked Tish.

'Just to get a coffee in the Buffet Car,' replied Rebecca.

'D'you want us to come with you?' asked Sue.

'I know I've never been to boarding school before,' said

Rebecca lightly, 'but I think I can find my way around a train.'

The Buffet Car was very nearly full. As Rebecca made her way down the central gangway, looking for an empty seat, she passed two senior Trebizon girls in navy jumpers and blue skirts, with a table to themselves. She recognized the prefect, Elizabeth Exton, and the girl called Emma. They had taken their coats off now and put them up on the rack.

They seemed settled there for the journey. The big black bag was open and up on the table. The two girls' heads were bent close together over some pictures that Elizabeth had spread out on the table. Although Elizabeth was shielding them, rather possessively, Rebecca caught a glimpse of some exquisite line drawings of birds, on artists' pasteboard, beautifully coloured in.

'Elizabeth, some of this stuff's sensational,' she heard Emma say. 'You've been really busy in the holidays.'

'I've met some super people, I can tell you.'

Rebecca found a seat, opposite an elderly gentleman, and ordered a coffee from a steward in a white coat. The coffee arrived in a white carton, with a lid, the cream in a miniature carton beside it; sugar lumps were in a bowl on the table, each lump separately wrapped.

The coffee tasted delicious. Looking out of the window, Rebecca saw rolling green fields, some houses and a church spire. They had left London behind and every minute took the high-speed train further west, towards Trebizon School and her new life.

'Elizabeth Exton must be an artist,' thought Rebecca. No wonder the prefect and her black bag appeared inseparable; it must contain all her holiday work. Was she specializing in Art perhaps, and hoping to go on to one of the big Art

Colleges? The thought that she could produce work like that made her seem an even more imposing and elevated person.

But before long, Rebecca fell to thinking of home, the town house in London where she had been born and brought up, and the sunny little bedroom with all her things in it. It would be strange sleeping in a dormitory with a lot of other girls and she shivered to think of her home, let out to strangers for many months of the year.

'Cheer up,' said the elderly gentleman. 'It won't be as bad as you think. My wife was an old Trebizonian, had the time of her life there. I expect you will, once you settle in.'

'Do I look new, then?' asked Rebecca in surprise.

'Brand new,' he replied, with a smile. 'So does the uniform.'

Rebecca made her way back down the train, feeling slightly more cheerful. For a few moments she had been made to feel as though she had joined a rather nice club, and one that had been going for a long time.

The door of her compartment was open and there was a large girl in there, standing over the other two, hanging on to the luggage rack with one hand and waving some sheets of paper in the other. The girl had brown plaits and a red, rather boyish face, and she was wearing the school uniform, without a cape.

'Honestly, Tish, I'm not asking you to read them this very minute – just put them in your bag –'

Rebecca decided to take her cape off, too. She rolled it up and climbed up on to the seat to put it on the luggage rack, at the same time taking a good squint at the top sheet of paper.

'My Dog' – a poem by Roberta Jones it said at the top.

'For the last time, Robert,' Tish said wearily, 'there is no point in putting them in my bag, as I haven't the slightest intention of reading them –'

'Daddy says they're the best poems I've ever written –'

'That's not saying much!' observed Sue Murdoch.

'And they *deserve* to go in the school magazine,' carried on Roberta, who really seemed to have a thick skin. 'In fact, he says they're a lot better than some of the things he's seen in the *Journal*.'

Rebecca settled back in her seat, rather enjoying this. So this was the Roberta Jones they had been trying to escape from! She could see their point of view.

'Look, Robert, I'll be holding a magazine meeting in the next couple of days and calling in all contributions. I'll read the poems then, along with the other stuff people have done in the holidays, and if we all agree with Daddy, they'll be chosen.'

'Of course, if we don't agree with Daddy,' said Sue, 'they won't.' So saying, she got up and took Roberta's elbow and pointedly escorted her out into the corridor.

'You'd better go – we're looking after a new girl – think she's got a headache,' she whispered loudly, and gave the big girl a push. ''Bye!' Then she slid the door firmly shut and threw herself down on her seat and laughed, looking across at Rebecca. 'Hope you didn't mind my saying that!'

'No,' replied Rebecca. But she was staring at Tish, almost eaten up with curiosity. She had hardly been able to believe her ears.

'Are *you* the Editor of *The Trebizon Journal*?' she asked.

The huge grin that was never long absent from Tish's face came back. She and Sue moved along to be opposite Rebecca.

'Good heavens, no!'

'Tish is the Magazine Officer for Juniper,' explained Sue. 'Mainly because she's good at English and very fair and nobody argues with her. It's like being an editor, only on a minor scale. At the start of term, she takes in all the contributions from the House and sifts through them, and asks people's opinions. Then there's another meeting and the best ones are passed round and we all vote –'

'And then two or three are chosen,' explained Tish, 'and the best of the lot has a gold star put on it, which means it's bound to go into the *Journal*. All the Houses do the same. It saves the Editor a lot of work, and makes it all democratic as well.'

'Who is the Editor?' asked Rebecca.

'A girl called Elizabeth Exton, way off in Upper Sixth.'

'Elizabeth –' exclaimed Rebecca. 'But her father –'

There was a moment's silence then, and the two friends looked at one another. They seemed almost embarrassed.

'You know about that then?'

'Well, yes. There was something about it in the Newsletter that was sent to us, with the school prospectus and all that stuff.'

'We think it looks pretty bad,' said Tish. 'And it's almost as bad as it looks! It wasn't that Freddie Exton attached any conditions when he offered to bale out the magazine. It's just that the cheque came through at the end of last term, just before the girls who were going to be in the Upper Sixth this year held their meeting to elect the new Editor.'

'They all knew how much Elizabeth wanted it,' said Sue, carrying on the story, 'and they just voted her in. They probably felt they couldn't do anything else. After all, without her father, there wouldn't be a *Journal* any more, or not as we know it, and now it can carry on for years.'

'But some of us thought she should have declined, all the same,' said Tish. 'Audrey Maxwell would make a much better Editor.'

'It was a proper election, though,' said Sue, 'and they

didn't *have* to vote for her. They must think she'll be pretty good.'

'She'd better be. It's the Golden Jubilee this term – a special issue. A lot of people will be looking at it.'

Rebecca now realized the full significance of Elizabeth Exton's big black bag. She realized she wasn't an artist, after all.

'I've met her,' she said. 'I think she's been working on it all over the holidays. I saw her down in the Buffet Car. She was showing someone some work, some beautiful drawings.'

'She must be keen,' frowned Tish, slightly perplexed, 'if she's been meeting some of the Seniors in the holidays and getting things together even before term starts. It goes to press early in the term, but the Editor doesn't usually collect stuff in till we all get back to school, the way I said.'

'I heard her say she'd met some super people.'

'I expect she has.' Tish wrinkled up her nose, unable to see any significance in that. 'She met the Queen once.'

They fell silent. Rebecca realized that, briefly, she had dropped her defences and had quite enjoyed talking to these two.

'Nice to talk to you,' said Tish then, as though reading her thoughts. 'You're the dead opposite of Roberta Jones and one or two others, who are so full of themselves they can never stop talking.'

'She seems to like herself,' murmured Rebecca.

'I suppose somebody has to,' laughed Tish, and added shrewdly, 'Do you do any writing yourself, poems or anything?'

Rebecca went pink to the roots of her fair hair. 'Of course not,' she said quickly. 'Not really. I just like reading, that's all.'

She got up and got her cape down and found her paperback in the pocket. She felt like being quiet now and settled down with her book while the others returned to their seats and began to chat.

Ishbel Anderson was quite a character, Rebecca decided, and she liked her. But she wanted to get to Trebizon now, and get it over with.

THREE

REBECCA'S POEM

The train pulled in to Trebizon Station at three o'clock in the afternoon. All the girls coming to school on the train from London had eaten a good lunch, some in relays in the Buffet Car and others, like Rebecca, a packed lunch. Now they spilled out on the platform in a crisp display of dark jumpers and blue skirts as porters unloaded dozens of suitcases and trunks from the luggage van on to station trolleys.

'Stick with us,' said Tish, steering Rebecca along the crowded platform. She and Sue were laden with their disorganized mess of carrier bags and hockey sticks and the violin case. Rebecca wore her denim bag slung over her shoulder and clutched her hockey stick and rolled up cape.

The dull September morning in London had turned into a warm, sunny afternoon here in the west country.

'Are you all right?' asked Miss Morgan, looking like a shepherd with the flock of First Years around her, as Rebecca went by. Rebecca nodded.

'Fill the front coach up first!' someone shouted.

'Let's try and grab a front seat,' said Tish, 'then you can get a really good view. Ever seen the place?'

'No, only pictures.'

To make room, the younger girls had to sit three to a seat and Rebecca rather liked being sandwiched between Tish and Sue in the first seat, right by the door. Tish seemed to be very popular.

'Hi, Tish!'

'Where were you on the train?'

'You promised to send me a card from France, you rotten thing!'

'Who's your friend?' asked a plump girl.

'Rebecca Mason,' Tish replied to this question. 'She's going to be in II Alpha with us. Rebecca – this is Sally Elphinstone.'

'Hallo,' said Rebecca shyly. She somehow felt that nothing was too bad while Tish was looking after her. It was a warm, secure feeling – while it lasted.

'Hi! Otherwise known as Elf,' giggled the girl Sally. 'And this is Margot. Margot Lawrence.'

A black girl. Nice. Fun-looking. Probably Elf's best friend. Rebecca dimly remembered seeing them together on the train.

'She'll be in our dormy, too, won't she Tish?' said the black girl. 'Wasn't there something about us getting some-one new in Second Year?'

'You're right, Margot,' said Tish in a matter-of-fact way. 'Hear that, Rebecca?'

'Mmmm,' replied Rebecca, trying not to look pleased or pathetic.

All the luggage loaded on, the double doors shut, the coach climbed steeply up the main street of the old stone-built town of Trebizon, with two more coaches behind. The sun slanted along the pavements and Rebecca noticed children with buckets and spades. This was the tag end of the holiday season and there were several beaches close to the town.

At the top of the town the coach turned left, down a winding road lined with small hotels, most of them set well back in gardens. At the edge of the road there were rhododendron bushes and, every so often, a small palm tree. The coach turned again, out into open country, and there –

'Trebizon Bay!' exclaimed Rebecca. 'Is that it?'

'Yes, that's it. Not bad, is it?'

Through the front window of the coach, Rebecca could see directly down across the fields to a huge bay, fringed with golden sand, the blue sea sparkling and dancing in the sunshine. Not bad? It was beautiful.

'And there's the school,' said Sue, pointing.

Rebecca glimpsed a mixture of white stone buildings and red brick, in amongst tall trees, set in many acres of parkland that ran down to the coast on the west side of Trebizon Bay. In the heart of the cluster of buildings, rising even above the trees, there was a tall tower with a clock, its hands caught brightly in the sun.

Shortly afterwards, the coach turned in through wrought iron entrance gates. White lettering on a large blue board beside the entrance said: TREBIZON SCHOOL. Another sign said: SPEED LIMIT 10 M.P.H. The drive was half a mile long and several times the convoy of coaches had to pull into the side, trees and bushes whispering against the windows, to let cars past, coming from the direction of the school.

'Chaos!' said Tish. 'It's always like this on the first day.'

The coach pulled up in front of the school's main building, a magnificent stone manor house of fine proportions, built for a local nobleman in the eighteenth century. It had a sweeping, gravelled forecourt so large that there was ample room for all.

The girls poured out of the coaches, milling around the parked cars and greeting friends who had been brought to school by road.

'Where are the coaches going off to now?' asked Rebecca.

'Round the back to unload all the luggage,' said Tish, but she was staring at a red mini that was pulling up nearby. Someone in it was waving to her. 'The school staff sort out all the trunks and cases and get them round to the various Houses. It's quite an operation, but with a bit of luck they all get to the right places in time for us to unpack before we have tea.'

'Tish!' cried a joyful voice.

A girl tumbled out of the red mini, parked incongruously beside a huge Rolls-Royce, and came rushing over. She had long black hair tied back, brown eyes and a very tanned skin. She flung her arms round Tish.

'Mara!' said Tish. 'How was Athens? Mara – this is Rebecca Mason, she's going to be in our Year. Rebecca – Mara Leonodis.'

'Hallo.'

'Hallo, Rebecca!' But the girl, who was Greek, had eyes only for Ishbel Anderson and Susan Murdoch. 'Tish – Sue – I've got it! I've got the machine!'

The other two shrieked and dropped their things on to the gravel.

'You haven't!'

'I promised, yes? Come quickly and see, it's in the boot. Soon Anestis will carry it in for us –'

All three of them rushed to the small red car, leaving Rebecca standing there wondering what the excitement was about. Suddenly, dwarfed in the shadow of the big school, of which she had only seen a small part so far, she felt lonely and frightened.

'Rebecca?'

Miss Morgan came striding over, followed by her large party of younger girls. They were lined up in pairs, carrying their hand luggage and their brand new hockey sticks, their blue capes folded over their arms.

'Walk with me,' the Junior House Mistress said kindly. 'I'm taking all you new girls to Juniper. Matron and her staff are waiting to meet you all, and they'll show you what's what.'

Rebecca fell into step beside Miss Morgan. Going up a long, low flight of stone steps to the main doors of the school, she glanced back and saw that the others were still by the red car, crowding round a large cardboard carton that stood on the ground. They had forgotten all about her.

'We'll cut through the old school,' said Miss Morgan, pushing back the large doors; and they all trooped into a magnificent entrance hall.

Coming into the cool building out of the sunshine, Rebecca shivered. The floor was of polished wood and the high ceilings were ornately moulded. The staircase was very grand, with oil-painted murals by an eighteenth-century artist rising up the side. She felt overwhelmed. Just because Tish and Sue had been nice to her – it didn't mean a thing. She was new and she had no friends and now she was actually here, it was terrifying.

Miss Morgan led them along a corridor and then out through a small glass door at the back of the building.

'These are the quadrangle gardens, and that's Juniper House opposite, where you are all going to be living from now on.'

'Going to be living,' thought Rebecca. She felt trapped.

They were in big square gardens, laid to lawn, but criss-crossed with flagstoned paths and dotted with flower beds. There were buildings all around the square: the main house, from which they had emerged, then to one side a converted stable block with the tall clock tower, added as a folly in Victorian times; to the other side a modern block in white stone which housed the school dining and assembly halls, with art rooms and science laboratories on the upper floors.

And directly opposite them, across the gardens forming the fourth side of the square, was Juniper House. It was a perfectly pleasant modern red brick building, that blended in well with the others, but to Rebecca's eyes it suddenly looked like a prison.

They crossed the gardens and entered Juniper House through open french doors at the far end of a long terrace. Matron and Miss Morgan took the main party up the east staircase to the First Year dormitories. They were beginning to chatter excitedly. Rebecca found herself abandoned to Mary, a young Assistant Matron, who took her the entire length of the ground floor and then up the west staircase.

'You're the only new Second Year,' said Mary. 'First, I'll show you your dormitory. You're in number six.'

Number six turned out to be a big room on the second floor, with primrose walls and big windows that faced due south, so that the sun dappled the counterpanes on the beds. There were eight beds in all, spaced well apart, in separate cubicles; each cubicle had its own chest of drawers, bedside locker and small hanging cupboard.

'You're here in the corner,' said Mary.

Rebecca put her bag and cape and hockey stick down on top of her chest of drawers, which was a pale pink. Although her bed was right underneath a large window, she still had the strange sensation of walls closing in on her.

'Have a wash, if you like,' said Mary. 'There'll be other girls coming up in a minute. You can meet them, then – if you like – I'll show you around Juniper, so you know the layout. Your trunk will be up here in about half an hour and you'll have plenty of time to unpack before tea.'

Rebecca's mind took little of this in. A strange whispering sound beyond the open window had caught her attention. She crossed to the window and looked out. What was it she could hear, coming from somewhere beyond those trees?

'Trebizon Bay!' she thought, catching a glimpse of sand and blue sea between the trees. The sound she could hear was the breaking of waves on the sea shore, for the back of Juniper House was less than two hundred yards from the most westerly corner of that huge, beautiful bay she had seen from the coach.

At the same time she heard voices: girls coming up west staircase.

'Please – may I just run down and look at the sea?'

The surprised look on Mary's face made Rebecca realize that she had betrayed something of her desperate impulse to escape.

'What I mean is,' said Rebecca, more calmly, 'I'm dying to stretch my legs after being cooped up in that train for hours.'

'Of course,' Mary nodded. In fact she had a lot of work to do. 'And the bay's lovely. Off you go then. Come back in half an hour, so you can unpack your trunk before tea.'

'Thanks!'

Rebecca snatched up her denim bag and flew out of the door at this end of the dormitory, just as she heard a clamour of voices outside the door at the opposite end. Dodged them! She couldn't bear the thought of being surrounded by them all, looking at her, asking questions. That could come later.

She came down the back stairs and let herself out of a back door. A coach was just turning out of the yard and some men were sorting through a stack of suitcases and trunks, all clearly labelled, and loading them on two land-rovers. Rebecca slipped past them and along a path that led downhill through the trees. There was the sea, beckoning her on.

She emerged from the trees and realized that she was fenced in from the sand dunes beyond by iron palings. Then she saw a small gate, open, with a sign on it: TREBIZON SCHOOL – PRIVATE. Joyfully she ran through the gate and up to the top of the nearest sand dune. She was free – she was back in the outside world! There was the bay spread before her, with deck chairs, and ice cream wrappers blowing about and a sprinkling of holiday-makers.

She ran down the other side of the dune and left her bag and socks and shoes at the bottom. Then she sprinted across the hard, golden sand barefoot, past a game of beach cricket, to the far distant sea. Her hair streamed out in the breeze and, because she loved running, she felt exhilarated. She paddled at the water's edge, squeezing wet sand through her toes and letting the salt water run over them. Enviously she watched some surfers. After some time, she walked slowly back across the sands to where she had left her things.

Sitting down at the foot of the sand dune, Rebecca took a thick notepad and ballpoint pen from her bag, filled with the urge to write something. She would make some notes of her first impressions of Trebizon, just like a real writer. She was safe here; nobody would ask her what she was writing.

A family came and settled down nearby, with sandwiches and a flask of tea: a London man and his wife with their two teenage daughters. The girls wore bikinis and found a sheltered hollow to sunbathe in. They hardly gave Rebecca a second glance.

She sat with her knees up, her notepad propped against them, wondering what to write. Her mood of exhilaration had been short-lived. The voices of the family nearby reminded her of London and made her feel homesick. Imperceptibly, the sun was sinking lower towards the green and white-flecked horizon. The rays of light slanted through the sand dunes, filling Rebecca with an ache.

She remembered the first line of a poem written long ago, and she wrote it down neatly, in block capitals:

THERE'S A CERTAIN SLANT OF LIGHT, ON
WINTER AFTERNOONS . . .

She followed this by writing:

IT FALLS THROUGH THE TREES, LIES HEAVY
ON THE DUNES

Unaware that one of the sunbathers was now watching her with curiosity, Rebecca decided to add some more. She wrote intently, wrinkling her nose in concentration, whispering the words aloud every so often. Sometimes she crossed words out and put in better ones, but on the whole, the poem came easily – it just seemed to flow from that opening line.

When at last it was finished to her satisfaction, Rebecca read it through and sighed. It was as though a heavy weight had been lifted from her shoulders. Writing the verses had somehow relieved her of the awful melancholy mood which had inspired them. She felt better now.

'She must be at that school,' she heard one of the teenagers comment. 'Bet she's brainy.'

Rebecca rummaged in her bag, lowering her eyes.

'It's famous, isn't it? Bet they have a marvellous time there.'

'Helen, Melissa!' That was the father's voice. 'Put something on, let's get back to the caravan before it gets cold.'

Startled, Rebecca looked up at the sky. The warmth was going from the sun. What was the time? How long had she been here? She scrambled into her shoes and socks and dropped her notepad and pen into her bag, first ripping out the page of verse. She read it for the last time, and smiled. Silly, gloomy poem!

'Stop feeling sorry for yourself!' she thought. 'It's *not* a prison. It's one of the best schools in England, and you've got to make a go of it. Mum and Dad expect it.'

There was a litter basket only ten yards away. She walked over to it and pushed her poem down between the squash cartons, cigarette packets and ice cream wrappers that filled the basket. Time to get back to school – to get unpacked – to meet the other girls in her dormitory! Maybe even tea time! She raced up to the top of the sand dune and down the other side, leaving her poem crushed amongst the litter. Dead and buried – best forgotten!

But although Rebecca's poem was buried, it was not dead, nor was it to be forgotten.

FOUR

THE MIGHTY EDITOR

As Rebecca let herself in through the small gate that said TREBIZON SCHOOL – PRIVATE, the holiday-makers had gathered their things together and were ready to leave the beach.

'What on earth are you rummaging around in that dirty litter basket for, Helen!' asked her father.

'I want to see what she was writing!'

'Come along at once, Helen!' said her mother. 'And put that piece of paper back!'

The family took the grassy track through the sand dunes that led in an easterly direction to the small caravan site where they were staying. Helen trailed along behind with her sister.

'Here, listen to this, Melissa. It's a poem. I told you she looked brainy.'

She started reading bits out loud, and giggling.

There was someone coming along the track towards them, head lowered, deep in thought. Elizabeth Exton, just like Rebecca, had felt the need to be alone. She had been out for a long walk, turning over and over in her mind a small problem that went with being the new Editor of *The Trebizon Journal*. She had enjoyed the summer holidays even more than usual; it had been wonderful to have something really important to do, something that had given her the opportunity of meeting and talking to famous people. Nevertheless, this one small problem remained. It was still not resolved – and now it was time to get back to school.

'Oh, chuck it away, Helen,' said Melissa.

The girl, bored with her find now, fluttered the paper in the air, opened her finger and thumb and let it fly away on the breeze. It fluttered straight down to Elizabeth Exton's feet. She picked it up indignantly. Holiday-makers! Litter bugs!

'Come back here!' she called as the girls passed her on the grassy track.

The girl, Helen, stopped, turned round, and stared at her.

'You dropped this.'

'Did I?'

About to give the girl a lecture, Elizabeth realized that it was a poem, quite a good one. The opening line was really most striking. The girl had obviously just written it.

'It – it's a poem,' said Elizabeth, rather feebly.

'Have it,' said the girl shortly. She turned on her heels and hurried on up the grassy track to catch up with her family.

As Elizabeth Exton walked back to school she read the poem over twice. It was all rather uncanny, she decided, and the more she thought about it, the stranger it seemed.

Meanwhile, Rebecca was racing up the back staircase of Juniper House in panic. A loud bell was clanging over in the dining hall block. Girls were rushing past her down the stairs, nearly knocking her over.

'Tea time!'

'You'll be late!'

'But I haven't even washed or unpacked yet!' thought Rebecca.

She charged through a door on the first landing. The dormitory was identical to her own, but the walls were pale green instead of primrose. Wrong floor! She backed out quickly, ran up another flight of stairs, and there was the right door with the number six on it.

Her trunk stood at the foot of her bed. It was neatly labelled REBECCA MASON, JUNIPER HOUSE, TREBIZON SCHOOL and was waiting to be unpacked.

Someone was standing there, her back turned to the door, surveying the trunk. Otherwise the dormitory was empty.

'Rebecca!' said Tish, turning round. 'Where on earth have you been? I've been looking for you.'

Rebecca was surprised and pleased. 'Down on the beach. So I am with you then?'

'That's my bed over there. Look, the bell's gone for tea –'

'I haven't unpacked –'

'Do it after tea. Quick, have a wash. You've got biro on your face. I'll take you over to the dining hall. Sue's saving us seats on Joss Vining's table, which is a good one.'

There was a mirror and handbasin in the dormitory and Rebecca washed her face and brushed her hair at speed. Her spirits lifted. She would have liked to have Tish Anderson as a special friend, but that was too much to hope for. On the other hand, Tish must quite like her or she would hardly be here now, and she certainly wouldn't have arranged for them to sit at the same table.

'Thanks for waiting for me,' said Rebecca. 'I'd have died if I'd had to walk in late on my own.'

'Sorry I lost you when we got off the coach. Come on.'

They hurried down west staircase and out on to the

terrace overlooking the quadrangle gardens. At the far end of the terrace, the modern white block that ran at right angles to the boarding house had its french windows open on the ground floor. A deep, continuous hum floated out, like the hum of thousands of wild bees swarming round nectar on a June evening. The girls of Trebizon School were in the dining hall and settling down to tea.

'Race you!' said Tish.

Rebecca hurtled along the terrace, which ran the length of the building, long legs fully stretched. She almost crashed into the wall of the white building at the end.

'Won!'

'You're fast!'

They walked – out of breath – into the big dining hall, where girls sat ten to a table. Josselyn Vining was at the head of their table serving grilled sausages and bacon from a large casserole dish onto plates.

'Sorry we're late, Rebecca got lost.'

'You're the new girl, are you? Hallo. Sausage or bacon or both?'

'Both, please,' said Rebecca hungrily.

'She's a good runner.' Tish looked at Rebecca, who was now piling runner beans onto her plate. 'Sliced tomatoes? Here, Joss was head of games last term and though she doesn't know it, she's going to be again.'

There was laughter round the table, and general approval.

'Good at hockey?' asked Joss.

'I – I don't know,' mumbled Rebecca.

Rebecca knew that she was a good runner. Although she would quite like to be good at organized games, she had not played them very much up till now, except netball.

'Well, if you can run that's a start.'

Sue Murdoch, who was sitting on the other side of Josselyn, said something then about hockey fixtures; Tish joined in, and quickly the three of them fell into animated conversation.

Rebecca felt an elbow nudging her ribs and for the first time became aware of the girl sitting on the other side of her. She had brown hair and a pretty, full-lipped face.

'You watch out,' she said in a conspiratorial whisper. 'You don't want to get in with the sporty brigade. Early morning runs before breakfast, extra hockey practice at weekends . . . once they think you're any good, there's no escape.'

'Thanks for the warning,' smiled Rebecca. It was nice to find someone being so friendly. At the same time, she felt a pang. She would like to be one of that little group talking about fixtures. They had obviously been in a junior team together last year, and travelled to other schools for matches. 'Do they really take it all that seriously?'

'You bet they do,' said the girl with feeling.

At that moment Rebecca saw Tish throw back her head and laugh about something, her mouth even wider than usual, her black curls bouncing. Did Tish go for runs before breakfast, too?

'Don't worry,' the girl was saying now, 'there's plenty of us who are normal here. I'm Debbie Rickard by the way – your name's Rebecca, isn't it?'

Although Rebecca did not know it at the time, Debbie Rickard was exaggerating wildly, and her attitude was coloured by the fact that she herself was hopeless at games of any kind.

She was happy to talk to Debbie for the rest of the meal; the girl was going out of her way to be friendly. Besides, everybody seemed to want to talk to Tish Anderson. When they had finished their fresh fruit and yoghurt, the Greek girl, Mara Leonodis, came over from the next table and grabbed the back of Tish's jumper.

'I've seen Miss Morgan!' she said. 'She's got a staff meeting after tea but she says she'll meet us in the Hobbies' Room later and arrange where we're to put it.'

'Good!' said Tish, obviously excited.

Rebecca thought again of the big carton that Mara had brought to school, containing some kind of 'machine'. What was it?

There was a deafening noise of scraping chairs all over the dining hall as girls started to disperse. Josselyn Vining was asking Sally Elphinstone to have a game of badminton with her, and Tish was deep in conversation with Mara Leonodis. Sue Murdoch said she was going to 'the Hilary', wherever that was.

'What are you going to do now?' asked Debbie.

'I've still got to unpack my trunk.'

'I'll come with you.'

In the dormitory, Rebecca soon sorted out her things. She placed her clothes neatly in the drawers of the pink chest and hung up her dressing gown. Her personal possessions she put in the locker beside her bed.

'Your trunk goes outside on the landing with the others,' said Debbie, dragging it out through the door. 'They'll collect them up soon and put them in store till the end of term. Your outdoor things –' she pointed to Wellington boots, raincoat and school cape, '– go downstairs. And there's a special locker for all your games stuff.'

Debbie helped her carry the clothes downstairs and showed her where to put them. Rebecca was very grateful for all this. But when Debbie dragged her along the corridor on the ground floor to a small room with a television set in it,

Rebecca pulled up short in the doorway. It was a nice evening and she didn't want to watch TV.

'I think I'd quite like to look round the grounds,' she said.

'But it's "Landslide"!' protested Debbie.

'Then don't miss it for me!' said Rebecca. 'I'll be fine.'

'Are you sure?' Debbie looked relieved. 'I'll see you later then – see you at cocoa time.'

As the door closed and Rebecca was left standing in the corridor, a voice behind her said, 'Come on, I'll give you a guided tour.'

'Oh –' Rebecca turned and saw Tish. 'Will you really?'

They went outside. Although the main school buildings were grouped around the quadrangle, there were other buildings in the grounds, too.

'That big white place in the trees is the sports centre. We hire it out quite a bit to help pay for the upkeep. It's got an indoor swimming pool, badminton, squash, the lot.' Tish kept up a fast pace. 'There's the hockey pitches, and the grass tennis courts – the hard courts are the other side of the sports centre, and we use them for netball this term. Come and look at the lake –'

They galloped along a flagstone path, through a shrubbery, and came out by water. The 'lake' was really a large pond, very reedy and beautiful with water lilies floating upon it. Beside the water stood a long low building; it had once been mews cottages and a coach-house, now modernized with plate glass windows, and a Spanish-style verandah overlooking the water. The whole scene was most attractive. Through the open windows came the strains of music, floating across the water.

'That's the Hilary,' explained Tish. 'The Hilary Camberwell Music School where we have our music lessons and people learn to play instruments. There are lots of little practice rooms. That violin you can hear might be Sue.'

On they went in a breathless whirl; it was really too much for Rebecca's mind to take in all at once. There were some very attractive houses set at various points in the grounds. Some, Tish explained, were staff houses and the larger ones were boarding houses for the Third Years upwards.

'After Juniper we go into smaller houses, thirty or forty girls, more free and easy, with shared studies. All the boarding houses have names – Willoughby, Chambers, Parkinson – you won't remember them yet. Look, there's Parkinson, that's the Upper Sixth's boarding house.'

They slowed down as they passed close to an attractive old Victorian house with large bay windows and walls covered in ivy. It had its own garden, with garden seats and a summerhouse. Somebody came out of the side gate and they stopped to let her cross their path. Rebecca at once recognized the tall, elegant figure with the striking bony features and long black hair. Her hair streamed out behind her. There was something rather witch-like about Elizabeth Exton when you looked at her from the side.

'Elizabeth?'

'What do you want Ishbel?' asked the prefect touchily. She was obviously in a hurry.

'How long have I got to collect Juniper's contributions, please?'

Rebecca thought she saw an annoyed frown cross the prefect's face; but, if so, it was quickly gone.

'About a fortnight. It'll be announced in Assembly. Are you still Magazine Officer then?'

'Yes, we're elected for two terms. It won't give the new girls much time. We had about four weeks last year when we were new.'

'New girls don't expect to get in the *Journal*, surely?'

'Two got in last year when Mary Green was Editor.'

'Well, just guess who's the Editor of *The Trebizon Journal* now – and it's not Mary Green.' Her eyes swept over Rebecca for a moment. She was about to say something, and then changed her mind. She spoke more reasonably. 'It goes to press early because it's the Golden Jubilee edition, remember? I'm sorry I can't give you longer. Everything will be considered on its merits.'

She hurried on her way.

'Piffling juniors,' she said, under her breath.

FIVE

THE BOX IS OPENED

'Come on,' said Tish, crisply. 'I'd better get notices up straight away. Seen round Juniper yet?'

Rebecca shook her head.

'Well, you can see it now.'

They hurried back to the red brick boarding house, went inside and along the corridor.

'This end of the building is the west wing, where all the Second Years live – the other end is the east wing, for the First Years. It's really two boarding houses in one building, joined by this corridor on the ground floor. This is our Hobbies' Room.'

She pushed open a modern glass door, like the one leading to the TV room. But unlike the tiny TV room, this was huge and airy, about the length of two classrooms. It was crammed with interesting things.

Rebecca noticed a table tennis table, a sewing table with two sewing machines on it and a potter's wheel. There was an Art corner with easels and a sink with a shelf of empty jam jars and poster paints above.

Then Rebecca saw the typewriter. It was on a table under

the window. Tish went over, sat down and fed in two sheets of typing paper with carbon paper in between them and rapidly typed some sentences.

'You can type!' exclaimed Rebecca.

'My sister's taught me,' said Tish, pulling the sheets out. 'A few mistakes, but not bad. I'm going to need to be able to type. Come on, we'll put one notice in the First Year Common Room and the carbon copy in ours.'

Rebecca's legs were beginning to feel weary and she would very much like to have stayed and tinkered with that typewriter, but she followed Tish out along the corridor, the length of the building, up east staircase and into the First Year Common Room.

It was a lovely light room on the first floor, overlooking the quadrangle gardens, with comfortable chairs, rugs on the floor, two tables and a piano in the corner. There was a large notice-board by the door. Tish took a spare drawing pin off the board and pinned up her notice. Rebecca read it with interest:

> Urgent. *Magazine Meeting 7 pm tomorrow (Wednesday) in the Second Year Common Room. Contributions for this term's* Trebizon Journal *required by next Monday. If you have anything suitable please bring it with you tomorrow. This will be the Golden Jubilee edition and we want our House represented.*
>
> Ishbel Anderson *Magazine Officer*
> *Juniper House*

'Pity there's no-one here to read it at the moment!' said Tish.

'Where are they all?' asked Rebecca, suddenly realizing. 'The place is deserted.'

'Most likely over in the library getting a pep talk from the Head. That's where we went on our first evening. She likes to see all the new girls when they arrive. Looks'em over!'

'Then –?'

'Don't worry, you'll get a message when she wants to see you,' said Tish. 'And don't look so scared. She's nice, really nice. Come on, you can see our Common Room now, it's just like this.'

They doubled back down east staircase, right along the ground floor corridor and up west. Tish threw open the door of the Second Year Common Room.

'Hi, Tish!'

'How are you?'

Girls were lounging around in chairs and some were lying on the rugs on the floor, reading. They crowded round the notice as it was pinned up. The notice-board was usually a great focal point of interest in their school life.

'The kitchen's just opposite, like to see it?' asked Tish, leading Rebecca out into the corridor. 'We make tea and coffee there, and our own cocoa at bed-time –'

She got no further. A tall, pretty girl of seventeen appeared at the top of the staircase. She was a prefect called Pippa Fellowes-Walker.

'Rebecca?' she asked. 'Rebecca Mason?'

Rebecca nodded, feeling scared.

'Run upstairs and wash, and brush your hair. I'll wait for you here. Miss Welbeck will see you in ten minutes.'

Rebecca's throat felt dry. She bolted upstairs. Summoned to see the Principal of Trebizon School! She collected her wash things from the dormitory and found a big wash room right next door. There was a long row of wash basins and a row of hooks to hang flannels on. There was also a toothbrush rack with brush handles hanging down all colours of the rainbow, and just one slot free for her own new, bright blue toothbrush.

When she returned to the landing below she found the prefect chatting amiably with Tish, not at all god-like and superior: not like Elizabeth Exton. She gave Rebecca a friendly smile. 'You'll do! Come on, follow me.'

Pippa liked the look of this new girl with the fair hair and the delicate features; there was something intelligent, and artistic-looking about her.

They went downstairs and out onto the terrace and crossed the quadrangle gardens to the back of the old school. Pippa took Rebecca in through the same glass door that she had passed through earlier with Miss Morgan, and back into that awe-inspiring entrance hall with its magnificent muralled staircase.

On the first floor, the prefect knocked on an oak-panelled door, and then looked into the room. Then she came out and spoke quietly.

'Miss Welbeck will see you now. Find your own way back? Okay. In you go.'

Afterwards, Rebecca always got a pleasant glow when she recalled that first meeting with Miss Madeleine Welbeck. Within moments of entering the panelled study, filled with the scent of roses, her fear left her. She saw a slim woman in tweeds, standing by a large window overlooking the entrance forecourt, watching a car drive off. She caught a glimpse of oak trees and park land in the distance and here in the room the evening light catching Miss Welbeck's fair-to-silver hair as she turned.

'Welcome to Trebizon, Rebecca.'

Rebecca felt herself to be in the presence of someone quiet and confident whom she could admire. She found Miss Welbeck had a tremendous effect on her, and when she emerged from her study, ten minutes later, she felt quite inspired. The Principal's last words were still ringing in her ears.

'Aim high, Rebecca. Don't expect success to come too easily, but keep on reaching up. Remember: "Two men looked through the prison bars, one saw mud and the other saw stars". Don't look down at the mud but reach up for the stars.'

What a clever thing to say! That bit about prison bars – could Miss Welbeck possibly have guessed how Rebecca had been feeling earlier? Reach up for the stars! Yes – why not? Why shouldn't she?

She walked down the magnificent staircase, gazing up at the richly coloured murals. She no longer felt overwhelmed by it, but inspired. Small and insignificant though she was, she must make her mark at Trebizon School, and justify her presence.

'Write something for that magazine!' had been her father's last words to her. What an honour it would be if she could get something printed in the Golden Jubilee edition of *The Trebizon Journal*! Of course, thinking of the mighty Elizabeth Exton, that wasn't just aiming high – it was aiming for the moon. But why not try? Why not?

When Rebecca re-entered Juniper House she heard a hubbub of voices echoing along the corridor, coming from the direction of the Hobbies' Room. The door was open and it sounded as though there was quite a crowd in there. What was going on? She decided to find out!

They were all gathered round the big table by the window, the typewriter table. There was a large carton near the door, its packing removed. Rebecca recognized it as the mysterious box that Mara had brought back to school with her. Miss Morgan and Tish had carried something over to the table and set it down next to the typewriter, and Mara was dusting it with a cloth.

'It's smashing!' said Josselyn Vining, tapping Mara on the shoulder with her badminton racquet. 'Do you mean to say your father didn't want it?'

'We were all expecting some grotty old thing!' laughed Tish. 'And Mara turns up with this.'

'It was down in the Southampton Office,' said Mara, with great pleasure. Her father was the owner of Leonodis Shipping Lines. 'It was much too small for them and now they have a new one as big –' Mara spread her arms out, '– as big as this.'

Rebecca's curiosity was at fever pitch – what was it? She stood on tip-toe behind the other girls and at last she could see. A duplicating machine! Just a little, hand-operated model, but quite modern. Beside it were boxes of stencils and duplicating paper, all that was required to put it into action.

'I think this is the best place, next to the typewriter,' said Miss Morgan. 'Now this corner of the Hobbies' Room can be your publishing office! I look forward to seeing what you publish!'

So saying, Miss Morgan moved away and, as the crowd parted to let her through, she walked past Rebecca and smiled and went over to the doorway. Before leaving, she called back, 'Cocoa time in ten minutes!'

'Yes, Miss Morgan,' responded the girls, already closing round the duplicator again.

Rebecca was beginning to feel quite excited. A miniature publishing office – what fun! – and what *were* they going to publish?

Even as she mentally asked that question, Tish jumped up on to a chair and answered it. 'Well, this is it! I've been practising typing in the holidays to be able to type the stencils. Mara has turned up with the machine, just as she said she would. From now on we can produce our own House publication – *The Juniper Journal*!'

'Hurray!' There was cheering and stamping of feet.

'I'll announce it properly at the magazine meeting tomorrow. We'll make it the best thing in the school –' She was interrupted by more cheers, but ended on a modest note. 'Except for *The Trebizon Journal* itself, of course.'

As Rebecca came out of the Hobbies' Room with a bunch of other girls, she was met by Debbie Rickard in the corridor. Debbie immediately put her arm through Rebecca's.

'Hallo! I've been looking for you. Where've you been?'

'I had to go and see the Principal.'

'Come and have cocoa, I'll show you where we make it.'

They made cocoa in the big warm kitchen on the first floor and sat and drank it, munching two digestive biscuits. Drinking cocoa, either in the kitchen or in the comfortable Common Room across the corridor, was a nightly ritual at Trebizon School.

'How did you get on with the Principal?'

'Fine,' said Rebecca, hugging to herself her secret resolve to make something of herself at her new school. 'She's nice.'

Debbie Rickard was in a different dormitory from Rebecca, but they were to be in the same form, II Alpha. Before they parted, Debbie said, 'Shall we sit next to each other in lessons tomorrow?'

'I'd like that,' said Rebecca gratefully. Tomorrow would be her first full day at Trebizon and she was pleased that she would not have to face it alone. She had already made a friend, of sorts.

She went up to her dormitory. When she had said

goodbye to her parents that morning, Rebecca had been dreading her first night at boarding school. She imagined that she might toss and turn all night in her strange surroundings, feeling terribly homesick. In fact, she lay in bed and tried to plan what she would write for the school magazine. Her eyelids got heavier and heavier.

All round her, girls were whispering and running about and discussing the holidays, until the duty prefect came in and said in a stern voice, 'Shut up! Lights out!'

But Rebecca knew nothing of this, for she was already fast asleep.

SIX

DEBBIE IS SPITEFUL

The first full day at Trebizon, Wednesday, Rebecca still did not feel a twinge of homesickness. The hours were too crowded for that and, in the few quiet times, she had something special to keep her thoughts occupied: her secret resolve to try and write something for *The Trebizon Journal.*

After the rising bell went, she knelt up on her pillow and pulled back the curtains. She stared in surprise at the trees and blue sea beyond and just for a moment wondered where she was.

Girls were hurrying to and from the wash room; some were already scrambling into their clothes.

'Where's my tie?' shouted someone.

'Hallo, Rebecca,' said a girl in a pale green dressing gown, with sandy hair, passing the foot of the bed. 'Sleep well?'

'Fine, thanks.'

It was only after she had gone that Rebecca realized the girl was Sue Murdoch, without her glasses. Spectacles suited her well, but without them she looked entirely different. She had rather a Slavonic face, with high cheekbones.

Rebecca could just imagine her on the platform in a big concert hall, playing the violin, when she was grown up.

Rebecca washed and dressed in a hurry, but she was still brushing her hair when Tish and Sue came past.

'Buck up! Breakfast in five minutes. You're on Joss Vining's table – where you sat last night, remember? Okay?'

Rebecca would have liked them to have waited for her, but told herself not to be such a baby. She went down and entered the dining hall with a throng of other girls; at least she wasn't late! She found the right table and an empty seat, next to Sally Elphinstone this time. To her regret, Tish was right at the other end of the table, talking madly as usual.

'Why's the seat next to me always left till last?' asked Sally in mock dismay. 'As if I didn't know.'

'You should go on a diet, Elf,' said Judy Sharp. 'Don't let her squeeze you off the table, Rebecca.'

'There's plenty of room!' laughed Rebecca, and turning said, 'Is that what they call you – Elf –?'

'That's right, because of my elfin figure,' said the plump girl cheerfully. 'Elfin Elphinstone, that's me. Help yourself to cereal and the milk's in the big jug. Oi – Tish – don't take all the muesli, pass it up this way. I'm fading away.'

Rebecca ate a hearty breakfast. There was much chatter and laughter on her table and so theirs was one of the last to finish. She was still eating toast when Debbie Rickard passed by from another table. Although she had sat there on the first evening, Joss Vining's table was not Debbie's proper one.

'Don't forget, Rebecca! We'll sit together in lessons.' She bent her head close for a second. 'See you after Assembly.'

Rebecca's pleasure was slightly marred by the look on Elf's face as she watched Debbie walk on. What was the plump girl raising her eyebrows about?

The assembly hall was immediately above the dining hall, and had a very high ceiling. Outside the french windows on either side of the hall, balconies ran its entire length. As the girls filed in, a mistress played stirring music on a grand piano.

When the whole school was assembled, the music stopped and the rows of girls stood silent as a figure entered. Miss Welbeck walked the length of the hall, her black gown flapping, went up on to the stage and stood behind a table. She placed her hymn book and some notices on the polished surface beside a bowl of chrysanthemums, then gazed around the hall.

'Good morning, girls.'

'Good morning, Miss Welbeck.'

The Principal of Trebizon School had arrived to take Assembly and the new school year had officially begun.

After Assembly, Rebecca was pleased to discover that most lessons took place in the old building, the 18th century manor house that formed the heart of the school. The science laboratories and home economics rooms were in the modern part of school, but the form rooms were in the old building and II Alpha was a quaint room with sloping, uneven floors and old-fashioned windows.

There were nine double desks in three rows in the room and Rebecca sat next to Debbie in the front row. Of the other sixteen girls in her form, Rebecca recognized several from her dining table, including Tish, Sue, Joss Vining, Judy Sharp and Sally Elphinstone and two more from her dormitory. She would soon get to know the others. Mara Leonodis was not there.

She liked Miss Heath, her form-mistress, at once and soon discovered that she also took them for English, Rebecca's favourite subject. At the end of the English lesson

Miss Heath said, 'Now for your prep. I want an essay written, please. All essays will be handed in on Friday morning. Here are the subjects.'

She chalked them up on the blackboard:

A WINTER'S MORNING.
MY ADVENTURE IN SPACE.
THE QUARREL.

The girls scribbled the headings down in their rough books as Miss Heath left the room. The maths mistress was waiting outside.

'Which one will you do?' asked Debbie.

'The first one,' replied Rebecca at once. She was glad they had until Friday to write the essay; today was only Wednesday. She wanted to make it really good. Once again her mind went back to her interview with the Principal, and her resolve to try and make her mark at her new school.

'Coming to watch TV?' asked Debbie after tea.

'I'm going to write my essay,' said Rebecca.

'But you can do it tomorrow night!' said Debbie in surprise. She always left her prep as long as possible. So did Rebecca, but only when the subject didn't interest her. 'Besides, you might miss the magazine meeting, if you're interested in that sort of thing.'

'I'll be back in time for that!' said Rebecca confidently.

'See you there, then.'

Rebecca wouldn't have missed the magazine meeting for anything. She would have liked to explain to Debbie that she wanted to make a start on her English essay because then, tomorrow, she might have time to start thinking about what she could write for *The Trebizon Journal*. But she said nothing; she had the feeling that Debbie might laugh at her for being so ambitious.

In the quiet peace of the library, Rebecca wrote her essay in rough. Older girls had studies in their boarding houses, but younger girls were required to do prep in their form rooms or in the school library. Since discovering the library during the course of the day, there had been no question in Rebecca's mind.

It was a beautiful room, the library of the original manor house, with some rare books housed there. French windows led out on to the terrace, overlooking the main forecourt of the school with a fine view of park land beyond. She worked out that Miss Welbeck's study must be immediately above the library. Occasionally, cars drew up as people came and went from the school and here Rebecca somehow felt in touch with the outside world.

It was nearly seven o'clock when she finished her essay. She could touch it up later, and copy it into her brand new English exercise book, but now she must go to the magazine meeting!

The Second Year Common Room was packed out with both First and Second Years, and Tish was kneeling up on a chair to take the meeting. There was a wire basket on the table beside her.

'This meeting is really to tell First Years about the school magazine, and how things are selected for it, and also to collect contributions from Second Years, who've had all the holidays to do something.'

Tish then quickly explained how her position as Magazine Officer made her a 'mini editor' of *The Trebizon Journal*, just as she had explained it to Rebecca on the train journey down.

'So you First Years have still got a few days,' she ended.

'But I must have everything in by eight o'clock next Monday evening, that's the final deadline. I'll be sitting in here from seven o'clock onwards. You, too, Rebecca –' she added, catching her eye encouragingly. 'You've still got time.'

Debbie nudged Rebecca hard. 'She's got a hope!' she whispered, and Rebecca went red. She had been quite uplifted by Tish's encouragement. She was glad, very glad, that she had confided nothing of her secret ambition to Debbie.

'We'll have another meeting next Wednesday,' Tish was saying. 'Same time, same place. I'll have a short list of the best entries and we'll pass them round and vote. The best one will be gold starred and one or two others will go up as well. Okay? Now, Second Years come and put your stuff in this basket – but nobody go yet, please.'

Girls shuffled up with their poems, essays and drawings and placed them in the wire basket. Roberta Jones hung back till last and then strode up and slapped her poems on top of the pile, looking satisfied. Now Tish would have to read hers first!

'The other thing I want to talk about is *The Juniper Journal*. We're going to have our own house publication this term. Even if you don't get anything in the school magazine, and most of you won't, we're going to need lots of stuff for *The J.J.* Verses, jokes, items of news. Be thinking about it. As soon as we've done our best, as far as this term's school magazine is concerned, we'll get *The J.J.* organized. That means a meeting some time next week to elect an editor and committee. I'll put a notice up in both Common Rooms.'

'Tish for Editor!' shouted Mara Leonodis, and the meeting broke up with clapping, laughter, and noise.

The word was passed round about the duplicator that had

arrived in the Second Year Hobbies' Room. Several of the new First Year girls rushed off to look at it.

'Thinks she's the Queen of England,' said Debbie suddenly, as they walked down the corridor. 'Tish Anderson, I mean.'

Rebecca was quite startled by the touch of venom.

As she got into bed that night, Tish came past in her dressing gown and stood for a moment at the foot of the bed. She had just cleaned her teeth and with her wide smile she looked rather like a toothpaste advertisement. 'I'm glad you came to the meeting. Going to try and do something for *The Trebizon*?'

'Yes,' Rebecca blurted out. 'As a matter of fact, I am!'

'Good.'

'I know – from what Elizabeth Exton said – that there isn't much chance. But there's no harm in trying.'

'There's not much chance but there's always *some* chance,' said Tish. Then very casually, 'Do you like Debbie Rickard?'

'Why, yes,' said Rebecca. 'She – she's fine.'

'Hockey tomorrow afternoon,' said Tish, changing the subject. 'I've forgotten – have you played before?'

'Hardly at all. I know the rules, and that's about all.'

'Well, you ought to be good.'

Rebecca knew that she was referring, once again, to the race they had run together when they had been late for tea yesterday. As she went to sleep she made up her mind to try and do well in the lesson tomorrow – she would try and be good at hockey! After all, if she wanted to get noticed at Trebizon it was no use pinning *all* her hopes on getting something published in the school magazine!

But the hockey lesson next day was a washout as far as Rebecca could see. She was given a red sash to wear by Miss

Willis, the games mistress, and put into a full-scale hockey game straight away, reds verses blues. The position chosen for her was left back, with Debbie Rickard playing at right back.

'Isn't this the biggest bore of all time?' said Debbie, as they hung around their end of the draughty field with only the goalkeeper for company. There was a biting east wind today.

'Yes,' said Rebecca, running up and down on the spot to keep warm. 'It is.'

The trouble was that reds had Josselyn Vining at centre forward, supported by Tish Anderson and Sue Murdoch at left and right inner, and the three of them made a winning combination. They attacked the opposing goal time and time again and the red defence had almost nothing to do. On a few occasions that the ball came her way, Rebecca was too cold and miserable to stop it in time.

As she watched the dazzling stick work and passing going on amongst the red forwards, Rebecca wondered how she could have been insane enough to think she might be good at hockey.

'And what does Tish Anderson look like in a games skirt!' giggled Debbie, after they had changed ends at half-time.

'Well, she's got thick legs for a start,' said Rebecca, feeling jaundiced. 'I suppose that's what playing hockey does for you.'

Rebecca did not mean the remark spitefully. In fact she had been surprised to notice that Tish had very thick, muscular legs when the rest of her was quite slim and graceful. She regretted the remark as soon as she had made it, especially when Debbie went off into peals of laughter.

'It's not that funny,' she said irritably.

Only once did Rebecca get a chance to warm up. The

opposing centre forward, Judy Sharp, came streaking through just before the end of the game and hit the ball a mighty whack with her hockey stick. It missed the goal and went racing away into the distance. The game came to a stop while Rebecca streaked off to retrieve the ball, running flat out all the way and just getting her stick to it before it rolled into a ditch full of brambles. Glad to get warm, she ran back with it all the way, tapping it ahead of her as she ran.

She would have been surprised if she could have looked upfield and seen the sudden interest on Josselyn Vining's face.

'Did you see that, Tish?'

'I told you she could run.'

That evening, some time after tea, Tish came into the TV room.

'Could you find Rebecca please, Debbie?' she asked. She was wearing a track suit, and as she was acting on the instructions of the hockey captain she was allowed to order people around, within reason. 'Tell her to be on school pitch with her hockey things in ten minutes for a trial game.'

Debbie was amazed, and deeply envious. She got to her feet. 'She won't come!' she burst out. 'She hates hockey. And do you know what she told me today? She said you've got thick legs because you play so much hockey, and she doesn't want to look like you.'

As Tish coloured deeply, Debbie felt a touch of satisfaction. 'But of course I'll tell her that Joss wants her,' she said sweetly. 'I'm just warning you that she probably won't turn up.'

SEVEN

END OF A FRIENDSHIP

Rebecca was in her favourite place, the library, and Debbie failed to find her. She looked into the Common Room on the first floor, then came back down and looked into the Hobbies' Room. She was alarmed to see from the clock on the wall that it was almost time for her favourite quiz programme on the TV.

'She must be doing her prep in the form room!' she thought and raced out and across the quadrangle gardens to the old school.

But of course Rebecca was not there either.

'Well, I've done my best,' thought Debbie virtuously, as she returned to the TV room and switched on the set. She picked up her English exercise book and ballpoint pen from a table and carried on writing, with half an eye on the programme. 'As if Rebecca would want to turn out, anyway. She'll be glad I couldn't find her.'

With that, Debbie put the whole matter right out of her mind.

In the library, Rebecca had her thick notepad open, the one she kept for her private writing, and was struggling with some lines of verse. If she were going to submit something for the school magazine, it had better be good. But – 'Awful', she groaned, when she read over her work.

She realized that the poem she had written on the beach had been better, although rather melancholy. But she couldn't remember it properly now, and besides, she wouldn't want to submit that for obvious reasons. She consoled herself with the thought that she had until Monday and it was still only Thursday. She would give up for tonight and turn her attention to her English essay instead.

She read through 'A Winter's Morning' and felt altogether more satisfied. It wasn't bad, but there were ways it could be improved. She spent a long time on the rough copy, changing words and phrases. Then, with a sigh of satisfaction she copied it out carefully in her best book and blotted it.

'Rebecca!' said an astonished voice. 'Have you seen the time?'

It was the prefect, Pippa Fellowes-Walker, who was on library duty that evening. She had only just noticed Rebecca, hidden behind a bookcase, working away as quiet as a mouse.

'Oh!' said Rebecca, looking at the clock. 'I've missed cocoa.'

'You certainly have,' said Pippa. 'You're supposed to be in bed in five minutes. You're not supposed to spend as long as this on prep! Go on – off you go!'

Rebecca rushed back to the boarding house and almost collided with Tish coming out of the wash room in pyjamas and dressing gown and ready for bed. 'Hallo!' she said. 'I missed cocoa –'

She got no further, for Tish walked straight past her in

stony silence. A coldness gripped Rebecca. What was the matter? What had she done wrong?

She was even more alarmed the following morning to find that both Tish and Sue were completely ignoring her, passing by her bed without a word, and hurrying down to breakfast together. Josselyn Vining was in a different dormitory but when Rebecca sat at the table in the dining hall, it struck her that Joss, too, seemed to be looking straight through her with a cold expression on her face.

Rebecca ate her cornflakes, feeling unhappy and confused. Were they being cool to her? Or was she imagining things? Was it simply that they had gone out of their way to be friendly because she was new, and now that she was settling in and had found a friend, they felt they didn't have to bother any more.

Whatever the reason, it cast a cloud over her entire day. Even the satisfaction of handing in her essay to Miss Heath was marred by her general feeling of unease.

As though to compensate for the unfriendliness of the other girls, Debbie Rickard was more friendly than ever before, as they sat together in lessons. Instead of finding this a comfort, Rebecca found that Debbie's constant chatter was beginning to get on her nerves.

'Please stop talking, Rebecca!' said Miss Gates, the maths mistress, turning round from the blackboard, and Rebecca went bright red. She hadn't been talking – Debbie had!

'Sorry,' whispered Debbie a little later.

The last lesson of the day was netball. This, at least, was a game that Rebecca had played many times before – not only at her London comprehensive school, but at her primary school before that. She was no good as a shooter but was very fast and useful in centre court positions. Unfortunately, as in the hockey game the previous day, she was put in a defence position.

Nevertheless, Rebecca had nothing to distract her, for Debbie Rickard was playing on another court, and she did her best. Although she was playing in her least favourite position she was fast on to the ball, and several times prevented Josselyn Vining getting hold of it in the shooting circle. This was tantamount to preventing goals, for Joss was the opposing shooter and every time she got the ball in the circle a goal would follow as sure as day follows night.

'I wonder if she hates netball, too?' Rebecca heard Joss say to Tish after the game.

'I expect so.'

'Pity.'

Rebecca, who had very sharp ears, saw them glance in her direction and knew at once that they had been referring to her. She could not bear their cold looks and, now, the growing feeling that something strange was going on. She walked over to them.

'I don't hate netball,' she blurted out. 'Why should I?'

'Well, you hate hockey, don't you?'

'Who told you that?'

'Your friend Debbie Rickard. It's true, isn't it?'

'I – I –' Rebecca broke off, feeling confused. It was certainly true that she had not enjoyed that first game yesterday, and she had told Debbie so.

She finished, lamely, 'I don't know yet whether I like it or not.'

She hurried away from the courts to the changing rooms in the sports centre. As she took a shower, various thoughts passed through her head. At last, she felt, she had some clue to Tish's cool behaviour. But it still didn't make sense. She felt a growing anger towards Debbie that she had told the others that she – Rebecca – 'hated' hockey, but she also felt sure that neither Tish nor Joss were the sort to lose much sleep over *that*. There must be more to it.

'What else has Debbie been saying?' wondered Rebecca.

When she got back to school, she found Debbie sitting on the terrace overlooking the quandrangle gardens, reading a book.

'Hallo, where have you been?' she asked Rebecca.

'Having a shower.'

'I can't bear showers,' said Debbie, screwing up her nose. 'Here, come and sit down. Tea bell should be going in a minute.'

But Rebecca did not sit down. She stood over Debbie. 'Why did you tell Josselyn Vining that I hate hockey?'

'I haven't even seen Joss Vining.'

'Well, Tish Anderson, then,' said Rebecca. Her feeling of uneasiness was growing every minute. 'How did it happen?'

'Oh, yes,' Debbie frowned, remembering. 'Tish was trying to rake you out for some game last night. She asked me to find you, but I told her you wouldn't want to play.'

'You might have asked me!' exclaimed Rebecca.

'I looked for you everywhere, absolutely everywhere!' said Debbie indignantly. 'I meant to tell you this morning, but I forgot. I'd have thought you'd be glad I couldn't find you.'

Rebecca realized that this must have been when she was in the library the previous evening; but her thoughts were already moving on with lightning speed.

'What else did you tell Tish?' she asked fiercely.

'Well,' Debbie started to laugh, but now that she could see the expression on Rebecca's face, the laughter was rather forced. 'I told her just what you thought of her legs and –'

'You *what*?'

'What's the matter with you?' said Debbie irritably. 'You thought it was funny enough yesterday. It's about time she was cut down to size. She's so full of herself, thinks she's so popular and that everybody likes her –'

'But I like her, too!' said Rebecca. 'And if she is popular she can't help that, any more than she can help having thick legs. I think that was really mean and spiteful.'

'Well, you shouldn't have said it then!' snapped Debbie. 'And if you like her so much, why don't you go off and be her friend. If she'll have you, that is,' she ended, with a sneer.

The tea bell sounded.

'I certainly don't want to be *your* friend,' said Rebecca, turning on her heel. 'I'm going.'

She marched off along the terrace towards the dining hall, with tears of anger pricking behind her eyes. So that was what her so-called friend was really like! Now things were beginning to fall into place. She knew why Sally Elphinstone had raised her eyebrows, and why Tish had asked that casual question, 'Do you like Debbie Rickard?' They had been surprised that Rebecca liked Debbie, and no wonder.

'It's better that I've found out now,' Rebecca told herself as she sat down to tea. She was trying to console herself. 'It's better to know sooner than later. Before she gets me into worse trouble.'

Even the fact that she'd been blamed for Debbie's talking in class that morning now caused Rebecca to feel angry. Some friend!

'Better to have no friends at all,' she thought, but at the same time a slight sense of panic overwhelmed her as she thought of the term stretching ahead of her, the many weeks before she would be going home for Christmas and seeing her family and old friends again. It gave her little appetite for tea.

Afterwards she went up to Joss and said awkwardly, 'I'm sorry I didn't turn up last night. I've only just heard about it. Debbie looked for me but wasn't able to find me.'

'Would you have come if you had known in time?' asked Joss.

Rebecca thought very hard. She still imagined that it had been a casual invitation to join in a game of hockey after school. Debbie had not explained to her that it was a trial game and that Joss was already beginning to think about picking the Under Fourteen school team for this season.

'Well, would you have come?' prompted Sue Murdoch, who was standing nearby. 'Honestly?'

Rebecca thought of what she had been doing in the library and how important it had been to her. She shook her head. 'No,' she said truthfully. 'There was something else I wanted to do. But I'd have come over to the pitch and explained.'

'Fair enough,' said Joss.

The two of them went off and joined up with Tish, reporting the conversation to her.

'You must admit she's frank,' said Joss.

'Too frank,' said Tish, with feeling. But she felt a little better towards Rebecca now. 'Trust Debbie Rickard not to bother to look for her properly. Can't think what Rebecca sees in her.'

For her part, Rebecca wished there were some way she could undo the hurt that her unkind remark must have caused Tish, once it had been relayed by Debbie, but it was something that could not be undone.

She went to her favourite place, the library. Somehow she must cling on to her resolve to write something for the school magazine. Drowning in homesickness, that was her one lifeline. She must be able to go home at the end of her first term and show them that she had achieved something: make them proud of her.

But nothing would come.

Rebecca had never found it difficult to compose poems before; she had won prizes for them. But they had never seemed so important before. Now that it really mattered, everything she wrote dissatisfied her.

She spent not only Friday evening, but most of the weekend trying to write the best poem she had ever written. The harder she tried, the worse her verses seemed to become.

She tried in the library, she tried in the school grounds; she even tried to write down on the beach, remembering how easily the words had flowed there when she had first arrived on the Tuesday. All the time she kept well out of Debbie Rickard's way, and everybody else's too. But still nothing would come.

On Sunday afternoon, Tish saw her sitting on the bank of the little lake by the music school, with her notepad on her knees, frowning and deep in concentration. Tish had come to the Hilary to meet Sue after violin practice, and just slipped silently through a side door without Rebecca seeing her. She felt obscurely pleased to see that she was not with Debbie Rickard, and also that she appeared to be writing something.

At bed-time that night she asked Rebecca, 'Got something to hand in to me tomorrow?'

'No.' Rebecca shook her head. 'Sorry.'

She turned and buried her face in her pillow. She was touched that Tish was still nice enough to show an interest, and it made it all ten times worse. Tomorrow was the deadline for handing in magazine entries and she had failed to produce anything. Her one hope of glory was fading away, in front of her eyes. A week of lessons stretched ahead of her, most of them to be spent – oh, horrors – sitting next to Debbie Rickard. Could anything be worse?

Rebecca thought, with longing, of home.

Although she did not know it, her spirits at that moment had reached their lowest ebb. They could sink no further. From now on they could only begin to rise.

EIGHT

JUNIPER VOTES

The first good thing that happened to Rebecca on Monday was supposed to be a 'punishment'. It took place after Miss Heath had called the register on Monday morning.

'Rebecca, Deborah,' said the form-mistress, sternly fixing her gaze on them, 'I have had complaints from three different mistresses about you two, talking during lessons, and I'm afraid I shall have to split you up.'

She looked all round the room at the pairs of girls seated at their double desks, thinking hard. Then she pointed: 'Susan and Ishbel, you tend to chatter rather a lot, too. So I think, let me see, Ishbel can sit in Margot's place at the back, next to Judith. I think it would be a good thing for Margot to come to the front. Margot come forward and sit in Rebecca's place next to Deborah, and you, Rebecca, collect up your books and sit at the back next to Susan.'

Rebecca felt weak all over. Some punishment! Not only was she being moved away from Debbie Rickard, but she was being told to sit next to Sue. She wondered if Tish would be furious at being split up from Sue but, as she went back there with her books, she could tell that she didn't mind. Sue, after all, would still be next door to her, just across the gangway, and Judy Sharp was pleased to have Tish sitting next to her. Debbie was relieved to be getting someone new, and the whole form was delighted at the distraction, which looked as though it would delay the start of the English lesson by at least five minutes as desk lids banged and girls shuffled around.

Only Margot Lawrence felt rather put out. She was not particularly fond of Debbie Rickard, and she liked sitting at the back. On the other hand, she was supposed to put some glasses on to look at the blackboard, and often didn't bother. Now she would not need to. Miss Heath was quite aware of this factor.

When the form had settled down, Miss Heath produced a thick pile of exercise books from her bag, and that was when the second nice thing happened to Rebecca.

'I have marked your essays over the weekend and one of them is so outstanding that I have awarded it an A. Rebecca, will you come up here and read it out to the rest of the form, please.'

Rebecca had to go up to the front. She took her open exercise book from Miss Heath and then turned to face the form. Her hand shook very slightly and the exercise book wobbled.

'A Winter's Morning,' she began, very fast.

'Don't gabble, Rebecca.'

Rebecca took a deep breath, and then read her essay slowly and carefully. The whole form listened in attentive silence. Nobody chattered or passed notes. Then Rebecca went back to her seat.

'Congratulations!' said Sue, out of the corner of her mouth, and Rebecca stared at the bright red A written boldly at the bottom of her essay, still not quite able to believe it.

But this was only the beginning of a day of excitement for Rebecca.

After English, Miss Heath left the room and a general babble broke forth, desk lids banged and chairs scraped. Next lesson was French and Ma'm'selle Giscard could always be relied upon to be late.

Tish got up and warmed her rear on the radiator, which was under the window and just behind Rebecca's chair. She grabbed the back of Rebecca's blue jumper and gave a tug.

'Hey, you!'

'Yes?' Rebecca turned round to see her smiling, one black curl out of place and hanging over her left eye. 'What?'

'You've got something to hand in tonight now.'

'For the magazine –? But I haven't.'

'That essay.'

'But –' Rebecca tried not to look too excited, 'is that allowed? I mean it was homework, not written for the magazine at all.'

'Of course it's allowed! You can submit anything you want. Copy it out on decent paper and have it ready by seven – okay?'

Tish shot back into her chair as Ma'm'selle entered the room, and the conversation came to an abrupt end.

'*Bon jour.*'

'*Bon jour*, Ma'm'selle.'

Rebecca found it hard to concentrate on lessons that day. She consulted the timetable at the front of her rough book and saw that the only prep for Monday evening was Geography. She hoped it would not be something long and arduous. She had to copy out her essay for Tish in her best handwriting by seven o'clock, and that was more important than anything else!

To her relief they were required only to draw some

common ordnance survey map signs and learn them. Rebecca knew them already, as they had done this work at her previous school.

She stayed on in the form room after the last lesson and drew the signs in her Geography exercise book quickly, finishing just before the tea bell went. She raced off and washed her hands and got to the dining hall in good time. Sardines on toast, good! Lots of fruit and stuff to follow, ginger cake and plenty of tea to drink.

'Where can I get some decent paper, Elf?' she asked. She had settled down more or less permanently at the opposite end of the table from Tish and Co., next to Sally Elphinstone, whom she liked. 'Somebody said there's a stationery room in old school.'

'Tiny little room next to the library,' said Elf, a second helping of ginger cake halfway to her mouth. 'There'll be a prefect on duty there after tea, and you have to sign for everything.'

It was Elizabeth Exton who was on duty. Just the sight of the tall, hawk-faced Sixth Former made Rebecca feel nervous.

'I want some sheets of best paper, please.'

'What do you mean, some? Be precise.'

'Four sheets, please.'

'Here you are.' The mighty Editor of the school magazine doled out the paper, wrote something in a ledger and handed Rebecca a pen. 'Sign here.'

Rebecca took the paper, signed for it, and escaped. Having already collected her English exercise book and yellow pencil case from the form room, she went straight into the library. She sat down and copied out her essay, neatly and carefully, in the best italic handwriting that she reserved for important occasions.

She then designed a title page on which were written the words: *A Winter's Morning by Rebecca Mason Form II Alpha.* She enclosed the words in a square box, carefully ruled, and then drew a little snowman underneath.

Just after seven o'clock she went to deliver the essay to Tish, who was sitting at the corner table in the Second Year Common Room, with her wire tray waiting. There were two First Years ahead of her, shyly depositing their contributions in the tray. Tish, in fact, was in the middle of sifting through the pile of contributions that had already been handed in at the magazine meeting the previous Wednesday, making still more notes.

But she looked up and caught Rebecca's eye. 'Well done,' she said, looking at the essay. 'I like the snowman. Just stick it in the tray with the other things.'

Rebecca went out quickly, trying hard not to show any sign of emotion. What were the other contributions like? How stiff was the competition? She would have to wait until Wednesday evening to find out.

Later, she made her cocoa and ate her biscuits alone. She wished she had a special friend, but not for a moment did she regret breaking up with Debbie Rickard. The terrible homesickness of the previous evening did not return; it had been an exciting day and now – although she hardly dare admit it – she was bubbling with hope. She wanted to write to her parents, but she must wait until after the second magazine meeting on Wednesday evening. Supposing, just supposing, she had some good news for them?

On Wednesday evening every chair was taken in the Second Year Common Room and Rebecca stood at the back with some First Years.

'Down to business,' said Tish briskly. She took a folder out of her bag and held it up. 'I've short listed six items and all of them are good enough to appear in this term's school magazine. But it's the Golden Jubilee edition and it's going to be very crowded, so I propose we send through four. That will be decided by vote. The best one will have a gold star put on it, as you know.'

Rebecca was very tense. She could not see all the items in the folder. Was her essay amongst them?

'First,' Tish held up a pen and ink drawing of the little church that stood in the school grounds, and Rebecca heard the fair-haired First Year standing beside her give a quick gasp of pleasure. 'Only one piece of artwork from the First Years, but it's outstanding. You can all recognize it, and it was done by Susannah Skelhorn over the weekend. I'm going to pass it round, but please be very careful not to mark it.'

She pulled another piece of artwork from the folder.

'Also we have this drawing by Verity Williams, Form II Beta, and I want you all to look at that closely, as well.'

Carefully the drawings were passed round the room and Tish took some sheets of paper from the folder. Rebecca thought she recognized her essay, but for a moment she could not be sure.

'Now the written contributions. I shall read them out, and then I shall pass them round as well. There are two poems, by Hilda Watkins and Judy Sharp, and two essays, by Jenny Brook-Hayes and Rebecca Mason.'

Rebecca felt slightly dizzy. The suspense was unbearable. In a blur she heard Tish read through the items, slowly and carefully. It seemed to take an age and although she could hear the words clearly, they refused to register on her brain, even the words of her own essay.

There was another long delay as the written work was passed round, so that girls who were undecided how to vote could read things through to themselves. During this period there was a lot of whispering and rustling of paper. At last Tish thumped on the table.

'I think you've all seen enough now,' she said. 'We'll have the vote. For the benefit of new girls, you are only allowed to vote for *one* item – the one you like best – and the six girls concerned are not allowed to vote at all. Okay? Let's start.'

She went through each item in turn. Hands were raised, votes were counted and written down. The first four items did not receive many votes, and Rebecca began to feel excited, even hopeful.

'Fifth, the drawing of St Mary's Church by Susannah Skelhorn.'

It seemed to Rebecca that a forest of hands shot up.

'. . . seven . . . eight . . . nine. Nine votes.'

She felt a huge lump coming into her throat. How silly of her to imagine that her essay might get the gold star! Would it even be selected to go through at all?

'Last, "A Winter's Morning" by Rebecca Mason.'

Rebecca closed her eyes. She heard Tish's voice.

'. . . seven . . . eight . . . nine . . . ten . . . eleven. Eleven votes.'

She opened her eyes again. Girls were turning round and looking at her, smiling and clapping.

Susannah Skelhorn, who was standing right beside her, said shyly, 'Congratulations. You deserved to win.'

Rebecca felt weak at the knees. She had no idea that there were so many girls in the room – that there were still eleven votes left for her! Her essay had been voted best, it would get the gold star!

Tish announced which four items would go through and the meeting broke up. Only one person looked really sour – Roberta Jones, who once again had failed to get anything short-listed for the school magazine. Debbie Rickard came up to Rebecca.

'Congratulations,' she said, but her smile was forced.

When Rebecca went up to the table, Tish was actually in the act of sticking a large gold star on the front of the essay, just above the snowman's head. A small crowd gathered round.

'Does this mean –' began Rebecca. Her voice faltered. She had meant to walk out with quiet dignity, but she *had* to be sure. 'Does the gold star mean that it'll definitely go in *The Trebizon Journal*?'

'Of course,' said Tish, and she gave Rebecca a dazzling smile. 'And I'm taking the stuff straight to Elizabeth Exton now. Well done, Bec, I knew you would win.'

NINE

THE MAGAZINE COMES OUT

Rebecca went out into the grounds. The sun was sinking low and a game of hockey was just finishing on school pitch. The birds were twittering and as she came within sight of Parkinson, the big Victorian house where the Upper Sixth boarded, she darted into some trees and kept watch.

Sure enough, Ishbel Anderson came hurrying along five minutes later, entered the garden of Parkinson House by the side gate and went across and rang the bell, her folder under her arm. After a few moments, the door opened and somebody let her in.

Rebecca came out of her hiding place. Her essay was being delivered to the Editor of the school magazine. She had seen so, with her own eyes. It was all real! She raced away, knowing that if by any chance Tish should catch sight of her gawping at Parkinson House, she would think her absolutely mad.

'It's twenty minutes till cocoa time!' thought Rebecca, running exhilarated as the breeze blew through her fair hair. 'I'll run down to the beach and look at the waves.'

In her study, Elizabeth Exton was pacing up and down. It

was a very large room, with a long mahogany table under the windows, and was not only Elizabeth's study but also the editorial office of *The Trebizon Journal.* There were four chairs set round the table which was piled high with papers and pieces of artwork. There had been a meeting of the Editorial Committee that evening. The Editor of the school magazine was always allocated this beautiful study as a matter of course. Last year its occupant had been Mary Green, who was now beginning an exciting career on a national newspaper.

Mary Green was very much in Elizabeth Exton's thoughts. She knew that Mary had got her start as a direct result of her work on *The Trebizon Journal*, and Elizabeth had similar ambitions. Although Freddie Exton had many contacts in the world of commerce, he had few in newspapers or magazines, a field Elizabeth badly wanted to enter when she left school.

Elizabeth had been told that she was unlikely to get to University, and she had decided to devote all her talents this year to the editorship of the school magazine. She felt sure that if she could produce three dazzling issues of the famous *Journal*, it would make a big impression on a future employer. This first issue, to mark the magazine's Golden Jubilee, must be the most dazzling of all.

Elizabeth felt very confident at the way things were going. What she planned to do with this issue was daring – ambitious – people were going to be very impressed! The meeting with the Editorial Committee this evening had been nerve-racking: especially that long argument with Audrey, trust Audrey to be difficult. The trouble was that she had wanted to be Editor herself! For a time, Elizabeth had had visions of her triumph slipping through her fingers, and all her hard work in the holidays going for nothing. But she had won the day! She had made the Committee see reason, and won them round completely to her way of thinking. Emma had been a great ally.

Now Elizabeth was convinced that this term's issue of *The Trebizon Journal* was going to put everything that had gone before in the shade. It would make Mary Green's efforts look dull and pedestrian by comparison. It was all very satisfying.

Only in one way did Mary Green have the edge, and it was this that was causing Elizabeth to pace up and down the floor. She was having a tremendous struggle with her conscience. By long tradition, the last page of *The Journal* always carried a personal contribution from the Editor herself. It could be prose or poetry or artwork, anything for which the Editor had a talent. Mary's special contribution had always been a crossword puzzle, with the clues written in verse, and they had won great acclaim. Elizabeth could produce nothing as good as that.

The last page of the magazine was still a yawning blank and, the more she thought about it, the more convinced Elizabeth became that there was only one way to solve the problem. But it would mean going against her conscience, and Elizabeth didn't like doing that.

'Who's that?' she asked, jumpily, as someone tapped on the door.

'Ishbel Anderson.'

'Come in.'

Elizabeth stared blankly for a moment as Tish walked in with her folder. What was a Junior coming to see her for?

'I've got Juniper's contribution, in this folder,' said Tish. 'Would you like to see them?' she asked eagerly. 'I got cracking quickly, because of what you said –'

'Just put the folder on the table,' said Elizabeth. 'I'm very busy right now. I'll look at them later.'

Tish placed the folder on the table, disappointed, as Elizabeth dismissed her.

'Thank you, Ishbel.'

As she left the room, Tish said, 'They're very good this term. They really are.'

'Yes, yes,' said Elizabeth abstractedly, 'I'm sure they are. Well done.'

After Tish had gone, Elizabeth walked over to the long mahogany table. She picked up the folder and then, restlessly, put it down again.

'House contributions,' she mused. 'More problems.'

She snapped her finger and thumb together and walked over to her portable typewriter, which was on a side table. She sat down and fed in a sheet of paper.

'About time I had a notice given out,' she thought. 'Forgotten all about it. So much to think about.'

She carefully typed a notice to be given out at Assembly the next day.

Sitting in the sand dunes, Rebecca watched the waves breaking on the shore of Trebizon Bay. The distant sea was stained red by the setting sun, and a solitary fishing boat bobbed upon it in dark silhouette. Rebecca felt happy and at peace. At last she could write to her parents, because she had something really good to tell them. Not tonight; it was almost cocoa time. Tomorrow. In the meantime, she composed the letter in her head.

Miss Welbeck read Elizabeth's notice at Assembly on Thursday morning.

'All contributions to *The Trebizon Journal* must be handed

to Elizabeth Exton by this weekend,' announced the Principal. 'It goes to the printers next week, a fortnight early, because for the first time it is carrying some colour pages to mark its Golden Jubilee.'

Rebecca could tell from the groans and whispers that some of the Magazine Officers were not going to have their House contributions ready in time. She caught Tish's eye. Tish was smiling and giving the thumbs-up sign. Elizabeth had certainly sprung her announcement at short notice. How sharp of Tish, thought Rebecca, to have found out in advance. At least Juniper House was going to be represented in *The Journal* – represented by her, Rebecca Mason! She still found that an amazing thought.

'Here is a further announcement,' said Miss Welbeck. '*The Journal* will be at the special price of £2.25 pence this term, and all copies must be ordered in advance. It can be posted direct to families and friends, and order forms are now available from the School Secretary. They must be completed and handed in by the end of the month.'

Miss Welbeck looked up from the typewritten sheet and added a comment of her own. 'Remember, you can pay for your copies out of pocket money, but if you are ordering more copies than you can pay for, you must write and ask for your parents' permission in advance, as they will be getting the bills!'

Subdued laughter echoed around the hall and Miss Welbeck passed on to other notices. Rebecca hardly took them in; she was doing a swift calculation. Her parents were in Saudi Arabia now. She had some airmail forms in her bedside locker. If she wrote to them in the dinner hour, and caught today's post, they could get the letter and send a reply by airmail by the end of the month – easily.

Rebecca wanted the magazine to go to at least ten people. Not just her parents, but her favourite uncles and aunts, and both her grandmothers would want a copy – and so would her friends in London, Claire and Amanda. It was such an honour getting into *The Trebizon Journal*! She had a whole mental list of people who would feel proud of her and want to have a copy to keep. But all those copies were going to cost her father a fortune!

On second thoughts, she would ask her father to pay for just four copies – his and Mum's, the two grandmothers' and one for Great Aunt Ivy, who definitely couldn't afford to buy one herself. Uncle Bill, and Godmother Joan, and Claire and Amanda and the rest she would write to herself and ask them to send through the money to her if they wanted one. Good, that was settled.

Rebecca dashed off the letter to her mother and father in the dinner hour, sealed up the airmail form and ran and dropped it in the school post box in the main entrance hall of old building. She tried to picture her parents' faces as they opened it and read it through. For a moment she felt an ache, missing them.

She wrote all the other letters the same evening, as soon as she had finished her French prep. She wrote to Claire and Amanda jointly and begged them for news; in return she told them about Trebizon and, in ironic tones, about the disastrous Debbie Rickard.

Not for a moment did Rebecca regret breaking up with Debbie, even though it meant she had no special friend to go around with at Trebizon. She would make her way as best she could, and try and get the most out of life at her new school, and perhaps friendships would follow. At least she was beginning to make her mark.

The following weeks were a little lonely at times, but one

thing made them less so. Her services were in demand in connection with *The Juniper Journal*.

It had been decided to bring out the House publication once a week, and an editorial committee of three had been elected. This comprised Tish Anderson and Mara Leonodis from the Second Year and Susannah Skelhorn from the First Year. Mara and Susannah were assistant editors, collecting in news items and other contributions from girls in their year, and Tish was Editor-in-chief, laying out the two pages and then typing the stencils. It was decided to produce *The Journal* on a single sheet of duplicating paper, using front and back. This would keep the cost down to five pence.

Everyone agreed that it was better to produce something cheap and simple once a week, full of up-to-date news, than a more ambitious publication that could only come out perhaps once a month.

The excitement in Juniper House as the first issue was being prepared was infectious, and a steady stream of contributions came in, some of them quite silly. It had been decided to make Sundays the press day for *The Journal*, as that was a day when Tish had plenty of free time to type out the stencils and run them off on the duplicator in the evening. *The Journal* would then be on sale every Monday morning.

On the Saturday night before the first press day, Tish was sitting having cocoa with Sue Murdoch in the Common Room.

'We've got stacks of news items,' she said. 'I mean Joss is announcing the Under-14 hockey team for a start. That's the lead story. We've also got a piece about the four items we've submitted to *The Trebizon* this term. That's a bit stale, but there are still some people who don't know.

Also one of the First Years has come up with a gem of a story . . .'

She lapsed into silence.

'What's the problem then?' asked Sue.

'The balance seems wrong. We haven't got what they call feature material – quizzes, crosswords, anything like that.'

At that moment the door opened and Rebecca and Sally Elphinstone came into the Common Room with cocoa and biscuits.

'You'd better have my biscuits, Rebecca,' said the plump girl mournfully. 'I just get fatter and fatter. It's just not fair, I mean look at you. You eat like a horse and you're skinny.'

'I burn it all up,' said Rebecca, taking the biscuits. 'You burn your food slowly, Elf, that's all. You'd have been the envy of all your friends if you'd lived in the Stone Age, when food was short. I mean they tried to be fat then. They really envied people who had an efficient system like yours, which could create energy from next to nothing.'

Sally snorted, but Tish's face lit up. 'Hey, that's interesting, Rebecca,' she said. 'Know any more useless facts like that?'

'She knows plenty,' giggled Sue, speaking from experience of sitting next to Rebecca in class. 'She's always churning them out. Tell Tish that one about lichen and pure air, Rebecca. Hey – I know what you're thinking, Tish!'

'What's going on?' asked Rebecca with a smile. It was true that she had a mind that stored up off-beat information; her father often teased her about it. 'Going to write a book?'

'No, you are!' said Tish. 'At least not a book. A regular piece for *The Juniper Journal* called "Did you know –? by Rebecca Mason"! Hmm? I'm serious. I've just thought of it. How about it?'

'Fine!' said Rebecca, trying to hide her delight.

'Good. Then write out three useless facts for me by tomorrow dinner hour, the weirder the better. Our first issue goes to press tomorrow afternoon, as if you didn't know.'

So Rebecca became a regular contributor to *The Juniper Journal*; she also helped to work the duplicator sometimes on a Sunday evening and was one of a team of girls selling copies around the school at five pence each.

The news-letter came in for a lot of praise, especially from Miss Morgan, their House Mistress. She herself undertook to sell two dozen copies a week in the Staff Room. It was all good fun.

But for Rebecca the high point of the next few weeks was the post. There was a long letter from her parents in Saudi Arabia, full of all their news, and scarcely concealing their happiness that she had made a good start at Trebizon School. They were immensely proud that her essay was going to appear in the school magazine and her father asked her to order eight copies, instead of the four she had suggested.

The letters from her Godmother Joan, her Uncle Bill and her Uncle David were lovely – they all wanted copies of the magazine and sent postal orders, with some extra spending money thrown in. Claire and Amanda each wrote a super letter, in the same envelope, and asked her to order an extra copy – for Mr Goodfellow, the Headmaster at her old school in London.

Rebecca was very excited, counting the days till half-term. The long-awaited Golden Jubilee edition of *The Trebizon Journal* was expected to arrive at the school from the printers' sometime over the half-term holiday. Rebecca was spending half-term with her grandmother in

Gloucestershire, and the magazines would be there, at the school, when she got back.

All through the half-term holiday at her grandmother's she felt a pleasurable sense of anticipation.

'You're sure your father's paid for my copy?' asked her grandmother anxiously. 'I'm well able to pay for it, you know, Becky. I certainly don't want you paying for it out of your pocket money.'

'Stop worrying, Gran,' laughed Rebecca. 'It's all ordered, and paid for, by Dad. I only wish it could have arrived from the printers in time for me to bring it with me. But it'll be posted to you in a few days, direct from school.'

Later, reading through the first three stencilled issues of *The Juniper Journal*, her grandmother said, 'And why aren't you in the hockey team, my girl?'

Rebecca was quite startled by the pang she felt. 'I'm – I'm just not,' she said.

She thought ruefully of her ambitions at the start of the term. She was beginning to like hockey a lot now, and knew that she was playing reasonably well, although she had still not been given a chance to play in a forward position. There were too many good forwards around for that.

She felt quite envious of the girls who were in the Under-14 team, going off in a mini-bus on Saturday afternoons to play matches against other schools. She still had no inkling that the game she had been asked to join during her first week at Trebizon had in fact been a trial game, and that Joss Vining had assumed that her interest was nil.

'You can't get in everything at a school like Trebizon, Gran,' said Rebecca. She smiled. 'At least I'm going to be in the school magazine, and that's something, isn't it!'

But Rebecca was wrong.

She learnt the awful news as soon as she got back to

school after the half-term holiday. She was late back because of the awkward journey from Gloucestershire, and went straight up to the dormitory with her denim bag to unpack her weekend things.

Tish was waiting for her there, holding a copy of the magazine. It was fresh from the printers and had a lovely gold cover. Rebecca had eyes for nothing else. She did not see that Tish's face was white with rage.

TEN

TISH DECLARES WAR

'You weren't on the London train,' said Tish.

'I haven't been to London,' said Rebecca. She was staring at the magazine, mesmerized. It looked beautiful! 'I've been to my grandmother's and that meant a bus that went halfway round England –'

'I've been waiting for you!'

'Miss Morgan knew I'd be late,' said Rebecca. What on earth was Tish so angry about, so very, very angry? 'The magazine's arrived from the printers' then? It really looks something –'

She reached out her hand eagerly. She *had* to see.

To her surprise Tish took a step backwards and put the magazine behind her back. She had difficulty in speaking.

'It's not in there. Your essay's not in.'

'Not in?' said Rebecca, dully.

'*Nothing's* in. Nothing from Juniper, almost nothing from any of the other Houses, a few Sixth Form things and *that's all.*'

'But – it's quite thick – there must be a lot of stuff in it – are you sure?'

'Of course I'm sure!' Tish produced the magazine and leafed over the pages in her hands. Rebecca caught a glimpse of beautifully laid out pages, some of them in full colour, thick and glossy. She recognized the exquisite bird pictures that Elizabeth had been carrying in her big black bag on the train, the very first time she had ever met her. 'It's thick all right and there's a lot of stuff in it, just nothing to do with Trebizon School, that's all!'

All Tish's pent up disgust poured out. 'It's full of big names, Rebeck. Famous writers, famous artists – okay, one or two of them old girls of the school, but not all of them, by any means. Elizabeth Exton's been having a ball! That's how she spent the summer holidays, dashing around meeting famous people, asking them to do things for the Golden Jubilee issue, making herself out to be someone really important. Here, take a look.'

Rebecca turned away.

'No thanks, Tish. I – I don't think I can bear to.'

'All right. But I'll just read what she says at the beginning, so you can have a really good vomit. Listen:

> It is a great honour and privilege to me to present this, our Golden Jubilee issue of *The Trebizon Journal*, marking its fifty years of continuous and unbroken production. This term contributions from the school were not quite up to the usual high standard, but no matter. The editorial committee and I decided to break with tradition and invite in outside contributors; how proud and honoured we are that such famous and illustrious names have agreed to grace our pages, a fitting birthday tribute to our famous *Journal*. Elizabeth Exton. Editor.

Rebecca sat down on the edge of her bed, feeling weepy.

'I've got friends and relations who've ordered it,' she said dismally. 'They'll all be getting it. Do I feel a fool. I just didn't think that my essay wasn't up to standard for the magazine, after –'

'It was up to standard!' snapped Tish. 'So was everything else, I expect – except a lot of stuff went in too late. Don't you see, that's just hot air? Elizabeth didn't *want* anything from the school! She'd got everything she needed before term even started – she had it on the train, remember? Talked about meeting super people.'

'Yes,' nodded Rebecca. 'I remember.'

'Being made Editor just went to her head. She raced around seeing all these big names in the holidays and getting them to do things. After that the committee hardly had any choice but to agree with her that they should be published in the magazine. I mean to say,' just for a moment a weaker version of Tish's usual grin appeared, 'imagine sending out a rejection slip to Nadine Rossiter.' The famous novelist had contributed a short story to *The Trebizon Journal*.

'Yes, imagine.' Rebecca managed to raise a smile, but she felt very depressed. 'All the same, I guess the stuff from the school really wasn't up to standard. They could have found room for it, if it had been. Even added a couple of extra pages.'

'Rubbish!' said Tish. 'Elizabeth just didn't want to find room for it. She didn't want anything that might spoil her grown-up looking magazine. I expect she's angling to get a good job somewhere on the strength of this,' she added darkly.

Silently, Rebecca unpacked her things. She was beginning to feel worse and worse; utterly humiliated. Tish was pacing up and down the dormitory, deep in thought. When she finally stopped, Rebecca looked at her and said, 'There's nothing you can do about it, Tish.'

'Oh, isn't there?' muttered Tish, and went out.

Brave words, thought Rebecca. As if there were anything Tish could possibly do. As if a mere Second Year could challenge the mighty Sixth Former who was Editor of the school magazine! After all, she *was* the Editor, and her decision was final. She said the school contributions weren't up to standard, and she should know best.

The more Rebecca thought about it, the more convinced she became that she had been conceited and overconfident about her essay. If it were a school tradition always to publish something with a gold star on it, then the Editor and her committee must have thought it *very* bad to reject it.

She ate tea in silence, grateful for the sympathetic comments from the girls on her table, but relieved not to be expected to talk. She was dimly aware that Tish arrived for tea very late, looking puffed and dishevelled, and left the minute she had finished her pudding, without even waiting for a cup of tea.

After tea, Rebecca didn't quite know what to do with herself. At a time like this she missed very much not having a special friend, someone to whom she could pour out her feelings. She felt such a failure! She would have liked Tish to talk to her again: somehow she did make it sound as though it was not a question of the essay being rubbish.

Rebecca went over to old school, carefully avoiding the Office where she knew that her personal copy of *The Trebizon Journal*, ordered so eagerly a month ago, was waiting to be collected. She didn't want to collect it – not ever! She wondered if there were any way she could stop all the other copies being posted off that she had ordered and paid for. There probably wasn't.

She borrowed a book from the library and went back across the quadrangle gardens to Juniper, having decided to find a quiet corner in the Second Year Common Room for the evening. There were too many people reading *The Trebizon Journal* in the library for her liking.

But as soon as she peered through the open door of the Common Room, she saw what looked like a forest of gold-covered Journals, glinting and shining in the light of the reading lamps, as though to mock her. Every seat was taken, every space on the rugs was taken, and there were even girls perched on the tables. It appeared to Rebecca's jaundiced eye that every single one of them was reading the school magazine, hot from the press.

'I think it's brilliant,' she heard Roberta Jones say smugly. 'Trust someone like Elizabeth Exton to do things in style. I'm not at all put out now that my poems weren't chosen to go forward.'

'Tish Anderson's like a bear with a sore head.' That was Debbie Rickard's voice, and there was a definite snigger in it. 'Her stuff's been rejected. The Editor's *dared* to question her judgement –!'

Rebecca didn't want to hear any more, and didn't want to be seen, either. She remembered how Debbie had come up and congratulated her, after the second magazine meeting. The hypocrite!

Where to go and read her book? Rebecca remembered the form room. There was no prep tonight and so it was deserted. She sat at her desk and read until a bell began to ring. She saw by the clock that it was bedtime, so she lifted the lid of her desk to put the library book inside.

'Who's been through my desk?' she wondered. 'What a mess.'

She decided to give cocoa a miss, and went straight to

bed. Tish and Sue were easily last in the dormitory, rushing in just before lights out.

'What have you two been up to?' asked someone.

'You'll see in the morning.'

'Sssh!'

'Shut up.'

'Have a biscuit, Tish.'

'Shut *up*, you lot!'

It took Rebecca a long time to get to sleep that night. She felt that she had only slept for a couple of hours when somebody drew the curtain behind her bed and shook her awake. It was Tish, already up and dressed.

'Here's your English exercise book, Rebecca,' she said, slamming it down on the locker. 'I borrowed it from your desk yesterday.'

'Whatever for?' asked Rebecca rubbing her eyes.

She stared at Tish, who seemed to be in a much better mood this morning. She seemed almost cheerful, and there was a strange light in her eyes. Rebecca also saw that she was holding some duplicated sheets in her hand.

'I needed to copy something out on to a stencil,' said Tish airily. 'Here you are, you may as well be the first to have one *J.J.* – special issue – free of charge, hot off the press last night. Five of us are off to disseminate it around the school now.' Bye. See you at breakfast!'

Rebecca found herself sitting up in bed, the stencilled sheet in her hands. Tish had gone. So had Sue. So had Margot Lawrence, Sally Elphinstone and Mara Leonodis. Joanna Thompson and Jenny Brook-Hayes were still fast asleep.

She stared at the sheet that had been thrust into her hands and, slowly at first, began to read it:

JUNIPER JOURNAL – Special Free Issue

We challenge The Trebizon Journal, it said. *Elizabeth Exton should resign. She's not fit to be Editor.*

Rebecca gasped and started to read much, much more quickly. Key phrases leapt out of the page at her.

For fifty years The Journal has been written by the school . . . for the school . . . not by outsiders . . . the Editor has no right to cast a slur on the school contributions . . . some Magazine Officers were not given time . . . As far as Juniper House goes, the slur is unfounded . . . We can prove it . . .

We throw open our editorial columns to all work that has been rejected by Elizabeth Exton. We will publish it for you! But first we start with Juniper's best –

The next line of type danced in front of Rebecca's eyes.

A WINTER'S MORNING – by REBECCA MASON, FORM II ALPHA

In growing excitement she read her own essay, printed out in full, right down to the bottom of the page and over on to the back. Tish had copied it word for word from her English exercise book.

At the bottom of the back page came a final exhortation:

Don't forget – send your rejected material to The J.J. We will print it and prove that the remark in the official school magazine is a slur on us all. This issue published by Ishbel Anderson – Magazine Officer – Juniper House.

Rebecca sank back weakly against her pillow. It was unbelievable. Tish had really done it. She had challenged no less mighty a person than Elizabeth Exton. Rebecca felt admiration for her courage, but it was mixed with dread.

What would happen to Ishbel Anderson now?

ELEVEN

REBECCA SEES A 'GHOST'

Rebecca got washed and dressed and kept out of everybody's way until breakfast time. She went and sat down by the lake, watched the ducks bobbing in and out of the reeds, and read the stencilled news-sheet over and over again.

She was excited to see her essay in print and to know that the whole school would be reading it. At the same time she was ashamed of feeling excited. What an incredible thing for Tish to do. Clearly there were others backing her up, people like Sue and Margot and dear old Elf. But the full wrath of those in authority would surely fall on Tish's head, and hers alone.

A group of Fourth Years went by, on their way to breakfast from their boarding house in the school grounds. They were crowding round the stencilled sheet as they walked along.

'I agree with every word she says!'

'So do I.'

'Suky Morris did a marvellous drawing and it should have gone in. Elizabeth Exton's just a big show-off.'

'But what's she going to do when she reads this? That's what I want to know . . .'

Their voices faded off into the distance. Rebecca got to her feet. She couldn't put off going to dining hall any longer, and besides, she wanted breakfast badly. It was an hour since Tish had shaken her awake. In that hour, Tish and Co. had certainly moved fast: the special issue of *The J.J.* had already been delivered to the boarding houses. People were already reading it.

Rebecca could tell, as soon as she entered the dining hall, that the news had travelled like wildfire. The stencilled sheets were in evidence everywhere and there was a tremendous buzz of talking. Tish, trying to sit down to have her breakfast, was involved in a quarrel with someone – it looked as though it might turn into a physical fight. And as Rebecca walked in, a group of First Years on the table nearest the door clapped her.

'Get your hands off me, Margaret Exton!' Tish was saying, as Rebecca approached. A tall girl with bony features, was gripping Tish's arm tightly and Tish was trying to tear her hand away. 'Get lost!'

Rebecca remembered that Elizabeth Exton had a younger sister in the Third Year. This must be her – white with fury, too.

'You'll pay for this, Tish Anderson,' she said threateningly.

'Go and sit at your proper table, Margaret,' said a prefect.

Margaret Exton walked across the hall to her table, where a group of Third Years banged their knives and forks and cheered her.

Miss Gates, the mistress on duty, blew a whistle loudly.

'Silence!' she said. 'Everyone will eat breakfast in silence!'

And so they did. Immediately afterwards, Rebecca approached Tish before she could leave the dining hall.

'Tish!'

'Are you angry, Rebecca?'

'No, I'm just scared for your sake.'

'I'm not scared. I just had to do something – and I feel great to have got it all off my chest. Sorry it happens to be your essay that's involved. Means your name's dragged into the whole thing.'

'I don't mind *that* at all!' said Rebecca, her eyes shining now. 'You've certainly got a lot of faith in that essay! Not only you, but the others who've helped you. I'd just about lost faith in it. But now, seeing it in print . . .'

'Six different people have already told me they think it's marvellous,' said Tish. 'I mean, older girls. Even a Sixth Former.'

As if to prove the very point that Tish was making, two older girls walked over and clapped Rebecca on the back.

'Good stuff that.'

'Should have gone in.'

But another girl, Lady Edwina Burton who was in the Fifth Year, came up to them and said quite angrily, 'Don't encourage these little berks. They're big-headed enough already. Who do they think they are, anyway?'

'Hear, hear!' said somebody else.

Fortunately, at that moment the bell went for Assembly.

During the course of the day, Rebecca came to realize that the school was split right down the middle, taking sides in the quarrel between the puny *Juniper Journal* and the mighty *Trebizon Journal*.

A lot of girls agreed with Tish's views, and were quietly pleased that she had expressed them. But there were others who admired the beautiful, lavish magazine that Elizabeth

Exton and her committee had produced to mark the Golden Jubilee, and thought the whole thing was rudeness and cheek beyond belief.

As for Elizabeth Exton, there was no doubt in her mind whatsoever. As soon as a copy of the offending sheet fell into her hands, at the end of a morning break, she went directly to see Miss Morgan, House Mistress of Juniper.

'I think this insolent little rag should be banned,' she informed Miss Morgan. 'These girls aren't sensible enough to have the use of a duplicating machine. They should never be allowed to use it again. Especially that Anderson girl.'

Miss Morgan read the news-sheet from start to finish.

'I see,' she said at length. 'Thank you for drawing this to my attention, Elizabeth. Perhaps you could arrange for Ishbel to be extracted from old school and brought over here to my office at once.'

'Yes, Miss Morgan,' said Elizabeth, with some satisfaction.

In spite of her protests to Rebecca about not being scared, Tish was only human. Her knees began to knock when she found herself hauled out of the French lesson and deposited in Miss Morgan's office on the ground floor of Juniper House. The room was empty but she could see the stencilled sheet lying on the desk.

Some time later, Miss Morgan walked in, sat down and picked up the sheet, fixing Tish with a stern eye.

'You shouldn't have done this, Ishbel.'

'But it wasn't fair!'

'You do realize, don't you, that if it were not for the generosity of Elizabeth's father, there would be no magazine at all this term?'

'Yes, but that shouldn't come into it –'

'Of course not. Except it should make you doubly careful

before you insult and vilify somebody without any possible justification, somebody much higher up the school than you who has worked extremely hard, in full and proper consultation with her editorial committee –'

'But –'

'Don't argue with me, Ishbel. That fact, I have just checked. And as you know, anybody elected to the high office of Editor of *The Journal* has, with her editorial committee, final responsibility for it. It's not up to any of us, least of all some insignificant members of the Second Year, to question her judgement in such personal terms.

'Elizabeth has asked me to ban your journal. I am not going to ban it. Indeed, you're free to publish any material you wish that did not reach the necessary standard for this term's magazine. But first you'll publish a full apology and retraction for this –' She tapped the sheet lying on the table. 'Draft something out and bring it to my office this evening.'

She got up and showed Tish to the door.

'Ishbel, I'm surprised at you,' were Miss Morgan's last words.

'Tish!' shouted Sue, hanging out of the form room window and waving. French had just ended and four of them, including Rebecca, were crowding round the window that looked down on to the quadrangle gardens, far below. At last Tish had emerged from Juniper House. 'Tish!'

'She's coming back, but she's not looking up,' said Margot Lawrence apprehensively. 'I don't think she's even heard us.'

'She looks really miserable,' said Elf. 'She's come into the building now. I wonder what the punishment is?'

'Whatever it is, we share it with her,' said Margot. 'We were all in it together.'

'I'll share it, too,' volunteered Rebecca.

They rushed over as Tish entered the form room, her cheeks red and her grin noticeably absent. Debbie Rickard, sat in the front row, all ears, pretending to sort out her history books for the next lesson.

'What happened?'

'What is it – lines? Detention? What?'

'Nothing like that,' began Tish. She was very subdued. 'Gosh, did I get an earful from Miss Morgan! She's backing up Elizabeth Exton completely. Won't hear a word against her.'

Debbie Rickard glanced across the form room and caught the eye of Roberta Jones. They exchanged satisfied nods.

'Look out!' shouted Judy Sharp, who was keeping watch in the corridor. 'Maggy's coming!'

There was a mad scramble for desks and books as Miss Magg, the history mistress, entered the form room.

'No whispering, please,' she said sternly.

Sitting next to Sue at the back, Rebecca tried to concentrate as Miss Magg wrote some facts about Ancient Egypt on the blackboard. Out of the corner of her eye she saw Tish pass Sue a note, across the gangway between their desks. Sue opened it out and let Rebecca read it with her. It said:

Have to apologize to E.E. in the J.J. or else . . .

Sue wrote underneath:

And will we?

She passed it to Tish, who wrote something and passed it back:

Horrible decision. I don't know.

All Rebecca's thoughts were with Tish now. Poor Tish. No wonder she looked so unhappy! She respected Miss Morgan and was obviously shattered that she sided with Elizabeth. But what else could the House Mistress do?

reflected Rebecca. No Second Year could insult an important School Officer and be allowed to get away with it. In her heart, she had guessed it would come to something like this.

'The tomb, Rebecca!' said Miss Magg sharply. 'What did they put in the tomb?'

'The – the body, I suppose,' said Rebecca weakly. There was laughter. Maggy had been asking her a question and she hadn't even heard it.

'Oh, really? The body?'

The mistress's voice was heavy with sarcasm and from then on Rebecca had to pay close attention to the lesson. At last the bell went. Morning lessons had ended; in fifteen minutes it would be dinner time.

Tish and Co. immediately went into a huddle over by the window. Rebecca wondered if she could join them, but Sue signalled her away. They were discussing whether Tish should write the apology.

'Action committee, Rebecca,' mouthed Tish. 'Clear off. We're mixed up in it, especially me, but you're not. Not fair to involve you.'

Rebecca wandered downstairs, thinking she wouldn't mind being mixed up in it. The Secretary popped her head out of the School Office and called her name. She was holding *The Trebizon Journal*.

'You've forgotten to collect your magazine, Rebecca.'

Rebecca had no choice but to take it. After all, she had paid for it. And as she sat in the weak November sunshine outside the dining hall, waiting for the bell to go, curiosity got the better of her at last. Gingerly, she began to leaf through the pages.

She was looking at the last page when Tish found her. The dinner bell had gone, but Rebecca hadn't even heard it.

Tish was feeling extremely angry and upset at the idea of having to write a public apology to Elizabeth Exton, and so far nothing had been resolved. But she was not so upset that she couldn't see there was something wrong.

'Reading that?' she asked. Then, 'What's the matter with you? You look as though you've seen a ghost.'

'My poem!' said Rebecca, hoarsely, almost too shocked to speak. It really was like seeing a ghost. 'She didn't write it. *I* did.'

TWELVE

OUT OF THE FRYING PAN . . .

'Your poem?' asked Tish, bewildered. 'What on earth are you talking about, Rebecca? Who didn't write what?'

'Elizabeth Exton didn't write my poem!' blurted out Rebecca. 'I wrote it! She's made up a title for it – "Solitude" – that's all. I called it "All Alone", but it's *my* poem. I wrote it! And she's put *her* name at the bottom of it!'

'Are you serious?' Tish said.

The last stragglers were going into the dining hall now and shortly a prefect would close the big glass doors. But neither Rebecca nor Tish were conscious of that. Tish snatched the gold-covered *Trebizon Journal* out of Rebecca's hands.

'You mean here on the last page, the place that's always reserved for the Editor's own personal work –'

Tish was speaking in a tremendous rush. She was outraged, but beneath the outrage there was a tinge of triumph and excitement in her voice.

'"Solitude",' she read out. Then, '"There's a certain slant of light, on winter afternoons. It falls through the trees, lies heavy on the . . ."'

'"Dunes."' Rebecca finished the line, automatically. She kept pushing a hand through her hair, wondering if she were dreaming the whole thing. 'That's exactly what I wrote – the whole thing. I don't believe she's altered a single word. It was the first day I arrived here. I was feeling really miserable. I went down to the bay, and sat in the dunes, and wrote it –'

'I remember!' said Tish. 'I looked for you. I was waiting for you when you came back and we were late for tea. And,' she ended triumphantly, 'you had biro on your face. You had to wash it off!'

She stared at the poem, in mounting excitement. 'Of course!' she said under her breath. 'I hadn't even read this, but now I have – it's not her at all, is it? It's much more you, Rebecca. How could she be so daft? Surely she knows she's going to be found out!' Tish grabbed Rebecca's arm. 'How did she get hold of it? Where was it? Have you kept a copy? Have you got your rough working out –?'

Rebecca just shook her head, the feeling of extreme unreality returning. That was what was so amazing about it all. 'I just wrote it on the beach,' she said dully. 'When I'd finished it, I felt a whole lot better. So I just ripped the page out of my notepad and put it in a litter basket.'

'What?' Tish's face fell. 'You didn't!'

Rebecca knew there was no need to reply. Tish believed her. She just shrugged her shoulders helplessly. And suddenly Tish saw the funny side of it.

'How ridiculous!' she laughed. She felt slightly hysterical. 'Do you mean to say Elizabeth Exton was so desperate to find something to pass off as her own work that she went poking around all the litter baskets in Trebizon Bay!'

'Looks like it!' Rebecca was beginning to feel hysterical herself. 'The latest craze – punk poetry!'

'It's a wonder she didn't print the words off an ice-cream

wrapper!' giggled Tish helplessly. 'Oh, Rebecca, this is all just too marvellous –'

'Marvellous?' said Rebecca, suddenly sober.

'Ishbel Anderson! Rebecca Mason! Come on – at once!'

The duty prefect had come over to close the doors and had seen the two of them still outside.

'Tish!' said Rebecca anxiously, as they hurried into the hall. 'Don't do anything silly. I know you believe me, but I don't think anybody else would. And there's not a hope of proving anything. You're in enough trouble already. I wish I hadn't told you. I'm not going to tell anybody else. I want to think it all over –'

'Yes, so do I,' said Tish suddenly.

'And you promise –?' began Rebecca. She was having to hurry to keep up with the dark-haired girl as they threaded their way through the crowded dining hall. 'You promise –?'

'I promise to do nothing silly this time,' said Tish.

As Rebecca and Tish sat down at opposite ends of the dinner table, Rebecca heaved a sigh of relief. Tish had given her promise not to do anything silly. Rebecca didn't want her getting into any more trouble on her account.

Maybe she, Rebecca, would have to summon up courage and confront the mighty Elizabeth Exton about the poem, but it would need some careful thought. Maybe she could have a meeting this evening with what Tish called her 'Action Committee', and see if *they* believed her. And if they did . . .

Maybe, maybe, maybe . . . All through the dinner hour Rebecca churned the problem round in her mind. She longed to talk it over with Tish. But Tish had gone off with Sue for a walk in the school grounds. Rebecca guessed that they would be talking over Tish's problem, whether or not to publish the apology to Elizabeth Exton in *The Juniper*

Journal. What would Sue advise? She felt deeply envious of their close friendship.

Rebecca also surmised that Tish would be telling Sue about her poem. Well, she didn't mind that. Would Sue believe it? As long as Tish didn't do anything reckless, that was the main thing! Rebecca felt fairly calm, because Tish had promised faithfully not to do anything silly. It never occurred to her that Tish had chosen her words with care. As far as Tish was concerned, what she had made up her mind to do was not silly at all – but perfectly sensible. And she certainly wasn't going to run the risk of Rebecca putting a stop to it.

It was a games afternoon, and Tish did not turn up. Even then, Rebecca suspected nothing. Sue told Miss Willis that Tish had a bad headache, and had gone to lie down in the sick room – and Rebecca believed it! She thought of the awful decision Tish had to make about the apology. That was enough to give anyone a bad headache.

After games, there was a whole free period before tea. Rebecca took a shower in the sports centre and planned to go and ask Matron how Tish was. But as she came out of the changing rooms, she heard a hubbub going on in the foyer where at least a dozen girls were crowding round the big notice-board.

'It's another special edition of *The J.J.*!'

'Tish Anderson's been pinning them up all over the school!'

'What does it say – here, let's have a look!'

'Is it true?'

'No, can't be!'

'She'll be rusticated now. That's for sure. She's mad!'

Rebecca walked slowly over to the notice-board, perspiration breaking out on the palms of her hands. She stood on tip-toe at the back of the crowd. There was a duplicated sheet pinned up but the stencil had obviously been made in a great hurry, because there were a lot of typing errors. However, what it had to say was clear and to the point:

JUNIPER JOURNAL – Special Issue No. 2

As the person mainly responsible for publishing Special Issue No. 1, I have been asked to retract and apologize to Elizabeth Exton. Before I will consider doing this, I must ask Elizabeth Exton to apologize to Rebecca Mason. In the Golden Jubilee edition of The Trebizon Journal, Elizabeth has published a poem called 'Solitude' as her own work. Below, I publish the poem under its real title, and under the name of the true author. Ishbel Anderson, Magazine Officer, Juniper House

Then came the title of the poem, and Rebecca's name: *ALL ALONE by REBECCA MASON FORM II ALPHA*, and then the poem in full.

Rebecca turned away, quickly. In the excitement, nobody had noticed her standing there. She hurried outside and into the grounds, and started walking. The trees were painted with the warm colours of autumn and leaves were falling. Her heart was beating very fast and she was gripped with exultation. And she had imagined Tish laid low with a headache!

She would never have dared to do something like this, but Tish certainly had! And now it had happened, Rebecca knew that it was right. The poem business justified every word Tish had put in the first Special Issue. Elizabeth Exton was *not* fit to be Editor of the school magazine. She *ought* to resign! And now the whole world would know it.

But Rebecca's exultant feelings were short-lived. Elizabeth Exton had also found a copy of the stencilled sheet, pinned on the notice-board in the entrance hall of Parkinson House. She took it down and went and made a strong cup of tea in the kitchen; she was glad that there was nobody else around as she gathered her wits together. How unlucky! What an awful bore! Her survival now depended on how ruthless she could be. It was them – or her. She imagined her father's anger if this should ever come to his ears, and she knew that she must stop at nothing.

Elizabeth marched straight across to see the Principal of Trebizon School, the stencilled sheet in her hand. As she entered the big study, she was surprised to find that Miss Welbeck already had copies of both Special Issues on her desk. They had been left with her, just before, by Miss Morgan.

'Come in, Elizabeth,' said Miss Welbeck, in calm tones. 'Miss Morgan has just been telling me about all this. I'd seen one of two of the early issues of their little House Journal and I must say I was quite impressed. Pity they have to spoil it with this sort of thing.'

The Principal of Trebizon School regarded her Sixth Formers as young adults which, indeed, they were. She trusted them completely and treated them as equals.

'I am very angry, Miss Welbeck, as you can well imagine.'

'I'm sure you are, Elizabeth. I shall see the culprit presently. I feel rather sorry for the little Mason girl, but I am very surprised at Ishbel Anderson's behaviour.'

'Quite,' said Elizabeth, pleased at the way things were going.

The Principal got up and walked to the window. A mist was coming down beyond the oak trees. The days were drawing in. She was feeling vexed and it would help to talk things over with Elizabeth.

'I'm afraid I myself encouraged Rebecca to have ambitions,' said Miss Welbeck ruefully. 'I imagine it was a great disappointment to her when her essay was not accepted for *The Trebizon*.' She glanced at Elizabeth. 'It is quite good, you know.'

'Indeed, yes. One of the few really good items this term,' lied Elizabeth. 'In a normal issue, it would have gone in. As a matter of fact, I had already decided to hold it over and use it in next term's *Trebizon*.'

'Good.' Miss Welbeck nodded her approval. 'The trouble is, the child is dying to make some sort of impression. I gather from Miss Morgan that she's something of a loner and has not made any special friends yet. She's completely unused to boarding school life, and her parents going abroad was no doubt a great shock to her . . .'

As Miss Welbeck continued to speak her thoughts aloud, Elizabeth listened demurely, nodding wisely at intervals.

'Clearly she admired your poem enormously, and has invented a little fantasy about it. She has pretended to Ishbel that she has written one just like it. Most disturbing really. As if –' the Principal turned away, looking out of the window across the park land. Elizabeth only just caught the next words. '– As if a girl of Rebecca's age would have met up with Emily Dickinson.'

Even as Elizabeth pondered over these last words and wondered what Miss Welbeck was talking about, the Principal turned and came back to her seat. With a heavy sigh, she sat down.

'No, it is Ishbel who has behaved outrageously. To have accepted this fantasy without question! I shall see Ishbel on her own. She will now have to make a double retraction and a double apology, instead of just the one that Miss Morgan called for. She will be the laughing stock of the school. So, unhappily, will Rebecca Mason, and I regard that as very unfortunate.'

Leaving the Principal's study, it was Elizabeth Exton who now felt exultant. She went back to her boarding house and made a fresh pot of tea in the kitchen, humming softly to herself. There was just one irritating little question that kept nagging at her mind.

When Audrey Maxwell came into the kitchen to get a biscuit, Elizabeth burst out, 'Audrey, have you ever met up with someone called Emily Dickinson?'

'You mean the poet?'

'Er – yes.'

'You must be off your rocker,' said Audrey. 'She's been dead for over a hundred years.'

Audrey went out nibbling the biscuit, thoughtfully. There was something very odd about the question Elizabeth had just asked her. It wasn't just her ignorance – Audrey was used to that. There was something particularly odd, but for the moment she couldn't quite put her finger on it.

THIRTEEN

...AND INTO THE FIRE

Tish spent only five minutes in the Principal's study. It was a close encounter of the bad kind.

'Come, come, Ishbel. You have made a silly accusation. You have spread it right round the school! And you have not one shred of evidence to back it up –'

'Then you haven't spoken to Elizabeth Exton?' said Tish. 'Please, Miss Welbeck, you should –'

'I have spoken to Elizabeth and she has reacted with a forbearance that would quite surprise you. You don't deserve it. I believe you have taken leave of your senses, Ishbel, to print this nonsense on your duplicator. You will go now and compose a full retraction and apology. After that has been printed you will never be allowed to use the machine again.'

'But I just *know* it's Rebecca's poem!' gasped Tish. 'I can't prove it, but I just believe her, that's all –'

'Stop this nonsense at once, please, Ishbel. Do as I tell you. Retract everything you have said in both issues of the news-sheet. Show the draft to Miss Morgan, as she asked you to this morning. That's all. You may go.'

Tish walked across to the door of the study, then stopped.

'And – and if I don't, Miss Welbeck?' she asked, in a very small voice.'

Miss Welbeck was picking up the internal telephone and dialling a number. She did not even look up as she replied.

'Then you will not be allowed to remain at Trebizon,' she said.

Tish went and stood outside, pressing her forehead against the wall for a few moments. In a blur, she could just hear Miss Welbeck speaking on the phone to Jacquinda Meredith, the Senior Prefect.

'Get some volunteers and see that every single copy is rounded up, please. Then make sure they are destroyed. What? You haven't seen it yet? You have missed nothing.'

Tish walked away, angry and tearful.

Later, Rebecca looked for her everywhere. She had been for a walk in the grounds and then raced back to Juniper. She had suddenly realized that there would be an almighty row about what Tish had done. And although Rebecca never doubted for a moment that Elizabeth Exton would confess, she wanted to be around when the whole thing blew up so that she could answer questions and back Tish up.

'She's with Miss Welbeck,' Sue Murdoch told her. Sue looked rather pale and tense. 'She's been there about fifteen minutes. I expect Elizabeth Exton's there, too. There'll be a big showdown going on.'

'Didn't – didn't Miss Welbeck want to see me, too?' asked Rebecca in concern. The storm broken already! She hated the idea of Tish seeing the whole thing through on her own. 'Was there a message?'

'Nope,' said Sue. 'She just wanted Tish.'

Rebecca raced over to old school. Girls advanced on her, some of them looking angry.

'You didn't really write that poem, did you?'

'What's Tish Anderson putting this sort of thing around for?'

But Rebecca dodged away from them. She had to know what was going on. At the foot of the main staircase she nearly collided with Pippa Fellowes-Walker, who was always friendly towards her.

'Pippa! Please, have you seen Tish? Is she still with the Head?'

'She came out a few minutes ago. She looked like death.'

Rebecca began to feel distinctly sick. Surely Elizabeth Exton had confessed? Surely Miss Welbeck couldn't be angry with Tish, when the truth was on her side? Had something gone wrong?

She searched for Tish in the old building, first in the form room and then the library. Then she went back to Juniper House. She pulled up short in the doorway. There was a crowd of girls outside the TV room, talking and banging on the closed door. Something very dramatic was going on. Suddenly, all together, they started to move away up the corridor, and Rebecca caught snatches of whispered conversation.

'Come on, the best thing we can do is leave Sue Murdoch in peace.'

'But she's locked herself in! Shouldn't we do something?'

'Of course not. She just wants to be left alone.'

'Who wouldn't? It's the most rotten thing that's ever happened.'

'It's all Rebecca Mason's fault!'

'You just shut up, Debbie Rickard!'

The moment they had gone upstairs, Rebecca ran forward and rattled the handle of the door to the TV room.

'Sue, it's me. Please let me in.'

She heard a muffled sob; then the catch inside the door was released and Sue opened it. Rebecca hardly recognized her; she had taken her spectacles off and her eyes were very red.

'What's happened? Where's Tish?'

'She's packed her things and now she's with Miss Morgan. She's asking Miss Morgan to ring her father to come and fetch her home. I expect Miss Morgan is trying to talk her round. But I know Tish. She's stubborn.'

Sue knelt on the floor and buried her face deep in the armchair. 'She's got to apologize to Elizabeth Exton or else leave the school. Well, Tish believes you wrote that poem and that's that. She'd rather be rusticated than apologize to that liar.'

'Sue!'

Rebecca sank down into the armchair. Her legs felt very weak and wobbly. So Elizabeth Exton had denied everything and Miss Welbeck believed her! It was Elizabeth's word against Rebecca's. The word of the mighty Editor of the school magazine against that of a pale and insignificant new girl. The chilling truth dawned on Rebecca at last.

'Miss Welbeck thinks I made the whole thing up!' she thought. 'She thinks I was just shooting a big line to Tish! She didn't even think it was worth calling me up to her study, to question me! I expect she feels sorry for me, and will give me a little talking-to sometime. It's Tish she's angry with, for believing me!'

Rebecca's head began to ache painfully.

'Sue,' she said numbly. 'You know I never wanted Tish to do anything like this. But to be honest, when I saw what she'd done, I was thrilled to bits. I just took it for granted that Elizabeth would own up. And then everyone would see that what Tish said about her not being fit to be Editor was true.'

'That's just how my mind worked,' said Sue. 'We talked about it at dinner break. I told her she was doing the right thing and that Elizabeth would be sure to own up –' She looked absolutely woebegone. '– but, she hasn't, and she never will. And Tish certainly won't apologize. So that's that. Tish is out.'

'But nobody's even talked to me yet!' cried Rebecca. She got up suddenly, and although the movement made her head throb, she rushed to the door. 'Doesn't anybody want to hear what I've got to say?'

She ran out of Juniper and on to the terrace. Small groups of girls were drifting about near the dining hall, waiting for the tea bell to go. But tea was the last thing on Rebecca's mind. She crossed the gardens and let herself into old school. The thought of going and knocking on the door of the Principal's study, completely uninvited, frightened her to death.

As she reached the top of the main staircase, she was just in time to see a tall figure entering Miss Welbeck's study. It was Elizabeth Exton. In that moment, fright left Rebecca and anger took over. She ran to the door before Elizabeth could close it.

'I'm coming in, too! I've a right to speak to Miss Welbeck, as well!'

'Wait outside, please, Rebecca,' came the Principal's calm voice. 'I thought you might turn up. But I'd like to speak to Elizabeth first.'

The door closed. Trembling, Rebecca sat down and waited. She wanted to yell and shout and rush in there and pull Elizabeth's hair. Somehow, she must control her feelings and wait until she was summoned.

FOURTEEN

THE MIGHTY FALLEN

Although Miss Welbeck had called out to Rebecca in a calm voice, she was less calm than she sounded. First of all, Miss Morgan had telephoned through to her from Juniper, and told her about Ishbel Anderson's stubborn and melodramatic behaviour. It seemed she had already packed her bags. The Principal had instructed the House Mistress on no account to telephone Ishbel's father, but to keep the girl in her office until she, Miss Welbeck, had had the opportunity of interviewing Rebecca Mason.

It was obvious that Ishbel was acting out of misguided loyalty to the new girl, and still believed her ridiculous story about the poem. Miss Welbeck decided that she must see Rebecca at once, and explain to her how serious the matter had now become. What had probably started as a silly piece of boasting on Rebecca's part had got completely out of hand. Rebecca must now admit the truth to Ishbel, and the sooner the better.

But before the Principal could arrange for Rebecca to be brought to her study, she had received an unexpected visitor in the shape of Audrey Maxwell. Audrey was someone whom Miss Welbeck held in high regard, and she was surprised to find her arriving without an appointment. She knew that it must be something important.

Earlier that afternoon, Audrey had been sitting in the comfortable little sitting room at Parkinson House, doing some private study, when Jacquinda Meredith had come in with a wad of papers. She had stuffed them in the fireplace and looked around for some matches.

'Lighting a fire before tea, Jackie?' Audrey had asked in surprise.

'The Head asked me to collect these up and burn them,' said the Senior Prefect. 'It's those Second Years again. They've really gone too far this time, sticking this up all round the school. I've heard that Tish Anderson's going to be rusticated.'

'Here, let's have a look,' said Audrey.

As soon as she had read the sheet that Jacquinda gave her, Audrey got to her feet, looking agitated. Now she remembered! She had felt there was something wrong when Elizabeth Exton had known nothing about Emily Dickinson – at last, she had pinpointed the reason!

'Did you ever read such rubbish?' Jacquinda was saying.

'I'm not sure it is rubbish,' said Audrey, keeping hold of the sheet. 'I'm going to see what Miss Heath thinks.'

Miss Heath was in the next room, giving two members of the Upper Sixth a tutorial in English Literature. It was on the advice of Miss Heath, who was of course Rebecca and Tish's form-mistress, that Audrey then went immediately across to old school and saw Miss Welbeck. As a direct result of Audrey's visit, Miss Welbeck had now summoned Elizabeth Exton to come and see her at once.

'Sit down, please Elizabeth.' The Principal fixed her gaze on her, and the Sixth Former returned it unflinchingly.

'When I saw you earlier I accepted without question that the poem "Solitude" was your own work. Can you, in fact, assure me that it is? Or are there any other factors that I ought to know about?'

'Of course it's my own work, Miss Welbeck.'

'Audrey Maxwell assures me that you know nothing about Emily Dickinson. If that is so, I find it very strange.'

Elizabeth took a deep breath. Miss Welbeck's reference to someone called Emily Dickinson earlier that afternoon had bothered her. It had bothered her still further to learn from Audrey Maxwell that Emily Dickinson had been a poet.

Although she was still baffled as to the significance of this person, Elizabeth had gone straight to the school library and read up about her. She was not going to be caught napping!

'I can't imagine why Audrey Maxwell should say that,' retorted Elizabeth. 'Of course I know about Emily Dickinson. She was an American poet who lived and died in the last century.'

Miss Welbeck made no reply.

Elizabeth was beginning to feel out of her depth. What was Miss Welbeck driving at? She turned to the attack. 'I'm surprised at Audrey if she's been saying things about me. Of course, it's common knowledge that she badly wanted to be Editor of *The Trebizon Journal* herself.'

'Yes,' Miss Welbeck got to her feet and walked over to the door. 'I daresay she did.' She opened the door. 'Rebecca, would you like to come in now, please?'

Rebecca was very overwrought. It had been agonizing, waiting outside. At last she was being summoned. She came into the panelled study, bursting to speak, and not quite sure where to begin.

'Miss Welbeck –'

'Sit down, please, Rebecca.' Miss Welbeck waved her to a chair, away from Elizabeth's. 'I can see that you have a lot of things to say to me, and you will have the chance to do so. But first, I want you to be very quiet until you are spoken to.'

Rebecca sat down, suddenly soothed by Miss Welbeck's presence. There was something so confident and reassuring about her, just as there had been the first time she had entered this study. Elizabeth Exton was looking tense and strained by comparison. Rebecca had the strange feeling that everything was going to be all right. The throbbing in her head began to subside.

'Elizabeth, let me ask you a question,' said the Principal. 'Let us take this first line of the poem: "There's a certain slant of light, on winter afternoons . . ." Now, how would you say it goes on from there?'

Elizabeth stared at the Principal. Surely she did not expect to catch her out as easily as that! Why, she knew the poem off by heart and back to front.

'"It falls through the trees, lies heavy on the dunes . . ."' began Elizabeth. Before she could get any further, Miss Welbeck signalled her to stop, with a sharp gesture.

'Thank you, Elizabeth.' She turned to Rebecca. 'And now your turn, Rebecca. "There's a certain slant of light, on winter afternoons . . ." How would you say the poem goes from there?'

Rebecca screwed up her eyes tightly for a moment, then said:

> '"*. . . That oppresses, like the weight of cathedral tunes.*
> *Heavenly hurt it gives us; we can find no scar,*
> *But internal difference where the meanings are.*
> *None may teach it anything . . .*"'

'Good!' exclaimed Miss Welbeck, cutting Rebecca off in mid-sentence. 'I see you know your Emily Dickinson. Do you admire her poems?'

'I find them rather difficult,' Rebecca admitted, speaking shyly. 'But I've always loved that first line, about a certain slant of light. It's sad and sends a little shiver down my spine. I wrote it down, my first day here, down on the beach – and then my own poem just sort of grew out of it.'

And then, staring joyfully at Miss Welbeck, she realized. 'You believe it was my poem then?'

'Yes, I do, Rebecca.'

All this time Elizabeth Exton had been sitting like someone turned to stone, except for a trembling of the lips that she was not able to control. As Miss Welbeck turned to her, she burst forth.

'I didn't know it was Rebecca's poem. I had no idea! A holidaymaker gave it to me down on the beach. I thought *she'd* written it. She said I could have it.'

'You took her advice very literally,' said Miss Welbeck in acid tones. 'Did you not recognize the handwriting?'

'It was written in block capitals,' said Elizabeth coldly. 'Of course, if only Rebecca had turned it in for the magazine, I would have known at once.' She turned on Rebecca quite savagely. 'Why didn't you do that?'

'I'd thrown it away – I couldn't remember it!' said Rebecca. She was no longer frightened or shy of the imposing Sixth Former. The mighty had fallen very low. 'Besides, as I'd taken the opening line from a proper poem, it wasn't really my own work.'

'True, true,' said Miss Welbeck. 'Though you could have made an acknowledgement. I was mildly surprised that it carried no acknowledgement when I first saw it. And that reminds me –'

Briskly Miss Welbeck picked up the telephone extension that went directly through to the School Secretary.

'Have any of the magazines been despatched yet, Sarah?' she asked. 'No? Good. Good. Hold them. None is to go out. I want some erratum slips printed. I'll give you details in the morning.' She put the telephone down and glanced at her watch. 'Elizabeth, you will remain with me. We must talk. Rebecca. You, I'm afraid, have completely missed your tea. So, I daresay, has Ishbel Anderson. Miss Morgan had instructions to keep her in her office.'

The Principal picked up the 'phone for the last time and dialled through to Miss Morgan's office at Juniper.

'Madeleine Welbeck here. The matter of the poem is resolved. Rebecca Mason is its author, with a little help from Emily Dickinson. Please tell Ishbel Anderson that I will see her in the morning. In the meantime I would like you to take both girls out to tea at the Vienna Restaurant. Charge it to the school account.'

'Please,' Rebecca blurted out shyly, 'Sue Murdoch hasn't had any tea either. She's Tish – she's Ishbel's best friend and she's been crying buckets.'

'Then she must go too,' said the Principal, with a hint of a smile. 'It may speed her recovery a little.'

She watched as Rebecca rushed out of the study, the last of the daylight catching her fair hair, and thought, 'What an interesting child she is.'

Then she turned to Elizabeth Exton and the disagreeable task ahead. 'Vaunting ambition,' thought Miss Welbeck. She must talk to Elizabeth about that. Some causes you won, and some you lost. Elizabeth, Miss Welbeck now realized, was a lost cause, cast too much in the Exton mould.

*

'Are you going to ring father now?' asked Tish sullenly, as Miss Morgan replaced the telephone receiver. 'What did Miss Welbeck say?'

As she waited for the House Mistress to reply, her mind went over the ground yet again. Why couldn't Miss Morgan have 'phoned her father straight away? Why didn't they just let her go? It was going to come to that in the end. Elizabeth Exton would never own up. Rebecca would stick to her guns, but it was only her word against Elizabeth's, and nobody would believe her. Well, Tish wasn't going to retract a thing. She'd rather leave Trebizon than do that, and that was saying something. It was the best place on earth, for a school.

Poor Rebecca. They weren't going to punish her, just treat her as some sort of nut case. Pack her off to see Dr Carson, that psychologist person, likely as not. Like they had Millicent Dawson when she had gone on that shop-lifting spree. Why wasn't Miss Morgan saying anything? She'd put the 'phone down hours ago. Why was she just staring into space with that red tinge creeping up her face?

'Can you get my father to come and fetch me now, please?'

Miss Morgan came to. She spoke in a voice full of emotion.

'Of course not, Ishbel. I've been told to take you and Rebecca out to tea at the Vienna Restaurant.'

'Tea –?'

'That's right. It seems we have misjudged you. Miss Welbeck has seen Rebecca and she is completely satisfied that she is the author of the poem.'

'She *is* –?'

Tish jumped to her feet and danced round and round the

office, flung open the door and danced into the corridor – and crashed into Rebecca.

'Tish!'

'Rebeck!'

They grabbed hands and twisted round and round outside Miss Morgan's office, until the walls spun. Rebecca felt delirious with happiness. Was it only dinner break when she had last seen Tish, and they had looked together at her poem in the school magazine? It seemed at least a fortnight ago. So much had happened since then.

'Stop it, you'll be sick,' said Miss Morgan, laughing, all the tension leaving her.

Rebecca very nearly was sick that evening. Miss Morgan took her and Tish and Sue down to the town for the most sumptuous tea at the Vienna Restaurant. They consumed hot toasted muffins and trifle and jelly and ice-cream and huge chocolate eclairs stuffed full of fresh dairy cream.

As if that weren't enough, the three girls rounded off the day with a celebration at Moffatt's, the school tuck shop, with the other members of Tish's 'Action Committee', Margot Lawrence and Sally Elphinstone and Mara Leonodis.

'Papa will laugh his head off when I tell him the excitement he has given us,' said the Greek girl. 'With the little duplicating machine, I mean. Who would have thought it could do so much good!'

'I bet Freddie Exton won't laugh,' said Margot, soberly.

'Do you think he'll ask for his money back?' asked Rebecca. 'All the money he put into the school magazine?'

'Not likely!' Tish's big laugh was back in place and the bounce was back in her bobbing curls. 'As if he'd dare. Besides, he's still got Margaret at the school.' She finished on a dry tone. 'Who knows, she might want to be Editor one day.'

Elizabeth Exton had already gone: she had caught the seven o'clock train to London. As she watched the lights of Trebizon town twinkling into the distance behind her, she wondered what the future held in store for her. She made a vow. If she ever met up with Tish Anderson again in the big wide world, she would find some way to get her revenge.

The mood in Juniper House that night was one of great jubilation and emotion. In both the Second Year and First Year dormitories the girls could talk of nothing but the great scandal of the day and the way that *The Juniper Journal* had, in the end, emerged with honour. Even those girls who had sided with Elizabeth Exton and authority, conveniently forgot about it or else had the grace to admit that they had been wrong.

Josselyn Vining met Rebecca on the second floor landing, just after she had cleaned her teeth for bed. For the umpteenth time that night, Rebecca found herself being congratulated on her poem.

'Of course, I'm not an expert, but it seems pretty good to me for someone of our age,' said Joss. She added ruefully, 'Wish you were as keen on hockey as you are on writing.'

'But I am,' said Rebecca.

'Then why didn't you come to the trial at the beginning of term?' asked Joss. 'That's what I can't understand.'

'Trial?' said Rebecca. '*Trial?* I thought it was just an ordinary practice game. That was the night I was trying to write something for *The Trebizon*. I mean, I'd never really played hockey before, and Debbie never told me it was a trial. I don't think I'd have believed her if she had!'

'So that was why!' exclaimed Joss, in some anger. 'It was a

trial all right. Judy's marvellous at right wing, but she's got a funny ankle and has to drop out of matches sometimes. I thought you might make a good reserve, especially for Judy. If I ask Miss Willis if you can play at right wing in games tomorrow, would you like that? We would see how you get on.'

'Like it?' said Rebecca. 'Of course, I'd like it!'

At Assembly next morning, Miss Welbeck announced Elizabeth Exton's departure and then hastily passed on to happier news.

'You all should know that the Upper Sixth Form held a special meeting last night and unanimously elected a new Editor for *The Trebizon Journal*. Audrey Maxwell will hold that post for the rest of the school year.'

Loud clapping burst out in the hall.

Audrey's first task in her new post was to go down to the printers and organize the printing of a batch of small gummed slips. The printer was able to run them off the same day.

That evening a large team of volunteers went through every single copy of the Golden Jubilee edition of *The Trebizon Journal* and stuck the gummed slips over Elizabeth Exton's name, at the end of the poem. It now read: *By Rebecca Mason Form II Alpha (with acknowledgements to Emily Dickinson)*. The magazines were now ready to be dispatched.

Rebecca played well in her trial position as right wing in the hockey lesson that afternoon. In due course, it was announced that she had been made a reserve for the school's Under-Fourteen team.

In the second half of the term, Judy Sharp's ankle only let her down once, just before a home match against Caxton High School. In her sole appearance in the school team,

Rebecca acquitted herself well – setting up one goal for Tish, at left inner, and another for Sue, at right.

There was something very pleasing about that, for the three girls were friends and inseparable now. By the end of term, Rebecca's first weeks at Trebizon, when she had had no special friends, were no more than a memory.

Her parents flew back to England for Christmas and met her off the train. They had already read *The Trebizon Journal*, which had been waiting for them at home, from cover to cover.

'I see you had a poem printed, Becky,' said her father proudly, as they drove away from the station. 'I thought it was going to be an essay.'

'It was,' said Rebecca. 'One day I'll tell you all about it.'

'Have you enjoyed your first term?' asked her mother anxiously. 'Have you really enjoyed it?'

'Yes, Mum. I really have.'

She was looking forward to Christmas at home. She was also looking forward to going back to school in January and seeing Tish and Sue, and seeing the winter sea through the bare trees from her dormitory window again.

What a contrast to her feelings when she had set off on the train for her first term at Trebizon! Would the second term be as good as the first?

Rebecca knew that she would have to wait and see.

SECOND TERM AT
TREBIZON

CONTENTS

ONE

BEFORE THE TERM BEGAN

Rebecca Mason's second term at Trebizon School was to be full of surprises. It was going to be the term in which Tish Anderson behaved in a way that had everybody baffled, including Rebecca, and drove Sue Murdoch almost to despair.

Rebecca sensed there was something different about Tish, even before the new term began.

The Christmas holidays were nearly over and Rebecca was at a loose end. Her London friends had already gone back to their school and her father had flown back to his job in Saudi Arabia. Her mother was dashing around getting their little terraced house in south London ready for the new tenants, before seeing Rebecca off to school and then joining up with Mr Mason abroad.

The previous September, Rebecca had dreaded going away to Trebizon, a boarding school in the west country. At the time, she didn't know a soul there and she was going to be the only new girl in the Second Year. Now, waiting for her second term to begin, she felt differently about Trebizon. In Ishbel Anderson (who was known as Tish) and

Sue Murdoch she had found the perfect friends. Tish and Sue had come to Trebizon as First Years and had been best friends from the start. But after a clash with a mighty Sixth Former called Elizabeth Exton, and a lot of drama and excitement, the other two had taken to Rebecca wholeheartedly and now they were a threesome.

It was Friday and Rebecca took it for granted that she wouldn't be meeting up with Tish and Sue again until the following Tuesday, on the London to Trebizon train. Sue lived right up in north London somewhere and Tish lived outside the city altogether.

So she was overjoyed when Sue rang her at home.

'Can you come for the weekend?' she asked. 'Tish is here already. I'm playing at a fairly crummy concert tomorrow afternoon, with Nicola Hodges – remember her? – but the main thing is that my parents are giving a party afterwards, you should see the food! Will your parents let you come? You can stay the night.'

'I'll go and ask!' said Rebecca.

Mrs Mason gave her permission at once and Rebecca returned to the 'phone. She felt pleased and excited.

'It's fine! I'll come to the concert, shall I? Where is it?'

'It's in a hall near Hendon Central underground station.'

'Hendon Central – that's straight through from here on the Northern Line!' said Rebecca.

'Tish can meet you outside the station at half-past two and bring you to the hall. The concert starts at three o'clock. Nicola and I will be trying to get our fiddles in tune. Don't expect anything good.'

'You can play as many wrong notes as you like,' said Rebecca. 'I won't be able to tell the difference.'

'That's exactly what Tish said!'

'Nicola Hodges – oh, I remember her now,' said Rebecca.

'She's in the First Year isn't she? I didn't know you knew her out of school.'

Nicola had flaxen hair in plaits and a round cherubic face. Like Sue, she was already good enough at the violin to be in the school orchestra, and she had played a solo at the school's Christmas concert.

'I *didn't* know her out of school,' said Sue. 'But last term I told her about this music place I go to in the holidays and the next thing I knew her father had got her into it. Then the two of us were chosen to play together at this concert tomorrow. There'll be lots of other turns, too, like recorders and ballet and tap.'

'Can't wait,' said Rebecca. 'Is Tish by the 'phone?'

'She's gone out,' said Sue. 'But don't worry. She's dying for you to come. She'll meet you all right.'

'Where's she gone?'

'Up to Hampstead. That Outer Space Art Exhibition.'

'*What?*' said Rebecca. 'The one that's been in the papers? Twisted lumps of metal suspended from the ceiling and flashing lights –'

'That's the one.'

'That's not like Tish!'

'She just marched out,' said Sue. Rebecca could tell that she, too, was baffled. 'Didn't seem to expect anyone would want to come. Said she suddenly felt like going to it.'

'Hope Tish isn't changing for the worse,' said Rebecca solemnly.

That evening she ironed her best pale green angora wool sweater, which went well with her fair hair, and hummed to herself. Then she ironed her trousers.

'Shouldn't you wear something smarter for a party?' inquired Mrs Mason anxiously. 'They're very well off, aren't they?'

Howard Murdoch, Sue's father, was the chairman of a big company called Metternex, though Rebecca had only found that out by chance once.

'Dead casual – that's what Sue said. She should know.'

'I expect they live in a lovely house,' sighed Mrs Mason.

'I'll describe it to you in tiny detail when I get back, Mum,' promised Rebecca. 'Even what sort of washing machine they have.'

Mrs Mason laughed. It was true, she loved to know such things.

Next day, after an early lunch, Rebecca set off across the common.

The January skies were grey and the trees on the common were bare, but she was in high spirits. She wore a thick navy-blue duffel coat over her clothes, her fair hair cascading over the thrown-back hood. She carried her night things in her denim shoulder bag. The day was cold and she was pleased to get down into the warm underground station, and into the train.

When she emerged in north London, forty minutes later, Tish was waiting for her beyond the ticket barrier.

She looked the same old Tish all right, except that instead of school uniform she was wearing bright red ski pants and a heavy, patterned black-and-yellow long jumper with hood attached. Slung from her shoulder she carried a small cassette player in a bright blue case. The grin was as big as ever, the black curls still as bouncy, although her face had a slight winter pallor.

'What have we here?' exclaimed Rebecca, pointing at the cassette recorder. 'You lucky thing!'

'Got it for Christmas,' said Tish. 'I thought we'd try and tape their duet for them! It's got a mike!'

The idea of recording Sue and Nicola's violin performance during the show appealed to Rebecca. As it turned out, it livened up the afternoon quite considerably.

Six budding ballerinas had come out on to the stage, and were dancing rather badly. According to the programme, Sue and Nicola would be on next. Tish sat fiddling with the cassette recorder in her lap, getting it ready. The tape was already half-filled with very tuneless pop music, Tish's favourite kind, which she had got from the radio earlier. She was trying to wind the tape on to a blank part, ready to record.

Unfortunately, she pressed the wrong button.

Suddenly, as the ballet reached its most delicate point, the hushed piano in the hall was drowned by loud, thumping pop music. People in the crowded hall turned at once, pulling threatening faces and making strangled shushing noises. Tish was so taken aback that the case slid right off her lap and under the chair in front, still thumping out the loud music. She rescued it and switched it off and the whole incident was over in a matter of seconds, but both girls were attacked by a giggling fit so severe that they had only just recovered their composure by the time Sue and Nicola appeared on the stage with their violins.

None of this was in the least untypical of Tish. Rebecca had no reason to think there was anything different about her at all.

The first slightly odd thing came during the interval.

Because the hall was so small and crowded, everybody had to stay in their seats, and cups of tea were brought round in paper cups. Rebecca and Tish talked about the holidays and then Rebecca, suddenly remembering, asked:

'What was the exhibition like?'

'What exhibition?' asked Tish.

'The funny one at Hampstead. Sue said you'd gone there yesterday. Was it weird and wonderful?'

Instead of laughing and joking about it, Tish just looked embarrassed. She stared down into her cup of tea.

'I didn't go to it after all. I just went for a walk.'

'Oh.'

There was an awkward silence. Rebecca tried to pick up the threads of conversation again, but Tish seemed to be sunk in thought. It was almost as though Rebecca had, unwittingly, touched on a very tender spot. But why? How? Finally she gave up and just drank her tea in silence. What on earth had got into Tish?

Her eyes strayed down to the front of the hall. The front rows were reserved for the people in the concert, who could take a place there once their own performances were over. Sue was sitting there with Nicola. Earlier Sue had turned and waved and signalled to them, but now she and the flaxen-haired girl were deep in conversation, their heads bent close together.

Could Tish and Sue have quarrelled in the last couple of days? Rebecca wondered, groping for an explanation. Had Sue got thick with Nicola Hodges in the holidays, over this concert? Serious music wasn't exactly Tish's scene. Maybe she felt left out . . .

The lights dimmed and the second half of the concert began. A particularly bad rendering of 'Oh, for the wings of a dove,' by an elderly soprano began to revive Tish. Rebecca noticed her taping it, surreptitiously. By the end of the show she seemed her normal self again.

A lot of people piled into cars afterwards to go to the party at the Murdochs' home. The house was everything Rebecca's mother could have imagined, high on a hill and standing in its own grounds, with far-reaching views of the lights of London. Rebecca made mental notes of some of the lovely furnishings and fabrics, in order not to disappoint her mother.

The food, as Sue had promised, was everything that Rebecca could have imagined. The trifle was the most mouth-wateringly sweet concoction she had ever tasted, and the pastries had real cream in them.

Sue introduced Rebecca to her parents and her two brothers, David and Edward. Mrs Murdoch, like Sue herself, wore spectacles and had the same sandy-coloured hair, delicate features and high cheekbones. The boys were dark like their father. Howard Murdoch was a big man, who had played rugby for Cambridge in his youth. He had very thick beetling eyebrows that, like his head of hair, were black touched with grey. His face was craggy and strong-looking, yet kind. Rebecca could see why Sue adored him.

Nicola Hodges's parents were a surprise. They travelled with Nicola to the party in a rather battered old lorry which said *Hodges Road Haulage* on the side. Brian Hodges had had to come straight to the hall, it seemed, from delivering a load of timber nearby and was still in his working clothes. He was a thin, spare little man whereas his wife was on the large side, and looked even larger in a bright pink coat and matching hat with feathers on it.

In spite of her size, Mrs Hodges was surprisingly fleet of foot and took the last second helping of trifle from under Rebecca's nose. Rebecca then heard her boasting about Nicola's brilliance as a violinist to the mother of one of the budding ballerinas.

'Poor Nicola!' she whispered to Tish.

'Takes all sorts,' Tish whispered back, with a tolerant grin. 'Doesn't seem to have affected Nicola. She seems quite sweet. Look at her now, with Sue, hanging on to every word Sue says. I can't remember looking up to the Second Years like that.'

Rebecca enjoyed the party and began to wonder if she had been imagining things earlier, in thinking there was something up with Tish. But when the party had ended, and all the guests had gone home, Tish said something that was completely out of character.

'I think I'll have an early night,' she said.

'Are you all right?' asked Rebecca, who had been looking forward to the three of them talking for hours, and playing back Tish's cassette recordings from the concert.

'Of course I'm all right,' said Tish. 'Just tired, that's all.'

Now Rebecca was convinced that something was wrong.

She was dragged off to play table tennis by David and Edward and Sue. The Murdoch home even had its own games room. They played good, fast games and worked off the excessive amount of food they had consumed. It was well past her usual bedtime when the party broke up.

'What's the matter with Tish?' asked Rebecca, as Sue led her upstairs and showed her to a little guest bedroom. 'Had a quarrel?'

'Of course not!' said Sue. Then added: 'But she's a bit quirky at the moment, isn't she?'

'Quirky – yes. That's the word.'

But what could she possibly have to be quirky about? wondered Rebecca, as she cleaned her teeth and got ready for bed.

Only Tish Anderson herself knew the answer to that. And she wasn't saying.

TWO

THREE SECRET WISHES

On the long journey down to Trebizon on Tuesday the three of them spent a lot of time running up and down the train, greeting old friends in other compartments. Then they settled down to a game called 'Confessions', a kind of forfeits game which they played with a pack of cards. If someone drew an ace the others could extract a 'confession' from her, and every word of it had to be true.

'Confess a secret wish to do with school,' said Tish, when Sue drew an ace.

'I can't!' said Sue, blushing. 'You'll laugh at me.'

'You've got to!' said Rebecca. 'It's the rule.' She was expecting Sue to say she would like to play a violin solo at the end-of-term concert, or something similar. So her words were quite a surprise.

'Well,' said Sue, taking a deep breath, 'I'd like to be junior head of games this term, now we've got into the Gold Cup. I'd make one or two interesting changes in the team, and then we'd be sure to win it!'

'Sue!' said Rebecca in amazement.

'You funny thing,' added Tish, giving her an odd look.

'I never knew you lay awake at night coveting Joss's job.'

'Well, I do,' said Sue, again going red, and Rebecca knew that it must be true. 'I know that Joss is the most brilliant player, and so nice it isn't true, and that she's going to be hockey captain for ever and ever, all the way up the school. But that only makes me long for the job all the more!'

'Well,' said Tish gently, 'you'll just have to make do with scoring dozens of goals this term instead.'

As soon as Rebecca drew an ace, Sue decided to get her own back. 'Confess *your* secret wish,' she said, and it was Rebecca's turn to be embarrassed, and the turn of the others to be surprised. Rebecca was especially gifted at writing things, and they expected her to say she wanted to get something in *The Trebizon Journal* again.

'Well, I'd be happy just to be in the Under-14 team,' she said. 'Like you two are. And stay in it. And play in the Gold Cup with you. But that's impossible and I know it is.'

The other two looked at her sympathetically. Rebecca was a fast runner, and a promising hockey player, and was one of a pool of reserves for the Under-14 team. She had played once last term and acquitted herself quite well. But the fact was that the team was full and, amongst the reserves, a First Year girl called Sheila Cummings had already emerged as outstanding and was now the official First Reserve.

'Of course, I could always poison a few of you,' said Rebecca, slightly nettled by their sympathetic looks. They all laughed.

She and Sue were just waiting to pounce on Tish when, at long last, she also drew an ace from the pack.

'Confess *your* secret wish!' they said in unison.

And suddenly she clammed right up.

'I can't,' she said. 'I just can't!'

'But you've got to!' exclaimed Sue.

'Can't.'

'You rotten cheat!' said Rebecca.

'Why did you ask me mine then?' complained Sue. She and Rebecca exchanged glances. Tish being quirky again! Not just quirky but downright infuriating, and not a bit like her usual self.

They ended the game, then, and turned to reading. There was a slightly frosty atmosphere for a while, but it soon thawed when Tish burst out laughing at something in her book.

'Here's a good one for *The J.J.*, Rebecca!' she said. She read it out aloud. *'There really is such a thing as a squirting cucumber. You only have to touch it lightly and it squirts its seeds at you. Sometimes you only have to walk past it for it to squirt you.'*

'Not bad,' conceded Rebecca. 'I'll add it to my list.'

'Let's grow one at school and put it in the staff room,' said Sue.

The J.J. that Tish referred to was *The Juniper Journal*, a duplicated news-sheet that they produced and sold around the school for five pence a copy. Tish, who was the only person who could type stencils properly, was its editor and Rebecca contributed a weekly piece called 'Did you Know?' consisting of two or three weird and little-known facts. Rebecca had the sort of mind that stored up useless information like a computer.

It was called *The Juniper Journal* because Juniper House was the junior boarding house at Trebizon, where all First Year and Second Year girls lived. It was a large modern block right in the centre of the main school complex. As the girls got older, they went into smaller boarding houses set in various parts of the grounds. But for the time being, Juniper House was the centre of Rebecca's world, and where everything happened out of school hours.

Juniper House had its own monitors and officers. Tish, for example, had been its Magazine Officer for two terms, in charge of deciding which contributions from the juniors went into the school's famous magazine, *The Trebizon Journal*. This term, a new Magazine Officer would be elected.

But the most important position, officially called Head of Games, was held by Josselyn Vining. Trebizon believed in giving girls a lot of responsibility from an early age, so that head of games picked the teams and ran things with the minimum of interference from Miss Willis, the games mistress. Joss was in charge of junior hockey, netball and swimming but informally she was just called hockey captain, as that was the major winter game. Similarly, the head of games in the summer term would be in charge of junior tennis, swimming and athletics but would simply be called tennis captain. It would probably be the same person: Joss Vining!

The train arrived at Trebizon station at three o'clock and coaches took them to the school. As they climbed up out of the old stone town and juddered along the country road, Rebecca felt pleased to see Trebizon Bay in the distance, even though the sea was grey and angry looking under the low January skies. Then she saw the familiar buildings again, a lovely blend of old and new, through the bare trees in the parkland that surrounded the school. What would her second term at Trebizon have in store for her? she wondered, as the coach turned in through the big entrance gates.

For Tish and Sue, the first thing it had in store was Joss Vining! She was waiting for them on the steps in front of old school, as they got off the coach. A lot of girls had come down on the train from London but many more, like Joss, had been driven from all parts of the country by car.

'Can you get your hockey stuff, you two, and come out on to school pitch right away?' she asked.

During the Christmas holidays the girls were allowed to leave their winter games' things in their lockers as they were needed again for the spring term.

'We've only just got here!' exclaimed Tish.

'Sorry, but there's a team practice,' said Joss. Rebecca noticed that Joss, usually the most relaxed of people, looked rather strained. 'We've been drawn in Group Two for the Gold Cup and we've got our first match exactly one week today – against Hillstone. So you see, we've got to get cracking. The trouble with this term is it gets dark after tea and a lot of practice will have to be done over in the sports hall, and that's never the same. In other words, this afternoon is too good to miss!'

'Of course, Joss. You're right as usual.'

Having recovered from their surprise, Tish and Sue agreed with her. On the first day back there was never much to do before tea except wait for the trunks to come up to the dormitories and unpack them. It was a dry afternoon and the pitch was firm.

'I'll take the stuff out of your trunks for you when they come up, if you like,' volunteered Rebecca, 'and that'll give you a bit longer. I'll come down and watch after that, if there's time.'

'You're an angel!' exclaimed Tish. 'Can you get these things upstairs as well?' Immediately Rebecca found dumped in her arms a load of hand luggage, additional to her own. There were two blue school capes, three carrier bags, Sue's violin case –

'Hey!' said Rebecca.

'I'll help!' cried Mara Leonodis, as her brother drove away in his red mini. She waved good-bye to him.

'Me, too,' said Sally Elphinstone, who was getting off the coach.

'Thanks Mara. Thanks Elf.' Both the Greek girl and plump Sally were in the same dormitory as Rebecca, Tish and Sue. They were a nice group in number six. Rebecca smiled in relief as they took some of her load.

'Okay?' asked Tish, as she and Sue went off with Joss.

'Just about!' said Rebecca.

'But if we're going to wait on you,' called Elf, 'you'd better win the Gold Cup and no excuses.'

Actually, Sally was only too happy to wait on them. She shuddered at the very thought of racing round a hockey pitch as soon as one got back. What a shock to the system! Rebecca, of course, merely envied them.

They trooped through the main school building, which was a converted manor house, out into the quadrangle gardens at the back and across to Juniper House. Up in the second floor dormitory they dumped everything on to the right beds and then lazed around and chatted. Rebecca knelt up on her bed and gazed out of the window. There was a little copse at the back, with a path leading through it down to the sand dunes and the sea. When the leaves were on the trees you could only catch glimpses of the sea, but now there was a wide view of the bay, with a big tanker on the horizon. It was good to be back!

'They're bringing the trunks up already!' exclaimed Rebecca, as she saw the men with trolleys down in the courtyard below and then heard the thud of footsteps on the stairs.

She unpacked her trunk and put everything away. Then she took all the stuff out of Tish's and Sue's trunks and piled it on to their beds, ready for them to sort it out after tea. Trunks had to be emptied quickly, and stacked on the landing, as the men would be coming back to take them down to the store-room.

'What's that?' asked Mara, as two pieces of paper fluttered on to the floor from the top of the pile on Tish's bed.

Rebecca picked them up.

'Notices about the election of a new Magazine Officer,' she said. 'Fancy Tish being so tidy-minded and typing them out in the holidays!'

The two notices were identical. One would go on the notice board in the First Year common room, which was at the opposite end of the building, and the other would go up in the Second Year common room, at this end of the building. They said:

Election of Magazine Officer
Having served two terms as Magazine Officer for Juniper House I am calling an open meeting. This will take place at 7 p.m. on Thursday in the Second Year common room. According to the school rules a new Magazine Officer must now be elected. She will serve for two terms. As there are two complete terms before anyone moves on from Juniper, this term only Second Years can stand. In the case of a vote, this will be taken on a show of hands.

Ishbel Anderson
Magazine Officer (Retiring)
Juniper House.

'Now I see how Tish got to be elected Magazine Officer when she was still a First Year!' exclaimed Rebecca with interest. 'Every other year an election falls at the beginning of the summer term, when the Second Years aren't going to be in Juniper for two terms, and that's when the First Years get a chance.'

'Rebecca!' said Mara. 'You are better than a pocket calculator. I was never able to work it out before.' The Greek girl shook her head. 'No wonder I am in *II Beta* when the rest of you are in *II Alpha*.' But she was smiling broadly.

'Don't think we're going to vote for you, Rebecca,' said Margot Lawrence who had just come in. 'Unless you want us to badly.'

'Eh?' Rebecca was surprised. 'I'm much too new to be anything like that.'

'It's not that,' said Elf. 'If you're Magazine Officer you can only choose other people's stuff for *The Trebizon*. You're automatically disqualified from choosing your own stuff!'

'And we all want that essay of yours to go in this term, the one that Elizabeth Exton kept out,' said Margot. Elizabeth, the former editor of the school magazine had left in disgrace and now there was a proper editor called Audrey Maxwell. 'Bet Audrey will agree.'

Rebecca felt a little rush of pleasure, and said nothing.

'Hey,' said Margot suddenly, 'it's going to be funny Tish not being something important this term. She was a First Year monitor all last year, and then Magazine Officer as well . . .'

'Tish is always important!' said Mara, with great affection. 'And besides, she's still editor-in-chief of *The J.J.* and that's something important!'

'I've got a good joke for it!' remembered Margot. 'Listen

to this: *How many girls at Caxton High School does it take to put a light bulb in?*'

'How many does it –?' giggled Rebecca and the others. Caxton were old rivals and insulting their intelligence was a favourite pastime at Trebizon.

'*1001!*' said Margot triumphantly. '*One to hold the light bulb in and a thousand to turn the school round.*'

They all hiccupped with laughter, and Rebecca had to tear herself away. She wanted to see how the Under-14 practice was going, and if she didn't hurry it would be over. Supposing half the team had gone off form! Supposing . . . Rebecca smiled at herself. What a hope!

There was just enough of the practice left for Rebecca to see that they were all in great form, especially Judy Sharp who played at right wing, Rebecca's natural position. The forward line was practising running, passing and shooting. Judy went at lightning speed, cracked the ball across to Sue who then in one sweet, deft movement shot it straight past Jenny Brook-Hayes in goal.

'Hurrah!' cried someone on the sidelines. 'Good old Sue!'

It was Nicola Hodges with a crowd of her First Year friends. They seemed to have formed a Sue Murdoch fan club.

Joss blew a whistle then and the practice ended. Nicola remembered Rebecca was at the party at Sue's house and came across to her. Her chubby, angelic face was pink and in spite of a frisky wind her beautifully brushed and plaited flaxen hair was as tidy as ever.

'Wasn't Sue marvellous?' said Nicola.

'Was she?' asked Rebecca. 'I've only just arrived.'

Rebecca was conscious of Joss and Tish standing talking together nearby and she wanted to go over and join them.

But Nicola was hanging around, as though anxious to have a long and earnest discussion about Sue. Then suddenly Rebecca realized that Joss was speaking to Tish very privately and had no idea she could be overheard.

'It may not happen, Tish. Don't tell anyone. Promise?'

'Of course I promise, Joss.'

Rebecca turned away quickly. She realized that Nicola had overheard, too. She took the younger girl by the arm.

'So you and your friends are hockey fans, Nicola?'

'Oh, we are now that Juniper's team's got into the Gold Cup!' said Nicola. 'And I've told the others how I've got to know Sue and what a great person she is – so we're going to turn up for every match, you wait and see.'

'Let's go over and talk to Sue then,' said Rebecca.

She was anxious to steer Nicola away. She had the clear impression that the younger girl was more than just interested in the conversation between Joss and Tish.

As they walked across to Sue, Rebecca glanced back over her shoulder. Joss, usually such a calm and relaxed person, was still talking to Tish and looking worried. More mysteries – more secrets! It was bad enough Tish being quirky – now there seemed to be something up with Joss!

THREE

THE TEAM IS PICKED

Whatever was up with Joss Vining, there were more surprises in store as far as Tish was concerned. On Wednesday the new and unpredictable Tish, whom previously Rebecca had regarded as such a steady person, suddenly seemed hysterically happy about nothing. And, as Rebecca was soon to discover, this new-found euphoria was going to spill out in all directions. Tish, to put it mildly, had hit a high.

They were back into lessons. English came first with their form-mistress, Miss Heath, followed up by a cold douche of mathematics from Miss Gates. She set them a complicated problem to work out in their heads. Rebecca was amazed when four girls, usually the slowest, smugly put their hands up first: Debbie Rickard, Joanna Thompson, Roberta Jones and Mary Bron. Tish started giggling but Rebecca realized nothing until Miss Gates suddenly clapped her hands, later in the lesson.

'Will the four girls who have been given pocket calculators for Christmas and have them on their laps please bring them up here and put them on the table.'

Sheepishly the four trudged up and handed them over.

'You may use your new-found brains in Chemistry, Physics and Biology. I believe the science staff approve. In my lessons you will learn to use your old brains until you are in the Fourth Year. Now, let's continue.'

Sitting in the back row, Tish doubled up with laughter until she started to choke. Judy Sharp, who shared a double desk with her, had to bang her hard on the back. Sue and Rebecca, in the adjacent desk, thought it was funny, too – and soon Tish had all three of them in hysterics.

'Let's go to Moffatt's!' she said at morning break, meaning the school tuck shop. 'I'll buy you lemonades.'

'It's not your birthday,' said Rebecca, in surprise.

At Moffatt's Tish drank her lemonade in one long draught, gave a contented sigh and leaned back in her chair.

'I think we're going to win the Gold Cup. I just have a feeling about it.'

'Good,' said Sue, humouring her.

'And what did you think about the Head's announcement in Assembly?' added Tish.

'What, about not leaving the taps running in the cloakroom?' asked Sue, puzzled.

Tish let out a shriek of laughter that made several Third Years at the next table turn round in surprise. She shook for some moments.

'What announcement do you mean, Tish?' asked Rebecca patiently.

'The Hilary Camberwell Music Scholarship of course,' said Tish, steadying herself, but with tears of laughter in her eyes. 'Oh, Sue, you are priceless.'

Rebecca remembered the announcement now. It had come somewhere in the middle of a long burble of notices read out by Miss Welbeck, the Principal, in the big Assembly Hall. *Will all girls entering for the Hilary Camberwell*

Music Scholarship shortly after half-term please note that the entry forms must be returned, signed by their parents, by January 30th.

'Oh, that,' said Sue.

'It was announced at the end of last term too, wasn't it?' said Rebecca. Her memory for detail, as usual, was good. 'It's for the best instrumentalist under 14 on September 1st and it carries up to full fees and free music tuition up the school.'

'Something like that,' said Tish airily. 'But the main thing is that the person who wins it is known as the Music Scholar of her year for the whole time she's at Trebizon! And they wear those lovely badges with HC on them. We've seen them Sue!'

'That's right. Moyra Milton's got one. She won it last year,' said Sue. Moyra was a talented clarinet player who was now in the Third Year. 'So what?'

'So *what*?' exclaimed Tish. 'Don't you realize this is your last chance to enter, Sue! Your very last chance. You're only just inside the age limit. Only *just*!'

'Enter?' Sue's mouth fell open in genuine amazement. 'Me?'

'Yes, you!' Tish looked at Sue as though she were a simpleton. 'Who else! You could win it, Sue! Easy!'

'But – but –' Sue looked bewildered, 'I don't see how I could win it for a start. I'd be the oldest, seeing when my birthday is –'

'You could still win it!' interrupted Tish, overflowing with largesse. Rebecca began to feel excited. There was something about Tish's mood today – it was catching!

'And secondly, even if I could win it, well . . .' Sue looked embarrassed, 'it wouldn't be fair. I mean, aren't the scholarships for people who are hard up. My parents don't need me to have a scholarship and –'

'That's got nothing to do with it, Sue!'

'Surely there's a means test or something?'

'Of course not. The honour's the main thing, being known as a Music Scholar all the time you're here. Imagine it, Sue!'

'I think Tish must be right,' said Rebecca. 'Why else would it be *up* to full fees awarded? Parents probably accept the fees if they need them, otherwise they don't. Then there's more money in the kitty for another year.'

'Of course I'm right!' exclaimed Tish. 'Look at Annie Lorrimer!'

'You're right about Annie!' gasped Sue. 'I'd never thought about it before.' Annie Lorrimer was in the Lower Sixth and was also the Music Scholar for her year. 'The Lorrimers are rolling.'

Sue, as a member of the school orchestra, was actually far more conscious of the Music Scholars than Tish had ever been. Their names were all up in gold letters on the honours board, over in the music school. She knew how respected they were, but it had never occurred to her that she could be one, too. Until now.

'There's the bell!' said Tish, jumping up. 'Let's go. It's all decided then!'

There was still a touch of frost on the lawns as she went dancing ahead to old school, back to lessons. Sue and Rebecca followed slowly in her footprints. Rebecca could tell that Sue was inwardly excited.

'What do you think?' asked Rebecca.

'I think Tish is on a high today!' said Sue, trying to keep sensible. 'First of all saying we're going to win the Gold Cup – now this.'

'But it *would* be a nice idea to enter, wouldn't it?'

'Yes,' said Sue. 'If I'm good enough. If I really stand a chance. That's the first thing I've got to find out. I know Mrs Borrelli will tell me honestly. Tish really has no idea!'

'Nor me,' confessed Rebecca. 'But you're right. Mrs Borrelli will know!' She was Sue's violin teacher. 'Is she in today?'

'Yes, I've seen her car.'

'Then you could see her at dinner break, Sue,' said Rebecca.

'You bet!' Sue's spectacles shone as a glimmer of sunlight caught them. 'That's just what I'm going to do!'

'You're late, Susan,' said Mr Douglas, the chemistry master, as Sue came into the science laboratory just after two. Her sandy hair was wind-blown and she had been running.

'I'm sorry, sir, I've been over at the Hilary, and then I had to go and see the school secretary and then I forgot my books –'

Tish and Rebecca, bending over a bunsen burner, nudged each other. Sue forgetting her books! Something exciting must have happened. Sue came and joined them at the long bench and they started whispering together at once.

'What did Mrs Borrelli say?'

'She was surprised at first but, yes!' Sue's face was shining. 'She says I do stand a chance if I work really hard, and she'll put me into the scholarship timetable. Then she asked me if I had my parents' permission and I told her they didn't know anything about it!'

'So what happens now?' hissed Tish.

'I'm going to ring them tonight, but I'm sure they'll agree! I'm so sure I've been and asked for an entry form to be posted off to them today!'

'So that's why you've been to see Mrs Devenshire –' began Rebecca.

'Stop talking!' ordered Mr Douglas. 'Now you've actually got here, Susan, I'd be grateful if you could get on with the experiment.'

The afternoon ended with a double lesson of hockey.

For once Joss Vining didn't play. She stood on the sidelines with Miss Willis, carefully noting form. So many girls played as forwards that Rebecca often had to be content with a half-back position during lessons. But today, with Joss missing, her chance came. Tish took over as centre-forward in the red team, Judy Sharp moved over to the left inner position, and Rebecca got the chance to play her best position, right wing.

She put everything she had into the game, feeling it just might be important. This feeling grew stronger when she saw Joss walk across to east pitch for ten minutes to watch a game going on amongst the First Years. Her suspicions were confirmed at the end of the lesson. Joss gathered everybody around her on the pitch.

'We had a good Under-14 team last term, but all the same I want to make one or two changes for the Gold Cup. I'll put the names up tonight, with the names of First reserve and Second reserve, who'll travel to matches with us. I'm also going to pick a Second Eleven for this term, which must be willing to play against the Under-14 team at certain times, and give them plenty of practice.'

Miss Willis, who had been keeping in the background, stepped forward.

'It's going to be a taxing term but it could be a marvellous one,' she said. 'We didn't think we'd qualify for the Gold Cup, but we have. It's a short term and it's going to be packed, because of course we have to fit in our normal fixtures as well. Everyone is going to have to work very hard, keep very fit and be dedicated to the idea that we bring the Gold Cup back to Trebizon for the first time in our history. The girls who will be in the Under-14 team will be expected to give quite a lot to their hockey for a while. Those who are going to be asked to be in the Second Eleven will also have an important role to play. A big burden is going to fall on your head of games this term –' she gave Joss Vining a solicitous glance, '– and I want you all to support her and back her up in every way.'

It was a stirring little speech, and Rebecca felt excited by it, though mildly surprised by that solicitous glance. Joss could look after herself, couldn't she? She was always in complete command, and nobody ever questioned it! That was why she was such a good captain.

'By the weekend I'll have the complete timetable sorted out of fixtures and practice matches up to half term,' Miss Willis was saying. She laughed. 'I'm booking time on the computer right now! As Joss says, she'll put the teams up tonight. If you're in them – I'm warning you – don't arrange too much for mid-week and weekends this term. I'll see you all again tomorrow. Dismiss.'

They went over to the sports centre to have a shower and change. Now it was Rebecca's turn to be at the receiving end of Tish's new-found euphoria.

'Rebecca! You heard what Joss said?' she asked, as they walked through an avenue of bare chestnut trees towards the main school buildings for tea. 'She's going to make some changes in the team.'

'About time,' Sue said softly.

Suddenly Rebecca was reminded of Sue's funny little confession in the train – her secret ambition to be in charge of the hockey team! Well, Sue had something else to occupy her mind now, something actually within the bounds of possibility. But Rebecca's own secret wish, simply to be *in* the team, burned inside her more strongly than ever. And she knew that Tish was referring to it.

'The changes won't include me,' she said realistically.

'What about the two reserves, though!' exclaimed Tish. 'Sheila Cummings will be one – but I bet you'll be the other! Judy's ankle will never stand the pace. If two reserves are allowed to travel to matches, one's just got to be a reserve for Judy! And that's you.'

Rebecca had been trying to dismiss the thought from her mind, ever since Joss had mentioned that two reserves would be travelling to all the Cup matches.

It was a fact that Judy had a funny ankle that let her down sometimes. It was also a fact that while some of the other reserves were better all-rounders than Rebecca, she was the one who excelled on the right wing, Judy's position. For the first time, Tish's confidence made Rebecca feel that she really might stand a chance.

'I hope you're right, Tish,' she said.

'I bet I'm right!'

After tea, Rebecca spent the evening in the Second Year common room. English prep was to read their set book. Normally Rebecca would have gone to the library in old school, her favourite place. But this evening she sat glued to a chair in the common room. She simply had to be there when Joss came and pinned the team list up on the big notice-board behind the door.

When Joss came in, a crowd appeared. As soon as she had pinned up the list and left the room, they clustered round it. Rebecca walked over, trying hard to look casual.

She saw at once that she was down as right wing for the Second Eleven, but that the two reserves for the Under-14 team were to be Sheila Cummings and Verity Williams, a Second Year girl who was in Form II Beta, and a good defence player. Tish and Sue still had their inside forward positions in the team. That went without saying.

Rebecca bit her lip and went over to the window, gazing out at the lights of the school buildings, twinkling round the quadrangle gardens. How dark and wintry it was outside! Tish and Sue came in a few moments later, looked at the notice-board and came straight over to her.

'It's not fair, Becky,' said Tish, with feeling.

'It looks as though Joss has decided to take a chance on Judy's ankle, after all,' said Rebecca. 'Rung your parents, Sue?'

'Just been ringing them,' she replied. 'My mother says she's sure Daddy will agree and she'll get him to fill in the form when it arrives tomorrow.' Sue smiled. 'She said it sounded like a great honour, but not to get myself in a stew about it. Oh, Rebecca, it is a shame about you.'

Rebecca glanced at Tish, who was looking sheepish. So much for her euphoria! She had been wrong about the team list. Rebecca hoped she wasn't wrong about Sue's chances, too. Entering for the scholarship was going to mean a lot of hard work for her, especially with all the extra hockey this term. Feeling slightly depressed, Rebecca decided that she liked Tish best when she was just being her normal self.

But she was going to have to wait some time for that.

FOUR

REBECCA COUNTS HER BLESSINGS

By Thursday afternoon, when it was double hockey again, Rebecca had put her disappointment behind her. Now that the team had been announced, there was a kind of Gold Cup fever in the air, and all the talk was of their first cup match against Hillstone the following Tuesday. To add to the excitement, it was going to take place on the Trebizon ground.

Even without being in the team, or a reserve, it was impossible not to be infected by it. Rebecca began to see that, as a member of the newly-created Second Eleven, she really would have a role to play.

In the interests of the Cup, Miss Willis explained, the First Years and Second Years were going to be mixed up together in the hockey lessons from now on. This was so that on Tuesdays, Wednesdays and Thursdays, which were the hockey afternoons, the full Under-14 team could have practice matches against the full Second Eleven. Although the Under-14 team itself was mainly made up of Second Year girls, it contained three players from the First Year, and there were several more First Years in the Second Eleven.

Before the first practice match began, on Thursday, Joss Vining gathered her team around her to discuss tactics. Miss Willis drew the Second Eleven over to the other side of the field.

'Play hard,' she told them. 'It really does matter. Not just in this match – every match. You've got to stretch our Juniper team, and keep on stretching them. That way you'll help bring them up to peak form for the cup matches – and keep them there.'

Rebecca, for one, played her hardest and it was an exhilarating game. Mara Leonodis had got into the Second Eleven, too, at right inner, and she and Rebecca discovered that they played very well together. There was a kind of telepathy between them when they occasionally managed to get a run up the field, and short clean passes whizzed backwards and forwards between them as they dodged round the Under-14 defence. It was from one of Rebecca's passes that Mara cracked a goal straight past Jenny Brook-Hayes, the Under-14 'keeper.

In reply the Under-14 team scored five good goals, two each from Tish and Sue, and a sheer beauty from the right-winger, Judy. Surprisingly Joss, at centre-forward, did not score. Rebecca noticed she was moving less fluently than usual but it was also a tribute to Verity Williams, playing at centre-half in the Second Eleven, who marked her well. Rebecca decided that Verity fully deserved her selection as second reserve for the Gold Cup.

That evening a different kind of selection took place: the choosing of a new Magazine Officer for Juniper House, for two terms. Tish, as retiring Officer, chaired the meeting and the Second Year common room was packed out, with a lot of girls standing.

Rebecca was mildly surprised to see Nicola Hodges and her First Year friends sitting in the best chairs, right in the front row. They had obviously arrived very early. But the reason, which she should have guessed, was made clear as soon as Tish asked for nominations.

'I propose Sue Murdoch!' said Nicola, leaping to her feet, flaxen plaits flying. She glanced eagerly across to Sue, who was standing by the door.

'And we second it!' chorused her friends.

Sue went a deep shade of pink and shook her head vigorously.

'I'm sorry, I just couldn't take it on this term,' she said, 'and besides I don't think I'm the right person. I'd like to propose Jenny Brook-Hayes, because I think she would be very good.'

'And I second that!' said Sally Elphinstone promptly.

'Are there any more nominations?' asked Tish.

Rebecca watched Jenny's face and felt for her at that moment. She wanted the job badly, and she would be good at it. Twice she had had something short-listed for *The Trebizon Journal*, without success, and to have something printed in the school magazine was a cherished ambition. Of course she would have to forego that for another two terms if she were elected Magazine Officer, but it meant she was the sort of person who would not turn down anybody else's work lightly. Everything would be considered very carefully.

'I propose Debbie Rickard,' said Roberta Jones, rather aggressively.

Roberta bitterly resented the way that her poems, which were awful, were never short-listed by Juniper House and sent through to the editor of the school magazine, way up in the Upper Sixth. Other people's were. With Debbie as Magazine Officer, things might be different.

'I second that,' said Mary Bron, who secretly thought that the gang in dormitory number six always seemed to have everything their own way.

But Jenny was not kept in suspense for very long. There were no more nominations and Tish took a vote. With Nicola and her friends following Sue's lead and voting for Jenny, and most of the Second Years present doing likewise, Debbie Rickard was defeated by a crushing 41 votes to 7.

Tish immediately handed over the chair to Jenny and gave her some notes. Jenny studied them and then, cheeks glowing with happiness, stood up.

'Thank you for electing me,' she said. 'I'll keep it brief. Audrey Maxwell, who as you know is the new editor of *The Trebizon*, wants our contributions in by the end of the month. The spring term issue is always a slim one, so I don't think we should send up more than four items. I would like to propose that two of those items should be our two outstanding ones from last term, which Elizabeth Exton deliberately kept out. The essay by Rebecca Mason and the drawing of the church by Susannah Skelhorn.'

There was a great roar of approval. A crowd of hands shot up and Rebecca felt herself going hot with pleasure. Jenny went on to ask for all contributions to be submitted within ten days, but Rebecca hardly heard her. First a poem in *The Trebizon Journal*, and now a real chance of her essay going in! Margot Lawrence had hinted at this, on their first day back, and it seemed that her hints were based on solid fact. Rebecca's pleasure was only equalled by that of Susannah Skelhorn, a First Year girl who was an artist of exceptional promise.

'Well,' said Tish after the meeting had broken up, 'that

went pretty well, didn't it? Especially the bit about your essay, Bec.'

They were drinking hot chocolate and eating biscuits in the kitchen, opposite the common room. Rebecca said nothing, still glowing pleasantly with the memory of it.

'Do you realize, Tish,' said Sue solemnly, 'that for the first time since you got to this place you're nobody important! Just plain Ishbel Anderson. It must feel funny!'

'I like it,' said Tish. She looked at Sue intently. '*You're* the one who's going to be somebody –' She flung up a hand, dramatically. '*Susan Murdoch – Music Scholar!*' she announced loudly to the empty room.

Rebecca and Sue laughed. She was off again! Although not quite as high up in the clouds as she had been the previous day, she was still impossibly good-humoured.

'Put those rose-coloured spectacles away, Tish,' said Sue. 'You haven't really got a clue whether I'll win or not. I've got a long way to go.'

'There's something that might help you,' said Tish mysteriously.

'What?'

'Oh, tell you later.'

'I've just thought of something,' said Rebecca. Actually it was Mara who had said it first, on Tuesday. 'You're still editor of *The J.J.*, so you *are* someone!'

'So I am!'

'Shall we do one this weekend or d'you think it's too early?'

'Of course we'll do one!' exclaimed Tish. 'There's tons of news to put in it already.' She held up her fingers and ticked the items off. 'There's Sue entering for this music thing. We'd better find out who else is, they'll all be in Juniper. There's the Gold Cup match on Tuesday, we can write up a bit about Hillstone's record. The Under-14 team list, of course. The Magazine Meeting tonight, and what was decided. That's four things for a start!'

'I'd better be thinking about my "Did-You-Knows" then,' said Rebecca.

Later, Rebecca cleaned her teeth and got ready for bed. She came into the dormitory in time to see Tish putting something on Sue's locker, and Sue protesting about it.

'I can't, Tish!'

'Look, Sue, stop arguing. Will it be useful, or won't it? There's a new tape in it, and you know how to work it. You can record when you want and then rub off and start again, until you get it perfect.'

At last Sue gave in. It was a marvellous idea. Tish wanted her to borrow her cassette recorder for as long as she needed it, so that she could record herself practising the violin. It would undoubtedly help her a great deal in the weeks ahead.

But it was noble of Tish to part with her favourite new possession like that! As Rebecca got into bed, she felt quite emotional. She began to feel slightly ashamed of herself, coveting Verity Williams' place on the team list yesterday, thinking she might have been good enough to have it herself! Wasn't it about time she shut her eyes and counted her blessings?

She had found two perfect friends at Trebizon. For all her odd ways lately, Tish was the nicest person she knew – not counting Sue. Everybody had been marvellous about her essay at the magazine meeting tonight. It hardly seemed credible that she might get something published two terms running! And Joss *had* selected her for the Second Eleven – that was quite an honour, too, when you thought about it. She'd only been playing proper hockey for a term . . .

Then there was *The Juniper Journal* . . . it was fun

bringing that out each week . . . having a regular piece to write for it.

Rebecca became sleepier and sleepier. The four news items that Tish had outlined and the people concerned became jumbled up in her mind . . . Sue was playing in goal . . . Jenny Brook-Hayes was holding a violin . . . and then she changed to Nicola Hodges. And Rebecca was fast asleep.

The Juniper Journal, in fact, never went to press before Sunday evenings. That was when it was typed and duplicated, ready to be sold around the school on Monday mornings. It was going to be nothing like what they had planned on Thursday night. By Sunday, a lot of the hot news that Tish had been talking about was going to be completely out of date. By then, like the changing images in Rebecca's mind, everything would be upside-down.

FIVE

THE FIRST QUARREL

'You've got a letter, Susan,' said Miss Morgan, as the girls trooped downstairs on their way to breakfast on Friday morning. She was the full-time house mistress in residence at Juniper House and had already sorted out the post. 'Here, read it over breakfast.'

Sue took the stout white envelope eagerly.

'It's from Daddy,' she told Rebecca, looking at the handwriting. 'Posted yesterday, first class mail from London. It'll be the form!'

The bell went for breakfast.

The girls rushed out of Juniper House and along the back terrace which overlooked the quadrangle gardens, to the big modern white building that stood at right angles to Juniper. Girls sat ten to a table in the dining hall and the three friends were on Joss Vining's table, as they had been last term.

'Is that your birth certificate, Sue?' asked Sally Elphinstone, as Sue slit open the envelope with a knife and pulled out the contents. 'Let's see!'

Sue's birth certificate was passed round the table while Sue examined the entry form that her father had completed.

There was a brief note attached to the front. She showed it to Rebecca and Tish.

'Daddy's pleased!'

'What does it say? I can't read it,' said Rebecca. Howard Murdoch's handwriting, as was often the case with busy and important people, was almost illegible. 'It looks like Grrrr hmhh Sue. What a sprrrr squiggle!'

Tish peered at the note eagerly, and interpreted.

'It says Good Luck, Sue. What a splendid idea!'

'What's a splendid idea?' asked Elf, all agog. She handed the birth certificate carefully back to Sue. 'And what's this for?'

'Sue's entering for the Hilary Camberwell Music Scholarship,' said Tish grandly, as though she personally had invented it. 'What's more, she's going to win it –'

'Oh, *Tish* –' protested Sue.

'Hope it's not going to interfere with hockey,' said Joss Vining suddenly, dishing out bacon and sausages from a big casserole. 'How often have you got to practise this term? How much has the orchestra got on?'

Rebecca was surprised by the unaccustomed sharpness in Joss's tone. She looked strained somehow. What *had* she been talking about to Tish the other day?

'Music times have never clashed with anything before,' said Sue, happily. 'I've got my first lesson this evening and Mrs Borrelli's promised to show me the new timetable.'

Sue carefully put the form and birth certificate back in the envelope. She would hand them in to the school secretary immediately before lessons.

'When you go over to the music school this evening,' said Tish, stuffing down the last of her cornflakes, 'find out who else is entering. It can only be people in Juniper because of the age limit, so it'll make a good item for *The J.J.*'

'You bet I will,' said Sue, pushing her spectacles up her nose. 'Never mind *The J.J.* I want to *know*!' She looked at her father's note again, which she had kept beside her plate, and then back to Tish. 'Thanks for the whole idea. I'd never have thought of it myself.'

Rebecca and Tish smiled at one another, and Tish winked. It really looked as though Sue were getting the bit between her teeth! Rebecca dismissed the slight doubts she had had on Wednesday evening. Yes – it was worth Sue trying for an honour like this, even if it did mean extra hard work!

Friday was the only netball afternoon and Joss Vining did not turn up. It was rumoured that she was in the sick room.

'I thought she might be going down with something!' said Rebecca. 'She hasn't looked too good lately.'

'Did you see her at dinner time?' exclaimed Elf. 'She gave me her shepherd's pie; she looked sort of in pain.'

'Enough to give anyone a pain, seeing you wade through a double helping of shepherd's pie, Elf,' said Tish. 'Honestly! What's happened to your diet?'

Sally Elphinstone looked guilty, but Rebecca had the impression that Tish was changing the subject. Then everyone started discussing anxiously whether Joss would be fit for the first cup-tie on Tuesday or not, and Tish said sharply:

'Come on, you lot. Are we playing netball or aren't we?'

After tea that evening, Sue went off to the Hilary in high spirits, taking her violin case with her. The Hilary, short for the Hilary Camberwell Music School, was a group of converted coach houses set by a small lake in the school grounds. It was a beautiful setting in which to learn music. There were a lot of small practice rooms where the girls had tuition in various instruments, and one large room where orchestra rehearsals took place. Trebizon was very strong in music, not least because Hilary Camberwell, a famous old girl of the school, had endowed these buildings as well as the annual Music Scholarship.

Sue's first violin lesson of the new term with her tutor, Anna Borrelli, went very well. She spoke warmly to Sue at the end.

'I can see you have kept up your playing during the holidays. Good. I am glad that you have decided you will enter for the Music Scholarship; it will extend you. A high standard is required. You will have to be very dedicated this term.'

'Who decides about the scholarship?' asked Sue, with interest.

'None of the Music School staff have any say in it!' explained Mrs Borrelli, with a laugh. 'That would be quite wrong. Three experts come down from London, and examine you all in turn, and their decision is final.'

'And parents' means don't come into it at all?' asked Sue anxiously.

'Not at all. The Music Scholar is quite simply the most promising young musician in any one year. She will automatically receive free music tuition for the rest of her school career. But the matter of the school fees – that is discretionary. For some people, they are very important. For others, less so.'

Sue nodded. So Tish and Rebecca had been quite correct.

'And who will I be competing against?' asked Sue. 'Am I allowed to know?'

'Of course! There are five of you altogether. You and Nicola Hodges are entering on the violin –'

'Nicola?' exclaimed Sue. She felt suddenly uneasy.

'And three girls on wind instruments. As you go out, you will see the list, and you will also see that a special timetable has been arranged for scholarship candidates this term. Copy all the details down. It's most important that you stick rigidly to the programme we have organized for you. The orchestra also has some important engagements this term, note those down as well, with practice times.'

Mrs Borrelli gave Sue a sheet of paper and a pencil and saw her out of the room. She was expecting her next pupil.

The next pupil was Nicola Hodges.

She came in by the side door, right by Sue. Sue was quickly jotting down the details of her timetable, from the Music School notice-board. Although Sue had felt buoyant earlier she now felt rather flat, and her brief conversation with Nicola did nothing to help.

'Hello, Sue.'

The two of them looked at the notice-board together.

'Timetable's up then,' said the younger girl.

'Looks like we're rivals,' said Sue, awkwardly. There was a long silence. 'When did you enter for it?'

'My parents entered my name for it as soon as I came to Trebizon last term. They'd read about it in the school prospectus.'

Sue looked at Nicola's cherubic face. She could tell the scholarship meant something to the Hodges – perhaps it meant a great deal.

'Nicola!' called Mrs Borrelli, looking out of Room 1. 'Are you ready?'

Nicola hurried across to her. Sue folded up her sheet of paper and put it in the pocket of her skirt. Then she walked out of the building and looked at the water. Street lamps illuminated the footpath alongside the lake, which led back to the main school buildings. Their reflections danced on the water.

Sue walked slowly back to school, her violin case hanging rather limply at her side.

Meanwhile, in the Second Year common room, there was a slight stir of interest. Miss Willis, the games mistress, had come in and pinned something on the noticeboard. She handed another sheet to Margot Lawrence.

'Margot, be a dear and go and pin this up for the First Years.'

It was the timetable that Miss Willis had promised to have ready by the weekend. She had managed to sort out the complicated tangle of cup matches and regular fixtures, though only after a great deal of telephoning to avoid clashes. And she had also managed to fit in a heavy programme of practice games and training sessions for the Under-14 team.

'Phew!' said Rebecca, gazing at it.

Tish had caught up with Miss Willis by the door.

'How's Joss?' she asked. 'Is she going to be all right?'

'We don't know yet,' said Miss Willis, going out.

'Look at this, Tish!' called Judy Sharp. 'We're going to be worn to a frazzle.'

There were only four of them in the common room and they were still discussing the timetable when Sue came in.

'Come and have a look at this, Sue!' said Rebecca.

Sue walked over and gazed at the notice-board, dully. Then she took a folded sheet of paper out of the pocket of her skirt and smoothed it out. She looked down at it, then up at the notice-board, checking back and forth, several times.

'What's the matter?' asked Tish.

'Well, that settles it!' said Sue.

'Settles what?'

'Come on, you two,' said Rebecca, 'let's go and make cocoa.'

They went across the corridor to the kitchen. They had it to themselves and Rebecca started to make three cups of cocoa. Sue had flung herself down at the table, staring at her piece of paper. Tish was craning her neck to get a good look at it.

'It's impossible!' said Sue. 'Look – all the times clash! Either I pull out of the scholarship or I pull out of the hockey team.'

'*Sue!*' said Tish, though Rebecca had already guessed.

'Well, I'm not going to give up my place in the team!' said Sue fiercely. There were tears starting up in her eyes. 'I'm not!'

'But, Sue you'll have to –' began Tish. She was pale.

Rebecca mixed the cocoa to a smooth paste and waited for the milk to boil. She wanted to cry with disappointment for Sue. What a horrible choice to have to make!

'What d'you mean I'll have to?' asked Sue. 'We've got into the Gold Cup!'

'But, Sue, you're being stupid! You've got the rest of your life to play hockey! You'll never ever have the chance of being a Music Scholar at Trebizon again, wearing that badge and having your name up on the honours board –'

'Oh, fiddle the honours board!' said Sue, but Rebecca knew that she didn't mean it. She had only once seen Sue as upset as this before. 'I'm going to pull out of the scholarship.'

'You *can't*!' Tish was angry now, beginning to lose her temper. 'I don't understand you. I thought you'd decided this was really important to you –'

'It is – it was,' said Sue, losing her temper back. 'Except I don't really need it, do I? As a matter of fact other people need it more than I do, people like Nicola Hodges –'

'Is she entering?' asked Tish sharply. 'What's she been saying?'

'She hasn't been saying anything!' retorted Sue. 'I just have a feeling it matters to her, that's all. And it might interest you to know, I feel rather mean.'

'Sue, don't be so utterly stupid,' said Tish.

Rebecca brought the cocoa over to the table. She was keeping out of the quarrel. The trouble was, she could see both points of view equally well, especially now Sue had said that about Nicola Hodges. It could be that Nicola's parents were really hard up! Well, Rebecca's own parents weren't exactly rich. She knew that she was only at Trebizon by courtesy of her father's firm, since they'd posted him overseas!

'Sorry, Rebecca, I don't feel like any cocoa,' said Sue, getting to her feet. 'I'm going up to bed.'

She went out through the door. Tish jumped up to follow her, looking annoyed.

'Come back, Sue. Talk about it properly –'

Rebecca grabbed the back of Tish's jumper and pulled her down into her seat again.

'Leave her alone, Tish!' she said. 'You can't run Sue's life for her. You can see she doesn't want to talk about it any more tonight.'

Tish looked so sorrowful that Rebecca added:

'Cheer up. Let her sleep on it. Maybe she'll see sense by the morning.'

'She'd better.'

That was all Tish said.

But the next morning there were other things to think about. The whole of Juniper House was buzzing with the sensational news. It buzzed along the corridors, through the washrooms and into the dormitories. By breakfast time, there wasn't a girl in the whole of the junior boarding house who didn't know about Joss Vining.

She had been taken to hospital in an ambulance. It seemed that an old back injury, which occasionally gave a little trouble and then quietened down again, was now causing serious pain. Joss's parents had been contacted and a specialist had been to see her. It seemed that a small operation could fix everything – that, and several weeks in hospital.

Afterwards, Joss would be as fit and strong as ever. But in the meantime, she would be absent from Trebizon for the rest of the term.

SIX

TOWARDS A BREAK-UP

'Cheer up, you lot, she isn't going to die, you know,' said Pippa Fellowes-Walker. Tall and pretty and a member of the Lower Sixth form, Pippa was Rebecca's favourite prefect. The seniors were allowed to wear what they liked at the weekends and Rebecca thought that Pippa looked as good as any model. She wore a flared corduroy skirt with big patch pockets and a russet-coloured polo neck jumper that toned in with her tan skirt. Her golden hair cascaded down over her shoulders. 'Muesli, Rebecca?'

Pippa was one of the prefects on duty in dining hall on Saturday morning. She felt sorry for the kids on Josselyn Vining's table and instead of parading up and down keeping law and order, she had slipped into Joss's old place at the head of the table and started serving out their breakfast to them.

'She's known she might have to have this operation for a long time,' said Tish, who was sitting next to Rebecca. 'She just hoped it wouldn't have to be this term, that's all.'

Rebecca looked at Tish and understood. So *that* was what

they had been talking about on the hockey pitch on Tuesday. Joss had made Tish promise not to tell anyone, and Tish had kept her promise.

'But it is!' said Sally Elphinstone, overhearing. She put into words what was in everybody else's mind. 'How are we going to win the Gold Cup now, without Joss?'

'I don't know,' said Tish, looking determined, 'but we are. Joss will be lying in hospital and just counting on it!'

'Who will be captain?' asked Sue suddenly.

'Goodness knows,' said Pippa. 'Come on, cheer up, shut up and eat up. Doesn't anyone want grilled bacon? What's the matter with you all?'

Towards the end of breakfast the duty mistress rang a small hand-bell, waited for silence, and then made an announcement. Mrs Beal's voice was very firm.

'Miss Willis has requested that *all* First Year and *all* Second Year girls remain seated at their tables when the breakfast things are cleared away. *Even* if you have activities arranged, none of you is to leave the hall before Miss Willis gets here.'

Chairs scraped and voices babbled and crockery clinked as one by one the older girls' tables were cleared away and abandoned. Obediently the First and Second Years remained behind, seated. Their tables were bare and wiped down now and there was a steady murmur of talk. An air of expectancy hung over all the tables. Rebecca, like everybody else, guessed that Miss Willis was going to talk to them about Joss. What was she going to say? Saturday morning was free time and it was very unusual not to be allowed to leave the dining hall. It had to be important.

As the tall games mistress strode in, wearing a blue Trebizon track suit, her short, curly fair hair looked unruly.

Sara Willis had not in fact had time to comb it that morning. There was an urgent, business-like air about her and everybody stopped talking at once.

'I wanted to corner you while you're all together,' she said crisply, 'and before the weekend starts in earnest. I expect you all know about Josselyn by now. I've just come back from the hospital.'

There were subdued whispers. Over by the door Pippa Fellowes-Walker and Annie Lorrimer, who was also on duty, hung on to listen to all this.

'Josselyn is in pain, but she is going to be fine,' said Miss Willis. 'I don't have to tell you how upset she is about the Gold Cup, and what a tonic it's going to be for her if we can go ahead and win it just the same. At the moment, Juniper House has no head of games and that means the Under-14 team has no captain. You're like a ship without a rudder and we've got to put that right as quickly as possible.'

Miss Willis's statement caused quite a stir and there was an immediate babble of talk and discussion on the other tables. Rebecca's own table, though, was oddly silent. A ripple of subdued excitement ran round it as they realized, some of them for the first time, what might be coming. Rebecca herself, still recovering from the shock of Joss's sudden departure, hadn't given a thought to the implications.

The games mistress deliberately let the noise run on for a while and then she clapped her hands for silence.

'There's a vacuum and let's fill it as quickly as possible,' she said. 'You all know the procedure for electing a head of games. Names are proposed and seconded and if more than one candidate decides to stand, we organize a ballot. I hope we can avoid that. I hope we can all reach agreement amongst ourselves, right now, on who should step into

Josselyn's shoes. I don't have to remind you that our first cup fixture is on Tuesday.'

Tish was looking at Sue, and Sue was looking at Tish. Rebecca's heart was beating very hard. She knew just what Miss Willis was going to say next, and she said it.

'It's between two girls, isn't it? Ishbel Anderson and Susan Murdoch are the only girls who have been in the team as long as Josselyn, from the time they started at Trebizon in fact. Both are outstanding players and have the experience to lead the team this term. And both of them, I know, would have your full support at a difficult time like this.'

There was an almost eerie silence. Then it was broken.

'I propose Sue Murdoch!' shouted Nicola Hodges.

A cheer went up from the First Year table where Nicola sat.

Sue looked amazed – and then thrilled. She simply could not hide her pleasure.

Debbie Rickard, sitting at the next table to Rebecca, looked across and saw the expression on Tish's face. Tish looked as though she wanted to kill Nicola Hodges! Debbie had always been jealous of Tish and now she could hardly keep the glee out of her voice.

'I second that!' she called out.

There was more applause and murmurs of approval. As Miss Willis had said, there was a vacuum and they all wanted it filled. It would be nice to get it over with at once, and get out and enjoy their Saturday morning, knowing that everything was neatly settled. Sue Murdoch was a fine player, and she was fair; she'd be okay as captain if that's what everyone wanted.

As more discussion broke out Rebecca saw Tish lean over to Sue, with a rather wild look, her black curls almost standing on end. She was mouthing the words, urgently.

'The music scholarship, Sue! *The music scholarship.*'

'I'm pulling out of that, Tish. *I told you that last night.*'

Miss Willis raised her voice above the babble. She was looking directly at Sue.

'Would you be willing to stand, Susan?'

'Yes,' said Sue.

'Is everyone content to leave it at that –?' began Miss Willis.

Suddenly Rebecca felt Tish's fingers gripping her arm, so tightly that it hurt. She whispered into Rebecca's ear. Sue saw, and so did some of the others.

'You've *got* to propose *me*,' she said.

'Tish –' began Rebecca, shocked.

'Please, *please* trust me.'

That was all she said. Rebecca didn't stop to think. It was all mad. Everything about Tish was mad this term. But she did trust her. She would have trusted her with her life.

'I propose Ishbel Anderson,' she said, voice shaking a little.

Mara Leonodis, who sat at the same table as Debbie Rickard, was waiting to release her pent up feelings. Of *course* Tish should be the new head of games. And Rebecca thought so, too! That was good enough for Mara.

'I second!' she cried.

There were some cheers now, and two whole tables applauded. Tish Anderson was very popular.

Miss Willis waited for the din to cease, and then she smiled.

'Now, which one of you is willing to stand down?' She said the words confidently. She knew that the two girls were best friends, and that they were both very sensible, and that they would hardly want to force an election over the issue.

There was silence, and her voice faltered a little.

'I'm sure one of you is?'

Sue stared at Tish, an expression of hurt disbelief on her face. Then she looked down at the table, resolutely.

Tish, equally resolute, sat with her arms folded, staring into space.

'Are there any more nominations?' asked Miss Willis.

There weren't.

'And Ishbel and Susan are both certain they want to stand?' asked Miss Willis. She stared at both of them, in turn. Both nodded their heads, very slightly, and said nothing. Everything was still in the dining hall. 'I see.' There was a hint of irritation in her voice. 'Then we shall have to organize a proper election,' she said. 'But we can't do anything over the weekend.'

She turned and saw the two prefects, who had been listening with great interest.

'You two,' she said briskly, 'organize a ballot in Juniper House on Monday evening. I suggest directly after tea. Ask Joanne to be there when the votes are counted.'

Joanne Hissup was in the Upper Sixth and was head of games of the entire school. It made the whole thing seem very important.

'Well,' said Miss Willis, turning back to the seated girls, 'with a bit of luck Juniper House will have a new head of games by Monday evening, and as we are meeting Hillstone on Tuesday, that won't be a moment too soon. I want the election to be conducted in a good atmosphere, with everybody pulling behind the new captain when she has been elected, and may the best girl win. You may go.'

Without a backward glance at Tish or Sue, she strode out of the hall. Pandemonium broke out as the girls scraped their chairs back, gabbling loudly as they left the dining hall in groups, discussing this extraordinary turn of events.

Tish Anderson and Sue Murdoch fighting each other for Joss Vining's old job! They were supposed to be best friends weren't they? It was Rebecca Mason's fault – that new girl who went around with them. What was she trying to do, stir up trouble between them?

'Tish Anderson *asked* Rebecca to propose her,' chipped in Nicola Hodges there. 'I saw her!'

'You didn't!'

'What a thing to do!'

'But Tish *would* be best!' said someone else. 'She always scores more goals than Sue!'

And so the argument and discussion raged on.

Tish went up to Sue and touched her on the shoulder, about to say something. But Sue angrily shook her off and marched out of the hall. Rebecca could see that she was on the verge of tears.

Tish started to follow her and then stopped. Nicola had caught up with Sue on the terrace outside, and was talking to her animatedly. They were joined by a crowd of Nicola's friends.

Mara Leonodis and some other girls mobbed round Tish, pledging their support.

Debbie Rickard came up to Rebecca and said sweetly:

'I suppose if Tish is elected you're hoping to get in the team?'

Rebecca felt sick, at that. She felt even sicker when she heard a First Year girl say to her friend:

'Do you know what Nicola Hodges thinks? She says Tish Anderson will go to any lengths to get it, even if it means breaking up with her best friend.'

Miss Willis wants the election to be conducted in a good atmosphere, thought Rebecca. *Some hopes of that!*

She had put Tish's name forward because she had begged her to. She had asked her to trust her, and Rebecca had complied. But Tish was baffling this term, she really was. Why did it all matter so much, anyway? And now people were starting to say horrible things. Hadn't Tish realized that they might?

Rebecca hovered by the glass doors of the dining hall. Sue was still on the terrace, surrounded by supporters. Rebecca longed to go out there and say something, but the look that Sue gave her chilled her to the bone. It was full of reproach. She quickly turned her face away.

There was Tish in the hall, talking to Mara, Sally and Margot. Tish looked quite sparkling, the light of battle in her eyes. She was sitting on one of the long dining tables swinging her legs.

Had Tish no idea how upset Sue was? Could she really be that insensitive? Had she forgotten about Sue's secret ambition to be a hockey captain – just for a term? Joss would get fit and well again, thank goodness, and she would be head of games all the way up the school. Everyone knew that. This was the only chance Sue would ever have.

Tish wasn't bothered about being anything this term. So why was she spoiling things for Sue? It could only be because she had this fixation about the Music Scholar business. Sue's name in gold letters on the honours board and all that. But Sue didn't want it! She had been excited at first, but she had soon changed her mind, when she had realized it was going to interfere with her hockey. Sue had already been planning to drop out of the Hilary Camberwell!

Doesn't Tish realize, thought Rebecca fiercely, *that this is going to break the three of us up? I've got to stop her. The whole idea of having an election is idiotic and I've got to stop it before it even starts.*

And then Mara called her over.

SEVEN

THE ELECTION IS ON

'Rebecca! You were marvellous!' Mara's large brown eyes were shining as she looked from Rebecca to Tish and then back to Rebecca. 'You were the only one of us who had the courage to do the right thing!'

'Tish made me,' said Rebecca. 'You all know she did!'

'And she was right!' said Margot.

The little group was quite alone in the vast dining hall now.

'Do you notice something, Rebecca?' asked Tish. 'The Action Committee has reactivated itself. Great minds thinking alike again.'

Subtly, Tish was reminding Rebecca of the events of last term. At that time, when there had been a clash with the mighty Elizabeth Exton over an injustice towards Rebecca, Tish had formed a little 'Action Committee'. It had consisted of herself, Sue, Mara, Margot and Sally 'Elf' Elphinstone and it had helped to win the battle against Elizabeth.

But Rebecca was in no mood for nostalgia.

'It's not quite the same committee this time, is it?' she said coolly. 'There's someone missing.'

'That's right,' said Tish, outrageously calm. 'Sue's missing. We're all going to gang up on her and stop her being daft. Are you going to join us?'

'No, I'm not!' Rebecca said furiously. The words poured out and she couldn't stop them. 'I don't know what's got into you this term, Tish. I don't know why you asked me to propose you just now, and heaven only knows why I did it! I must have been mad! You've taken it into your head to run Sue's life for her. *You've* made up your mind that she's going to be the Music Scholar this year, when she doesn't even want to be any more –'

'That's only part of it,' said Tish hastily.

'Then what's the rest of it?' asked Rebecca. Tish being baffling again! 'Whatever it is, it's not worth it. Do you realize people are already starting to say nasty things about you –'

'So what, as long as they're not true.'

'And about me,' added Rebecca.

'Are they?' Tish was taken aback.

'But the worst thing is *Sue*. We've made her utterly miserable. She was so amazed and thrilled when it looked as though she was going to be given Joss's job, and she just can't understand what you're up to. She's hurt, Tish. *Please* drop it – just drop the whole thing.'

There was so much emotion in Rebecca's voice that the others were embarrassed and silent. She hadn't intended to say so much. Tish looked upset and for a moment Rebecca thought she might have won the day. But when Tish finally spoke, her hopes were crushed.

'Not a chance,' she said. 'Of course Sue was amazed and thrilled, as you put it. Amazed, especially. It had just been a day-dream of hers. She's not cut out to run things while Joss is away, especially not to win the Gold Cup. She's not aggressive enough. You can see it when she plays. She's clever and skilful and she makes a lot of goals for other people, but she doesn't go crashing through and scoring them. Another thing is, she can't take too much pressure. She gets uptight. Her mother's always telling her off about it.'

'And you wouldn't?' said Rebecca scornfully. Did Tish really believe all that stuff? 'Stop electioneering, for heaven's sake!'

'Me?' said Tish, unabashed. 'I'd be okay. I've got more will to win than Sue has. Take the Hilary Camberwell.' A note of rebuke crept into her voice. 'One look from Nicola Hodges and Sue wants to back down.'

'*That* girl has the will to win all right,' said Mara Leonodis darkly. 'Who stuffed the idea into Sue's head that she should be a busy little hockey captain? What a strange coincidence, hey?'

'Oh, I don't think Nicola planned that,' said Tish quickly. 'She's not the sort. She looks a sweet, innocent sort of girl to me. The trouble is she worships the ground Sue walks on and it goes to Sue's head. The main thing now is to nip this whole thing in the bud.'

'You've got to win the election on Monday, Tish!' said Margot Lawrence. 'Aren't we supposed to be going over to Moffatt's to plan out our campaign?'

'I haven't just got to win,' said Tish calmly. 'I've got to crush her. Nothing else will do.'

'*Why?*' asked Rebecca, aghast. 'Why do you have to do *that*?'

'So she'll realize, once and for all, that the whole idea was silly. Then maybe she'll get down to what really matters, working hard for the Hilary Camberwell.'

'That she *can* win,' said Mara. Mara herself had a lovely singing voice and, unlike Tish and Rebecca, a good musical ear.

'You really think so, Mara?' asked Tish.

'I know it!' said Mara and added, under her breath: 'And so does Nicola Hodges.'

'Oh, come off it, Mara!' For the first time that morning Tish's grin was back in place, huge and irrepressible. 'I'm sure you're wrong about Nicola.' She slid down off the table, ready to go, and turned to Rebecca. The others were already walking towards the doors. 'You won't join us then?'

'Tish,' said Rebecca, close to despair, 'maybe you'd do the job better than Sue, maybe you wouldn't. But none of it matters. If the election goes ahead, it's going to break us three up. Please call it off. Anything's better than you two fighting each other.'

'It won't break us up,' said Tish. Rebecca was amazed. She sounded so sure, so confident! She grabbed hold of Rebecca's arm, and lowered her voice. The others were over by the door, waiting for her. 'I asked you to trust me before, and you've got to go on trusting me. I don't want this election, any more than you do. I tried to talk to Sue earlier, but she wouldn't listen. She might listen to you. If you really want to make yourself useful, go and find her. Try and get it into her thick head that I care about her and I'm trying to stop her doing something she'll regret . . .'

'Come on, Tish!' called Elf. 'I'm starving.'

'And tell her to drop out of the contest!' finished Tish. 'Coming, you greedy pig!' she called. 'You've only just had breakfast!'

Rebecca watched as they all went outside. A few snowflakes were falling and some landed and shimmered briefly on the back of Tish's dark curly head. She heard their voices going off into the distance, across quadrangle gardens.

She came out and shut the doors carefully behind her. She stood on the terrace, uncertain, undecided. Then she made up her mind.

'I believe you, Tish,' she thought. 'Thousands wouldn't. I still don't know what you're really up to, and why it all matters so much. But whatever it is, I don't think you're doing it for yourself.'

For the second time that morning she found herself doing Tish Anderson's bidding. She set off to find Sue Murdoch.

'Tish has put you up to this, hasn't she?' said Sue, furiously. 'Of course I'm not going to drop out of the contest! Why should I?'

Rebecca's heart sank.

She had tracked Sue down to one of the small practice rooms at the Hilary. She had glimpsed her through an open door, head bent over her violin, playing a haunting piece of music. She had waited outside for her to finish the piece, somehow comforted by the sounds. Sue was not ignoring her timetable then.

That was the beginning and end of any comfort that Rebecca Mason was going to receive from Sue Murdoch that morning.

'Don't get so angry, Sue,' begged Rebecca. The cold glint of the eyes behind the spectacles was almost more than she could bear. 'Tish honestly believes she's doing you a favour. She thinks you'd make a mess of Joss's job and you'd kick yourself for ever more, when you looked back and saw what you'd given up.'

'She does, does she?' said Sue. 'Of course, it couldn't possibly be that she wants to be head of games herself –'

'Sue!'

Rebecca was shaken.

She had naturally expected Sue to be hopping mad with Tish for interfering in her life and trying to decide what was good for her. Who wouldn't be! She was also waiting to be mowed down in a hail of verbal bullets for putting Tish's name up for captain.

But this – It was completely unexpected.

'Tish is a hypocrite!' Sue burst out.

'Sue . . .'

'I'm sorry, but it's true.' A look of utter incomprehension came across the sandy-haired girl's face. Rebecca realized that, beneath the anger, she was on the verge of tears. 'She knew all along that Joss might be going!'

'What do you mean, Sue? What are you driving at?'

'Look, Rebecca, do I have to spell it out? Tish is quirky when we see her in the holidays. Why? She's suddenly realized she's coming back to school this term without a job to come to! She feels lost. She's a born organizer, is Tish! She loves to be at the centre of things – in charge –'

'Oh, Sue!' Rebecca laughed out loud. Could this really be Sue talking? 'Of course she does, but –'

'Don't laugh. Just listen. As soon as she gets back to school she finds out that Joss is in a bad way and someone may have to take her place –'

'Hey!' said Rebecca. But Sue would not be silenced.

'And suddenly she's up in the clouds! You remember! Says we're going to win the Gold Cup! Suddenly becomes wildly interested in Hilary Camberwell Music Scholars, badges, names up in gold, me playing the violin all hours of the day and night. Tish! Who hardly knows one end of a violin from the other! Be honest, Rebecca. Has Tish ever taken the slightest interest in the Hilary Camberwell Music

Scholarship before? Has she ever mentioned it? Did she even notice when Miss Welbeck explained all about it at the end of last term?'

Rebecca shook her head.

'No,' she agreed. 'She hasn't. She didn't.'

'And suddenly – she acts as though my life depended on it. It all fits together, doesn't it. Admit it, Rebecca.'

'It fits together fine,' said Rebecca, slowly. 'It's just –'

'If only she'd *said*, right at the beginning!' interrupted Sue. 'If she'd just had the guts to admit that she wanted to take Joss's place, I wouldn't have dreamt of standing against her! I'd have backed her up all the way. That's the silly thing about it. But all this stuff about the scholarship! Shunting me off here –' Sue gave her violin case a small kick – 'getting me out of the way! The hypocrite!'

Sue fell silent, tearful and angry. Rebecca felt bemused. How damning the evidence against Tish looked, when Sue spelt it out like that!

'It all fits together fine,' repeated Rebecca, finding her voice at last. 'Except I don't believe a word of it. Not one single word. I know Tish has been behaving mysteriously, and I still don't really know what goes on in her mind, but I'm sure it's not the sort of things you're describing. I trust her, Sue, so why can't you?'

Sue looked at Rebecca reproachfully.

'You're on her side. You want her to win. You haven't been listening to a word I've said. Well you're wasting your time if you think I'm going to drop out of the contest, I've got a lot of support.' There was a light in Sue's eyes. 'I'm going to beat her, after this. It would give me great pleasure.'

'I'm not on anybody's side,' said Rebecca quietly. 'How did you find out that Tish knew about Joss long before the rest of us?'

'I – I –' For a moment Sue was thrown into confusion. She looked embarrassed. And then she snapped her fingers. 'Tish said so. At breakfast. I heard her say so, to you.'

'True,' said Rebecca, thoughtfully. 'She did mention it.'

Sue picked up her violin and bow, ready to continue. She was anxious to bring the discussion to an end. Rebecca made one last attempt.

'Sue,' she pleaded. 'I'm *not* on Tish's side. I proposed her because she made me. But I'm sure she thinks she's acting for the best. What you've been suggesting is rubbish and I think when you cool down a bit, you'll see it is. I'm not on *anybody's* side. I just want you two to stop fighting each other. Can't you drop out? It's still not too late.'

'No,' said Sue. 'Why should I?' Pointedly she drew the bow across the strings and started to play. Rebecca walked to the door.

'The election's on then?' she said, dolefully.

'The election is on.'

When Tish went up to the dormitory at mid-day, there was something standing on her bedside locker. It was the smart little cassette recorder in the blue case that she had lent Sue on Thursday. Sue had returned it, without a word, and Tish knew that Rebecca had failed.

EIGHT

A DIRTY ELECTION

Rebecca realized it was going to be a dirty election from the moment the first posters went up, late on Saturday afternoon. She saw them when she came back to Juniper after playing hockey.

Now that the election was inevitable, the First Years were throwing themselves into it with gusto. They were split into two camps and there was no limit to their zeal. It was no holds barred! What really shook her, though, were the tactics adopted by Tish Anderson. It was going to be just one more surprise in a long line of surprises; yet another sign that something peculiar had got into Tish this term.

The hockey game lacked excitement. It was the second of the practice matches ordered by Miss Willis, between the Under-14 team and the newly-formed Second Eleven. The atmosphere between Tish and Sue did not help, and the team was conscious of it. They were also missing Joss badly. It had been decided to try Sheila Cummings, the first reserve and a good all-round player, in Joss's position – centre forward. But she really didn't compare. The game was a dull affair.

The only exciting thing that happened was the sudden appearance of Mr Barrington on school pitch at the end of the game. He was the Director of Music at Trebizon, always impeccably dressed, and he looked most out of place as he walked to the touchline on tip-toe, trying not to get his shoes muddy.

'Susan!' he admonished. 'You were supposed to be at orchestra practice. This is no way for a potential Music Scholar to behave.'

'I may be voted head of games, sir, now Josselyn's in hospital,' said Sue. 'If I am, I won't be entering for the Hilary Camberwell and I'll be getting written permission to drop out of the orchestra this term as well.'

'Head of games?' Mr Barrington shook his head. 'Tcchh! Tcchh! Anybody can be head of games.'

He went away, still shaking his head, looking quite comical as he stepped from one dry patch to the next. Everybody was grinning – except Tish.

When Rebecca got back to the junior house, the posters were starting to appear. Sue's supporters had taken over the First Year Hobbies' Room and were turning them out at speed; Tish's supporters had moved into the Second Year's Hobbies' Room and were doing likewise.

Some were quite innocuous like VOTE X MURDOCH, with crossed hockey sticks forming the 'X'. Others were less than friendly. SUE WHO? screamed a poster stuck to the door of the television room and, half-way up west staircase, another one said STOP TISH ANDERSON!

At teatime Sue asked the duty mistress if she could change tables. She did a swap with Mara Leonodis who sat on the next-door table, and everyone on Joss Vining's old table could breathe freely again. There had been an atmosphere you could have cut with a knife.

'Though I don't know why it had to be *Sue* to go,' observed Judy Sharp as she doled out pieces of spam from a large plate. She had taken over Josselyn's place as head of table.

'One of us had to,' said Tish blandly. 'Sue's with her friend Debbie Rickard now.'

Several girls giggled. Sure enough, at the next table, Debbie Rickard was fussing around Sue like a mother hen. Rebecca lowered her eyes. Nobody liked Debbie Rickard, including Sue. It wasn't her fault that Debbie had been the person to support her nomination this morning. Tish was using anything to gain support!

That evening the poster war hotted up. Two awful caricatures were pinned up; one showed Sue with her spectacles dropping off and the other showed Tish with legs like tree trunks. Her legs *were* very thick and muscular compared to the rest of her, and Rebecca knew the picture must have hurt. Even more hurtful was the slogan under the picture of Sue: BUT CAN SHE SEE THE BALL?

The two rival camps also started scribbling on each other's posters. To the slogan VOTE FOR SUE were added the words AND THEN COMMIT SUICIDE, and beneath the simple exhortation TISH! was written something outrageous.

The First Years were having the time of their lives, until Miss Morgan toured the building and took all the posters down except for four respectable ones. Rebecca felt miserable. Her long hair felt lank and greasy and she could feel a spot coming up on her chin. She shampooed her hair and gave it a conditioner, bathed her spot, blow-dried her hair and went to bed early.

Her suspicions that Tish would stoop to anything to gain support were confirmed on Sunday.

After church, Rebecca spent the morning in the library composing the 'Did You Know?' piece that she wrote regularly for *The Juniper Journal.* Sunday was its press day, and it was a relief to have something to take her mind off the election.

As this was to be the first issue of term, she wanted to make her piece really good. She decided to write about the squirting cucumber that Tish and Sue had laughed about on the train journey down (how long ago that seemed! But Tish had been rather odd, even then –) and three other useless facts that she selected from the recesses of her mind. Her favourite was the one about the Gimyak tribe in Siberia. *Did you know*, she wrote, *that Siberian Gimyak women have the longest fingers in the world? They are often eight or nine inches long* . . . She had no idea where she had read that, but with Rebecca it was a case of once read, never forgotten.

'You're a walking data bank of useless information!' laughed Judy, when Rebecca showed her the piece over Sunday dinner. 'It's a good batch this week. Even better than usual!'

But when Rebecca took the piece along to *The J.J.'s* 'publishing office' during the afternoon she received a rebuff. The 'publishing office' was simply a large table in the corner of the Second Year Hobbies' Room. On it stood a typewriter, on which were typed out the stencil skins, and next to it a small, modern duplicating machine on which the news-sheets were run off. There was a small crowd of Tish's supporters gathered round it, with Tish in the centre, and there was excitement in the air.

'Sorry, Rebecca,' said Tish, 'but there just won't be room for it in *The J.J.* this week. Hold it over until next week.'

'No room –?' began Rebecca.

'*Election Special!*' said Tish crisply. 'Just a short run this week, to be sold around Juniper. To help everyone make their minds up!' She looked across to Mara Leonodis, who was carefully composing something in an exercise book at a small table nearby. 'How's it coming along, Mara?'

'Fine, Tish.'

Rebecca immediately felt suspicious. She felt even more suspicious when Debbie Rickard walked into the Hobbies' Room at that moment, looking incredibly self-important. She was holding a sheet of paper.

'I've written the article, don't forget to put my name on it.'

As she handed it over, Rebecca caught sight of the heading: *Why I supported Sue Murdoch for Head of Games – by Deborah Rickard.*

'Don't you dare cheat, Tish Anderson,' said Debbie. 'Don't you dare forget to put it in. And Mara's piece about you has got to be exactly the same length, remember?'

'Of course I won't forget to put it in!' said Tish, glancing at the paper she had been handed. She kept a very deadpan expression. 'What's more I'll run Mara's piece first, and yours underneath. That way you have the last word – what could be fairer than that?'

'Hmmm,' said Debbie. She was obviously worried at the back of her mind that there could be some catch. 'Don't you change a single word!'

'Of course not!' and Tish. 'I'll try not to make any typing errors, either.'

'Has Sue agreed to this?' blurted out Rebecca.

'Of course she has,' said Debbie importantly, and went out of the room. Rebecca followed her out, thinking: Poor Sue! I suppose she just didn't have any choice, now Tish has dreamt this up.

She stood outside in the corridor for a few moments, watching Debbie go up east staircase. She felt suddenly angry with Tish. Nobody liked Debbie Rickard, and Tish knew it! If she were after the floating voters, this was certainly the way to get them! Whatever Debbie had written for the *Election Special* it was bound to be nauseating – and bound to put people off voting for Sue.

She heard subdued laughter coming from inside the Hobbies' Room and feared the worst.

By breakfast time on Monday morning, the special election edition of *The J.J.* was already in circulation. And it certainly did nothing to help Sue's cause, as Rebecca had rightly guessed.

The first article was entitled *Why I supported T. Anderson for Head of Games – by Mara Leonodis.* The writing was not inspired, but it was sensible and factual, listing Tish's good record as a member of the under-14 hockey team for the past two seasons, especially with regard to the number of goals she had scored. It pointed out that she had natural leadership qualities and had excelled when given responsibilty, first as a monitor in the First Year and latterly as the Magazine Officer for the whole of Juniper House. It did not denigrate Sue in any way.

Debbie Rickard's article came after it, and contrasted badly. It gave very little factual information about Sue, or what her qualifications were for being made head of games this term, but contained some silly and rather spiteful remarks about Tish. It was also most unfortunate that there was a typing error in the very first sentence so that the article began: *Sue Murdoch is very good at playing hookey* . . . This soon became the standing joke of the moment and made Sue seem slightly ridiculous. Rebecca was quite sure that the so-called error had been deliberate!

She looked across at Sue's face, pale and drawn, in Assembly that morning and her heart went out to her.

'No wonder she thinks Tish is just out for herself, and that's all there is to it. It looks more and more like that, all the time. I know Tish thinks that, for her own good, Sue's got to be crushed – but she doesn't have to fight a dirty election!'

All along Rebecca had been baffled by Tish. Now, just for a moment, as she looked at Sue's face, she came very close to disillusionment. Could Sue be right? Was Tish a hypocrite?

And then she caught sight of Tish looking at Sue. Tish's face was completely unguarded. There was no grin there, just an expression of great anxiety and with it a certain affection. In spite of everything, Rebecca's trust in Tish came rushing back and she felt ashamed for having doubted her.

Monday was the only day when they did not have Games – just a whole lot of lessons to slog through. First lesson was English with the form-mistress and Sue asked Miss Heath if she could come and sit in the front. She changed places with one of the Nathan twins, and so Rebecca found that she and Sue were no longer sitting together. It somehow seemed to make the break-up complete.

The election took place immediately after tea. Pippa Fellowes-Walker and Annie Lorrimer organized it very well. They took over the Second Year Hobbies' Room, which was the largest room in Juniper House, and set up a ballot box. For half an hour, girls filed in and recorded their votes on special slips of paper, put them in the box, had their names ticked off the register and then left.

Rebecca did not vote. Instead, she stayed in the common room and did her geography prep, which was to read about the wool trade. Not a single word of it sank in. For company she had several members of the Under-14 team, who were not voting either. Most of them found the idea of having to choose between Tish or Sue rather distasteful.

'Not voting, Rebecca?' asked Jenny Brook-Hayes, who was the team's goalkeeper. 'But you started the whole thing.'

Rebecca just went on staring at her book.

But they all went down when the result was due to be announced. The Hobbies' Room was packed and girls overflowed into the corridor. Joanne Hissup, as requested, had come over specially from Parkinson House to supervise the count and make the announcement. Rebecca's hands felt rather clammy as Joanne stood up, with a piece of paper in her hand. The room went so still that they could hear the clock on the wall ticking.

'Here is the result,' she said. 'There were 19 abstentions. Susan Murdoch – 23 votes. Ishbel Anderson – 76 votes.'

A tremendous roar went up. A crowd of girls mobbed round Tish. The Senior girls smiled and pushed their way out of the room.

'Well, that's settled,' said Joanne. 'And Miss Willis will be relieved. Now they can get themselves organized for the Gold Cup. They've got their first match tomorrow afternoon!'

Rebecca saw a small group round Sue, with Nicola Hodges prominent amongst them. Sue looked utterly crushed. Nicola was looking flustered for once. Sue spoke just one sentence, and Rebecca overheard it:

'I blame myself most, Nicola, but let's face it – I look a real fool, don't I?'

It had dawned upon both Sue and Rebecca at the same moment. The result had been a foregone conclusion, right from the beginning. Although – to those who knew her –

Sue was well-liked in Juniper House, some girls hardly knew who she was. Tish was universally popular, in a way that Sue could never be. Tish had had no need to resort to her dirty tricks! She would have won the election by a wide margin in any case!

Which only made it all the odder.

'Speech!' shouted someone.

Tish stood up on a chair, giving her widest smile. Her black curls were full of bounce. She waited for the noise to die down.

'Not so much a speech,' she said, 'more just a couple of quick sentences. First, thanks for electing me. Second, I've got to rearrange the team now we've lost Joss – and if you'll leave me in peace with the typewriter for half an hour, I'll sort it out. I'll pin the list up in both common rooms straight after.'

There was some clapping and then the meeting broke up. Girls went out chattering happily. The rank-and-file of Juniper House had enjoyed the election, but they were glad that it was over now. Someone was in charge of the hockey team again. It was nice that it had all been so decisive, with the obvious person emerging as captain. They could forget all about it now, and let's hope they did well in the Gold Cup! Soon, the large room was almost empty.

Rebecca hovered. She had to decide whether or not to congratulate Tish. It was a bit difficult with Sue standing there. Tish was seated at the typewriter now, frowning as she fed in a sheet of paper. Then slowly, very slowly, Sue walked across to her.

'I'll say one thing, Tish,' she said, awkwardly. 'You've proved your point. Nobody wanted me as head of games except for a few infants and lunatics. They all wanted you. I have to hand that to you. I allowed myself to get carried away. Nicola told me I had a lot of support, and I believed her.'

It was all so humbling for Sue. It was taking a lot of courage on her part. To Rebecca's amazement, Tish waved her away.

'Sorry, Sue. I must concentrate on this.'

Sue looked as though she had been slapped in the face. She turned on her heel and walked out of the room. Rebecca followed soon after, seething with indignation. What was the matter with Tish? In spite of what Sue believed to be totally selfish behaviour on Tish's part, she had been trying to make it up. She had been trying to say that the result was right and she accepted Tish as captain.

Tish had got what she wanted, hadn't she? Surely she could relax a bit now?

But Rebecca was not thinking clearly enough. She should have guessed what was coming next.

NINE

RIGHT OUT ON A LIMB

The first Rebecca knew about it was when Sue came rushing into the dormitory, half an hour later, with the tears streaming down her cheeks. It was not yet bed-time, but Rebecca had sneaked up there to try and read her geography book. She just hadn't wanted to be in the common room when Tish came in to pin up the team list. It might look as though she were hoping to be on it, when, obviously, she couldn't possibly be.

'Sue!' exclaimed Rebecca, dropping her book on the floor and jumping off her bed. 'Whatever's wrong?'

She ran round her cubicle and along to Sue's, but Sue was already pulling her curtain across with a savage wrench. Girls hardly ever bothered to pull their curtains across.

'Sue,' said Rebecca through the curtain. 'What –'

'Go away!' sobbed Sue. 'You've got my place in the team, isn't that enough!' And she flung herself face downwards on her bed.

Rebecca gasped. She turned and ran out of the dormitory, took the stairs two at a time to the floor below, and walked into the Second Year common room. There was an icy silence as she came in. Several members of the Under-14 team were clustered round the notice board but now, as Rebecca walked in, they all walked out.

'What a rotten trick!' said someone.

'Winning the election must have gone to her head!' said another. 'It's the meanest thing I've ever seen.'

'But it's not like Tish!' said Jenny Brook-Hayes.

Rebecca stared at the sheet on the notice board, going hot and then cold. She had been left completely alone in the common room, as though she suffered from the plague. This is what she read:

Under-14 Team List

Trebizon U-14 v. Hillstone U-15
Tuesday 2.30 p.m.

Home

This is match 1 in Group 2 in the West of England Junior Gold Cup and the team and reserves are as follows:

G.K. J. Brook-Hayes
R.B. J. Thompson L.B. R. Jones
R.H. E. Keating C.H. S. Cummings L.H. W. Gorski
R.W. J. Sharp R.I. R. Mason C.F. I. Anderson (Capt.)
L.I. L. Wilkins L.W. M. Spar

1st Reserve V. Williams *2nd Reserve* S. Murdoch

(Signed) *Ishbel Anderson*
Head of Games: Juniper House

So it was true! She had been given Sue's place in the team.

Rebecca looked for a long time and then she went and slumped in a chair, over by the big window overlooking the school quadrangle. Its gardens were shadowy in the darkness. Most of the lights were out in old building, across the way. She could just make out the silhouette of the sundial, set in the centre of the lawns. The building she was in was itself ablaze with light, glowing out into the darkness and lighting up the terrace below. Nobody would be going to sleep early in Juniper House tonight.

For a long time Rebecca had wanted to be in the team. If that wish would ever come true, she used to think, how she would jump for joy! Now it actually had come true, a less joyful sight than Rebecca Mason in that chair would be hard to imagine.

'You look as though you've just been to a funeral,' said Tish, coming in and shutting the door.

'How do you expect me to look?' asked Rebecca, still slumped. 'What do you think you're doing?'

'Making the best of a bad job, of course,' said Tish, in her most matter-of-fact tone. She seemed completely confident that what she was doing was right. She paced up and down the long carpet, enumerating on her fingers as she talked, a favourite habit of hers.

'For a start, I'm the best centre-forward now we haven't got Joss so I've moved over from left inner. I've switched Laura Wilkins to left inner from centre half – I think she'd be good in the forward line. I've put Sheila Cummings at centre half, she's good all round and is wasted as first reserve –'

Rebecca wasn't listening to any of this, which she agreed with anyway.

'– and I've put you in, instead of Sue. Otherwise the team is just as Joss had it.'

'You've put *me* in – oh, Tish, I like the casual way you say it.'

'You mean you weren't even a reserve and Verity Williams was?' asked Tish. 'But she's a defence player –'

'*I mean you've dropped Sue!*' yelled Rebecca.

'Of course I have!' snapped Tish. She looked at Rebecca in despair. Why didn't she understand? 'What did you expect me to do, once I was captain? Have you seen the timetable over at the Hilary –?'

'No,' said Rebecca, wearily. 'It's none of my business.'

'Mrs Borrelli started Sue on her first scholarship piece on Friday,' said Tish. 'She's supposed to practise it every day, and two hours tomorrow afternoon instead of games. If she doesn't know it by Friday she can't go on to her next piece. Do you realize, Becky, she's got to know *four* new pieces for the scholarship and she's only got six weeks to learn them in?' Tish sounded so strange! 'There's no way she can play against Hillstone tomorrow. I've only put her down as second reserve so that it doesn't look too awful. The whole team can break their legs, but she's not going to play.'

'It looks awful already,' said Rebecca. She was still completely mystified by Tish. 'Can't you get it into your head that Sue doesn't want to be a Music Scholar? She did at first, but not any more. I know you think it's important for her, and you're probably right. She can play hockey for ever more, whereas this chance will never come again. It *is* a distinction.' Rebecca had been taking note of the Music Scholars in the past two days, the proud way they wore their badges. She had found out about all the special opportunities they were given to develop as musicians, higher up the school. She sighed. 'Yes, Tish, I know all the arguments. But the fact is that Sue isn't interested and you just can't force her to be.'

'I can't force her, but I can persuade her,' said Tish. 'She hates me at the moment. I've just been up in the dormitory trying to talk to her, and she won't listen to a word I say. But give her twenty-four hours to cool down, and she'll listen. Somehow –' there was a look of utter determination on Tish's face '– somehow I *will* get it through to her that everything I'm doing is for her own good. She'll buckle down all right then.'

'You sound very sure,' said Rebecca.

'I am very sure. We've been such close friends, she's always listened to me before.' A bewildered expression crossed Tish's face, as though she couldn't understand why Sue hadn't been listening this time. 'She's always trusted me before, too. Once I make her see . . . once she accepts she's out of the team, and I'm not going to let her in, she'll start trying hard for the Hilary Camberwell because it'll be the only thing she has left.'

'And even if Sue wants to run her own life, and run it quite differently, nothing will shift you?'

'Nothing,' said Tish, with passion.

Rebecca shook her head, helplessly. She started on a new tack.

'The team's taken it very badly,' she said.

'I know,' said Tish, and she looked worried for the first time. 'I can't hope to make them understand. But you understand, don't you, Rebecca?'

'No,' said Rebecca, a lump coming to her throat. 'I'm afraid I don't, Tish. But the funny thing is I trust you.' It was true. She trusted her more than ever now, for the simple reason that she was so burning with passion over the whole thing that somehow she must have right on her side! Also, she was prepared to go right out on a limb. 'You realize, Tish, that some people think you're just being nasty.'

'Of course I realize. And I didn't want to put you in the team, either, because a lot of it will rub off on you. It's just that, with Joss and Sue out, you happen to be the very best person we have now to put in the forward line, after Laura Wilkins.' Tish looked Rebecca straight in the eye. 'If you want to chicken out, just say so. I'll understand.'

For all her dismay at the events of the past few minutes, Rebecca felt a sudden surge of elation. *The very best person we have now* . . . Tish had said it, and she had meant it!

'Chicken out?' she said. 'Not me.'

The atmosphere in the dormitory was fraught that night. There was Sue's cubicle, curtained off in silent reproach. There were Jenny and Joanna, both members of the team, and also occupants of dormitory number six, glaring at Rebecca and Tish as they came in. Even the other three occupants of the dormitory, Margot and Elf and Mara, all staunch Tish Anderson loyalists, were dreadfully subdued.

Rebecca tossed and turned and woke up several times during the night. Tomorrow she was playing in the Gold Cup in Sue Murdoch's place. Sue was the better player and everybody knew it! Every move she made would be watched, every mistake noted! This was their first match in Group 2 and if they lost it they could be on their way out of the Cup! She didn't want to play. She was terrified.

She was up and dressed early. She knelt on her bed by the window and gazed through the bare trees behind Juniper House, to the sand dunes and sea beyond. And she saw that Sue Murdoch had got up even earlier.

She was walking slowly back from the direction of the sand dunes with a companion. The companion was Nicola Hodges. They had obviously been for an early morning walk along the seashore together. They were in deep and earnest conversation. An orange winter sun was rising over Trebizon Bay.

Poor Sue, thought Rebecca. After all she had suffered at Tish's hands, it must be a relief to turn to someone like Nicola Hodges who appeared to offer the unfailing devotion one would normally expect from a faithful spaniel.

'That Nicola!' sniffed Mara Leonodis, who had silently appeared at Rebecca's shoulder. 'That Nicola Hodges girl, she gives me the creeps. She is at the root of all the trouble, you mark my words.'

'What on earth do you mean?'

'I don't know what I mean, Rebecca,' said Mara. 'I just go by instinct in this life. All I know is that there has been nothing but trouble between Tish and Sue since that girl appeared on the scene.'

'Oh, Mara. You're just being silly,' said Rebecca.

She watched them. Sue was putting an arm round the younger girl's shoulders now, as though to comfort her. 'At least,' thought Rebecca, 'I suppose Mara is just being silly.'

TEN

A VISIT TO THE HILARY

Juniper House had talked about it half the night. Tish Anderson and Sue Murdoch were enemies now! Tish had dropped Sue, the star of the team, and put Rebecca Mason in, in her place! By the morning, Tish Anderson's stock had suddenly fallen very low.

'Let's boycott the match!' Nicola Hodges said to the First Years, and Debbie Rickard took up the same cry amongst the Seconds.

'Nobody will listen to them,' Tish told Rebecca.

'I think they will,' she replied.

Miss Willis was already in a bad temper, even before Tish told her (by way of explanation) that Sue's schedule for the next few weeks was going to clash with her being a regular member of the team.

'I had no idea she was even a candidate for the Hilary Camberwell, until Mr Barrington told me last night,' frowned the games mistress. 'He was annoyed that she intended to withdraw if she were made head of games this term – and now I daresay he's pleased. This is all very sudden! There are plenty of suitable candidates for Music

Scholar without Susan deciding to add herself to that number. You apart, she's our strongest player.'

At dinner time Rebecca was issued with her own official team sweater which had TREBIZON in large white letters on a blue background. She had played for the team once before, as a last minute substitute when Judy Sharp's ankle had swollen up. But this was more like the real thing, and the sweater proved it. At half-past two she would run out on to the pitch with the rest of the team, wearing that sweater. 'The stuff of my dreams,' thought Rebecca, with bitter humour. As each minute passed, she dreaded the match more.

As dreams went, this turned out to be a very bad one.

The whole of Juniper House had been let off games, to be able to come and cheer. But the whole of Juniper House did not turn up. Not even half of it. Not even a quarter of it. Hillstone, who had brought two coachloads all of fifty miles, had more supporters lining the pitch than Trebizon, the home team!

Miss Willis was annoyed. 'I suppose they think that without Josselyn and Susan we haven't a chance,' she thought. 'What the dickens are they all doing? Watching TV?'

Tish looked round the thinly-lined pitch and was shaken rigid. But she was made of stern stuff. When the starting whistle blew, she just put her head down and stick down for the bully-off, got possession and streaked away. If everybody could have played like Tish, they would have won.

They lost, and for one small mercy Rebecca could be grateful. The rest of the team played as badly as she did! They were all hopelessly out of touch with each other and they just couldn't get going. Again and again Tish tried to get them working together as a team, but they just wouldn't gel. Hillstone won the match by 3 goals to nil.

'What a mess!' Miss Willis shouted at them, afterwards. 'Call yourself a hockey team. You're on your way out of the cup, before you've even started!' She was angry and disappointed. Trebizon was the youngest team to have qualified for the Gold Cup. On last term's form, she had felt excited about their prospects. 'We're down to play three more matches in our Group. But if you get another result like this against Caxton High next week, you might as well quit!'

'The new forward line's got to come together –' began Tish.

'If there hadn't been an election the team could have been settled on Saturday morning!' said Miss Willis sharply. 'Not late last night. You would have had three whole days to come together, as you put it –'

She stopped. The team was dejected and exhausted. They had played their hardest, they had run themselves into the ground, and they had nothing to show for it. Now they all seemed to be glaring at Tish, as if everything were her fault. Miss Willis sensed an undercurrent of bad feeling. She didn't want that. She didn't want Ishbel Anderson to be made a scapegoat.

'I'm sorry,' she said. 'The election was your business, not mine. I'm sure it was quite right to hold one, with both Ishbel and Susan keen to do the job. But now it's all settled, for heaven's sake make it work. Now go and get cleaned up and changed and take those miserable looks off your faces, or you'll put the Hillstone girls off their tea. Miss Morgan's organized quite a spread, and she suggests five o'clock. You know what you have to do, Ishbel?'

Tish nodded. As captain of the home team she would be

acting as hostess at the hockey tea. Hockey teas took place at the boarding house, instead of in the dining hall, and they were always something special!

'Pass them lots of grub and be terribly polite and see that our lot don't pinch all the best cakes,' said Tish.

The others laughed. That sounded a bit more like the Tish they knew and loved. Even Rebecca raised a smile.

But Tish didn't exactly rush to get back to Juniper House. She was still stuck in a changing room, long after the two teams had showered and dressed and left the sports centre. Rebecca was getting fed up with waiting for her.

'Come on, Tish,' she opened the door and looked in, 'what –' Tish was sitting on the bench. She had obviously been dressed for some time. She was just sitting there, staring into space, a picture of dejection. 'Oh, poor Tish,' she said, and came and sat next to her. 'Cheer up.'

Tish buried her face in her hands.

'Do you think Sue's over at the Hilary?' she said. 'Do you think she's bothering? Because if she isn't I might just as well go and shoot myself!'

Rebecca put an arm round Tish's shoulders.

'Why don't we go and see?' she said. 'And isn't it about time you two got on speaking terms again?'

'You're right.' Tish got to her feet. Some of her old certainty was coming back. 'Perhaps she's stopped hating me and is ready to listen. The sooner that happens the better. Come on!'

She grabbed Rebecca's hand and they ran out of the big white building and along the winding footpath that led to the Hilary. As they came out of the shrubbery and around the little lake, they saw Nicola Hodges come out of the side door of the building, carrying her violin case. She passed quite close to them.

'Hello, Nicola. Is Sue in there?' asked Tish.

'Yes,' said Nicola. There was a wary expression on her face.

She's ubiquitous! thought Rebecca. *She's always around Sue!* Then she chided herself. If Sue had been told to do two hours' violin practice this afternoon then, obviously, so had Nicola. And, as for the other times, who could blame Sue for going round with Nicola? Tish drove her to despair so what else was she supposed to do with herself?

'That kid just worships Sue, doesn't she?' said Tish ruefully, when Nicola had passed out of earshot. 'That's why she got the First Years to boycott the match. I must say, I could have done without that.'

'Come on,' said Rebecca. 'Let's find Sue.'

Tish was worried that the building seemed very silent and she couldn't hear a violin playing anywhere.

They found Sue in practice room number four. She wasn't playing but was standing over by the window, looking out across the little lake. She had obviously been trying to work, because there was some music up on the stand. But her violin and bow lay discarded on a table, with a sealed envelope lying beside it.

'How's it going, Sue?' asked Tish.

'It's not,' said Sue, without turning round. 'And how did the match go?'

'We lost 3-nil.'

There was something so utterly despondent in Tish's tone that Sue turned round then. 'I'm sorry,' she said simply. 'I really am. And it wasn't my idea that they should all boycott the match. That was stupid.'

'You don't have ideas like that,' said Tish.

It was clear to Rebecca that Sue had stopped hating Tish.

She seemed to have something bigger on her mind. 'What do you want?' she asked.

'I just want to tell you what you wouldn't let me tell you last night. Everything I've done has been so you can forget about hockey this term and settle down and win the Hilary Camberwell music scholarship. Okay?'

'That's your theory,' said Sue.

'It isn't a theory, Sue!' Rebecca burst out. 'It's a fact!'

'Whatever it is, it's all been a waste of time!' snapped Sue. She was very tense and irritable. She walked over to the table and picked up the white envelope. 'I've just written this. It's formal notice in writing that I'm pulling out of the scholarship.'

Tish then behaved in a really amazing manner. She lunged at Sue and grabbed the envelope from her hand, shouting furiously all the time. 'What do you think you're playing at! I haven't gone through all this for nothing! You're going to win that thing, you *are*!' She ripped the letter to pieces and flung it up in the air before Sue could stop her. 'There!'

'Tish!' Sue stared at her in amazement. 'You *do* mean it. It hasn't just been an act . . .'

Tish had slumped into a chair, breathing heavily, spent by her furious outburst and trying to recover. It was left to Rebecca to speak.

'Of course it hasn't been an act, Sue! Tish is obsessed about it! She's put herself out on a limb over this. The whole team's turned against her – as well as most of Juniper. Or hadn't you noticed? She may be nuts, but she isn't acting!'

'Tish.' Sue stared at her friend, and her lips were starting to tremble. 'You really are a stubborn pig. I *told* you I'd gone off the idea, once I found out I'd be competing against Nicola.'

'Nicola?' Tish was very alert again. She gathered all her wits together. Then she spoke fast and compellingly. 'I know how you feel, Sue. I'm sure Nicola's a very nice kid, and maybe the money would be useful to her parents. But you can't back down because of that, and she shouldn't expect you to –'

'She doesn't –' began Sue.

'A competition's a competition,' said Tish fiercely, 'and the best person has got to win. I think Mr Barrington thinks you're the best person, as a matter of fact, but the experts from London will decide that. Nicola's got to take her chance, fair and square. The Music Scholar's got to be the *best* person, that's the whole idea, otherwise the whole thing's a farce . . .'

'Tish!' Sue was trying to break in. Rebecca could see that she was becoming very distressed.

'And look at it this way, Sue, if you do win it won't be a disaster for Nicola. She'll be young enough to enter again next year, but this is your last chance.' Tish got up and went and gripped Sue's arm. 'Your very last chance.'

There was silence. At last Sue spoke.

'I'd worked all that out for myself, Tish. I woke up early this morning and went up for a long walk along the beach. I realized that my dream of stepping into Joss's shoes had all been a total fantasy. I wasn't cut out for the job. It was you they wanted. And that I might as well try for something that I actually am cut out for, Nicola or no Nicola –'

'Then?' Tish's eyes were wide with hope for a moment. She looked at the floor and saw the torn-up pieces of the letter lying there. Her voice faltered. 'Then why did you write out your notice?'

'I met Nicola on the beach,' said Sue.

'And –'

'I can't really tell you. It's not my secret. She didn't mean to tell me. It just came out in a kind of rush.'

'You'd *better* tell me,' said Tish.

'Okay.' Sue took a deep breath. 'You may as well know. If Nicola doesn't win the Hilary Camberwell she'll have to leave Trebizon. You won't tell anyone?' She looked at Rebecca. 'Nor you?'

'No, I won't tell anyone,' said Rebecca. 'Are we allowed to know why? It's money presumably.'

'Yes,' said Sue. 'Her parents knew it was going to be a struggle to send her here, but her mother works as a manageress in a shop and her salary has been paying the fees.' Rebecca nodded. She could just imagine Mrs Hodges in charge of a shop, probably a dress shop. 'Well, just before Christmas they discovered she's got a serious illness and she's had to give up work. So you see –' She spread out her hands in an expressive gesture, '– the scholarship means absolutely everything to Nicola.'

'Yes, I see,' said Rebecca.

Sue bent down and picked up the pieces of torn letter from the carpet and looked at Tish. Tish had not spoken a word.

'There wasn't much point in tearing this up, you know. I've only got to write it out again.'

Still Tish said nothing and Rebecca realized it was because she was dumbfounded. She seemed to be in a state of shock.

'Poor Tish,' thought Rebecca. 'This really is the end of a dream. She's taking it very hard.'

And suddenly Annie Lorrimer appeared in the doorway, arms akimbo.

'Tish Anderson!' exclaimed the duty prefect. 'I've been

sent to look for you! They're waiting to start the hockey tea, and they can't start without you! Come on!'

She took Tish by the arm and started to haul her out of the room. The cheerful prefect was never angry with anyone for very long. 'Okay, so you lost the match! What are you doing skulking over here!' Tish was staring, mesmerized, at the lovely mother-of-pearl badge on Annie's jumper with the monogram HC – the badge that only Music Scholars were allowed to wear. She was very close to tears.

Rebecca was left behind, forgotten. She knew she should be at the tea too, but she wanted to stay and talk.

'Poor Sue,' she said. 'You've ended up with nothing you wanted. And we've probably lost the Gold Cup. As for Tish . . .'

'Poor Nicola,' said Sue.

'Is her mother very ill?'

'Yes. It's a serious form of diabetes. She's always been a diabetic, but just before Christmas it got much worse.'

'I won't say a word –' began Rebecca. She stopped. A certain part of her brain started ticking over and sending out signals. It was that curious little bit of Rebecca's brain that stored up useless information. This was to be its big day.

ELEVEN

THE BIG SHOWDOWN

'I totally misjudged Tish, didn't I?' Sue was saying.

'Yes,' said Rebecca. And all the time that word *diabetes* kept going round and round in her brain. 'And she has to take insulin every day? Mrs Hodges I mean.'

'Yes! And lots of tablets as well. Isn't it terrible!'

'Awful,' said Rebecca. *Only I don't think it's true*, she thought.

'But you must admit she's quirky this term,' said Sue. 'Tish. She's really got me baffled. I don't feel I know her any more . . .'

'True,' said Rebecca, but her thoughts were elsewhere.

The tea bell went in the far distance, over in the main block.

'I'd better dash!' exclaimed Sue. 'And you, Rebecca – you're supposed to be at the hockey tea!' She hurriedly gathered up her music and rolled it up and put it with the violin and bow in the case. The walked across the grounds to the main school buildings and drew apart near the dining hall.

'Who do you have to give your notice to?' asked Rebecca,

suddenly, pulling Sue back. 'Don't you have to tell your parents first?'

'I'm writing a letter to them tonight,' said Sue. 'They'll understand.' She was irritable but she tried to hide it. She knew her parents were going to be disappointed. But it couldn't be helped. 'And I give my notice in to Mrs Devenshire. I've missed the office now. I'll write it out again tonight and hand it in first thing in the morning. Hadn't you better hurry, Rebecca?'

But Rebecca didn't go to the hockey tea. Even if she'd felt hungry, which she didn't, she would never have had the nerve to walk in so late. And besides – she had urgent things to do. She hurried over to the school library in old building, got out a large encyclopaedia and checked through it.

She was right, of course she was right! If you suffered from diabetes then you weren't allowed to eat sugary things. You just weren't allowed to! But at that party at Sue's house, Mrs Hodges had been stuffing herself silly with cakes and trifles. Rebecca could picture her now, in the bright pink coat, whipping the last helping of trifle from right under her nose. Diabetes.

Rebecca put the book back on the shelf. She was trembling a little. What to do now? She thought of Nicola with her flaxen hair and her round cherubic face, looking as though butter wouldn't melt in her mouth. It was incredible! But she had to find out more – she had to be sure!

How could she find out about Mr Hodges? She remembered the battered old lorry he had brought to the party with *Hodges Road Haulage* on the side. He obviously worked hard – he'd come straight from a delivery job! Was that one lorry the extent of his business, or were there more? Suddenly she remembered that Annie Lorrimer's father was in road haulage – in a big way. She'd seen the lorries around

London, with the word *Lorrimers* on the side, and an arrow symbol. Would Annie know anything?

She found the prefect making her own tea over in Willoughby, the Lower Sixth boarding house. She had to screw up all her courage to ask.

'Know the Hodges? Yes, of course we do. They live down the road. What's all this about, Rebecca?'

'I just wanted to know – I mean, do you happen to know if he makes a lot of money?'

'Really!' Annie looked shocked. 'What's that got to do with you? It's none of my business, and it's certainly none of yours, Rebecca. What are you doing over here, anyway? You're supposed to be at the hockey tea!'

'Perhaps she wants to touch Nicola for a loan,' said an amused voice. Pippa Fellowes-Walker had just come in. But she noted the fraught expression on Rebecca's face. As Rebecca walked out of Willoughby, dejected, half a minute later, a hand touched her shoulder. Pippa was right behind her.

'What's going on Rebecca?'

'I wasn't just being nosey!' Rebecca blurted out. 'I've just got to know whether Nicola's parents are rich or not and whether her mother used to be manageress of a shop!'

Pippa was marvellous. She didn't find that in the least extraordinary. She didn't ask questions. 'Leave it to me,' she said. 'You're too late for the hockey tea. Go and get yourself something to eat at Moffatt's. I'll see you there in a few minutes.'

Rebecca sat in the school shop drinking endless cups of tea. She still didn't feel hungry. Would Pippa never come? The place was empty. Then, at last, a tall and elegant silhouette appeared against the frosted glass panel of the door and Pippa entered.

'Well?' asked Rebecca, very pent up.

'They're rolling,' said Pippa. 'And I gather Mrs Hodges has never done a day's work in her life. In fact, Brian Hodges and John Lorrimer are business rivals –'

'You would never think it to look at him!' exclaimed Rebecca.

'Annie says he goes around looking like a tramp and keeps all his money under the bed!' laughed Pippa. 'And he works day and night as though he's right on the brink of poverty, but actually he owns a lot of lorries and half of Tottenham as well.'

'Well, I'll be blowed,' said Rebecca.

'It's something to do with the Music Scholarship, isn't it?' said Pippa shrewdly. 'Annie says Mrs Hodges is the most awful woman, who's always boasting and trying to keep up with the Joneses. Because Annie came to Trebizon then *naturally* Nicola had to come here. And four years ago, when Mrs Hodges heard that Annie had been elected the Music Scholar for her year, she started Nicola on the violin the very same week! Now's she told half of Tottenham that Nicola's going to be this year's Music Scholar. Poor kid!'

'Hmm,' said Rebecca.

'Has she been telling your friend Sue a hard luck story?'

'Something like that.'

'I must go, Rebecca, I'm on library duty,' said Pippa. 'Whatever was on your mind, it's nice to see some colour's come back to your cheeks!'

The colour in Rebecca's cheeks, although Pippa did not know it, was caused by blazing hot anger! She sat there, outraged. Poor kid, indeed! As she pieced together the events of the past week, step by step, it occurred to her that Nicola Hodges wasn't devoted to Sue at all. It had all been a pretence. Those angelic looks, the flaxen hair and the baby-blue eyes, concealed a clever, calculating little personality. The only person Nicola Hodges was devoted to was herself.

She must have been nervous about Sue from the start. Violinists were given preference in the scholarship. Rebecca had read that somewhere. Nicola was the only girl entering on violin this year, the other three played wind instruments! But was Sue Murdoch going to put in for it? She had managed to get friendly with Sue in the holidays, and had reassured herself that she was safe. The scholarship hadn't entered Sue's head!

And then that idiot Tish Anderson had *put* the idea into her head – made her really keen! From that moment on, Nicola had tried every trick in the book to steer Sue into other paths. She had even proposed her for Magazine Officer, last Thursday evening! On Friday evening she had looked at Sue with those big blue eyes of hers and made her feel mean for entering. *That* was the moment when Sue went off the idea, Rebecca decided; the hockey timetable was merely an additional sore. 'That settles it,' Sue had said. Her mind had been made up already. The hockey timetable, on its own, would never have settled it. Sue would probably have decided to put the scholarship first.

But Nicola was still nervous. On the first day of term she'd got wind of the fact that there was something wrong with Joss. Rebecca had been with her when they'd heard Joss and Tish talking about it, on school pitch. Tish was the natural person to step into Joss's shoes – and that would give her the power to drop Sue from the hockey team and persuade her, all over again, to put the music thing first! Nicola was ready for that. On Saturday morning, when Miss Willis raised the subject in dining hall, she jumped in straight away with the proposal that Sue would be the new head of games!

She'd been able at the same time to poison Sue's mind against Tish, by pointing out that Tish had already known about Joss and hence the sudden enthusiasm for Sue to be a Music Scholar! But Tish had won the election, and Nicola was back to square one. Sue had been dropped from the team and her thoughts were going back to the music scholarship – so Nicola had played her last card, this ridiculous story about her mother's illness!

'And just to clinch things, she's been stirring up trouble all day – getting people to boycott the match – so all the pressure's going to be on Tish to put Sue back in the team,' realized Rebecca. It was incredible, all right.

'You let your tea get cold!' said Mrs Moffatt, as Rebecca suddenly got to her feet. Rebecca glanced back at it. So she had! Then she ran out of the tuck shop and over to Juniper House. She took the stairs two at a time, up to the dormitory.

'A cool customer, Nicola,' she thought. 'She's not going to be easy to pin down. But I'm going to settle this!'

She took something small out of Tish's locker and slipped it in her pocket. 'Tell Tish I've borrowed this,' she said to Mara, who was staring gloomily out of the window at the dusk gathering over Trebizon bay.

'I wonder if Sue will draw her curtains round again tonight?' sighed the Greek girl. 'It is all so terrible, this bad atmosphere.'

'Clever Mara!' observed Rebecca, rushing out of the dormitory.

'Me – clever?' said Mara, but the door had slammed. What on earth was Rebecca talking about?

Downstairs, Rebecca pounced on Nicola. She had just got back from tea. She pushed her along the corridor and into the small television room. Then she shut the door. They were alone.

'You've been telling Sue a lot of lies haven't you!' she said to the startled Nicola. 'You've told her your mother's very ill and had to give up her job. I've checked up, and I know that not a word of it is true.'

Nicola's mind worked quickly. Where had Rebecca got this from? It couldn't have been from Sue. She had sworn Sue to secrecy! Rebecca must have overheard something.

'Surely Sue hasn't told you that?' she asked, her eyes wide and innocent. 'I told her my mother hasn't been very well lately, and that's perfectly true.' She didn't like the expression on Rebecca's face. It was grim! She burst out petulantly: 'It doesn't matter to Sue whether she wins the Hilary Camberwell or not.'

'She can decide that,' said Rebecca. 'You go and find her right now and confess to her about all the lies you've been telling –'

'I shan't!' Nicola stamped her foot. 'I want to be chosen as Music Scholar, my mother's *counting* on it! I'm not going to confess anything. I haven't been telling any lies! Sue didn't even know about the scholarship until that stupid Tish Anderson –'

'Stop it,' shouted Rebecca. She walked across and shook Nicola hard. 'That's for being a liar! And thank you for breaking up my two best friends!'

She took something out of her pocket and held it up.

'I know every word you've said to Sue!'

Nicola gasped, her senses still shaken. Rebecca was holding up a small cassette. Tish Anderson had a cassette recorder, she'd seen it! They must have planted it somewhere today, and left it running. At the Hilary, perhaps! She'd had so many conversations with Sue, she couldn't remember where they'd all taken place. Now it was all on tape . . .

'You shouldn't be allowed to enter at all!' said Rebecca. 'You should be made to withdraw at once. I've a good mind to hand this cassette over to Mr Barrington and get it played through –'

'No!' Nicola dived at Rebecca, who sidestepped. The younger girl stumbled against the wall. Coolly Rebecca put the cassette back in her pocket. Nicola turned round, tears streaming down her cheeks. 'No, *please*! *Please* don't do that. I'll do anything –'

'Just go and find Sue then,' said Rebecca. 'I expect she's writing her letter of withdrawal right now. Stop her. Tell her the truth – why you wanted her to have Joss's job – why you turned her against Tish – everything.'

As Nicola walked to the door, with leaden footsteps, Rebecca felt a twinge of pity for her.

'If you're going to win, it's better that you win fairly. If you're not going to win, it'll teach your mother not to go round boasting about you! Next time she starts, you can tell her to shut up.'

The members of the Hillstone hockey team were on the coach, ready to start the long journey back. It had been a delicious tea, and records had been played afterwards, but they weren't very impressed with Trebizon's captain.

'Did you ever see such a misery?' said one girl. 'She was supposed to be cheerful and act as hostess. She didn't even seem to want to talk to us.'

'Just because we beat them!'

'The rest of the team thought she was a bit off. You could tell.'

'One of them didn't even bother to turn up – the fairhaired one. Wonder what happened to her?'

Tish stood in the cobbled yard at the back of Juniper House, seeing the coach off. She watched it draw away. She hadn't even the strength to wave. What a mess she'd made of her duties as head of games. If only Joss were back. Calm, happy Joss – she'd have put the visitors at their ease, everything would have gone smoothly. Joss! What was she going to think, lying in hospital, when she heard that they'd lost the match 3 – nil? Of course, it would be all right to put Sue back in the team now. Except it was probably too late to make any difference to the Cup. Everything had been in vain. Everything was a mess . . .

She turned to walk back into Juniper, curls damped down by the fine, drizzling rain. Somebody was waiting for her in the lighted doorway, arms outstretched. 'Oh, Tish! You poor thing!' There were tears of emotion in Sue's eyes. 'Tish . . . I've been so stupid it isn't true! *You're* the one who's been bothering about me, all along. Not – not Nicola – she was out for herself . . .'

'Nicola was?' asked Tish in amazement. 'But her mother . . .'

'It was all lies. Rebecca found out. Rebecca made her confess.'

'Lies?'

'So I am going to enter, after all. The minute I sat down and tried to write to my parents, and imagined their faces, I *knew* you'd got it right. From the beginning. But there just didn't seem any choice. And then Nicola walked in, looking like a sick cat.' Anger crossed Sue's face. 'Oh, Tish, she's been the most incredible little two-faced hypocrite and I was completely taken in by her! I began to believe awful things about you – I even started to hate Rebecca . . . I thought she was on your side, against me. When all the time it was just that she trusted you, and I didn't. Please say you'll make it up.'

'Make it up?' Tish was feeling rather dazed by all this, and full of joy. 'Of course I will. Clever old Rebecca. How on earth did she do it?'

'I don't know. Oh, Tish, let's get her and hear all about it and go and buy some stuff and have a party in the dormitory tonight! I feel like blowing my whole allowance in one big bang! I'll tell Jenny and Joanna the whole sordid story, and they'll tell the rest of the team, and they'll all see that you're really a *saint* and –'

'No, don't let's. No parties,' said Tish briefly. She was frowning. 'Nicola Hodges has been a grotty little nuisance, hasn't she?'

'Well, yes –' Sue felt flattened.

'You didn't do much practice this afternoon. Hadn't you better get over to the Hilary and make up for lost time? You've got the rest of the evening.'

'If you think I should – yes.'

Sue was disconcerted. Tish, turning down the chance of a party! Just when they had something marvellous to celebrate. Tish being baffling again! Well, she wasn't going to question it. She was glad to have Tish back on any terms. But it was curious, just the same.

TWELVE

HEADLINE NEWS

For the next few weeks, Rebecca and Sue continued to be baffled by Tish from time to time. It wasn't that things weren't going well. They were going marvellously.

Once she had got the Nicola affair right out of her system, Sue threw herself into her music with complete dedication. All of that very early enthusiasm she'd felt, wanting to be the Music Scholar for this year, returned in abundance. Rebecca explained to the hockey team that Sue had been conned by Nicola Hodges, though she spared them the gory details, and they could see it was true. Tish had known what was best for Sue all along. The glow on Sue's face as she went about her scholarship work proved that. When she wasn't over at the Hilary, dashing away at her fiddle, she was playing back tapes of herself on Tish's cassette recorder, over and over again, anxiously asking the opinion of people like Mara, who had a good ear for music.

All that apart, it was quite obvious that Rebecca and Sue and Tish were just as close as they'd ever been. By the Wednesday morning Sue was sitting next to Rebecca in class again, with Tish just across the gangway, whispering and cracking jokes and passing notes between the three of them, as ever. The Nathan twins were quite pleased to be reunited after two whole days apart.

Neither the team nor Miss Willis were exactly pleased to lose Sue from the Under-14, but they accepted it as inevitable. After the misunderstanding surrounding the first cup match, the team wanted to make it up to Tish. They took to the field for the second cup match, against Caxton High School, in the mood to win. It was a resounding victory, 5 goals to 1 in Trebizon's favour. It had been an inspired idea of Tish's to move Laura Wilkins from centre half to left inner, for three of those goals were scored by Laura.

They were back in the Gold Cup with a real chance and the joyful letter they received from Joss Vining, in hospital, was pinned on the notice-board to spur them on.

In the third cup match, against a very good team, they drew 1–1, so everything depended on their fourth and final match in Group 2 against Helenbury. Not only must they defeat Helenbury, but they must score at least 4 goals. If they could do it, that would make them winners of Group 2! They would then go through to play the winners of Group 1 in the final of the Gold Cup!

The Helenbury match was immediately after half-term, which Rebecca had spent with her grandmother. Sue, along with other scholarship candidates, had remained at Trebizon over the half-term holiday for extra music study. There was only a week to go now until the scholarship. Sue seemed very happy. But Judy Sharp, on the other hand, came back to school in the depths of misery.

Her troublesome ankle, which had held out so well for the packed hockey programme up to half-term, was swollen and painful after a weekend's ski-ing on some high ground near her home! She was out of the Helenbury match.

Tish immediately switched Rebecca to Judy's right wing position. Miss Willis, with Tish's agreement, persuaded Mr Barrington to allow Sue to miss orchestra practice – just this once – and she was back in her old position of right inner. It was a home match and not only were Juniper House allowed to turn out to support the team, but some of the older girls were let off lessons as well. Rebecca was keyed up. She had not been playing badly for the team, but she had never really adjusted to an inside-forward position, finding in-field play too crowded for her liking. As a born sprinter she longed for the wide open spaces on the wing. She wanted to shine against Helenbury – and she did!

It was a most thrilling match with the score standing at 3–3 only five minutes before the end. Tish, Sue and Laura had all scored. But they needed four goals – to win the match and to top the table on goals – if they were to qualify for the final! Just when hope was fading, Sue won a tussle for the ball with the opposing centre half, started to run up field and then – about to be tackled – shot the ball out to Rebecca. Rebecca was already racing up the field with her opposing wing half in hot pursuit, and caught the ball on her stick in mid-stride, accelerating past a helpless opponent. Her speed was untouchable all the way up the wing and the crack of stick on ball as she whacked it hard into goal, from the very edge of the circle, made the sweetest sound.

They had won! They were through to the final!

But Tish was still baffling.

On that particular evening, for instance, she decided, half-way through the celebration at Moffatt's, to go to bed early! She just seemed suddenly to switch off, exactly as she had the night Rebecca stayed at Sue's house at the end of the Christmas holidays. But at least, on that occasion, she had waited until the party was over!

These odd moods came and went – and were nearly always in the evening. She would be grinning around the place as usual during the day. It seemed to Rebecca that Tish was like someone carrying a burden. It felt light enough in the morning, but sometimes it got heavy by nightfall.

The other strange thing about her was that she started going to the library a lot. Rebecca had always loved the library, in the old manor part of the school, overlooking the parkland. It housed some wonderful books, and she nearly always did her prep there. But not Tish. Her thing was to dash through prep as quickly as possible in the form room, or maybe the common room if it were just reading, and then shoot off and do things, like playing badminton over at the sports centre or table tennis down in the Hobbies' Room.

Now Tish went to the library nearly every day. Not to read books – but newspapers! Trebizon took daily newspapers, the important-looking, serious ones, and they were laid out on a big table in the library. Tish used to read them all the way through, even the city pages and the sports pages, though she never seemed to know what was in them afterwards! She just said she found she liked them. Rebecca and Sue were utterly baffled.

Everything became crystal clear on the day of the music scholarship. The timing of the whole thing was, in fact, rather extraordinary.

Three adjudicators from London, who had close connections with the school, had travelled down to Trebizon on the Monday night. The scholarship examination would take place on Tuesday morning, over in the Hilary Camberwell Music School. The five candidates would have to play the pieces they'd prepared and do aural and theory tests. They'd also have to play a piece on sight, which meant playing music that they'd never seen before. Sue had spent a lot of time practising her 'sight reading' as that was the thing she found hardest.

After the formal examination the girls would then have lunch with the visitors, over in the Principal's house, and would no doubt be subjected to further scrutiny. Then they would return to school for normal afternoon lessons, while the experts added up the points scored and came to their decision.

As soon as the successful candidate's parents or guardian had been contacted by telephone and informed of the result, she herself would be told – probably during the course of the afternoon.

'Good luck, Sue!' said Tish, after Assembly on Tuesday morning. 'Just think, you're missing Maths, Biology, French and History! See you after lunch!'

The five candidates were waiting with their instruments in the entrance hall of Juniper House, faces washed and hair brushed. Sue's shoulder-length hair was gleaming and she looked spruce, but Nicola Hodges put them all in the shade. She had taken her flaxen hair out of plaits and it fell to her shoulders in lovely little waves against the dark blue background of her school jumper. She looked suitably nervous, like an anxious little cherub, and at her most appealing. She had been working very hard all term and had kept right out of Sue's way since the day of the big showdown. The other three candidates, with their clarinets and flute, were all tall Second Year girls like Sue, and beside them Nicola looked small and dainty.

'Good luck, Sue,' echoed Rebecca.

Mrs Borrelli arrived with Mr Hobday, the woodwind

teacher, and they took their five pupils off to the music school. Everyone but Sue had received flowers and good luck telegrams from their families. It seemed that her parents hadn't thought of it.

'Do you think she minds!' Rebecca asked Tish, as they went off to lessons.

'I'm sure she doesn't!' said Tish. 'She wouldn't be half so relaxed if they'd made a fuss.'

The casual manner that she had adopted in front of Sue had already disappeared and she became quite tense during the morning.

'Relax, yourself!' said Rebecca, after biology. 'Anyone would think *you* were taking the scholarship, not Sue!'

'I feel as though I am,' said Tish.

She didn't eat much at dinner time and straight afterwards said:

'I'm going to the library.'

'Oh no,' thought Rebecca. 'Not the newspapers again.'

But she trailed after Tish and settled down with a book by the big french windows. The library was a lovely, comfortable place. Outside, violent gusts of wind were catching up stray tendrils of ivy and rattling them against the glass. March was coming in like a lion.

Over at the big table, Tish was scanning through a large newspaper. Then suddenly she groaned.

'Ssssh!' said the prefect on duty, and turned back to rearranging some books on a shelf. But Rebecca looked across towards Tish in alarm. She was staring at something in the newspaper and looking strange.

Rebecca tip-toed over. Tish tried to cover something up with her hands, but Rebecca forced them away. The newspaper was open at the financial pages, and there were two small headlines:

METTERNEX (GLASSWARE) DEALINGS
SUSPENDED
HOWARD MURDOCH COMES UNDER FIRE

Rebecca read the news item in a hurry, not understanding some of it. But the main message was clear. Sue's father's company had crashed, its shares had become worthless overnight, and people had lost their savings.

She closed the newspaper and dragged Tish outside.

'You've been waiting for this Tish! You knew?'

'I didn't know for certain.'

She sank down at the foot of the main staircase in old building, sitting on the bottom stair, and Rebecca sat beside her. Above them the magnificent muralled walls towered up to the ornate moulding of the ceiling above. Tish stared up at the chandeliers, moving almost imperceptibly as a draught whistled through a high-up window. She was very upset.

'My legs feel weak, do yours?'

'A bit. How are Sue's legs going to feel?'

'This means they've lost everything,' said Tish soberly. 'When I was there in the holidays, her parents were sinking every penny they had into the company to try and save it. They'd mortgaged the house, the cars, furniture, paintings, jewellery – the lot. Mr Murdoch thought he could stop the crash.'

'How did you find out?' asked Rebecca. The mystery of Tish's baffling behaviour was solved at last! Everything fell into place.

'It was the most stupid thing,' said Tish. 'It was the night I arrived. The boys were chasing me, we were fooling around, and I went and hid from them – behind the long curtains in the little sitting room. Then suddenly Mr and Mrs Murdoch came in and they shut the door and he said: "Well, darling, the bankers have agreed to an enormous loan, but I've had to put the house and everything else in hock to get it!" I was stuck there, behind the curtains, just frozen to the spot. I didn't dare move or breathe after that. Mrs Murdoch was very nervy and kept asking him what would happen if it didn't work. And he said: "It's got to work. If I can't save Metternex a lot of little people are going to be ruined." He's a good person, really, Rebecca.'

'Did they say anything about Sue?'

'Just touched on it. Mrs Murdoch said, "If it doesn't work, what about the children? The boys will be all right but Sue will have to leave Trebizon." And he replied, "I'm afraid so, but for heaven's sake let's look on the bright side" or something like that. Rebecca, that was the most horrible ten minutes of my life.'

There was silence. Rebecca gazed at Tish. What an amazing person she was. She had been carrying this burden around with her all term, hoping things might come right, dreading that they wouldn't. What a weight – and she'd carried it quite alone!

'You should have told me –' she began.

'I've been longing to! But how could I? It was bad enough me having to put on an act all the time, just imagine both of us at it!'

'You did it pretty well,' said Rebecca, in awe. 'The way you handled the music scholarship – making Sue see it was important, and yet never once letting her suspect . . . I could never have kept it up . . . Oh, Tish, what you must have been through.'

'The scholarship!' said Tish. 'As far as Sue's concerned, it's her only chance. If she's won it, she won't have to leave

Trebizon. Otherwise –' Tish couldn't bring herself to finish the sentence.

'It must be over now,' realized Rebecca. 'Supposing she'd got wind of this before she went in there this morning!'

'She'd have gone to pieces,' said Tish.

Miss Gates, the maths mistress, appeared at the top of the wide staircase and gazed down at them.

'What do you two girls think you're doing –' she asked pleasantly. 'Since when you have been allowed to sit on the main stairs?'

The girls got up and walked away.

'Sue should be back soon. Let's go and wait for her.'

'Are we going to tell her?' asked Rebecca.

'I think we should. Obviously her parents will be writing or telephoning, but when? She could easily hear it from some big-mouth. I think she'd rather hear it from us than from Debbie Rickard or someone.'

Sue arrived back at Juniper House just before two o'clock.

'It was quite good fun!' she told them. 'I quite enjoyed some bits of it – I never thought I would. And you should've seen the lunch they've just given us at Miss Welbeck's house! Talk about two classes of citizen at Trebizon – why can't they make school dinners like that –'

'Sue,' said Rebecca.

They told her everything. It was a tremendous shock and Sue swayed as though she were going to faint. Rebecca and Tish helped her up to the sick room, and Matron made her lie down.

'Just let her be quiet with me for a while,' said Matron..

They returned immediately after games. Sue was sitting up, the colour back in her cheeks. In spite of her obvious distress, she managed to raise a smile. Matron had fetched the offending newspaper and it was lying on the bed. 'No wonder they didn't have time to think about flowers,' Sue said. And then she added: 'I think my father has behaved very correctly and I think I can bear almost anything, as long as I'm able to stay on at Trebizon. If I *have* won, they will know where to find me, won't they?' she asked anxiously.

'We've told Miss Morgan,' said Rebecca.

There was silence and they listened to the ticking of the clock.

By now the judges would certainly have come to their decision. It was simply a matter of the Principal contacting the winning girl's parents, and then informing the girl herself. Why was nothing happening?

At teatime Sue came with the others to the dining hall, though she ate very little. After tea they went back to Juniper House. Still nobody had heard anything.

'It didn't take as long as this last year,' said Mara Leonodis, who had a good memory for anything connected with music. 'Don't you remember Moyra Milton's friends coming into the dining hall at teatime, dancing in a long line, after they'd heard she'd got it!'

Tish and Sue remembered that dance, though not the reason for it. The Third Years, who were Second Years then, had knocked a jug of milk off a table and got into trouble.

'I wonder what the delay is?' Tish said.

'It must be very close,' said Mara. 'It must be neck and neck. Perhaps the judges are having an argument.' She and Rebecca exchanged wary looks as they thought about Nicola Hodges and all her charms.

Sue was very quiet. As yet, none of the others knew just what the scholarship meant to her. No-one had any idea that Howard Murdoch was now a bankrupt man. Sue had missed games and gone to lie down in the sick room, and that was all they knew.

The friends sat down on the sofa in the common room, Sue in the middle. They put their arms round her, and waited.

THIRTEEN

THE RESULT OF THE MUSIC SCHOLARSHIP

They waited an hour. No news came through. It was awful. Then they learnt that the judges had gone back to London before tea. Someone had seen them go! So it *must* be decided. What had gone wrong?

Sue watched the minute hand of her watch creeping slowly, slowly round. Her head was bent, her hair flopping dejectedly.

'The only thing I can think,' she said, almost inaudibly, 'is that no-one's up to standard this year. When that happens, they don't award it . . .'

Her voice trailed away.

'Stuff!' said Tish. But she was scared.

'I think I'll go to bed early,' said Sue. 'I don't know what's the matter with me. I feel terribly tired, all of a sudden.'

'Doing a Tish on us!' said Rebecca suddenly.

'That's right,' said Sue. 'She's had quite a load to carry this term hasn't she?'

'St Tish!' said the same, with an embarrassed laugh.

'Don't laugh, Tish,' said Sue. She walked towards the door. 'It hasn't really been funny for you, has it?'

'No,' agreed Tish. 'Nor Rebecca.'

'It hasn't been funny for any of us,' said Rebecca. 'Especially that dirty election. Come to think of it, *that* wasn't very saintly.'

'Even saints can be as tough as old boots,' said Sue. 'She just wasn't taking any chances.'

'Let's hope it's all been worth it,' shrugged Tish. She was thinking – *Surely it can't be because no-one's good enough this year? There must be some other reason! Why haven't we heard yet?*

'Yes,' said Rebecca. And she was thinking – *Why is it taking so long? Is it something to do with Nicola? Please let Sue win.*

And Sue just said:

'I'm going to bed.'

Mrs Murdoch's car was racing along the motorway in the fast lane, heading west. What time was it Lights Out at Trebizon these days? It had been eight-thirty in her day. She was going to miss this car. It would have to be handed over to the bank, along with the house and everything else. She must see Sue before she went to bed! It was no use writing or 'phoning, she must *see* her. She'd telephoned the boys at their school; they were going to be all right. With the money their grandfather had left them, they would just scrape through.

But not Sue. There was no way they could keep her at Trebizon now. She had to break the news to her gently, put her arms round her . . . tell her what had happened to her father . . . tell her, before she found out some other way.

Wasn't it round about now she was hoping to be a Trebizon Music Scholar? What an irony if she were elected, just when she had to leave. It was such a distinction – free music tuition – special opportunities, no doubt. But that wasn't going to pay the fees. *Come on, come on. Must get there.*

At least Howard was resting. After working through the night and most of the morning, he'd let her drive him down to friends in the country, where he could get some much needed sleep and escape the 'phone for a few hours. He was a very exhausted man.

At a quarter to nine, when the car screeched to a halt in front of the main Trebizon building, Mrs Murdoch was on the edge of exhaustion herself. She got out and stared up through the shadows at the façade of the lovely manor house. The wind lifted up the edges of her headscarf. There was a light still burning in the Principal's study, upstairs, and a soft glow coming from the tall windows of the library on the ground floor. She could see some senior girls moving around inside. Two had their heads together, bent over a book. She felt a wave of nostalgia for her own schooldays at Trebizon and then, thinking of Sue, a great sadness.

'Mrs Murdoch?'

Entering the building, she was amazed to see the Principal of Trebizon School descending the main staircase, a hand stretched out in greeting. Mrs Murdoch had meant to telephone the school to warn them that she was coming, and for a moment she wondered if she'd done so after all! Everything today had been such a frantic rush . . .

'I've just been trying to telephone you,' said Miss Welbeck.

'To telephone *me*?'

They met at the foot of the stairs.

'You've driven down to see Susan?'

'Yes! I'm sorry, I should have let you know. Will she have gone to bed? I wanted to break some news to her . . .' Mrs

Murdoch lowered her eyes. 'I didn't want her to hear it by chance.'

'About Metternex? She does know about that,' said Miss Welbeck. 'We've been trying to contact you about something else. Since three o'clock this afternoon, as a matter of fact, at both the telephone numbers that you gave on the form –'

'The form, Miss Welbeck?'

'The entry form for the Hilary Camberwell Music Scholarship. I need hardly tell you that the five candidates are in great suspense, waiting to hear the result of the competition, and none of them more so than your daughter. But, of course, we never inform the winner until her parents have been told and the scholarship has been formally accepted on her behalf.'

'Then –?' Mrs Murdoch felt only dismay.

'Susan was a clear 20 points ahead of her nearest rival in the competition this morning. Are you willing that she be elected the Hilary Camberwell Music Scholar for this year?'

Mrs Murdoch shook her head. She felt like weeping. She had driven all the way from London – to hear this!

'I'm sorry, Miss Welbeck –'

'You do realize, of course, that the scholarship carries with it free music tuition and up to full fees for the rest of a girl's time at the school?'

'Full fees?' gasped Mrs Murdoch. 'No. No, I – I hadn't realized.'

'I thought perhaps you hadn't,' said Miss Welbeck. At last her face had relaxed into a smile. 'I suggest we go across to Juniper House and break the good news to your daughter. We may, of course, have to ask Matron to wake her up first.'

But Sue was not asleep when Matron walked in and told her to put her dressing gown on and come downstairs.

Neither were Rebecca, nor Tish, nor any of the occupants of dormitory number six. All the girls now knew about Sue's father. It just had to come out. And they had been discussing, endlessly, the question of the scholarship.

'Your mother's driven all the way down from London to see you. Miss Welbeck has brought her over and they're waiting to see you downstairs,' said Matron. She couldn't hide her excitement. 'I think they've both got a very nice piece of news for you, after all that bad news you've had today.'

One look at Matron's smiling face was enough.

As Sue scrambled into her dressing gown and stumbled towards the door, Tish ran after her. She was laughing and crying at the same time.

'Your glasses, Sue!' And then: 'You've done it, Sue! You've won!'

When Sue had gone, Tish turned on her cassette recorder and it played some music at full volume. She grabbed hold of Rebecca's hand and together they raced round and round the dormitory, jumping over beds, whooping with joy. To complete their happiness, they then had their first good pillow fight for weeks, and the rest of dormitory number six joined in.

FOURTEEN

HOW THE WISHES TURNED OUT

Rebecca didn't get her wish. She didn't stay in the Under-14 hockey team. Her second term at Trebizon had its disappointments, as well as its surprises.

For the final of the Gold Cup, against Skinnerton School, Dorset, Rebecca was dropped from the Trebizon team and wasn't even a reserve. Judy's ankle was completely better and she was back as right wing. Sue was back as right inner. Right-half Eleanor Keating, one of the four First Years now in the team, showed unexpected brilliance as a winger in one of the practice games. If anything went wrong with Judy, Tish realized, she could substitute Eleanor. So – after much heart-searching – she picked another defence player to join Verity Williams as a reserve. 'The slightest chink in our defence, and we've had it,' she explained to Rebecca. 'I've got to have strong replacements lined up for Robert or Joanna or Sheila – or the Skinnies will be in there scoring! Their centre forward's quite a girl!'

The final was played at a neutral ground, outside Exeter, and three coachloads from Trebizon went to cheer. Trebizon's tactics were defensive ones – the opposing centre-forward couldn't get near the ball. Then Tish broke through after half-time and scored the only goal of the match.

Trebizon had won the West of England Junior Gold Cup, against older teams, for the first time ever! Rebecca cheered until she was hoarse. At the end Tish, having been presented with the cup, walked over and gave it to somebody who was sitting in a chair near the touchline, wrapped up warmly. Joss Vining had just come out of hospital, and her parents had driven her to Exeter to see the final.

Singing loudly in the coach on the way back, Rebecca remembered that inspired goal she had managed to score against Helenbury, which had got them to the final. That had been *her* moment of glory and she would always cherish it!

The main surprises of the term had been those created by Tish's baffling behaviour – that went without saying. But another surprise for Rebecca, the one when Juniper House had decided to submit her essay to the school magazine, turned out to be even more thrilling than she had contemplated. When the spring term edition of *The Trebizon Journal* was delivered from the printers, in a lovely glossy blue and white cover, Rebecca found that 'A Winter's Morning' had been set up right across the centre pages, and was delicately illustrated with line drawings. They had been done by Pippa Fellowes-Walker, and were so good they made Rebecca admire her all the more!

Audrey Maxwell and her editorial committee then decided to submit Rebecca's essay to a national newspaper competition for the best work published in a school magazine. It won Third Prize and at prize-giving, towards the end of term, Rebecca had to go up to receive a framed certificate from Miss Welbeck, in front of the whole school.

'The first day you arrived at Trebizon, do you remember Rebecca, I told you to aim high?' smiled the Principal, firmly clasping her by the hand. 'Well done. Keep it up.'

Rebecca shook a strand of hair out of her eyes. Could that really have been her, that funny new girl of last September, so anxious to make her mark at Trebizon?

Prizes were given in alphabetical order and straight after Rebecca came Sue, to be presented with her Hilary Camberwell badge. As Miss Welbeck fastened on the distinctive piece of jewellery, there was some very special applause for Sue.

Another person to receive a surprise that term was Nicola Hodges. She came up to Rebecca, a week after the result of the music scholarship had been announced, and spoke to her in honeyed tones.

'Have you still got that cassette?' she asked.

'Tish has got it,' said Rebecca.

'Well, I was wondering –' Nicola smiled her most appealing smile, '– now that it's all over, could you rub it clean please?'

'Has your mother stopped boasting?' inquired Rebecca.

'She's talking about next year now,' said Nicola.

'Well, remember what I told you,' said Rebecca. 'Tell her to shut up.'

'But what about that tape?' asked Nicola anxiously. 'Those things I said to Sue. Can you rub them off now?'

'There's nothing to rub off,' said Rebecca. 'The tape was blank.'

She walked away, leaving Nicola rooted to the spot.

On the last morning of term, the three friends packed their trunks after breakfast and then went down the path through the trees, for a last look at the bay.

They watched the waves breaking against the sea shore.

'None of our wishes came true!' Tish said suddenly. 'Sue wanted to be head of games, and she's ended up Music Scholar. Rebecca wanted to be in the team and she's ended up winning a prize for writing, instead . . .'

'That's the way it goes,' said Rebecca. 'And what was *your* secret wish? Though I think I can guess.'

'I just wanted Sue's father to save Metternex,' said Tish.

'You can't say he didn't try,' observed Sue. She would be going home to a much smaller, rented house. 'You can't change fate, though. *Que sera, sera* . . . whatever will be, will be. It just goes to show that all three of us wished for the very things that were impossible.'

'Doesn't everyone?' said Tish. 'There's something up-side down about life. Nothing ever turns out quite how you expect.'

'Yes,' agreed Rebecca. She thought of that party at Sue's lovely big house in the Christmas holidays. Who would ever have dreamt that it was Nicola's father who was rolling in money and Sue's father who was going broke! But that was all history now. And, one day, Sue's father would be successful again. Rebecca felt sure of that.

'Come on, you two,' she said. 'You've got to get your train and I've got to get my 'bus.'

Her parents weren't able to come home for Easter. She was going to her grandmother's once more. As she ran to the top of a sand dune and waited, she could smell that spring was in the air. In the little wood behind her the birds were twittering; soon the trees would be bursting into leaf again. In front of her the sea looked quite blue for once, the sun dazzling on to it. March had come in like a lion, but now it was going out like a lamb.

Rebecca had joined the school Gardening Club and sown

things in the big walled garden behind the stable block: lettuce, parsley, onions, leeks, carrots and spinach. She hoped they would grow well! Mrs Dalzeil, who was in charge of home economics, had promised to teach them how to make delicious soups from vegetables they had grown themselves, next term! She was also going to show them how to prepare things for the freezer.

The other two joined her up on top of the dune.

'You'll like the summer term, Becky,' said Tish. 'The sea's warm enough to swim in . . . and there's tennis . . . and picnics and . . .'

'Exams!' laughed Sue.

'. . . and athletics,' finished Tish.

'I like the sound of athletics!' said Rebecca.

The long 'bus journey to Gloucestershire was a peaceful interlude. Rebecca thought about home and she thought about the past term and she tried to imagine the summer term. She would enjoy the Easter holidays while they lasted and soon she would be seeing all her friends again. Tish, and Sue, and Mara and Elf and Margot. And Joss would be back. And of course – there was Pippa. She liked her more than ever now.

It would be her third term.

SUMMER TERM AT
TREBIZON

For Tessa and Anna

CONTENTS

ONE

A MATHS PROBLEM

For Rebecca Mason there were going to be a lot of good things about the summer term at Trebizon – and a few bad ones, too. The bad things all seemed to have a connection with the letter 'M'.

M stood for maths. It also stood for Maxwell. Worst of all, it stood for Mason, her own surname, and that was going to create its own problems.

Rebecca suspected none of this as the long distance bus trundled through the green English countryside. She had spent the Easter holidays at her grandmother's home in Gloucestershire, one of a group of 'retirement bungalows' on a small housing estate. She loved her Gran but she had missed seeing London and her parents. The London house was let out until July, and her parents were in Saudi Arabia. Her father had been posted there by his firm the previous September and Rebecca had been transferred from her local day school to Trebizon, a boarding school in the west country. She had been lonely there at first, until she had made some friends. Her two best friends were Tish Anderson and Sue Murdoch.

Now she was travelling back to Trebizon for the summer

term, and although to her grandmother she had pretended to groan about going back to school, she was secretly quite looking forward to it.

As yet, the letter 'M' had no significance in her life. She couldn't have cared less what letter her surname began with. As for Mr Maxwell-beginning-with-M (who liked to be called Max), she had never even met him. So that left only maths.

She did spare a few brief thoughts to those, as well she might in view of the warning letter she had had from her father. The question of maths crossed her mind as, her luggage having been transferred from the coach at Trebizon Bus Station to a waiting taxi, she was being driven at speed out of the top end of town in the direction of school. Rebecca's thoughts lingered just long enough on the subject of maths to wish that they had never been invented, then quickly passed on.

There was Trebizon Bay! As the taxi passed the last of the hotels on the fringe of the town and turned into open country she could see the waters of the big, blue bay in the distance, across the fields. Although it was still only the end of April, there was a glorious sun this afternoon, dazzling on the sea, and the air was warm. Rebecca knew that they were allowed to swim in the sea during the summer term.

'I wonder if we'd be allowed to today, after tea?' she thought. She felt sticky after her long journey. 'I'd like that.' She wound down the window of the taxi half-way and stuck her head out, so that the rushing air blew her long fair hair around her face. Now she could just glimpse the school buildings in the parkland over on the west side of the bay, old roofs and white stone gables amongst tall trees that had recently burst into leaf. Trebizon School was still there then, as solid as ever.

Soon the taxi turned in through the main school gates,

slowed down to 10 m.p.h., as instructed, then dawdled along the long leafy lane that led to the main school building, which had once been a manor house. They passed one or two cars coming from the direction of the school, but most girls had arrived back in the early afternoon. The taxi-driver knew the ropes and crawled straight past old school and right round behind the dining hall block, eventually pulling up in the cobbled yard at the back of Juniper House: the long red-brick boarding house where all the junior girls at Trebizon, including Rebecca, lived. The driver opened the rear door of the taxi while Rebecca got out, arms laden with carrier bags and a tennis racket, the overspill from her trunk.

'Rebecca!' shrieked several voices at once.

'Tish!' laughed Rebecca. 'Sue! Mara –!'

They were all running towards her. In front was Ishbel Anderson, Tish for short, her dark curly hair badly in need of a comb. Behind her Sue Murdoch, Mara Leonodis and Margot Lawrence looked equally dishevelled. They had just finished a game of tennis and were carrying rackets. 'Elf' – chubby Sally Elphinstone – brought up the rear, carrying some tennis balls. She had been keeping score and was not sweaty and untidy like the others.

'About time you got here,' said Tish.

'It was that bus again,' said Rebecca. 'What a journey!'

'Where's this to, miss?' asked the taxi-driver. He was getting Rebecca's trunk out of the large boot. 'Upstairs?'

'Second floor!' interjected Sue promptly. 'Dormitory number six. We'll show you. You won't believe this but she's supposed to be unpacked by teatime!'

Sue led the way to the back door of Juniper House, followed by three of them, chattering. Tish hung back with Rebecca and the taxi man and yelled out:

'Catch, Margot!'

She hurled her tennis racket through the air as the black girl turned swiftly. Deftly Margot caught it.

'Now I can help you hump this trunk upstairs,' said Tish to the man.

With a great deal of awkwardness and laughter she did so, once colliding with Rebecca who was just behind them so that Rebecca dropped her things all over the stairs. Tish seemed to think that was hilarious. On the second floor landing they picked their way through the empty cases and trunks that were waiting to be collected and at last deposited the trunk safely inside dormitory six, at the foot of Rebecca's bed.

'Thanks!' said the taxi-driver to Tish. 'Your friend can get unpacked now.'

Rebecca dumped her other things on her bed and scrabbled around to find her purse. She paid the taxi-driver self-consciously, as she was not very used to hiring taxis, and just guessed wildly when it came to the tip, hoping it was neither too generous nor too mean.

'Thank you, darling,' he said, to Rebecca's relief. He thought she seemed a pretty youngster, athletic-looking, too. He glanced at the tennis racket on her bed and winked. 'You off to Wimbledon then?'

'Some hopes!' laughed Rebecca, blushing.

'Rebecca's going to be a sprinter!' said Tish.

'A sprinter, eh? You'll have your eye on the Olympics then.'

They all laughed, and as he left Elf called out:

'Someone in our form really has been to Wimbledon. Junior Wimbledon.'

'Hope she got a good seat,' he observed.

'No –' Elf started to follow him. 'She *played* there –'

'Now, now, Elf,' said Sue, hauling her back. 'He knows. Stop showing off about Joss. She wouldn't like it.'

'How is Joss?' asked Rebecca. 'Seen her yet?'

Josselyn Vining was head of games in the junior house, but had been away most of last term after a minor back operation.

'Fitter than ever!' said Sue. 'Saw her down on the courts –'

'Beating Miss Willis,' added Tish.

Rebecca sighed. It must be very satisfying to be like Joss Vining, brilliant at any game she turned her hand to and a natural leader. Or was it? It must set you just a little apart from everyone else.

All five girls rallied round to help Rebecca get unpacked at speed, then dragged her empty trunk out on to the landing just as the first tea bell went. There were squeals then and a stampede into the washroom; hands and faces were washed and hair combed, Rebecca's included.

'Nice to see you back, Rebecca,' said Mara, waiting for her comb.

'Nice to *be* back,' confessed Rebecca.

Even better than being like Josselyn Vining, Rebecca decided, was being one of a crowd. Tish and Sue were her best friends because dramatic happenings in her first two terms had drawn them very close together. But the other three, Mara Leonodis, Margot Lawrence and Sally Elphinstone, were the sort Rebecca liked too. They all joined forces sometimes, especially when things needed doing – the 'Action Committee' Tish called it – and they certainly got things done. There were two other girls in the dormitory, both very pleasant, but it was these five she was with now that Rebecca liked best of all.

'I wonder if we'll need the Action Committee for anything this term?' said Rebecca, working furiously at a tangle.

'Only Charity Week,' said Mara.

'Charity Week?'

'Yes,' smiled Mara. 'And that'll be enough excitement for me.' There was a light in the Greek girl's eyes. 'This term I'm going to work very, very hard.'

'You *are*?' exclaimed Tish, with interest.

Mara had to burst out with it.

'If I work very hard, I may go into the A stream when we move up into the Third Year next term! It was in my report!'

'Oh, Mara!'

'Great!'

They all crowded round, patting Mara on the back. They were all Second Years at present and in the same form together, II Alpha, with the sole exception of Mara, who was in II Beta. She so much wanted to be in the same form as the rest of them. Now perhaps, when they moved up into III Alpha, Mara would be joining them!

'Anything wrong, Rebeck?' asked Tish, a moment later.

There was a funny look on Rebecca's face, for she had been reminded of something that she distinctly wanted to forget. But she quickly shook her head.

'Hey, listen!' said Sue, opening wide the washroom door. 'It's the second bell. We're late!'

They all rushed down the west staircase, out of the front of Juniper House, which overlooked the quadrangle gardens and old school opposite, and along the terrace to the modern dining hall block. The doors were open and the clamour of noise hit Rebecca like a tidal wave. It sounded like four hundred girls talking at once which was, very roughly, the position.

The next day, Wednesday, when the term really started, they would have to sit at their proper tables. Today, girls could sit where they liked. The six latecomers had to take seats where they could find them and Rebecca found herself sitting with Mara and Sue at the same table as Roberta Jones, who had written a play in the Easter holidays.

'I shall be inviting people to be in it,' she said stolidly.

'But what's it for exactly, Roberta?' asked Rebecca.

'For Juniper's Charity Week of course,' said Roberta.

This being Rebecca's first summer at Trebizon, Sue had to explain to her that early in May each year Juniper House organized a Charity Week. All the members of the junior boarding house, the entire First and Second Years, split up into small groups. Each group had to think of a fund-raising idea and organize it, outside of lesson times, and then carry it out during the course of the week. 'It's quite fun,' Sue explained. 'There are different things going on every day.'

The girls in the group that raised the most money would get special merit marks from the principal.

'I see what you mean about the Action Committee now!' said Rebecca, turning to Mara.

'That's a thought,' said Sue. 'We'd be good together. We'll get Tish to revive it, shall we?'

'Let's have a meeting and try and think of something really different,' said Rebecca, pushing her bowl forward for another helping of fruit salad and whipped cream. 'When?'

'I've got to go and do some music practice in a minute,' said Sue.

'I've got to check all my maths holiday work with my new calculator,' said the new, industrious Mara. 'Let's all be thinking of some ideas and talk about it tonight!'

'Right,' agreed Rebecca, but she felt suddenly depressed. Maths!

Her father's letter came back to her mind with a jolt.

Your maths are letting you down, Becky. You must try very hard next term.

Enclosed with the letter had been a photo-copy of her school report, which had been sent out to her parents. On the whole it had been good, but beside *Mathematics* Miss

Gates had written: *Generally poor. Some improvement this term but Rebecca has a great deal of ground to make up.*

However, it wasn't that which had filled her with alarm. It was the principal's comment, right at the bottom of the report:

> *Rebecca has high ability in some subjects, but unless she makes noticeable progress in Maths next term it may be advisable for her to spend the next academic year in the Beta stream, where she can receive extra maths teaching*
>
> (Signed) Madeleine Welbeck. *Principal.*

So, just as Mara was excited at the possibility of going up next year, Rebecca was dismayed at the possibility of going down. No wonder Tish had noticed a funny look on her face. Now Sue noticed something, too.

'Anything wrong?'

'Tell you later.'

Rebecca decided she would tell both Sue and Tish about it, straight after tea. That's what best friends were for. They would find some way of cheering her up.

She was right about that.

TWO

LEARNING TO SURF

Tea was over. Rebecca and Sue waited outside the dining hall, on the terrace, for Tish. Through the glass doors they could see that she was talking to Zrina Singh, one of the prefects on duty. When she was happy, Tish Anderson had the biggest grin in the whole school and it was very much in evidence as she charged through the door to join them.

'Still feel like going in the sea, Rebecca?'

'Yes!' Rebecca had mentioned swimming to Tish, almost as soon as she'd got out of the taxi. 'Why? Can we?'

'Anybody who's got their swimming certificate can! Zrina says we've got to wait for our tea to go down, but there's plenty of time because Harry's on duty till half-past seven. He's the lifeguard.'

Rebecca felt excited. She was a good swimmer and had gained her swimming certificate during the winter term. There was an indoor pool in the school sports centre. But she had yet to swim in Trebizon Bay. She hadn't really thought they would be allowed to yet! In spite of the warm, sunny day, the sea was bound to be cold until the summer got under way.

'We won't want to swim, of course,' said Tish surprisingly. 'Too cold.'

'We won't?' asked Rebecca, baffled. 'Then –'

'Surfing!' said Tish. 'In wet suits! The school's got all its own stuff, in that white shed next to our beach huts. Harry looks after it for us. Ever done it?'

'No –' *Surfing!*

'Wait till you try. Harry'll show you!'

'Blow,' said Sue. 'I've got music practice.'

The three of them walked along the terrace and into Juniper House and then they went up to the dormitory. Sue changed out of her tennis things and into her school skirt and blue striped summer blouse. It had a V neck and short sleeves; the girls didn't have to wear a tie in the summer term. To the lapel she pinned the pretty little badge with the monogram HC that showed that she was now one of the school's Music Scholars. As Tish and Sue chattered about the Juniper House Charity Week and the need to get the Action Committee going again, Rebecca fell silent.

'Terrific!' said Tish. 'Let's try and think of a really good fund-raising idea tonight. Let's try and be the winning group.'

Sue picked up her violin case. It was time for her to go over to the Hilary Camberwell Music School, but she glanced at Rebecca.

'Come on, Rebecca. Out with it.'

Rebecca had been just waiting for the chance to tell them about her maths problem. Now she did, gloomily.

She wasn't gloomy for very long.

'What rubbish!' exclaimed Tish. 'So that's what you've been brooding about! They won't put you in the B stream next year! You're good at everything else and you just need to catch up on maths, that's all.'

'It's just to get you working, Rebecca,' said Sue. 'They

threaten you! They did exactly the same thing to me last year – said I'd go into II Beta if I wasn't careful. I was miles behind the others because we had a crazy kind of maths teacher at my last school, and I never knew what Miss Gates was talking about half the time –'

'That's just it!' said Rebecca with feeling. 'And I don't this year. All the maths was different at my day school and the trouble with Gatesy is she takes it for granted that we know all the back work. Well, I *don't*. So how am I ever going to catch up?'

'Because we have Mrs Shaw this term!' explained Sue, in triumph.

'That's what saved Sue's bacon last year,' said Tish.

'Mrs Shaw?'

'Yes,' said Tish. 'You haven't met her yet. She comes in every summer term to teach the juniors because Gatesy gets all tied up with the seniors and their big exams.'

'The nice thing about Mrs Shaw,' explained Sue, 'is that instead of taking it for granted that everyone's brilliant she takes it for granted that everyone's as thick as two short planks. She explains things over and over again!'

'Phew!' Rebecca laughed. She was overcome by a feeling of utmost relief. 'Mrs Shaw.' She repeated the name, with gratitude. What a friendly comforting name it began to seem. Shaw. Sure. Safe. 'Just the person I need!'

'Just the person we all need, seeing there's exams at the end of term,' said Sue. She moved away from the other two. 'I'd better get along to the Hilary. Everything'll be all right, Rebecca, you'll see.'

'Bound to be,' said Tish. 'Hey, Margot!' As Sue went out of the dormitory, Margot Lawrence came in. 'We can surf! Coming? Help teach Rebecca!'

A quarter of an hour later, the three of them strolled through the leafy little wood at the back of Juniper House and came out through a private gate into Trebizon Bay. There was still some sun. They had been trying to think of a fund-raising idea for Charity Week, without success, and now all they could think about was surfing. They could change into wet suits in the school beach huts. They had brought towels to dry themselves with, after they came out of the sea, and jumpers in case they felt cold later on.

They clambered through the dunes and out on to the open expanse of sand. Rebecca was beginning to feel very happy, looking around her as they walked across the sand to the white shed by the beach huts, where the lifeguard kept the school wet suits and Malibu boards.

'Just look at that man!' exclaimed Rebecca. 'Isn't he good!'

A sinewy young man, with MAX in white letters across the chest of his wet suit, was riding in on the surf from a long way out. He stood balanced sideways on his Malibu board, legs apart, coming in at great speed, the spray kicking up in front of him – at the same time managing to wave to his girlfriend who was watching him admiringly from the shore.

All the other surfers were Trebizon girls, about a dozen of them. It was a huge bay, the sand hard and golden down near the sea. The waves broke far out and came rolling in, in a long and seemingly unbroken line, to make it a surfers' paradise. In this corner of the bay, where the girls were allowed to surf ride this evening, the waves were breaking closer in to shore, making the run-ins shorter, but very exciting nevertheless. Here, Harry was able to keep a watchful eye on them all. The school's white Malibu boards lay in a row on the sand, their fins uppermost, looking like a row of sleeping sharks.

When Rebecca had changed into a wet suit he selected her a board and took her in hand, wading into the shallows with her. He was a tough, weatherbeaten man whose skin looked almost as dark as Margot's against his faded blue denim swimming shorts and white tee shirt. First Rebecca tried riding in on the edge of the waves, flat on her stomach, hands gripping the two edges of the hollow fibreglass board, and that was easy. Then she tried to stand up on the board in the eddying, swirling shallows, with plenty of encouragement from Tish and Margot, until they went off to do some real surfing.

After a few minutes, Rebecca was keeping her balance well and longed to get out of the shallows. The fin at the back of the board kept scraping into the sand and bringing her to a halt. She could see the others surfing. Tish was good, so was Margot. They could do it!

'Come on, Rebecca!'

'Shall I?' she asked Harry eagerly. He nodded.

'Go and have a try. You have to get out to beyond the breakers.'

Rebecca lay flat on the board, as she had seen the others do, then propelled it forward by paddling with her hands to get beyond the breaker line. She enjoyed rising up through the big waves and feeling the sting of the spray on her cheeks and the salty tang of the sea on her lips. The sun was getting low in the west now, blood red, turning to pink some little clouds on the horizon. She kept going until she was out beyond the breakers and level with Tish.

'Get the board like this,' Tish shouted, and demonstrated, 'and when a big one comes – just get on, and go!'

Rebecca waited for the next big breaker.

As it came, she sprang on to the board in front of it and then felt herself being lifted high into the air. Then she started to shoot forward at speed.

'Fantastic!' she shrieked. She wobbled from crouching to standing position, sideways on. 'I'm standing up!' she cried in disbelief. 'I'm actually –'

She wobbled perilously on the Malibu board, struggling to keep her balance as it raced along in front of the surging breaker. The shore was rushing towards her. She could see Harry waving. She tried to change position.

'Ohhh!'

Rebecca lost her balance and went keeling into the sea with a great splash. The big wave went right over her head. After a few moments she bobbed up on to the surface of the sea, laughing and gasping for breath, her eyes screwed up tight and full of salt water.

She opened them and started to thrash around to get a grip on her Malibu board. She never even saw the fast approaching surfer. He was going extremely gracefully and he didn't want to spoil it.

'Look out!' he yelled.

Even as Rebecca was still blinking the water out of her eyes and wondering from which direction the voice was coming, he went straight over her board in a somersault and took a nose dive into the sea. When he came up he was gulping for air and looking cross. He swam to get his own red surfboard, painted to look like a fish. Bobbing on the sea, fin uppermost, it looked quite alarming.

He started to laugh. He was really very good looking.

'Are you all right, darling?' called his girlfriend from the beach. He turned his back on Rebecca and kickpaddled himself and his board towards the shore. Rebecca followed, slowly. She heard him call out.

'I'm fine, Katie. Some of these girls aren't very bright! How about a drink now?'

That was Rebecca's very first meeting with Max.

A minute later, Harry blew a long blast on the whistle and it was time for them all to come out of the sea.

THREE

ROBERTA FALLS IN LOVE

'Well, what did you think of it?' asked Tish.

'Need you ask!' exclaimed Rebecca.

The three of them were warmly dressed now, walking back along the beach to school. Harry was locking all the equipment away in the white shed, ready for another day. Rebecca's cheeks were aglow.

'You certainly look cheerful!' said Margot. 'Even if you did come off!'

'Right in front of that man!' giggled Tish.

'When can we come again?' asked Rebecca, rapturously. 'Now I've tried it I really want to get good at it, like you two. What a sensation! Did you know –' she said suddenly, 'that in 1936 a man rode a wave a distance of 4,500 feet?'

'Oh, Rebecca!' laughed Margot. 'Where?'

'Off the coast of Hawaii,' said Rebecca solemnly. She had a mind that hoarded useless snippets of information. Each week she wrote a little piece called 'Did You Know?' for the *Juniper Journal*, a newsletter that the juniors produced themselves. She never seemed to run out of facts for it.

'4,500 feet!' said Tish. 'Lucky for him you weren't around then, or you might have spoiled the whole thing.'

They all started to smile. 'Just imagine –' Tish threw her arms wide '– all set to break the world record, the crowds cheering, the flags waving and then suddenly, up pops Rebecca, looking for her Malibu board . . .!'

'Ooops – crash! – sorry!' laughed Rebecca.

They had just reached the sand dunes. Margot suddenly thought of something. She turned and looked at the bay, beautiful and empty now. The sea was reddening in the setting sun and the long line of white breakers had never looked more racy.

'Got it!' she exclaimed. 'Stop a minute, you two.'

'Got what?' they asked, stopping.

'Record-breakers! Raising money. Charity Week!' said Margot.

'Surfing!' yelled Tish. 'Yes, you *have* got it –'

'Maybe one of us could try and set some kind of record –' began Margot.

'What, a long-distance record?' asked Rebecca, in disbelief.

'No, no,' said Tish. 'Wait, I'm thinking.' She stared at the distant breakers and then clapped her hands. 'Just the number of trips! The number of times we can come in from beyond the breakers to the shore, without falling off. If you come off, you're out!'

'And we can each get sponsors!' said Margot eagerly. 'People have to promise to pay a penny for each ride we make –'

'Or even two pence,' said Tish in delight. 'The rich ones.'

'That's really good,' admitted Rebecca. 'Sponsored surfing. Bet no one else will think of it! Oh, I wish I could go in for it!'

'Maybe you can!' said Tish. 'You've got a couple of weeks to learn!'

'What about the others?' asked Rebecca, meaning the rest of the 'Action Committee'.

'Couldn't be better,' said Margot. 'Sue's good and so's Elf. Mara, well –'

'Mara hates surfing,' realized Tish. 'But she can be in charge. Somebody's got to be. Somebody's got to have a chart and tick off each time we ride in without falling off. Come on! Let's find them and see what they think!'

They turned their eyes away from the sea and ran back to school.

They found Mara Leonodis and Sally Elphinstone straight away. They were leaning against a radiator in the corridor outside the Second Year Common Room gossiping.

'Action Committee all ready?' asked Mara.

'Let's go in and find some armchairs!' suggested Tish. 'We'll tell you what we've thought of. Besides, we've been surfing and our legs are aching.'

'No fear!' said Elf. 'Roberta's in there, jabbering about her play for Charity Week. She's had loads of copies typed out in the holidays –'

'She'll put one into your hand the minute you walk in,' warned Mara. 'Apparently it needs a cast of at least twenty people!'

'We've thought of our own thing to do!' said Tish. 'At least, Margot has. Here, let's go in the kitchen.'

'Sue!' said Rebecca as she opened the door of the kitchen. Sue was munching sandwiches. 'Who you hiding from?'

'Who d'you think?' mumbled Sue.

'Don't you *want* to be in *A Midsummer Night's Nightmare* then?' asked Tish. 'Hey! Where did you get those sandwiches?'

'Left over from the train – here, have some.'

The three girls who had been surfing grabbed at the food

eagerly: Rebecca was amazed to find herself so hungry again. She had eaten a big tea. Between delicious mouthfuls of bread and butter and cream cheese they expounded the 'sponsored surfing' plan. It was an immediate hit.

'Perfect!' said Sue. Then, gazing at the empty place where her sandwiches had been: 'And afterwards we'd better have some sponsored sandwich cutting, at the rate you three can eat.'

'You'll get fat!' said Elf virtuously and then laughed. She felt quite excited. She was terrible at organized games but she enjoyed swimming and surf riding and was quite good at both. This was due – the others said – to her being more buoyant than average because she had a built-in tyre round her middle.

'What about you, Mara?' Tish asked anxiously.

'Fine!' smiled Mara, who liked Tish very much and would always follow her lead. 'Like you say, I can keep count, and help collect the money up afterwards and all that sort of thing.'

'We could raise pounds!' said Rebecca eagerly. Secretly she was determined to get good at surfing in time for Charity Week, and intended to practise whenever she possibly could. She wanted to take part and at least do a few rides without falling off!

'It's all settled then,' said Tish. She gazed round at the group and said humorously: 'I hereby declare the Action Committee re-awakened!'

There was a happy hum of conversation as they moved around the kitchen making cocoa and finding biscuits. There would be quite a lot of things to do. They would have to get permission, naturally, and Miss Morgan – their House Mistress – would want to make sure that the surfing was all properly supervised. Then they would need to make sponsorship forms. Tish could type those out on a stencil and run them off on the little duplicator that Mara's father had given to the junior boarding house, the machine they used when printing the *Juniper Journal*.

After a while, Rebecca heard voices in the corridor and peeped out of the kitchen door, her cocoa in her hand. Roberta Jones was leaving the Second Year Common Room at last, accompanied by Debbie Rickard and the Nathan twins. They were all holding copies of the play.

'I expect everyone will want to be in it,' Debbie was saying. 'How will you choose?'

'I shall hold auditions if that happens,' said Roberta.

'Coast is clear!' said Rebecca, when they'd gone. 'Now we can go and drink our cocoa in there.'

They trooped into the big, comfortable Common Room with its armchairs and rugs and big windows. It was up on the first floor of Juniper House. Through the windows Rebecca could see the school's formal gardens, set within the quadrangle of buildings, shadowy and peaceful in the dusk. Here and there a lighted window in the old school opposite illuminated a rose bush, a flagstone, or a triangle of lawn.

'It's nearly dark,' said Sue, switching on the lights.

Over by a window, Jenny Brook-Hayes got up from her chair, put down her book, and started to draw the long curtains.

'Look, Robert's put a notice up,' said Tish.

They crowded round the big notice-board behind the door. The notice said:

Important *Charity Week*

The Fairy Queen *by Roberta Jones*

The first reading of my one-act play will take place in here, Friday dinner hour. Everyone who wants a part please sign below and then come along to the play-reading. Make this play a success and be one of the group that raises the most funds for Charity Week.

(Signed) R. Jones

'Nobody's signed yet,' observed Rebecca. 'What's it like?' she asked, wandering across to Jenny, who had settled back with her novel.

'Not much good,' Jenny grunted, still reading.

'I don't mean your book, I mean the play,' said Rebecca.

'So do I,' said Jenny. She looked up and sighed. 'She's actually hoping we might pass it forward to be considered for the *Trebizon*, too.'

'Not again,' groaned someone. Every term Roberta Jones tried to get something on the short-list for the *Trebizon Journal*, the school's official magazine. At present Jenny was the Magazine Officer for Juniper House and decided which junior contributions should go on the short-list. A vote was taken on the short-list and the best ones submitted. They usually then appeared in the magazine, a great honour.

'Hope people will find time to do some good things,' said Jenny suddenly. 'I mean, with Charity Week coming up. This'll be Audrey's last term and she'll want it to be her best issue.'

Audrey Maxwell, the Editor of the *Trebizon Journal*, was in the Upper Sixth and would be going up to University in the autumn.

'Oh, they'll find time,' said Rebecca. People always clamoured to get in the *Trebizon*. Rebecca herself wouldn't be trying this term, having already had two pieces of writing published – the first in very unusual circumstances, in her first term. But there were plenty of others who were dying to get into print. She settled on the arm of Jenny's chair. 'So you're not thinking of being in the play?'

'Joanna and Joss and I have decided to run a cake stall.'

'We're doing something else, too,' said Sue, coming up and joining them. 'Just thought of it this evening.'

Rebecca sighed and sipped her cocoa. The sponsored surfing was going to be marvellous, but she felt a twinge of sympathy for Roberta. She was large and not very pretty and always rather full of herself. She had the idea that she was a great writer, although she was actually much better at other things, like netball and hockey. She was quite good at lessons, too, except for maths – like Rebecca. But she had this terrible urge to write things and show people how good they were all the time. Would anybody even want to be in *The Fairy Queen* except the Nathan twins, who were loyal friends of Roberta's, and maybe Debbie Rickard?

Rebecca was feeling sleepier and sleepier and the hum of conversation in the Common Room was getting blurred. When Miss Morgan put her head round the door and said 'Bed time!' she roused herself and went straight up to the dormitory, without even waiting for the others. It had been a long day.

'Hello, Rebecca, good holidays?' asked a slim, pretty girl as the Second Years filed into the assembly hall next morning.

'Yes thanks, Pippa!' said Rebecca shyly.

Pippa Fellowes-Walker was in the Lower Sixth and was already a prefect: Rebecca's favourite one. Rebecca was an only child and if she could have had an older sister, she would have wanted her to be like Pippa.

As the big hall filled up, Mr Barrington, the school's Director of Music, played the grand piano and the girls shuffled and chattered and scraped chairs as they got into their proper places. It was another warm day and the whole school wore summer uniform, open-necked striped blouses crisp and clean, blue skirts spotless, a few blue jumpers here and there for those who felt the cold. Silence fell as the principal arrived to take Assembly, walking the hall in easy strides and mounting the stage.

'Good morning, girls.'

'Good morning, Miss Welbeck.'

As it was the first morning of term there were a lot of notices to give out and Rebecca still felt sleepy. She went off into a daydream. She came to just in time to hear Miss Welbeck finishing off an announcement:

'. . . So although we are sorry that Mrs Shaw, who as you know comes here as a relief teacher every summer term, cannot be with us this year, we are indeed lucky to have procured his services at such short notice. He holds a First Class Honours degree in mathematics.'

Although a lot of the younger girls were bored and fidgety by this stage, and some of them looked half asleep, Rebecca was suddenly wide awake. Mrs Shaw not coming! A man coming in her place! A First Class Honours graduate – a high-powered mind – brilliant, wise, erudite. Rebecca's shoulders sagged.

'He'll probably be even worse than Miss Gates,' she said to Tish gloomily as they all trooped across to the form room in old building, after Assembly. 'Fancy someone like that needing a job, anyway.'

'Some old chap they've dragged out of retirement, I expect,' said Tish.

Sue glanced at Rebecca sympathetically.

'Cheer up. One thing about men teachers is they usually take pity on you more than women. They usually help you more. I mean, look at Mr Douglas.'

That raised Rebecca's spirits. It was true, their chemistry master was very kind and avuncular. At her London comprehensive school, too, there had been a lot of men teachers and on the whole she had got on very well with them.

'I'd still rather have Mrs Shaw,' said a voice behind them.

It belonged to Roberta Jones. Her plaits, which never suited her at the best of times, looked particularly droopy this morning. 'She helped me a lot last summer. I don't like men teaching you, they never take any notice of you.'

'You ought to make yourself look glamorous, Robert,' said Tish with a giggle. 'Wear your hair loose and all that.'

Roberta scowled. 'Shut up!' She was in no mood for Ishbel Anderson's funny remarks. The truth, although she was not going to admit it to a soul, was that she was worried. She had received a report very similar to Rebecca's and her parents were going to be annoyed if she had to go into the B stream next year. She had to do well at maths this term!

A new teacher was always interesting. The eighteen girls in Rebecca's form could hardly wait for maths, which was second lesson on a Wednesday. No sooner had Miss Heath, their form mistress, gone out of the room after taking them for English, than Tish and some others rushed for the door. The II Alpha form room was right at the top of the old manor house and with luck if they hung over the banisters they might catch a glimpse of the new master coming up the stairs.

Rebecca and Sue, who shared a desk at the back, remained seated however, getting their maths things ready. Rebecca felt slightly anxious.

'I thought all my problems were over when you told me about Mrs Shaw!' she said. 'Now I don't know.'

'Don't worry, Rebecca.' Sue nudged her arm. 'He'll probably be all right. And even if he isn't, they just threaten you in school reports. They don't mean it.'

There was a lot of din outside, like a stampede. The door burst open and the girls came rushing back in to their desks, shouting and laughing.

'He's coming!'

'You should see him!'

'What's he like, Tish?' asked Rebecca, as Tish scrambled into her chair and rummaged around in her desk for her maths things. Tish looked across the gangway at Sue and Rebecca and her eyes were sparkling with fun. 'He's young! Dark hair. Looks like –'

'Ssssshhh!'

The new maths master walked in, tall and sinewy and very good looking, with dark curly hair. Rebecca recognized him at once. It was the brilliant surf-rider who had been down in Trebizon Bay.

'Hello,' he said, with an engaging smile. He went and sat on the edge of the table in front of the blackboard and surveyed the girls. They surveyed him back. 'I'm Mr Maxwell. My friends call me Max. You can, too.'

The girls of Form II Alpha grinned and whispered and nudged each other, hardly able to believe their luck. Not only did Mr Maxwell – Max – look dishy but he seemed easy-going, too. Rebecca, on the other hand, felt rather disconcerted – especially as, only last night, she had sent the new maths master toppling into the sea. She hoped he wouldn't hold it against her.

Meanwhile Roberta Jones was staring at him. She shared a desk in the front row with Aba Amori, the Nigerian girl, just next to her friends, the Nathan twins. So she had a really good view of the new master. Her rather red, stolid face was getting redder and redder with pleasure and self-importance.

'Haven't I met you somewhere before?' she blurted out.

Max looked at her from under his long, dark lashes, hesitated for a moment, then gave her a flashing smile.

'That's what all the girls say.'

Everyone giggled.

'But I have!' protested Roberta, frowning hard in concentration, trying to remember. She wasn't going to have her moment of importance snatched away from her. 'I'm trying to think –'

Max stood up, picked up a piece of chalk and walked to the blackboard, firmly turning his back on Roberta. He began to write.

'Right. Let's start today by refreshing our minds on the binary and denary systems . . .'

'I remember!' Roberta shouted. 'You were at Greencourt!'

The master's hand stopped in the middle of chalking up some numbers. His back view remained frozen for a moment then, slowly, he lowered his arm, turned round, and walked over to Roberta. Her face was upturned, as she gazed at him.

'You never taught me but you used to teach the top class. I remember! You weren't there very long, but I remember you!'

'And you are –?'

'Roberta Jones!' she said eagerly.

'Of course!' He looked down at her upturned face and touched the tip of her nose with his forefinger and gave a very special smile. 'Little Bobbie Jones! Of course I remember you now. I did teach at your Prep School for a while – a term or two, wasn't it? – and, my, how you have grown! Well, isn't it a small world.'

'Yes,' breathed Roberta, almost speechless with pleasure.

'Ahem!' coughed Tish and there was some suppressed giggling.

'Well, to work,' said Max brightly, striding to the blackboard, but looking back over his shoulder to give Roberta a friendly nod. 'I'm sure Bobbie will make quick work of this exercise. How about the rest of you?'

Roberta watched, transfixed, as he wrote the numbers up on the board.

'Robert's fallen in love,' whispered Sue across the gangway to Tish.

'She and Max are going to have a *special relationship*, you can tell,' grinned Tish. 'What a hoot!'

Rebecca smiled rather weakly. Roberta was having some luck for once. How was she going to get on with the new master? Would he remember her from last night?

What were the binary and denary systems anyway?

FOUR

TWO VIEWS ON MAX

Rebecca watched the rows of figures appearing on the blackboard.

1011 . . . What on earth were they meant to represent?

'Start copying them down in your exercise books,' Max said, as the chalk squeaked across the board: 10011, 100111 . . . The rows seemed to be getting longer all the time! There was some bustle and the sound of flicking pages as the girls got their books open and started to write. Rebecca copied the numbers down from the blackboard as carefully as she could, at the same time whispering to Sue:

'What are they?'

'Binary numbers!' hissed Sue, as though that explained everything.

'Be quiet!' said Max, squatting to finish off the column of figures, which almost ran off the bottom of the blackboard. He got up, turned round, placed the chalk on his table and dusted his hands off. Then he lolled against the wall beside the blackboard, waiting for them to finish writing. Once or twice his gaze strayed to Roberta, and he seemed to be deep in thought.

'Right.' He came out of his reverie. A lot of the girls had

put their ballpoint pens down and were gazing at him expectantly. 'Let me explain. I'm not going to do any new work with you this term. We're just going to go through everything step by step, that you've learnt in your first two years here. We're going to consolidate. Come the exams and you'll be tested on the whole lot. If you don't know it all by then, heaven help you. Anyone who gets less than 50% in the maths exam, or bad marks in term time, or both, will go into the Beta stream next year! Or the Gamma stream! You're supposed to be the clever lot in this room.'

There was some slightly excited laughter. Max was acting. They rather liked it. One or two rewarded his performance with long, realistic groans.

'Now, somebody tell me what these numbers are –' He pointed to Tish. 'You at the back with the curly hair. Name?'

'Ishbel Anderson.'

'Tish!' shouted several voices at once.

'Right, Tish. You tell me. What are they called and what will you do with them?'

'Binary numbers,' said Tish, happily. She had already decided that Max's lessons were going to be an improvement on those that Miss Gates dished out. 'And we're going to put them into denary numbers.'

'Precisely! Our minds are meeting!' said Max, giving her a dazzling smile. He then gazed round the room. 'You are to take each binary number in turn, work out its denary equivalent and write it alongside. Any girl not able to perform this simple task, put her hand up.' He waited.

All over the room, heads were quickly lowered over maths exercise books and girls began writing. Just two hands were raised. One was Roberta's and the other was Rebecca's.

'Please, Max,' said Roberta, 'it's over a year since we did this and I just can't quite remember.'

'Okay, Bobbie,' he spoke soothingly. 'Come and sit beside me and we'll talk. It'll soon come back to you.'

'Thanks!' Roberta said, adding hastily: 'I just need to brush up – I know how to do it really.'

Max was staring fixedly at Rebecca.

'You are –?'

'Rebecca Mason.'

She knew at once that he had recognized her.

'Didn't I bump into you last night?' he said wittily.

'That's right,' said Rebecca. 'I fell off my Malibu board – I'm sorry.'

There were a few snorts.

'What's the problem now?'

'The problem is that I've never done it before.'

'Surfing?' asked Max and the whole class burst out laughing.

'No, I mean –' Rebecca began, her colour rising, 'I was at a different school last year and –'

'All right.' Max hardly seemed to be listening. 'I'll deal with Roberta first as she's only got a minor problem and then I'll get round to you.'

Max thinks I'm dumb, I can tell, thought Rebecca.

Roberta had already scuttled up to his table. He drew up a spare chair and they sat there together, talking very quietly, heads close together. Sue and Tish made some wildly comic faces at each other and at Rebecca and then bent over their work. Rebecca idly doodled a picture of a Malibu board with shark's teeth and waited for Max to finish with Roberta. She waited a long time. *She's only supposed to have a minor problem!* thought Rebecca as she watched. Max kept scribbling numbers down on a notepad and explaining them in a low patient voice. As soon as he finished, Roberta would pipe up again with another question. Rebecca began to wonder if it might take the whole lesson.

Tish passed Rebecca a note, straight across Sue.

How long does it take when she's got a MAJOR problem? T.

They both hiccupped with laughter. Rebecca showed Sue the note and she laughed, too. 'Shut up!' requested Max. He continued to speak to Roberta and Rebecca continued to doodle on the cover of her book until, at long last, she heard the scraping of a chair up at the front of the class. Roberta returned to her desk, a self-satisfied smile on her face. She looked – Tish said later – as though she had just cracked Einstein's theory of relativity, single-handed.

With a sigh of relief, Rebecca waited to be summoned. Max sat behind his table sideways on, his long legs elegantly crossed, frowning in concentration. He seemed to be making some workings-out on his notepad. Rebecca gained the impression that he had completely forgotten her existence. Finally, too shy to call out, she scraped her chair back and started to get to her feet. Even as she did so, the door opened and Mrs Devenshire, the school secretary, appeared. She was out of breath and slightly cross at having to climb so many stairs. Her office was at the bottom of old school and the II Alpha form room, with its sloping ceilings and funny little windows, was right up at the top.

'You're wanted on the telephone, Mr Maxwell,' she said.

'Am I?' He beamed and sprang up and headed for the door, then stopped as he remembered his class. He turned to them. 'Work on. I'll be taking your books in at the end of the lesson and the marks will be going down on your weekly mark sheet. If any girl hasn't managed to finish I'll want to know what she's been doing – oh,' he realized for the first time that Rebecca was standing up. 'Look on my table and you'll find your last year's text book. Chapter 5 I think it is. It'll refresh your memory.'

'I was at a different school last year –' Rebecca began again.

He shot out of the doorway. Rebecca walked up to his table and noticed that he'd been making a diagram on his notepad. It looked like a hang-glider, with a lot of measurements and calculations jotted all round it. She found a First Year Maths text book, took it back and turned to Chapter 5.

'I think he's designing a hang-glider,' she whispered to Sue.

'Really?' said Sue.

'Hang-glider?' exclaimed Tish. 'Must have a look in a minute.' She bent her head over her work, going steadily through the numbers.

'Isn't he athletic looking?' said Judy Sharp, who sat the other side of Tish. 'Was he out surfing last night then?'

'Yes. And he's really good. Rebecca got in his way!'

'I bet hang-gliding's fun.' That was Josselyn Vining's voice, from further along the back row. 'I'd love to try it.' Trust Joss!

Soon, there was so much chattering and whispering going on at the back of the form room that Rebecca couldn't take in a word of Chapter 5. She envied the ease with which the others could do the work and discuss Max at the same time! She must find out about these wretched numbers!

'Sue!' she pleaded, as soon as Sue had put her pen down. 'Help me!'

'It's easy,' said Sue, pointing to the first row of figures. 'See that 1? Well it's not a 1 really, it's a 2. Get it?'

Rebecca didn't. Now there was a fresh diversion.

Tish had gone up to the front of the room and had found Max's design and was showing it round the class. Then she put it back and perched on the edge of the table. She swung her legs and surveyed everyone, just as Max had done when he first arrived.

'Hallo,' she declaimed, giving a horrible sickly grin and

imitating Miss Gates' voice. 'My name's Miss Gates. My friends call me Gatesy. You can, too.'

Everyone hooted with laughter, even Debbie Rickard, who usually hated Tish. Roberta Jones actually smiled and her eyes sparkled a little. Tish carried on in this vein, getting wilder and wilder, finally climbing up on to the table and flapping her arms up and down. 'Don't mind me, girls, but I'm just going off to do a little hang-gliding.'

The girls were almost in hysterics and Rebecca could feel the tears of mirth running down her cheeks. Crash! Tish leapt high into the air from the table, flapping her arms, and landed almost at the door.

'Bye, bye, girls!'

The door burst open. Tish found herself face to face with none other than Miss Gates herself, who had been just passing by. Tish's arms were still upraised. Slowly, very slowly, she lowered them to her sides. Slowly, too, the uproar in the form-room subsided until it was no more than a few sniffs and snorts.

'Go to your desk, Ishbel,' said the grey-haired senior mistress. 'Who is taking this class?'

'I am,' said Max, sauntering in. 'What a racket!'

'I see you left them unattended,' commented Miss Gates icily.

'I'm sure they've all finished the work I set them,' said Max, quite unperturbed. 'Have you, girls?'

'Yes!' they all roared, anxious to protect Max from Miss Gates.

The bell for morning break sounded.

Miss Gates marched out of the room. As she went, Max gave her back view a solemn salute. It was all the girls could do to hold in their laughter. He then faced the class and clapped his hands.

'Books in, please.'

The eighteen members of Form II Alpha filed up with their maths exercise books and placed them in a pile. Roberta had hers open and showed it to Max. There was a very happy smile on her face.

'Done the whole lot, eh, Bobbie?' he said, abstractedly. 'Good for you.'

'I haven't done any at all,' said Rebecca apologetically, holding the text book. 'I'm afraid I still don't understand them.'

'Keep the book and learn Chapter 5 off by heart,' he said briefly. 'It's all explained in words of one syllable. I'll test you tomorrow, if there's time.'

'It's not fair!' exclaimed Rebecca later, as she and Tish and Sue collected their orange squash and biscuits in the dining hall. 'He spends all that time with Roberta, who's done it before.'

'Robert's hopeless at maths,' interrupted Tish.

'– and then when it comes to me, he tells me to read it all up in a book. Now I've got some extra prep to do!'

'It hasn't really dawned on him yet that you weren't here last year,' said Sue. 'But he would have shown you, if his girlfriend hadn't rung him up in the middle of the lesson!'

They all laughed, but Rebecca said wryly:

'If I'd twisted his arm, he would. He thinks I'm useless, I can tell.'

At that moment Roberta walked into the dining hall with the Nathan twins. She looked like someone in a happy daze.

'Robert's still glowing from it all!' said Tish. 'She can't believe her luck.'

'Glowing? Undoubtedly the Max factor,' cracked Sue. Tish and Rebecca groaned.

'What's Roberta got that I haven't?' inquired Rebecca, later. 'Whatever it is, I must try and cultivate it.'

'You'll be all right, Becky, don't worry,' said Tish, as they drank their squash. You heard what he said – he's going to go through everything we've done, step by step. You'll soon catch up. And you must admit it's going to be a lot of fun having him.'

'I suppose so,' nodded Rebecca. 'Though I'd like to have seen this Mrs Shaw. The one you said was so good.'

'Maybe,' conceded Sue. 'But I'll tell you something –' she pushed her spectacles up her nose and grinned, 'Max is better looking than Mrs Shaw.'

'*And* Miss Gates,' said Tish. 'Put together.'

'Especially put together, I should think,' said Rebecca.

They laughed.

Evelyn Gates spent the morning break with Madeleine Welbeck, the principal of Trebizon. They had been drinking coffee together in Miss Welbeck's panelled study in the school's main building, once an eighteenth-century manor house. The study's first floor windows overlooked ancient parkland. The huge oaks had lost their bare brown winter outlines and were dense with young green leaves. The morning sun slanted amongst them on to rolling hillocks of grass and Miss Welbeck, half-closing her eyes, could imagine herself back in the Middle Ages, walking in that lovely parkland. There had been a house on this site even then.

She returned to the twentieth century. The two women had been sorting out a timetable problem for the advanced maths group, who had important exams looming up. When that had been resolved, Miss Gates got up to go.

'That young man, Dennis Maxwell, has the right name,' she said suddenly. 'I think he's going to be a bit of a menace.'

'Really?' said Miss Welbeck, in surprise. 'I think we're lucky to have got him, Evelyn. He has much charm – and a brilliant mind.' She gave a teasing smile. 'His knowledge of new advances in the field of pure mathematics outstrips mine – and probably yours, too!'

'Why's he not got a permanent post somewhere then?'

Miss Welbeck gazed out of her window and smiled.

'He's young. He doesn't want to settle anywhere yet. He enjoys life! Trebizon's a very pleasant spot in the summer, especially when he has a girlfriend in the town here. He's quite a find, Evelyn! I'm sure the girls will respond to him.'

'I'm sure they will,' nodded Miss Gates, sagely.

'Dennis,' she muttered, as she left the room. 'Dennis the Menace.'

FIVE

TWO TRIUMPHS

Wednesday turned out very well in the end. After break, there was German with Herr Fischer. No-one started German until the Second Year, so Rebecca was up with the rest. Then there was double French with Ma'm'selle Giscard, who always made her lessons interesting, when she remembered where they were. Dinner was only passable although the gravy was better than usual, but pudding was a light treacle sponge and custard – delicious. It was good to have Joss Vining back at the head of the table and she told Rebecca about the Athletics Club that met every Saturday afternoon in the summer term.

'I'll be joining that!' said Rebecca promptly.

She knew she could run well – but how well? She had never tested herself against proper competition. This would be her chance to find out.

After lunch came chemistry with Mr Douglas, in the laboratory at the top of the modern block that housed the dining and assembly halls. Rebecca was at the bench nearest the window, where she could keep a watchful eye on the weather. The sun had gone in and a cool breeze had sprung up. She hoped it wouldn't rain, because the last lesson was double games and it seemed that in the summer term they did tennis on a Wednesday.

The rain held off and they were able to go out on to the courts in track suits. Rebecca loved tennis, both watching it on TV and trying to play it. But sometimes her play drove her to despair.

'Have you played much?' asked Miss Willis, the games mistress. She was sorting them out into fours. 'Have you had any coaching at *all*?'

'I've just played in the park with friends, in London.'

Rebecca was put in a four with three girls from Form II Gamma, Susan McTavish, Anne Brett and Jane O'Hara. They went to Court 9 and then they started to knock the ball to one another. Rebecca quickly realized that she had been put in a 'weak' group for although she hit the ball wildly and could never make it go where she wanted it to, she could at least hit it much harder than the other three. Susan McTavish kept skying the ball high into the air and Jane O'Hara couldn't get it over the net at all.

There was a great deal of hilarity, but for twenty minutes Rebecca's knowledge of the game remained at a standstill. All that changed when Miss Willis came striding over from court 8, where she had been teaching four girls backhand volley.

'You three are hopeless,' she said to Susan, Jane and Anne. 'You've forgotten everything you learnt last summer. As for you, Rebecca,' she walked up to her, 'has nobody ever taught you how to grip the racket for the forehand?'

She held out her right hand.

'Shake hands with me.'

Puzzled, Rebecca did so, while the other three giggled. Then Miss Willis took Rebecca's racket from her, held it by the head and proffered the handle.

'Now shake hands with your racket. A good, hard, firm handshake.'

As Rebecca obeyed, Miss Willis nodded in satisfaction.

'That's it. The forehand grip. That's all there is to it. Now, let me show you what you should do with your feet as you come up to make a forehand drive – be quiet, you three, and watch, you might learn something –'

Ten minutes later, Rebecca was hitting good low, straight forehands over the net every time Miss Willis threw a ball to her. It was unbelievable! It was like magic! It was all a matter of doing it the right way, instead of the wrong way.

'I've got to try and get round,' Miss Willis said then. 'The Sixth Form run tennis coaching sessions for the juniors, all through the summer term. I suggest you put your name down, Rebecca.'

'I will!' said Rebecca in delight. Five minutes later it began to pour with rain and they all dashed back to Juniper House.

With time to kill before tea, she and Tish and Sue went to the library, in old school, to do their English prep. They found Mara had got there ahead of them. She was poring over some reference books and making notes.

'It's for a history project we've been set,' explained Mara. The Beta form had already had their first history lesson of the term. 'I want to get an A.'

'You really *have* made up your mind, haven't you?' said Tish fondly. 'Hey, maybe it's a good thing you don't like surfing. At least there won't be that to distract you!'

'Surfing!' The very mention of it filled Rebecca with excitement. She walked over to the long elegant windows. The library was on the ground floor and overlooked the main forecourt of old school; it had once been the drawing room of the big house. The rain was beating against the windows now and the wind was getting up.

There wouldn't be any surfing this evening.

Tish and Sue joined her and they watched the rain.

'Look, isn't that Max's girlfriend?' said Rebecca. 'In that red sports car parked near the wall. Remember her on the beach last night? Gorgeous looking, isn't she!'

'She's come to pick him up after work!' said Sue.

'She's not wasting any time then,' said Tish, looking round at the library clock. 'Lessons aren't over yet –'

Even as she spoke, a bell began to ring outside, signalling the end of afternoon lessons. It had scarcely finished reverberating when a figure came bounding out of the main school building, collar turned up against the rain, bulging briefcase in his hand. The girl at once threw open the passenger door of the sports car.

'Max isn't wasting any time either!' laughed Sue.

'Look!' exclaimed Rebecca. 'There's Roberta!'

Roberta Jones had appeared from nowhere, at a run, and headed Max off just before he could get into the car. She thrust an envelope into his hands, speaking eagerly, drops of rain running down her face. Max listened, smiled, nodded and took the envelope and stuck it under his jacket. His girlfriend, Kate, sounded the car horn noisily and Max promptly shunted Roberta off in the direction of the school and climbed into the car.

As it drove away, he waved to her and she waved back. There was a soppy look on her face and she hardly seemed aware of the rain.

'She was lying in wait for him!' giggled Sue.

'I wonder what was in that envelope?' asked Rebecca.

'A passionate love poem I expect,' snorted Tish. 'Gosh, he's soon going to get fed up with her if she carries on like this.'

They walked back to the long table where Mara was working and settled down alongside her and opened their English books. English was Rebecca's favourite subject, but now she couldn't settle down to her prep. She gave a heavy sigh.

'What's the matter?' asked Tish, always ready and eager to be distracted.

'Still can't understand that stuff about binary numbers. And he's going to test me tomorrow.'

Rebecca had been dipping into the maths text book all day, on and off, even in chemistry. She'd wanted to learn it and get it over with, especially as she'd thought there might be some surfing after tea.

'Oh, thought you were going to say something interesting!' wailed Tish.

'This is the library!' said a prefect who had just come in. 'Don't make so much noise.'

'Come on, Rebeck!' Tish's voice dropped to a very low whisper. She pulled her chair close to Rebecca's and put an arm round her shoulders. 'Here, give me your English book.'

She carefully extracted the centre pages from Rebecca's English exercise book, picked up her pen, and wrote down 1111.

'Now in ordinary numbers, denary that is, those four figures'd be thousands, hundreds, tens and units,' she whispered. 'After the units column, everything is to the power of ten. 1111 is 1 plus 10^1 plus 10^2 plus 10^3. Well, with binary numbers, instead of thinking in powers of ten you think in powers of two, except in the units column.' She was writing figures down as she spoke. 'So 1111, when it's a binary number, become 1 plus 2^1 plus 2^2 plus 2^3. Work out what that is in ordinary numbers.'

She thrust the pen and paper in front of Rebecca, who

frowned hard at what Tish had written down and thought about what she had been saying. She did some workings out and then scribbled an answer. 15.

'That's right!' exclaimed Tish.

'Sssssh!' said the prefect.

Tish leant over and wrote some more numbers down. 'Now try those!' she mouthed. Rebecca worked away in silence. As she got each answer correct, Tish grinned and put a thumb up. A feeling of relief swept over Rebecca. The book made it seem so difficult. But it was easy when someone explained it properly. Like that tennis forehand!

She'd just finished when the first tea bell rang. They all left their prep in the library and rushed outside. They'd have to come back and finish it after tea. Right now, they were hungry – and happy, especially Rebecca.

'Thanks!' she said to Tish. 'I still can't believe it's that simple! What do we need to know them for anyway?'

'Search me,' grinned Tish. 'Why do we need to know how to find the area of a trapezium, or how to prove triangles are congruent . . .'

'If you're an acrobat-ium,' said Sue, keeping a straight face, 'it's *vital* you know the area of a trapezium.'

'Arrgh.' They all groaned at such a terrible joke. But it was Mara, surprisingly, who answered Rebecca's question.

'Binary numbers are needed for computers,' she said. 'It means you can take any number at all and break it down into just ones and noughts. The computers prefer it that way!'

'Any number at all?' Rebecca thought about it for a moment. 'Yes, I suppose you can. Mara, you're brilliant! Have you had a brain transplant in the holidays?'

Mara shrieked and threw her history book at Rebecca. Rebecca ducked and it hit the wall, just as a prefect came round the corner.

'Pick that book up and go across and have your tea. Don't run! Walk.'

Yes, today had turned out well, Rebecca decided as she drank her cocoa in the Common Room, just before bedtime. She had marvellous friends and a lot of things to look forward to.

She walked across to the notice-board and looked at Roberta's play announcement. Only three people had signed up to be in it – Debbie Rickard and Sarah and Ruth Nathan. It was a shame, really. Poor old Roberta!

Roberta Jones created a minor sensation on Thursday morning. She arrived for breakfast wearing her hair loose. Rebecca had never seen her in anything but thick, droopy plaits before. Now her hair cascaded round her shoulders, brown and gleaming and well-brushed.

'Ye gods,' said Tish, as Roberta took her seat at the next table.

'It's maths first lesson,' observed Sue calmly.

It got the day off to a merry start, though Roberta was going to spring a much bigger surprise than that before the day was out.

It was another good day for Rebecca, in fact it was a superlative day, because it was on Thursday afternoon that she really got the hang of surfing.

Once again, the only jarring note of the day was struck by the maths lesson. Rebecca was almost looking forward to being tested on binary numbers, now she understood them. But Max forgot all about her. After handing them back their maths exercise books – and Rebecca's had a large red nought written on it – Max pressed straight on to talk about factorizing. This was something else that Rebecca had never done. Max rattled on about it at such speed that she still only half understood it when he wrote up an exercise on the blackboard and told them to get on with it.

Rebecca kept putting her hand up but although he briefly answered questions from Anne Finch and Aba Amori and Margot Lawrence, he just ignored her. Finally he settled down for another long session with Roberta. They seemed to be going through something together. At the time, Rebecca assumed it was yesterday's binary numbers and that Roberta had still managed to get them wrong.

'She's hopeless, isn't she?' whispered Sue. 'Come on, I'll help you.'

With Sue's help, Rebecca managed to do four of the ten questions on the board. Then the bell went and they had to hand their books in for marking.

The sun broke through the clouds just before dinner time and after that the friends could talk of nothing but surfing. It was double games again in the afternoon and on Thursdays, Tish told Rebecca, they could choose between several activities – including going in the sea, if they had their swimming certificates and the weather was good enough, with Harry supervising them.

Mara managed to get excused from games because she wanted to finish her history project ('Isn't she keen!' said someone) but the other five members of the 'Action Committee' couldn't wait to get down to the beach and into wet suits. They needed plenty of practice if they were going to raise a lot of money doing a Sponsored Surf for Charity Week. As for Rebecca, she was determined to master the art. Then she could get some sponsorships and be in it with the other four.

'Elf, you amaze me!' she shouted as the plump girl came streaking past her on her Malibu board, heading inshore, while she was still hard at work paddling hers out to beyond the breaker line. Sue, Tish and Margot rode in just behind

Elf, on the next breaker. They stood on their boards in a line like circus bareback riders – experts, all of them! *'Come on, Rebeck!'*

Gasping for breath, the salt spray in her face, lying tight to her board, Rebecca got out behind the breakers at last. She turned, gripped the board and waited for a big wave. As it came, she missed her footing on the Malibu and instead of riding in with the wave, it washed right over her. But she was still holding her board. The next wave came, not quite so big – she took it!

Gloriously, Rebecca felt herself being lifted high in the air. Like a tightrope walker she struggled to an upright position, arms outstretched, legs wobbling, getting her weight distributed evenly on the board . . . now it felt right! She was shooting in on the breaker at speed – it was sensational fun – she wasn't going to fall off this time! It was all a matter of balance.

'I can do it! I can do it!' she cried as she glided into the shallows. The others were holding their boards aloft, cheering her. Harry came wading into the water to meet her, smiling broadly.

'You're a natural, you are. You're well away now!'

'I can do it!' Rebecca said, yet again.

It was a moment of sweet triumph.

Roberta Jones's triumph – her big surprise – was yet to come.

The gang from dormitory six had enjoyed their surf riding so much that they collared Mara afterwards and walked along to the Hobbies' Room in Juniper House. 'You'd better help with the sponsorship form, Mara,' said Tish, 'as you're going to be the steward. Say how you'd like it set out and I'll type it out on a stencil skin. Then we can run all the forms off on the duplicator straight after tea.'

'And start finding people to sponsor us!' said Rebecca eagerly. She'd made six successful surf-rides in all. Now she was confident that she could take part. 'Some of the first years are planning to have a Sponsored Walk.'

'We'd better get in quickly then!' said Margot. 'We don't want everyone pledging their money to them first!'

But when they entered the Hobbies' Room, they found that Roberta Jones was using the typewriter. Sarah Nathan was reading a typescript to her and Roberta was laboriously transcribing it on to a stencil skin. She had already completed four stencils and this was the fifth. Ruth Nathan was fixing the first stencil up on to the duplicator. Debbie Rickard was hanging round watching. There was a general air of suppressed excitement.

'They've been here all afternoon,' Verity Williams told them, in a whisper. She was painting a water-colour in the Art Corner. 'Miss Morgan got them off games so they could do this.'

'How long are you going to be with the typewriter, Robert?' asked Tish, marching over. 'We need it for something.'

'Hours yet,' replied Roberta happily. 'We're duplicating my play. Miss Morgan's given permission.'

'Come on,' said Rebecca, taking Tish by the arm. 'Let's just rough out the sponsorship form somewhere. We can run it off tomorrow.'

'It's nearly teatime anyway,' said Sue. 'I'm starving.'

'It's the magazine meeting after tea,' remembered Margot.

'What on earth's she getting her play duplicated for?' exploded Tish, once they were out in the corridor. 'She's already had a lot of copies typed out in the holidays. Now she's running it off on the duplicator. Nobody wants to be in it, in any case.'

'Maybe she thinks they will if it's printed!' laughed Mara.

Rebecca was very surprised when Roberta didn't turn up for the magazine meeting, later. Jenny was there with her wire tray, collecting in contributions for the *Trebizon Journal* from girls who had brought them. She then told the assembled first years and second years that they still had a fortnight to submit something and they'd better try hard because this would be Audrey Maxwell's last issue. Roberta Jones turned up right at the end of the meeting.

'Hallo,' said Jenny, in a resigned voice. 'Have you got something?'

Roberta was usually the first person to plonk something in the wire tray. Every term she tried to get something shortlisted for the *Trebizon Journal*. But this time she just waved her hand, airily.

'Sorry, Jenny. Too busy. I just wondered if I might make a quick announcement. While there's a good crowd here.'

'Go ahead.'

'Well,' said Roberta, taking a deep breath, 'it's about my play.' People began to fidget but Roberta raised her voice. 'I know a lot of you haven't had time to sign up for tomorrow's auditions.' Everyone giggled at that word *auditions*. 'Well, don't bother to sign up, just come along. And by the way,' she backed towards the door of the Common Room and made her dramatic exit line:

'In case you think the play isn't much good, you might like to know that Mr Maxwell likes it very much and has agreed to act as producer. In fact he'll be taking tomorrow's meeting.'

She left behind her a stunned silence.

Rebecca's moment of triumph in Trebizon Bay had been sweet. But Roberta's was even sweeter.

SIX

LOOKING FORWARD TO CHARITY WEEK

'He must be mad,' said Sue, for about the tenth time, as the whole dormitory discussed it, long after lights out. 'Fancy wanting to produce *A Midsummer Night's Nightmare* or whatever it's called.'

'Stark, staring mad,' agreed Elf, who had read the play.

'I think I'll go along all the same,' giggled Joanna Thompson, up in the corner. 'This should be funny.'

'Who won't be going along?' said Rebecca, sleepily. 'I mean, who's going to miss this? I can't wait!'

Similar conversations were taking place all over Juniper House, with the result that the Second Year Common Room was packed out for Roberta's play meeting the next day, more packed than Rebecca had ever seen it. In fact the six of them hadn't bothered to rush over their school dinner, and now found it quite impossible to get in. They joined the jostling throng in the corridor, crowding round the door, up on tip-toes to try and get a look.

Max was taking the meeting, standing behind a table at the top end of the room. Roberta was seated demurely beside him. The freshly-stencilled copies of the play had already been handed out, one between three, and were being eagerly read. Just inside the door, Jenny Brook-Hayes had managed to get one and was flicking through it rapidly.

'Still the same play, Jenny?' asked Sue in a loud whisper.

'No fear!' said Jenny. 'He's just about rewritten it!'

Max began to speak loudly and the room fell quiet.

'This play is going to be a lot of fun and I'm sure it'll raise a lot of money for Charity Week. So here's a chance for any girl who likes acting and isn't already fixed up in a group, to do her bit. Bobbie and I have decided to change the title to *A Woodland Comedy*.'

'It was a tragedy before!' Sally Elphinstone hissed to Rebecca, on the verge of laughter.

'You've rewritten it, sir,' piped up a first year girl in the room.

'No, no, not at all,' said Max, glancing at Roberta. 'Just a few minor changes, with Bobbie's permission. We've cut down the number of parts to ten and introduced a little light-hearted dialogue.'

Roberta nodded happily. She was wearing her hair loose for the second day running.

'By the way,' Max continued, 'it occurred to me that the play should be performed in the open air and that South Terrace by the Music School would be the perfect setting. The trees and lake there will give us the rustic atmosphere, in fact it makes a perfect open-air theatre – as long as the weather's kind to us –'

They laughed as they looked at the rain beating on the windows.

His enthusiasm was infectious. A stir of interest was running round the room. When he asked how many people would like to be in the play about twenty hands shot up. 'Okay, everyone who's put their hand up had better take a copy of the play away with them. Look at it carefully. We'll have another meeting after school and hold auditions. Where do you suggest, Bobbie –?'

He turned to her deferentially.

'I'll ask Miss Willis if we can use the gym, shall I?' said Roberta.

'For those who don't get a part in the play, there'll be plenty of other jobs,' said Max. 'We'll need help with props and costumes and –'

'Come on,' said Tish, as the meeting continued. 'I'm getting a crick in my neck. Let's do the sponsorship form now, shall we?'

'We've heard enough!' said Mara, with a smile.

As they moved off down the corridor Rebecca heard Debbie Rickard's voice raised in the meeting:

'Please, Max, I've already been given the part of fairy queen. Roberta promised it to me.'

They all laughed and jostled and shoved each other down the stairs to the Hobbies' Room on the ground floor. They were very impressed, all the same.

'So that's what she gave him on Wednesday!' said Rebecca. 'Her play. She must have asked him for suggestions.'

'He rewrote it and then they went through it together, in the lesson yesterday morning!' Tish realized. 'He was showing her all the changes.'

'But fancy him agreeing to produce it as well!' said Margot. 'It'll be good now! Roberta's group will probably raise the most money.'

'Not if we can help it!' said Tish, pushing open the door of the Hobbies' Room. 'Come on, let's get this form worked out and then I'll make a stencil for it.'

Mara worked out a layout quickly and Tish just managed to finish typing the stencil when the bell went for afternoon school. First lesson was physics and then there would be double games.

'We'll come back straight after games and run it off on the duplicator. There's room for ten sponsors on each form and as we'll each want to try and get loads, we'd better have several forms each.'

The weather was very bad again, so although Friday was another tennis afternoon, it was called off and the girls did PE in the gym, instead. Rebecca was disappointed about that. Obviously there would be no surfing that evening, either. Well, they could get the forms run off and start collecting some sponsorships, instead.

They had showers after the PE lesson, and before leaving the sports centre Rebecca looked back in the gym. She saw that Roberta was arranging chairs in a big circle. She was getting everything ready for Max and company. She usually looked so stolid but now, with her hair loose and a soft expression on her face, she looked quite different.

On the way back, Rebecca and Tish met Sue outside the Hilary. Sue had orchestra practice on Friday afternoons, instead of games. They looked across at South Terrace, on the far side of the Music School. It was framed by trees that overhung the waters of the little lake. The leaves were dripping after the recent downpours, but as she gazed dreamily at the scene, Rebecca could imagine it in sunshine, peopled by goblins and elves and a fairy queen.

'You've got to hand it to Max,' she said. 'It'll make a lovely setting for the play. I bet a lot of people will turn up.'

Max's girlfriend wasn't very pleased about the play.

Rebecca discovered that quite by accident. When they got to the Hobbies' Room they found that Roberta had used up the last of the duplicating paper and they needed some more. It was kept in a cupboard in the school office and Rebecca offered to run over to the old building and get some. If Mrs Devenshire had gone home she wouldn't mind them taking some. Rebecca had often done it before, on a Sunday. They always seemed to run out of paper on Sunday evenings, in the middle of printing the *Juniper Journal*!

The door of the school office was ajar. Rebecca was about to go in when she heard Max's voice. He had nipped in to use the phone! She hung around in the corridor, waiting for him to come out. He and Katie were having a shouting match.

'I did *not* spend all evening on that play, I spent about an hour on it . . . and only because it was a mess . . .' Then: 'Look, Katie, be reasonable, the kids are trying to raise some money for charity. They need some help with this play. Yes, sure it means staying late a few afternoons . . . but the whole thing'll be over in a fortnight . . . sorry, Katie. I've said I'll do it now and that's that. I'll see you later.'

As Rebecca heard the phone slam down, she walked heavily up to the door, as though she'd just that minute arrived. She marched in as Max marched out. He hardly noticed her. He just went off down the corridor with long, easy strides, his dark hair looking rather rumpled. He was whistling.

After she'd had tea and done her prep, Rebecca wandered round Juniper House collecting up sponsorships. Josselyn Vining was amazed that she'd learnt to surf ride so quickly and signed up her name on Rebecca's form, pledging two pence for each ride Rebecca could make before she fell off.

'Who'll be there to see you don't cheat?'

'Well Mara will be keeping score, as she doesn't like surfing, but Joanne Hissup is drafting in some prefects as well. They'll supervise and double-check. It should turn into quite a contest between Tish and Margot!'

'Could I be in it, too?' asked Joss suddenly. 'I was going to run a cake stall with Jenny and Co., but the wretches have gone and got themselves in this play!'

'I'm sure you can, Joss!' said Rebecca in delight. 'I'll ask the others when I see them.'

'Don't forget Athletics Club's tomorrow afternoon,' the junior school head of games said, as she walked away. 'Let's see what your sprinting times are like.'

Rebecca had no intention of forgetting.

That night, in the dormitory, Jenny Brook-Hayes and Joanna Thompson confessed that they had gone along to the second play meeting, just for interest. But the auditions had been such fun, they'd decided to join in, and Max had given them each a part. They were slightly shamefaced about it.

'We found out that some of the first years are planning a cake stall, anyway.'

'No point in duplicating.'

'Of course not!' said Tish. 'Let's face it, the play's going to be quite good now.'

She was feeling happy because Joss was going to join them in the Sponsored Surf. It was a feather in their caps. What a contest it would be now! A big crowd would come to watch and that meant they should be able to pull in a lot of last-minute sponsorships on the day.

'Have you noticed, Becky, Robert's suddenly got nicer,' Tish said, at bedtime. They were both gazing out of the window by Rebecca's bed. 'She came up to me at cocoa time – and you know how you have to twist everyone's arm – well, she offered to sponsor me, without me even asking! Two pence a ride!'

'I had noticed,' said Rebecca. She gazed out at the night sky. The heavy cloud that had lain above Trebizon Bay all day had now cleared away and she could see the stars quite clearly. 'It's obvious why.'

'Yes,' said Tish. 'Somebody really likes her at last.'

'I wish Max liked me,' Rebecca said with a sigh. The maths lesson that morning had been yet another disaster. Max had demonstrated a lot of instructive games they could play with calculators. The only trouble was that Rebecca didn't have a calculator. When it came to setting prep for the weekend it was some horrible algebra that she hadn't the faintest idea how to do.

'Don't think about maths,' said Tish.

'Don't worry, I'm not going to,' replied Rebecca.

There were too many other things to think about. All of them were preferable to maths.

SEVEN

ALL SET

It was a hectic weekend. It was so hectic that Rebecca completely forgot to do her maths prep. She remembered it late on Sunday evening, just before she fell asleep, by which time it was too late to do anything about it!

The weather was good that weekend. The rainclouds had disappeared and clear blue skies and sunshine appeared, to welcome in the month of May.

'I've got a feeling it's going to be a long, hot summer!' said Tish after breakfast on Saturday morning. 'Wouldn't that be nice?'

'Yes,' nodded Rebecca. At the end of spring term she'd joined the Gardening Club. She'd planted seeds in her own patch in the walled kitchen gardens at the back of the stable block. Sometime over the weekend she must go and see how they were getting on! A sunny May coming after a fairly wet April would do them the world of good.

'What are you two doing after we've seen the film?' asked Tish.

'I'm going to the Hilary,' said Sue. 'Mr Barrington wants to see all the Music Scholars at eleven o'clock. It's something to do with a Youth Music Festival in the summer holidays.'

Life was exciting for Sue since she'd been elected one of the school's Music Scholars at the end of last term.

'I've got my first tennis coaching!' said Rebecca. 'I'm in Pippa's group and we're to meet on court number three.'

'I'll do my prep maybe,' said Tish.

First they went to see the film, in the assembly hall. All the juniors had been ordered to go. It was followed by a talk. Although most of Juniper House turned up, a few girls had skived off because it was such a lovely morning. If it had been Walt Disney or Laurel and Hardy it might have been different, but this film was called 'Animals need Real Kindness' and had a serious message throughout.

Animals need Real Kindness, ARK for short, was a well-known charity. It was never easy to decide which charity should benefit from the special fund-raising week that the juniors organized each May. There were so many deserving causes. This year ARK had been chosen and now the charity's west country organizer, a lady called Julia White, had come to show the film to the girls and talk to them afterwards.

It was a good charity, efficiently run, with the aim of alleviating any kind of unnecessary suffering amongst animals. The film 'Animals need Real Kindness' showed the wide range of its activities. These included providing free vets for people too poor to have their pets made better, saving old horses and looking after animals that had been neglected or ill-treated. Some parts of the film brought Rebecca close to tears, especially the sight of a tiny puppy that had been abandoned and would have died if it hadn't been brought to an ARK centre in the nick of time.

'The whole school should have come!' whispered Sue indignantly, as soon as the film had ended. 'Then they'd really want to give all the cash they've got to Charity Week!

'We ought to write it up in the *J.J.*!' said Tish at once. 'We're compiling a list of the fund-raising events. We ought to describe ARK properly – this film and everything.'

'Yes!' said Mara. 'Let's ask Susannah what she thinks!'

The juniors' weekly news-sheet, the *Juniper Journal*, was produced by an editorial committee of three consisting of Mara, Tish and Susannah Skelhorn, who represented the first years and collected in all their contributions. Tish typed the stencils and they printed it on the duplicator on Sunday evenings, front and back of a single sheet of paper, to be sold around the school for five pence a copy on Monday. It even had quite a good sale in the Staff Room.

'Rebecca must write it!' said Susannah when Tish ran over to her. 'She's the best writer.'

Mrs Beal, about to introduce the speaker, clapped her hands for order. Tish ran back to her seat and spoke quickly behind her hand.

'Ask questions at the end, Rebeck. Write it all down.'

'Okay!' said Rebecca, feeling flustered and pleased. She found some scraps of paper in the pocket of her skirt and Sue produced a ballpoint pen. After that, she carefully noted down points from the charity worker's talk and asked two questions at the end, feeling like a proper reporter. Sue also stood up and asked a question:

'Can you tell us how much £1 could do and how much £5 could do and how much £10 could do?'

'That's a very good question,' said Julia White. 'I'll give you some examples.'

Rebecca wrote them down as quickly as she could. That would fit in well to the piece she was going to write!

For the rest of the morning she kept planning out what she would say. It was there in the back of her mind, all the time, even when she was at tennis coaching.

'Throw the ball up straight, Rebecca. You'll never, never have a good service if you don't learn to throw the ball up straight.'

'Sorry, Pippa.'

But at the end of the session she was surprised and faintly excited when Pippa took her aside for a moment and said:

'Rebecca Mason, I think you might make a tennis player one day.'

'Me?'

'Yes, you. Practise throwing things up straight whenever you can. Just use a shoe, anything that's handy. See you next Saturday?'

'Yes!'

Rebecca wrote her first rough draft in the dinner hour. It was rushed and a bit of a jumble, but she wanted to get her thoughts down about ARK and why it was important. She mustn't make it boring! She badly wanted all the people who hadn't been to the film to read about it and not just skip over it. Juniper House wanted their pocket money: this was the reason why! Once she'd got something down on paper she felt better and she hurried off to the Athletics Club.

The Club meeting was the high point of the day. The school was lucky. Angela Hessel, who had twice represented Great Britain in the pentathlon in the Olympic Games, actually lived near Trebizon these days with her husband and three children. She came in as Athletics Coach every summer term. For most of the afternoon she was busy coaching some of the seniors in the high jump – Joanne Hissup, the senior Head of Games, was regarded as an England prospect. While that was going on, Joss Vining timed Rebecca's running over four different distances – 100 metres, 200 metres, 400 metres and 800 metres. That just confirmed what they'd guessed. Rebecca was best at sprinting, not the middle distances.

At the end of the afternoon Angela Hessel spent five whole minutes with her, showing her how to start from blocks. Rebecca practised starting for a while and then did the 100 metres again. Tish timed her this time.

'What did I do?' gasped Rebecca after she'd crossed the 100 metres line, slowing down and looking back over her shoulder.

'Fourteen seconds!' yelled Tish, looking at the stop-watch.

'Is that good?' asked Rebecca. Heaving for breath, she walked back to pick her track suit up off the grass. 'I'm shattered. I thought I was quite fit, but I can't be.'

'Nobody is at the beginning of term,' said Judy Sharp coming over from the long jump pit. She watched Rebecca put her track suit on over her shorts and blue tee shirt. Athletics Club was over for the afternoon. 'What time did she do, Tish?'

'14.'

'Hey, that's quite good for a start!'

'Is it really quite good?' asked Rebecca as they walked away from the sports field. Tish liked distance running and had spent the afternoon fairly gently, just jogging round and round the track. 'What do you think?'

'Yes. You only have to do 13.5 seconds and you'll qualify for the junior 100 metres on Sports Day.'

'When is Sports Day?' asked Rebecca.

'Friday before half-term. A lot of parents come down for it and then take us back home afterwards. Will yours –?'

One look at Rebecca's face was enough. Her parents were due for two months' leave in the summer, but they'd still be in Saudi Arabia at the end of May. She would have liked them to come to Sports Day!

'13.5?' repeated Rebecca, when the miserable feeling had subsided.

Silently she vowed that, parents or no parents, she was going to qualify for the 100 metres sprint on Sports Day – and the 200 metres, too!

'The junior record's 12.4,' Tish added casually. 'Get near that and you'd go through to the Area Sports after half-term, then probably the County Sports at the end of term.'

'Let's go and find Sue,' Rebecca said, changing the subject. 'She's probably finished playing tennis by now. Let's all have some fizzy at Moffatt's.'

From that moment onwards, Rebecca decided that although she wanted to learn how to play tennis properly, and surf-riding was the most exciting new thing she had ever done, only one thing really mattered this term. She wanted to run in the County Sports, at the end of term, when her parents would be back in England to see her!

She spent Saturday evening in the library, alone. She wanted it that way. After rushing through some French prep as fast as she possibly could, she worked on the piece about ARK. One of the problems was getting it all into 400 words, which was the most she could be allowed in the little news-sheet. She polished the phrases up, rewrote some bits and cut others. At last she was satisfied with it. The bedtime bell was going. She would copy it out neatly some time tomorrow and then hand it to Tish to go into the *Juniper Journal*.

Sunday morning the weather was still fine and they went surfing after church and before Sunday lunch. The sunshine and clear skies were deceptive for the breakers were much higher than they'd been on Thursday afternoon, when Rebecca had done so well. She kept coming off her

Malibu board at first, but she finished the morning with two glorious rides.

'I hope the waves aren't as high as that on the day we do it,' she said to Margot afterwards. 'I won't raise a penny if I come off first time, like this morning.'

'You'll be all right if you keep practising!' said Margot, droplets of salt water on her gleaming skin. In her wet suit she was all black sheen.

They saw Roberta Jones coming back across the sands with Sarah and Ruth Nathan. They'd been for a walk right across the bay. Shading her eyes and looking into the distance, Rebecca saw the reason. Max was surfing on the far side of the bay on his unmistakable red Malibu board. They had been to watch him.

They all met Mara as they went into the dining hall. In contrast to their healthy open-air glow she looked frowsy and her large brown eyes lacked their usual lustre. She had spent the morning on some difficult prep, determined to get good marks for it.

On Sunday afternoon Rebecca copied out her piece for the *J.J.* and took it along to the Hobbies' Room. Tish was busy sorting out all the material that Mara and Susannah had gathered up, putting it into some sort of order. Then she would begin to type the stencils. Her sister had taught her how to type properly which was how she came to be editor of the *J.J.* Susannah, who was very good at art, was roughing out a layout for the news-sheet with some possible headlines such as: BEST EVER CHARITY WEEK PLANNED and START SAVING YOUR MONEY NOW. It had been decided to turn the whole issue over to Charity Week, with a complete list of all the events that the First and Second Years were planning.

'Hey, this is you at your best,' said Tish, quickly reading through Rebecca's piece. 'This should come first, before anything else, with a really eye-catching headline. Something like: ANIMALS NEED REAL KINDNESS – DON'T READ THIS IF YOU'RE SQUEAMISH.'

When the issue went on sale on Monday, a lot of people congratulated Tish – and Rebecca – but not Debbie Rickard. She came up at morning break with Roberta Jones.

'Fancy putting that gruesome piece in as the main story. You know full well the play's the big story – but you've just shoved it in a list with all the other things that are happening. You jealous or something?'

'Shut up, you silly fool,' was Tish's comment.

Debbie took it for granted that Roberta felt the way she did. She was amazed when Roberta suddenly touched Rebecca's arm.

'It's a beautiful piece,' she said. 'Now the whole school will known what Charity Week's all about this year.'

'Hasn't she changed!' whispered Sue, as the pair walked away.

'It's Max,' said Tish.

Rebecca smiled. But she was touched. It made her hard work seem worthwhile. She was even more touched in maths, which was the first lesson after break, when Roberta said:

'*Don't* give her a penalty mark, Max! She really didn't have time to do her prep. She was writing up something for Charity Week, a lovely piece about . . .'

But for once Max cut Roberta short.

'I don't care if Rebecca was writing the Domesday Book. She was supposed to do some algebra.'

During the next two weeks the excitement in Juniper House increased as Charity Week drew near. In spite of rain, and Athletics Club was cancelled two Saturdays running, Rebecca got some more surf-riding in. She was getting quite good at the art of remaining upright on a speeding Malibu board. Battling against tough opposition from those First Years who were organizing a sponsored walk, Rebecca managed to get 34 sponsors in all. She worked out that she would raise, in one and two pences, forty pence for each ride she could make before she either fell off or got exhausted. Two of the others had done even better. Joss would be making forty-six pence a ride! Their great ambition still was to raise more money than any other group, even the play crowd.

During the fortnight, maths lessons were a riot. There were nine girls in II Alpha involved with the play, one half of the class. At every opportunity they sidetracked Max into talking about it. There was a kind of carnival atmosphere in the air. Once Miss Gates walked in just as Max was demonstrating to Judy Sharp how to do a little goblin dance. She silenced the hilarity with an unusual display of anger.

'I am trying to give a lesson in the next room!' she said to the girls. At Max she directed a look that would have withered the sun. He became very brisk and strict for the rest of the lesson.

Rebecca enjoyed these diversions as much as anyone, but she felt uneasy, sometimes, come evening when she was struggling with maths prep. She always seemed to be doing things again.

'Don't worry,' said Sue once. 'Everything'll settle down once Charity Week's over.'

The surfing gang were overjoyed when it was agreed that the Sponsored Surf should take place on Sunday morning. So it would be the very first event of the Week!

They suffered agonies on the Saturday when wind and rain came. They'd put up posters all over the school and they knew that plenty of people wanted to come, especially to see Joss, Tish and Margot fighting it out. It was bound to develop into a marathon between these three, long after the others had dropped out. How many pounds might they not raise between them! But if the weather was bad the whole thing would have to be postponed until later in the week when there would be counter-attractions, including prep.

To their utter relief, Sunday morning dawned clear.

Tish and Rebecca went down to the beach early and planted a big banner they had made: SUPPORT THE SPONSORED SURF FOR ARK. The bay was deserted and the waves rolled in long, unbroken lines of white foam on to golden sand. Perfect conditions! They heard a faint cry high above them. For a moment Rebecca thought it was a seagull and then, looking up, she saw a solitary hang-glider sailing past, high above them. The cry came again and it sounded like 'Good Luck!'

'It's Max – it must be!' exclaimed Tish, staring upwards.

They both waved feverishly, laughing in delight.

'Nothing can go wrong now!' exclaimed Rebecca. 'Even Max is on our side.'

'Not to mention over your head as usual!'

He went drifting gently onwards, towards a patch of rosy sky.

EIGHT

THE BITTER END

'We've even had a visitation from the sky!' Tish said to the others, as they all went down to the beach at nine o'clock. 'A guardian angel flew over!'

There was excited laughter. Max belonged to the Hang-Gliding Club over at Mulberry but no-one had actually seen him airborne until today. It was just the right, zany start to what proved to be a wonderful morning.

The six surfers got there early and changed into wet suits. Dozens of girls from the school, as well as members of staff, were soon joined by local people and some early holidaymakers about in Trebizon Bay. They all gathered around the big banner and waited.

Mara had some spare forms down on the beach and Rebecca and Co. moved amongst the bystanders, collecting more signatures.

'How long have you been surfing?' asked a good-looking boy whom Rebecca had noticed around the town occasionally. He was preparing to sign her form, tapping his chin with end of a pencil.

'Less than three weeks!' said Rebecca.

'Is that all? Then I bet you don't do more than three rides

without falling off!' He laughed. 'Here, I'll sponsor you for three pence a ride.'

'Thanks,' said Rebecca, demurely, determined to surprise him.

She found seven more sponsors at a penny a ride, bringing the money pledged up to a grand total of fifty pence a ride. What an incentive to do well! Joss managed to get her total up to eighty pence a ride.

Everything was ready. Mara and a prefect called Della Thomas were up on high umpire chairs, borrowed from the tennis courts. The chairs stood squarely on the sand, looking out to sea. As stewards, they had blue cards on which they'd tick off the number of rides each girl made. Joanna Hissup herself had turned up and took charge of the metal cash box, so that money could be collected quickly from the new sponsors, as soon as a girl's score was known.

'All set?' Harry blew his whistle. 'Go!'

The six girls ran into the water, splashing and laughing and holding their Malibu boards aloft. As soon as the water was above the waist they jumped themselves flat on to their boards and paddled furiously with their hands to get out beyond the breaker line.

'The waves are breaking miles out today!' gasped Rebecca to Sue, who was alongside her, looking different without her glasses. 'It's going to take longer to get out!'

'Longer rides coming in!' yelled Sue eagerly.

'Long enough to fall off, too!' shouted Rebecca, in some trepidation. She thought of all the people watching from the shore. Now that the moment had come she dreaded making a fool of herself. Supposing she fell off on her first ride? Then she would have to come out – without having raised a single penny for ARK. 'Look at those three!'

Margot, Tish and Joss were forging ahead. They were almost out beyond the breakers. Elf wasn't very far behind them. Rebecca redoubled her efforts, battling through the spray. This was going to be the hardest part, getting out each time!

Rebecca rose to the occasion. Tish, Margot and Joss made a superb first ride in, all in a line, and a cheer went up for them. Sue, Rebecca and Elf followed a few breakers later, not quite so expert, and a bit raggedy-looking, but they made it and another cheer went up! Elf raised a hand to acknowledge the cheers and slipped off the Malibu at the water's edge, but no-one counted that as a fall.

'I've raised fifty pence!' thought Rebecca in relief, turning round and heading straight back out to sea again. 'Now for the next one!'

By the eighth ride, Rebecca was exhausted, but she hadn't come off yet. This time, though, she wobbled badly, half-way back to shore. Her arms flailed round and round like windmill sails as she fought to keep upright on the speeding board. Then, nerve-rackingly, she steadied herself and managed to complete the ride. A crowd of First Years shouted and cheered.

On the ninth ride a big breaker took her up before she had properly got her balance and tossed Rebecca in one direction and the Malibu in another. It was all over! She shook the water out of her eyes and minutes later carried the Malibu on her back, up the sandy shore, to cheers intermingled with a slow handclap. She was first out. But she hadn't disgraced herself by any means! The nice boy came up.

'You've been doing it more than three weeks, I bet!' But he was smiling and digging his hand into his pocket. 'Who do I give the twenty-four pence to, anyway?'

'That tall girl with the cash box, please!'

In spite of the sun, Rebecca felt cold and rushed to

change in the end beach hut. She mustn't miss the rest of the contest!

As she came out, Miss Morgan had hot soup ready for her and she gulped it gratefully. Nothing had ever tasted so delicious!

'Well done, Rebecca. How much have you raised?'

'Four pounds!' It wasn't just the soup that was making her glow. 'Four whole pounds!'

'The first four pounds of Charity Week!' the House Mistress pointed out, as Rebecca handed back the empty carton.

It was an exciting contest. Elf dropped out after twelve rides, too tired to go on. Then Sue got a slight attack of cramp after her thirteenth ride and came straight out. Now, as everyone had expected, the marathon developed between Joss and Tish and Margot. Joss was piling up rides faster than the other two by getting out more quickly. After her sixteenth ride she stood in the shallows, recovering her breath and arching her back, hands on her hips.

'Out, Joss!' shouted Joanne Hissup. 'That's enough.'

There were a few boos as Joss came out because some of the local boys had started laying bets amongst themselves and three of them had backed her to win! But Rebecca could tell from the way Joss was walking that her back had stiffened up slightly. It wasn't so very long since her spell in hospital.

'I can go on a long time yet,' she protested.

'You can, but you're not going to,' said Joanne.

That left Tish and Margot to battle it out. Soon they had overtaken Joss's score of 16 rides. 17 ... 18 ... 19 ...

'Surely they can't go on much longer!' Rebecca said to Sue.

'They can!' said Sue. 'Look at their faces. Neither of

them wants to be the first to give in. At this rate, Harry will just have to blow his whistle and – oh! Tish!'

It was over. A moment's loss of concentration on her twentieth ride and Tish keeled off her board and Margot went shooting ahead of her with a yell of triumph. 'I've won!' she cried. Loud cheers went up and then Harry really did blow his whistle. It was time for Sunday lunch.

After dinner, Mara checked all the sponsorship forms against the number of rides and did a lot of calculations on a piece of paper. The gang were lying sleepily around the Common Room, mainly on the floor.

'We've raised £49.20!' she announced. They all cheered. 'Now I'm going to check it with my calculator.'

'Well?' they asked excitedly, when she'd pressed all the buttons.

'It's still £49.20,' said Mara in delight. 'I shall come into III Alpha next term, you see. Just wait and see if I don't.'

Later in the afternoon, Tish and Mara vanished into the Hobbies' Room with Susannah Skelhorn to get the *Juniper Journal* ready. Rebecca's regular 'Did-You-Know?' piece wasn't needed because the weekly sheet was again crowded out with Charity Week news. So she and Sue and Elf and Margot spent the rest of Sunday collecting up sponsorship money in the metal cash box.

It was easy to find people because Juniper House was full of Middle School and Senior girls supporting the first day of Charity Week. Cakes were being sold at the cake stall, Hoop-la and darts and roll-a-penny had been set up in the First Year Common Room and Verity Williams was doing lightning portraits for ten pence a time.

A lot of the sponsors were surprised at the amount they owed, especially those who'd recklessly promised a penny or even two pence a ride to people like Tish and Margot.

Roberta Jones could hardly believe she owed thirty-eight pence! Some of the First Years, especially, looked worried – like Sheila Cummings and her friend Eleanor Keating.

'Can I pay half now and half next Saturday, when Morgy pays out next week's allowance?' wailed Sheila. 'If I pay it all now I'll have nothing left for anything else!'

'We wouldn't even have enough to go and see the play on Friday!' added Eleanor.

'Of course,' smiled Rebecca. 'A lot of people are doing that. If you're really going to be skint, you can leave it all till next Saturday. Cheer up!'

By evening the friends had collected up almost £24, with the rest promised for the following Saturday. The box felt beautifully heavy. Rebecca put her head round the corner of the Hobbies' Room and told Tish. 'Late news! We've already got in £24 and, by the way, the cake stall's sold out and they raised £14.60.'

'Terrific!' said Tish. 'I'll just squeeze it in at the end of the stencil.'

By Friday, no other group had raised as much as the 'Action Committee', although the girls who did the sponsored walk came close with £41.60. Whether or not Rebecca and Co. would be the winning group depended very much on the play.

It took place after tea on Friday and made a fitting climax to Charity Week. The weather was kind, as it had been ever since the previous Saturday. Whether it was the beautiful May evening, with a balmy breeze in the air, or sheer curiosity, or both, that drew the crowds, it would be difficult to say. But row upon row of girls sat on the green grass in front of South Terrace waiting eagerly for the play to begin. They had all paid thirty pence for the privilege.

The comedy began with no sign of the players, just the

gay, jaunty sound of a violin playing in the trees behind the terrace. Then the figure of Nicola Hodges appeared, dressed as a strolling minstrel, with the instrument tucked beneath her chin, the bow dancing backwards and forwards over the strings. The doors of the Music School were thrown open and out came an assortment of 'woodland folk' dancing comically to the music. The stage was set for fifteen minutes of uproarious fun.

At the end, the audience gave the players a standing ovation and Rebecca clapped as loudly as anyone. Max had taken Roberta's shapeless, wooden play and turned it into something light and magical.

There were loud cheers as the elves and goblins dragged Max out to take a bow. He, in his turn, disappeared into the Music School and reappeared a minute later. He was dragging Roberta Jones forward and holding something behind his back.

'I may have produced the play,' he shouted, 'but here is the person who wrote it, whose brainchild the whole entertainment has been – Bobbie Jones.'

There was polite applause and Roberta stood there blushing. Then a gasp went up as Max produced, from behind his back, a large bouquet of flowers, all wrapped in cellophane. Rebecca had seen the sort in the florist's shop in town, with large price tag to match.

'For all the fun you've given me, Bobbie,' said Max, bowing low. 'For all the fun you've given all of us.'

Everybody entered into the spirit of the thing and cheered loudly. Roberta took the bouquet, clumsily, almost dropping it, her eyes glazed. She couldn't quite believe this was really happening to her. Then the audience, restless now that the fun was over, got to its feet and scattered in all directions. But Roberta just stood there by the little lake, the bouquet clutched to her chest, staring down at her reflection in the water. Was that her, down there? Was it really her?

'Max certainly does everything in style!' exclaimed Sue admiringly, as they walked away. 'And Jenny told me that he's going to treat the whole cast to fizzy drinks at Moffatt's afterwards.'

The celebration was still going on in Moffatt's an hour later. The three friends wanted to go and buy a squash and found they couldn't get in the door. There was a singsong going on, with Max's baritone voice clearly audible.

As they smiled and walked away, Rebecca heard a car screech to a halt on the gravel in front of the tuck shop. They looked back and saw the red sports car that always collected Max from school. The hood was down and as usual the glamorous girl called Katie was at the steering wheel.

She looked furious. As she heard the singing, she did a strange thing. She just put her hand on the car's horn and kept it there. HOONNNNNNNKKKKKKKK! Max came running out. She let go of the horn.

'For goodness' sake!' she yelled. 'We're supposed to be taking the Mulliners out for a meal! They're waiting for us!'

'The Mulliners!' Max looked horrified. 'I thought that was next week!'

'Well, it's not. It's now. It's half an hour ago. For heaven's sake get your stuff.'

'It's over in the Staff Room, give me five minutes.'

When Rebecca and Co. went up the steps of old building a little later, Max came flying out, his bag bulging with books to mark, nearly knocking them over. Katie juddered the car over to him and he jumped in.

'Bye, Bobbie!' he shouted as they drove away.

Rebecca saw Roberta Jones standing under the big cedar tree on the far side of the school forecourt. She was still clutching the flowers. On impulse, she walked across to her and glanced at her stricken face.

'Hadn't you better put those in water?' she said kindly. 'Come on, bring them over to Juniper. They'll make a lovely arrangement.'

Roberta cheered up then.

On the way to the boarding house she said, wistfully:

'The play was fun, wasn't it?'

'Terrific fun,' said Sue.

'The whole of Charity Week's been fun!' said Tish suddenly.

It was true. It had been marvellous. So much so that none of them really minded when the principal announced on Saturday morning that Roberta's had been the winning group. The play had raised £60. Much more important, a grand total of £292 had been raised for the Animals need Real Kindness Fund.

Somebody went and stole the surfing money.

Rebecca wandered along to the School Office, later Saturday morning, to pick up the cash box. There was £30 in it now and they wanted to collect the rest of the money that was owed and hand in the total to Miss Morgan.

Round about Thursday she had left it as usual with Mrs Devenshire, who had told her to put it on the table by the door.

It wasn't on the table. It wasn't anywhere in the office. It had gone.

NINE

M FOR MASON

As soon as it became known that the cash box containing the £30 surfing money had been stolen, a sense of outrage ran through Juniper House. It was mean, despicable, unbelievable! Who could have gone into the School Office and calmly lifted it just like that? Who was the creeping, rotten girl responsible?

Mrs Devenshire confirmed that the cash box had been on the table last thing Friday afternoon, before she went home for the weekend. Straight after phoning Mrs Devenshire, Miss Welbeck phoned the police. Two policemen came to the school and asked questions and took notes. Then they drove away again.

'It's horrible, isn't it?' said Joss, serving out the slices of cold meat at lunch time. There was salad to go with it and potatoes baked in their jackets. 'It must be somebody in the school.'

'I wonder how she's feeling now?' said Rebecca, angrily.

'I don't think the police will catch them,' said Tish. 'I mean, it could be anybody. Anyone at school could have nipped into the School Office. It's never locked or anything.

I hate the feeling that it's . . .' she screwed up her nose and glanced round the full dining hall. 'Well, it must be somebody in this hall.'

'I wonder who?' Rebecca paused. 'Maybe it's somebody who's overspent themselves, on sponsorships and things. Just can't find the money and feels panicky. Took the cash box on impulse –'

'It must have been impulse,' agreed Sue. 'A proper thief would have looked to see if the box was locked –'

'Which it wasn't because it's never had a key!' interposed Rebecca.

'Then they'd take the money out quickly. Just the large money like the £1 coins and the fifty pence pieces, and leave all the two pences and stuff. I mean who'd want to take the box as well! What a risk! It *must* have been impulse.'

'We'll write something for the *J.J.* tomorrow!' said Tish. 'Ask the guilty person to own up and not to be so stupid.'

'And we could do some detective work as well!' suggested Rebecca. 'The thief must have dumped the empty cash box somewhere. We could search for that. And they might have tried to get rid of the small change, in Moffatt's maybe. We could ask Mrs Moffat –'

'Detective work!' Tish nodded vigorously. 'Yes. Action Committee again. I mean, it was us six that raised all that money and it's up to us to try and get it back! Let's start this afternoon!'

'I ought to help, too,' said Joss, listening. 'As I was in the surf. But I'm supervising First Year sprinting this afternoon. Athletics Club. The whole programme's behind. You're behind, too, you know, Rebecca. Sports Day's on Friday week and if you want to be in the 100 and the 200 you've still got to qualify.'

Rebecca was well aware of that. She had cursed there being two wet Saturdays in a row, so that Angela Hessel hadn't come. Athletics Club's activities had been limited to keep-fit training over in the sports centre. She wanted to get out on the track again and had been looking forward to it ever since the fine weather arrived last Sunday. But now –

'Sorry, Joss. I'll have to leave it. I'll make Athletics my option on games afternoons and I'll come next week to Club. But we have to try and do something about this. At least, I do, seeing I was daft enough to leave the cash box there in the first place. If only I hadn't been too lazy to get Miss Morgan to lock it up each time we'd finished collecting . . .'

'Oh, stuff!' said Tish. 'Nobody ever bothers.'

'It's not your fault, Rebecca!' said Elf. She'd finished her jacket potato at last and there was some butter on her chin. 'In fact we could manage without you this afternoon, if it weren't for your fantastic memory.' The detective idea had really captured her imagination. 'Knowing you, you'll remember some vital little detail about somebody's behaviour on Friday –'

'It's okay, Elf. I'm coming this afternoon,' said Rebecca, laughing. 'I've made my mind up about it.'

She did want to go to Athletics Club and get some more coaching from Angela Hessel and run 13.5 seconds – but she wouldn't. They must try and do *something* to find the money. It made her hate the thief all the more.

As it turned out, they didn't find the box, or any clues, that afternoon – although they ransacked the school grounds. Rebecca's photographic memory *didn't* recall any vital little detail. It was all, in short, a waste of time.

Nor did anybody respond to Tish's appeal when it was published in the *Juniper Journal* on Monday. Nor did the police have any success. They soon had to move on to more important crimes.

There was no way of replacing the money, without writing home. Miss Morgan refused to allow them to do that. The cheque just had to go to London £30 smaller than it should have been.

'I feel in my heart that the person with the guilty conscience will own up, sooner or later,' said the junior House Mistress. The theft had distressed her very much for it carried the hallmark of somebody young and impulsive, possibly one of her First Years. 'I think they'll own up, sometime before the end of term. A guilty conscience is a terrible burden to carry around. The best thing you girls can do now is to forget about it.'

But Rebecca and the others from dormitory number six had no intention of forgetting about it. In the fortnight before half-term they went around in a gang more than they'd ever done before. The sponsored surf had brought them close together, but the theft of the money brought them even closer. 'The six detectives', Roberta Jones called them, though not jeeringly, as she might have done once. Roberta was still blossoming and, secretly, she never ceased to marvel at how much Max seemed to like her.

The six concentrated their activities on trying to find the missing metal box, which they felt sure the thief must have hidden somewhere in the school buildings or grounds. And although it was like looking for a needle in a haystack, they secretly began to get satisfaction from these activities.

'We've got to persevere,' Tish would say. 'Then sooner or later we'll crack the mystery.'

It was during that fortnight that the question of the new boarding houses first entered Rebecca's mind. She was beginning to despair of maths and dimly in the back of her mind she began to acknowledge that she might have to go into the Beta stream next year. So the question of being in the same boarding house as her friends began to assume importance.

In September all the Second Years would be leaving

Juniper House. They would no longer be juniors, but Third Years and therefore members of the Middle School. The Middle School comprised all the girls in the Third, Fourth and Fifth Years at Trebizon. They were split up equally between five different boarding houses, situated in the school grounds. These were very small units compared with Juniper House, where one hundred and twenty girls lived. Each one housed no more than about thirty-six girls.

'How's it decided which Middle School house we go in?' asked Rebecca.

'Dunno, exactly,' said Tish, who was cleaning her teeth at the time. 'I think we all put our names down at the end of term and they try and keep friends together. But that's years away yet.'

'But they let friends keep together?' asked Rebecca eagerly.

'Pretty sure that's always been the system. It'd better be!'

Rebecca comforted herself with the thought that if by any chance she was put down into III Beta next term, at least she and Sue and Tish would be together other times. How rambling and friendly the Middle School boarding houses looked, with only three dozen girls living in them. She'd heard they had studies, that three or four of you shared together. Mara and Margot and Elf – they must come, too. She was getting fonder of those three all the time. Tish's Action Committee. It was a silly name, but it stuck.

She threw herself into athletics. One afternoon, to her delight, Angela Hessel came to take the group doing athletics, to make up for the two missed Saturdays. She timed Rebecca over the 100 metres sprint.

'13.8 seconds. Get some running spikes by Saturday,' she said. Then added, quite casually: 'They'll make a big difference. You should qualify for Sports Day quite easily.'

Rebecca was overjoyed. She hadn't any money but she

got hold of a secondhand pair of running shoes from Miss Willis and asked for them to be put down on her school bill. When she wrote her weekly letter to her parents, she told them what she'd done. She did not, of course, tell them about her secret ambition to run in the County Sports at the end of term, when they would be home from Saudi Arabia. She dreamt of surprising them with that. It was becoming a favourite daydream.

Wearing running spikes at Saturday's Athletics Club meeting she ran the 100 metres in 13.2 seconds, thus fulfilling Angela Hessel's prophecy. She rested for a few minutes and then went straight on to qualify for the 200 metres as well.

'You've got six days until Sports Day,' was all Joss said. 'So you'd better work! You'll have to get below 13 if you want to be in the first three. Aba can do 12.9 and so can Laura Wilkins in II Beta. Also it's not even worth going through to the Area Sports if you can't get below 13 seconds.'

'Then I'm going to get below 13 seconds!' said Rebecca.

Rebecca and Tish trained together. Tish had also qualified for Sports Day – the 800 metres. Sue might have got into the long jump but she had so much music on that she decided to opt out of Athletics. The school orchestra was going to be playing in Exeter over half-term. Any spare time she had, she played tennis.

So the two of them trained like fanatics for six days. They did the special exercises that Angela Hessel recommended, over in the sports centre, as well as athletics every Games afternoon. Morning and evening they went jogging, to the far side of Trebizon Bay and back again.

The days were getting hot now but the mornings and evenings were pleasant for running, the sand golden and damp beneath their bare feet.

On the Monday evening, after a particularly sunny day, the heat stayed in the sun quite late. By the time they reached the far side of the bay they were uncomfortably sweaty, even in tee shirts and shorts and bare feet. The sight of the sparkling blue sea and the gulls wheeling above the headland was too much for them. There was nobody around. They broke all the school rules and plunged into the waves just as they were and swam round the headland into Mulberry Cove. They threw themselves on to a flat slab of rock, licked by salt spray, feeling the sun on their backs. Rebecca let her feet trail in the water. She could have lain there for ever.

'Voices!' said Tish suddenly, lifting her head.

They crept towards a pile of rocks and peered through them. There, less than twenty yards away, was Max! He, too, was lying outstretched on a slab of rock, in swimming trunks, with his girlfriend, Katie. He was busily marking homework, while the sea water eddied around his feet and threw spray all over the books. He was talking and laughing as he worked and Katie was smoking a cigarette, flicking the ash over the edge of the rock, into the sea.

The girls crept away, plunged into the water and swam back round the headland into Trebizon Bay as fast as they could. They stumbled up on to the sand laughing, supporting each other.

'So that's where he marks our books!'

'I noticed some funny marks on mine the other day!' said Tish. 'He must have got the cover wet!'

'I wish he'd drop mine in the sea!' exclaimed Rebecca.

By the time they'd jogged back to school, right back across the bay, their clothes were almost dry. When Matron saw them in their pyjamas and dressing gowns, drinking cocoa with their hair wet, she presumed they'd just had a shower. 'You should have worn shower caps, you silly girls,' she scolded. 'Hurry up and dry your hair now. It's late.'

One day, before breakfast, they saw Roberta out jogging. She wasn't in Sports Day.

'Making herself beautiful for Max,' whispered Rebecca.

'How's your maths?' Tish asked suddenly.

'Oh, Tish, don't let's talk about maths. It's glorious this morning – I'm going to sprint!'

Rebecca streaked away across the sand, her fair hair flowing out behind her like a windsock, straight up a sand dune and on to the top. She threw her arms up and gazed up at the sky. 'Just glorious!'

However, when Rebecca's form mistress, Miss Heath, got hold of her on Friday morning and said 'Let's talk about your maths', there was no such escape. The girls would be breaking up for half-term at the end of the afternoon, after Sports Day, and Miss Heath was anxious to speak to Rebecca.

'I've been looking at your marks so far this term,' she said. 'They're abominable. It would be a pity for a girl of your intelligence to have to go into III Beta next term, but that's what's going to happen, Rebecca, if you don't pull your socks up.'

'Threats!' said Sue, at morning break. 'Just threats!'

'I'm not so sure,' said Rebecca, uncomfortably.

Mara's news was the reverse of Rebecca's. She was elated because Mrs Beal, her form mistress, had taken her and another girl called Jane Bowen on one side after the geography lesson.

'She as good as said that Jane Bowen and I'll go up into the Alpha class in September, just as long as our exam marks are as good as our term work!'

'Oh, Mara!' Elf hugged her. 'Good. Good!'

'Swot!' teased Tish.

'Once we're all together, I'll never swot again!' promised Mara. 'I just hate being the odd one out.'

'It'll be perfect, us all being together,' said Sue.

'I know,' nodded Tish. But she glanced across at Rebecca, with a slightly worried expression on her face.

Rebecca was downcast by Miss Heath's words. Sue refused to believe it and Tish was unsure. But Rebecca knew it had to be faced; she might go down. Her parents would be disappointed if that happened. But it was no use, she just couldn't get on with Max's way of teaching. If only that Mrs Shaw person had been able to come this term!

She was further downcast when all the parents started arriving for Sports Day, straight after lunch. She wished hers were in England. Sue's weren't coming, either, because none of the school orchestra would be going home for half-term. Tish's parents were the next best thing. They knew Sue well, but they'd never met Rebecca before. They took both girls under their wing.

'So this is Rebecca!' said Doctor Anderson, who had a lovely crinkled up face. 'Here, have some chocolate. Give you energy.'

'You said she was brainy, Tish,' came a boy's voice, just behind Rebecca. 'You never told us she looked quite normal.'

Rebecca turned round and found herself shaking hands with a tall, strong-looking boy who had a big laughing mouth, just like Tish's, and the same humorous brown eyes.

'I'm not brainy,' Rebecca said quickly, hating herself for blushing.

'This is my brother Robbie,' said Tish. 'It's his half-term, too. My parents have just picked him up.' His own boarding school, Garth College, was just on the other side of town. A lot of Trebizon girls seemed to have brothers there.

'You two had better win,' said Robbie, 'seeing we've come to watch.'

'The tea's quite good,' riposted Rebecca.

But she suddenly felt cheerful again. She had to win something this afternoon! If she could get into the County Sports at the end of term, that would make up to her parents for anything else! It suddenly seemed the most important thing in the world.

The day was sunny again and the ground was firm. There was almost no breeze. Her first race – the 100 metres junior sprint – was nearly due. There were crowds of girls and parents lining the running track, a lot of them bunched up by the finishing line. She'd pretend her parents were there, amongst them. She'd pretend it was the County Sports.

The starting pistol cracked. They were off first time!

Rebecca knew she'd started well. She was in the first four and the pace was terrific. Straight all the way! No bends! She hurtled along and at the half-way point she could see Laura Wilkins to her left and Aba Amori to her right, the rest of the field drumming along behind the three of them. There was a lot of cheering and noise. Rebecca was conscious of only one thing now, the dominating presence of the Nigerian girl at her right shoulder – the long dark legs striking out, head, neck and shoulders forward.

The tape was coming up and Rebecca knew that she must accelerate or Aba would leave her for dead. For two electrifying seconds they fought it out, shoulder to shoulder. 'REBECK!' that was Tish's voice. *'Come on Rebecca!'* – her brother's! Rebecca edged in front and hurled herself forward at the tape. She felt it touch her and she ran on through it, arms raised, gasping for air.

She'd won!

'12.7 seconds, Rebecca. Very well done!' said Miss

Willis, soon after. Joanne Hissup herself came and threw an arm round her shoulders.

'You're a County prospect, Rebecca!' she said in delight.

Aba hugged her sportingly. Joss Vining, Tish, Sue – they were all converging! 'Marvellous!' said Joss.

'Whatever happens in the 200, you've got through to the Area Sports!' exclaimed Tish. 'Oh, gosh, it's my race soon!'

Rebecca felt elated. If only her parents could have seen her run! Funnily enough, she would have liked Max to have seen her, too. She'd have liked him to see that there was *something* she was good at. But Max had vanished. Roberta Jones had been looking all over for him, to introduce her parents, until Debbie Rickard had informed her that the red sports car had carried him away directly after morning lessons.

Tish won the junior 800 metres and she, too, qualified for the Area Sports. Aba and Laura also qualified. They got their revenge in the 200 metres by beating Rebecca into third place. That didn't dampen Rebecca's spirits in the least. Now she knew that she must concentrate all her efforts on the 100 metres. She would work and work at it between now and the Area Sports – the last barrier between her and the County Sports, when her parents would be home!

There was a party atmosphere that afternoon, not least because the senior girls had finished their big exams the very same morning.

Tea was set out on the big terrace in front of the dining hall, overlooking the quadrangle gardens. It was eaten and enjoyed in brilliant sunshine. The dainty sandwiches, sausage rolls and delicious pastries were, by amazing sleight of hand, conjured from the school kitchens – the same place from which stews and bean bakes and other stolid fare so often emanated.

'Why do the cooks hide their light under a bushel?' asked Rebecca, sinking her teeth into a third chocolate eclair.

'It's just to impress visitors,' said Tish.

'Then I'm impressed,' said Robbie, through a mouthful of gateau.

'Have a happy half-term!' said Pippa Fellowes-Walker later.

'I shall!' replied Rebecca.

But when she arrived at her grandmother's the next day and was shown the circular letter, all her happiness evaporated.

Rebecca's grandmother, who was her guardian while her parents were abroad, had received the notice earlier in the week. She showed it to Rebecca on the Saturday evening, quite casually:

> ARRANGEMENTS FOR TRANSFER OF SECOND YEAR GIRLS TO NEW BOARDING HOUSES IN SEPTEMBER.
>
> *Your daughter will be leaving the junior boarding house at the end of this term, having completed her first two years at Trebizon. She will be transferred to one of five middle school boarding houses, where she will remain for her next three years. These are smaller units with a family atmosphere where girls are allowed a greater degree of freedom than in Juniper House.*
>
> *We have tried in the past to accommodate the wishes of girls and their parents in the matter of choice of boarding house, but we have found this system to be unworkable because some houses are always oversubscribed. We have, therefore, decided to allocate the girls to the five boarding houses in groups of 12, taken in strict alphabetical order down through the three streams as follows:*

Girls 1–12 (III Alpha): COURT HOUSE
Girls 13–18 (III Alpha) and 1–6 (III Beta): NORRIS HOUSE
Girls 7–18 (III Beta): STERNDALE HOUSE
Girls 19–21 (III Beta) and 1–9 (III Gamma): TAVISTOCK HOUSE
Girls 10–21 (III Gamma): CHAMBERS HOUSE
These numbers are based on present streaming and do not allow for end-of-term adjustments. The general principle is clear: to allow most girls to be with a group from their own form in their new boarding house. Arrangements will also be made for sisters to remain together. House lists will be posted up at school after Summer Exams when Third Year streaming has been finalized.

Madeleine Welbeck, *Principal*

Rebecca read the notice through three times.

'What's the matter, Rebecca?'

'Er – nothing, Gran.'

She got out a pencil from the jar on the kitchen dresser and wrote down the names of the girls in her form – in alphabetical order:

Aba Amori, Tish Anderson, Mary Bron, Jenny Brook-Hayes, Sally Elphinstone, Ann Ferguson, Anne Finch, Roberta Jones, Elizabeth Kendall, Margot Lawrence, Rebecca Mason, Sue Murdoch, Ruth Nathan, Sarah Nathan, Debbie Rickard, Judy Sharp, Joanna Thompson, Joss Vining.

She sectioned off the first twelve names in II Alpha by putting a stroke after Sue's name. If the whole form went up to III Alpha, just as it stood, she and Sue would go into

Court House with Tish and Margot and Elf – they'd all be together, with the exception of Mara.

But that wasn't going to happen! Jane and Mara were coming up to III Alpha, it was as good as settled. Jane *B*owen and Mara *L*eonodis. So they would be in the first twelve! They'd go into Court House with Tish and the others, while Rebecca and Sue would go into Norris House.

That was bad enough, but there was something infinitely worse.

Rebecca might go into III Beta!

Would she still then go into Norris House with Sue? The names of present Beta form girls ran through her mind . . . *Susan Carter, Elizabeth Fichumi, Jane Ford, Helena King, Penny Leason, Rachel Lee.* There were at least 6 before Mason! She wouldn't go into Norris House with Sue. She'd go into Sterndale House, on her own.

It was bad enough for Sue, but at least she'd be seeing Tish and the others in lessons every day. If Rebecca went into the Beta stream next term she'd be separated from the others all the time! The very name Sterndale House sounded hateful – like a prison!

The letter 'M' was even more hateful – M for Mason – and maths.

She worried about it all weekend. When she got back to school after half-term, the crowd in dormitory six could talk of nothing else. It was like trying to do a difficult crossword puzzle, working out all the possible combinations – who might go up, who might go down – who had a sister – who would go into which house. Rebecca couldn't bring herself to join in. Then Sue said something which proved to be the last straw.

'Cheer up, Rebecca. It's maddening, I know. But Court and Norris are right next door to each other – not like

Sterndale or somewhere, stuck away on its own. And we'll all be together for lessons.'

'I used to think you were bright!' snapped Rebecca, miserably. She stalked off. 'I'm going to the library.'

Tish and Sue followed her there, two minutes later, and found her in floods of tears.

TEN

THE HOUSE LISTS GO UP

'I'm sorry, Sue,' sniffed Rebecca, 'but it was just too much when you said that. I just *know* I'll be going into Beta and that means I *will* end up in Sterndale, stuck away on my own . . .'

She was crying like a baby and she couldn't stop it! It was humiliating. Tish and Sue put their arms around her waist and walked her over to the window. Pippa Fellowes-Walker was on library duty, sorting out some books on a shelf, looking their way.

'Ssssh! Pippa'll chuck us out of the library,' soothed Tish.

'This idea you've got! About going into Beta! It's really stupid!' said Sue stubbornly.

'My marks!' gulped Rebecca. 'The highest I've had in maths all term is 7 out of 20! You should see my book!'

'That's only because Max doesn't bother with anyone, except Robert!' said Tish. 'Miss Gates won't worry about your term's work – she doesn't like him! As long as you can scrape together about 45% in the exam, they won't dream of putting you down –'

'Or even 40%,' said Sue triumphantly, glad that Tish

seemed to agree with her. 'Because you're okay at everything else!'

'How am I going to do that?' asked Rebecca helplessly. She'd stopped crying now She just felt fatalistic. She was never, never going to be any good at maths, no matter how hard she tried!

'Because we're going to help you, silly,' said Tish.

'You can't!' said Rebecca, shocked. Then she realized what Tish meant.

They all started laughing. Pippa was standing right behind them and she was laughing, too. For the first time, Rebecca began to feel better.

'I don't think anyone can help you in the exam itself!' said Pippa. 'But if you're going to have some maths coaching, it'd be better from somebody older. I've finished my big exams, so I could do it. I'll have to ask Miss Gates, of course.'

'You!' exclaimed Rebecca. Had she heard right? 'Do you mean it?'

'Of course I mean it! Now shut up making such a noise in here, you three, and go and make a noise somewhere else.'

'Yes, that girl Mason's got a lot of ground to make up,' said Miss Gates, when Pippa came to see her. 'If I weren't so busy with the GCSE Year, I'd try and take her in hand myself. Of course, Dennis Maxwell should do it really. The trouble with that young man,' she said acidly, 'is that as soon as the afternoon bell goes he's out of the front door like a scalded cat. Not that I should be discussing that with you.'

Pippa hid a smile. The friction between Miss Gates and the temporary maths master had reached almost legendary proportions. It was early June and Max spent every spare moment swimming and sunbathing in Mulberry Cove. His tan won admiration from the girls, but further hostility from Miss Gates.

'Now I'm convinced of it!' she told Miss Welbeck. 'He may have a brilliant brain, but he's just a layabout like all the rest who come down here for the summer. He's taken this job to get some stamps on his card! He's probably counting the days to the end of term, when he'll be able to draw unemployment benefit and have a jolly good time of it, like all the rest of them. I don't know what you see in him, Madeleine.'

'He has splendid references, Evelyn.'

'Written by his Cambridge friends, I daresay!'

'One or two girls have come along remarkably under him. Roberta Jones, for instance.'

'Roberta Jones!' Snort! 'I'll believe that when I see her exam result.'

Having written Max off as a lost cause, Miss Gates readily agreed to the prefect's suggestion.

'It's very kind of you, Pippa. It might give Miss Hort a few less pieces to pick up when the new academic year arrives and Dennis Maxwell is no longer with us.'

Miss Hort was in charge of maths in the Middle School.

The month of June was glorious. The long, hot summer that Tish had hopefully predicted at the beginning of term was really coming to pass. Most evenings Rebecca had to go and water her plants in the kitchen garden, or they'd have died. She enjoyed that peaceful task at the end of the busy days, when the heat had gone out of the sun. She could watch the martins darting in and out of their nests under the eaves of the old stables, which overlooked the big walled garden.

She was happy again now. Pippa was coaching her and maths had lost some of their mystery – like the time Tish had explained to her about the binary system. It was all very hard work, but things were beginning to fall into place.

The days were too crowded and busy to think about her

parents, but she would think about them those evenings when the garden was heavy with summer scents and the spraying water made a cool sound. They were coming back to England soon for their summer leave! If she won her race in the Area Sports, at the beginning of July, she'd write and tell them that they could come and see her run in the County Sports, on July 15th. They'd be home by then!

It was a bit of a daydream, really.

Rebecca was getting nowhere near as much athletics training as she needed. In the second half of term, games lessons were taken up with swimming in the sea and surfing and tennis. Rebecca was starting to love tennis. The afternoons spent in the sea were sheer paradise. But with Sports Day over, athletics no longer figured in the official timetable. Athletics Club, training sessions in the gym, matches with other schools – all these took place out of school hours. Rebecca was offered a place in the athletics team and she had to turn it down. With all the extra maths, she simply didn't have the time. She went jogging with Tish most mornings before breakfast and hoped that would be enough.

'It won't be!' Miss Willis told her, rather sharply. 'You need to run against some good competition before the Area Sports. But if you can't come to training sessions and fixtures then you can't, I suppose.'

Rebecca worked hard, all through June. Pippa was patient and explained things well, going over the groundwork that Rebecca had missed in the First Year. The maths syllabus at her London school had been completely different. She began to enjoy maths lessons more, now that she could sometimes understand what Max was talking about. Slowly her marks began to improve. She worked hard revising for the other exams, too. A few evenings the others would drag her away from her books to go surf-riding. Mara would come, too, though she would sometimes bring her school books down to the beach, as she couldn't surf. She was working at least as hard as Rebecca, leaving nothing to chance.

They always came back to Juniper House starving hungry and raided the kitchen and talked and laughed long after Lights Out.

Those evenings were such fun that it made Rebecca sad to think that the six of them could never be in the same boarding house again, let alone in the same dormitory. The best she could hope for was to be with them in III Alpha next year and go into Norris House with Sue. But with Tish, in particular, in a different house, nothing would be quite the same again. Rebecca knew that Sue felt the same way, although they never spoke about it.

The June roses in the quadrangle gardens began to wilt; the days got still hotter. Suddenly it was the first week of July – summer exams week. Exams lasted from Monday to Friday and the Area Sports meeting was on the Saturday.

For five days the girls of II Alpha bent their heads over examination papers, in a room silent except for the scratching of cartridge pens and the buzzing of flies. The little room, high up in old building, seemed to get hotter and stuffier each day. Rebecca would gaze out at the bright sky and the little scudding clouds, thinking with longing of the blue waters of Trebizon Bay. But she was glad that she'd worked for the exams. On the whole, they didn't seem too bad.

Her greatest sense of relief came with the last exam, on Friday. It was the maths paper. It covered two years' work and lasted 2½ hours. As she worked her way through the questions, Rebecca felt grateful to Pippa. She was on familiar ground with a lot of the problems that had been set, though there were some she couldn't do. Tish, Sue, Margot and Elf crowded round her afterwards, eager to know how she'd got on.

'I think –' Rebecca swallowed hard. She didn't want to tempt providence. 'I *think* I may have passed.'

'If *you* think so, then you must have done!' said Tish jubilantly.

'Look at Robert's long face!' whispered Elf. 'I don't think she's done very well, in spite of all the help she's had from Max.'

'What about Mary Bron then – and Joanna – they both looked as though they could burst into tears!' said Margot, as the five came out of the form room in a knot. 'Let's go and see how Mara's got on!'

Mara had got on famously.

That was the best evening Rebecca could remember. About twenty of them went swimming and surfing and finished up with a barbecue on the beach: an end-of-exams celebration, with Miss Morgan's permission.

They cooked sausages on the fire and watched a magnificent sunset over the sea. It was getting late.

'Come on, Becky,' said Tish. 'We'd better go now. We've got to run tomorrow, this lot haven't!'

'Coming!' said Rebecca. She could hear the distant sound of the waves and her face was glowing in the firelight. She had to drag herself away. She wanted the party to go on for ever because she felt as though she had a lot to celebrate. Afterwards, she wondered what could have made her feel that way.

Probably because she hadn't done enough training, Rebecca flopped at the Area Sports. She ran the 100 metres junior sprint in 13.2 seconds and there were five girls ahead of her. So she didn't qualify for the County Sports.

Tish fared better, coming second in the 800 metres, and

Aba Amori actually won the 200 metres, which was her best distance. Joanna Hissup cleared 1.74 metres to win the senior high jump event with ease and Joss Vining won the junior long jump.

'We've done pretty well as a school,' said Tish, on the long minibus journey back to Trebizon. Miss Willis was driving. 'But it's a shame about you.'

'I'm furious with myself,' said Rebecca. A cloud of depression was settling over her. 'I never told you, did I, but my parents will be back here by July 15th – you know, the County Sports . . .' Her voice trailed away. 'I'd been hoping all along . . .'

She lapsed into silence and Tish let her brood. But after a while Tish said: 'There's always next year. Much better to pass the maths exam this year.' Rebecca cheered up a little after that.

But it seemed that her confidence was ill-founded.

When Max read out the results of the maths exam the following Wednesday, they were not, admittedly, very brilliant. Only three girls, Tish and Anne Finch and Joss Vining, had got over 70%. Nevertheless, the rest of the form had all scraped above 50% – including Roberta Jones – with the exception of four girls. Debbie Rickard had 45%, Joanna Thompson had 41%, Mary Bron had 32% and last of all came Rebecca with 28%.

28%! At first Rebecca's mind simply couldn't take it in. She thought she must have misheard. But one look at Sue's face was enough. Sue had never been seriously worried about Rebecca. But she was now. In fact she was gaping at her in amazement, her jaw sagging. Tish was aghast.

The rest of the lesson passed in a blur for Rebecca. As the bell went, they started to crowd round her, to sympathize – not just her friends but people like Anne Finch and the Nathan twins. They all knew how hard she'd worked. Even

Roberta Jones was coming over. She was in a daze for a different reason. She'd got 61% in the exam and still couldn't quite believe it.

Rebecca couldn't stand sympathy from anybody, not even her best friends. What point was there in talking about it? There was nothing more to say! She'd known all along she would never be any good at maths! Whatever had made her think otherwise? The whole thing had been an illusion!

She shot away out of the form room and down the stairs. It was morning break and she went to find Pippa, who was out in the grounds, sketching.

'I've let you down,' she said, flatly. 'I got 28% and came bottom.'

'Rebecca!' The prefect stared at her. 'I don't believe it.'

'It's true.'

'Oh.' Pippa was really surprised. 'Bottom! After all that slogging! And you seemed to be getting on so well!' She stood up and put an arm round Rebecca's shoulders. 'Were you nervous?'

'Not particularly. I'm not good at maths, that's all.'

'No, Rebecca! It's not that.' Pippa searched for an explanation. 'I suppose,' she said, becoming resigned, 'that a month just wasn't long enough. You'll catch up in the end.'

'But I'll have to go into III Beta now,' said Rebecca, trying very hard not to cry.

'Perhaps,' said Pippa. 'I know it's hard to take, but maths is so important and you've got to learn it. It's no use going faster than you can cope with. Wait and see what happens.'

She watched Rebecca walk away, very nearly in tears herself. What a shame! She'd done her best to help, but it hadn't made any difference. She was surprised, all the same. She would tell Miss Gates how surprised she was.

*

The House Lists were posted up on the noticeboards, the last weekend of term. The school would break up the following Thursday. Knowing the lists were going to be put up, Rebecca could hardly eat any lunch on Saturday, though Elf tried to coax her, telling her how delicious the cold savoury pie was. Tish and Sue said nothing. They weren't very hungry themselves. Sue hated herself for never having taken Rebecca's fears seriously, right through the term. Now, with Rebecca and the others, she feared the worst.

On the next dinner table, Roberta Jones was on tenterhooks.

'I'll die if I'm not put in III Beta,' she announced.

'III Beta?' asked Mara in amazement. It was common knowledge by now that Roberta had been trying hard all term, especially with maths, in order to stay in the Alpha stream.

Roberta and Debbie Rickard exchanged meaningful looks.

Previously, in spite of frequent overtures from Debbie, the ungainly Roberta had been far too lacking in confidence herself to go around with someone as unpopular as Debbie Rickard. She had just formed a trio with the quiet Nathan twins. Not any longer. Max, and the play, had changed so much! As Roberta had blossomed she'd taken Debbie under her wing, with the result that Debbie Rickard had become a much nicer person, especially after winning a lot of praise for her performance in the play. Now Roberta had what she'd always wanted, a best friend of her own.

'If I stay in the Alpha form I'll go in Court House,' said Roberta, making a face. 'I want to go in Norris! Debbie and me and the twins have just worked it all out. If I go into III Beta we can all be in Norris together!'

'But you'd be in a different form from them –' began Mara.

'Who minds about that!' said Roberta stolidly. 'You can't have any fun in lessons. They've got studies for four in Norris and we'd all share one – we're planning to start a middle school drama group –'

'What about your parents?' asked Laura Wilkins. 'They'd mind!'

'No they wouldn't!' said Roberta. 'I thought they would but Daddy wrote to me during exams and told me not to worry. He said there's a lot more to life than having your head in books – and things like writing the play and raising the most money were actually more important.'

'He's got something there,' nodded Mara. She'd long ago decided that she'd done enough swotting this term to last an entire lifetime. Just as long as she could be with the others now!

So when the House Lists went up, a cry of disappointment came from Roberta. She was going to be in III Alpha – and Court House.

'It's not fair!' She went storming off. 'I'm going to find Gatesy! I'm going to tell her that maths exam was just a fluke!'

There was a lot of laughter. It was such an amazing turnabout.

Rebecca and her friends weren't laughing at the House Lists. They were looking at them leadenly.

It could have been wonderful. Mara had won her place in III Alpha and was down to be in Court House with Tish and Margot and Elf – and Sue as well!

Sue couldn't quite believe her eyes. She wasn't going to be in Norris House on her own, after all. Mary Bron had been put down to III Beta and placed in Norris House, which meant that Sue just scraped into Court House with the others, as number 12!

It wasn't wonderful, though. For there was Rebecca,

down in III Beta, in the Sterndale House group – all on her own. It spoilt everything.

'Oh, Rebecca,' whispered Mara.

Her father, the shipowner, had sent a magnificent iced cake to school for them all. It was in a box in Miss Morgan's office and there, as far as Mara was concerned, it could stay.

ELEVEN

THE CASH BOX COMES BACK

On Saturday afternoon, instead of getting the cake, the six of them wandered around the school grounds trying to think of something to do. The fact that Rebecca was going to be separated from the rest of them, next term, just didn't bear thinking about. Nobody was willing to refer to it.

Rebecca was relieved about that. She just wanted to shut it out of her mind now. But it wouldn't go away. It hung silently in the air.

'Shall we go surfing,' suggested Margot. 'Harry's on duty.'

Tish looked up at the sky and made a face. For the first time in weeks the weather looked threatening. The clouds were a navy-blue colour over Trebizon Bay. The others looked up, too.

'No,' sighed Margot. 'Don't let's.'

'What about badminton?' said Sue, trying to sound bright.

Thumbs down to badminton.

They mooched along the paths that led to the Hilary, kicking bits of gravel as they went, and then stood for a while by the little lake. Rebecca tried to make some stones skim on the water, but they wouldn't. Tish took pot shots at a clump of water weed in the middle and missed.

'We've got to do the *J.J.* this weekend,' she said suddenly.'

'It's funny to think it's our Farewell Issue.'

It was Mara's father who had given the little duplicator to Juniper House but next term, when they moved on to the middle school boarding houses, they'd be leaving it behind. The *Juniper Journal*, which Tish and Mara had started in Rebecca's first term, would carry on under different editors.

'Our last issue,' said Rebecca.

'We must try and make it good!' said Tish quickly, anxious not to strike a down-note. 'Some really crazy Did-You-Knows, for a start.'

'Can't think of any,' replied Rebecca, listlessly.

They wandered on.

'We never did find out who took the surfing money,' said Elf.

'We never even found a single clue!' added Sue. 'And we swore we'd solve the mystery before the end of term!'

'Let's search the grounds again!' said Tish resolutely.

'Good idea!' agreed Rebecca. 'Let's really search! She *must* have dumped the cash box somewhere – the thief – she wouldn't dare keep it in school.' They'd been over this so often before. But now Rebecca felt angry, all over again. 'We swore we'd never give up.'

They searched in some really weird places for they had long ago exhausted the more obvious ones. Rebecca climbed the big cedar tree by the main school forecourt and looked along the huge, spreading branches. There was no sign of the cash box, but she was pleased to have something active to do – and at least it was something worthwhile. They even searched St Mary's, the little church that was set in a secluded, tree-shaded corner of the school grounds and was never kept locked. Rebecca felt slightly sacrilegious as she and Sue crawled along on hands and knees, looking under the pews, while Tish and Margot and Mara hunted in the bell tower and Elf kept guard. But, as always, they drew a blank.

They were half-way back to school when a livid scar of lightning lit up the sky; then came a great crash of thunder and the heavens opened. They went running into the sports centre for shelter, at just the same time as Roberta Jones, who came running in on her way back from Willoughby House. She'd heard Miss Gates was over there, giving a Lower Sixth girl a maths tutorial. She'd waited a whole hour, determined to catch the senior mistress when she came out, for she was still upset about the House Lists. Her patience had been rewarded.

'What on earth did Gatesy say?' asked Tish, curiously.

'She listened to me very carefully,' said Roberta. Her hair was wet and she looked bedraggled. 'She asked me a whole lot of questions, she even asked me the name of my last school and whether Max actually taught me there. I can't see what that's got to do with it, mind you. But the main point is,' Roberta's eyes were bright with hope, 'I think maybe I've convinced her that I'm not all that good at maths and would do better in the Beta stream. She's taking a special interest in my case.'

'Poor old Robert!' said Tish, as the big girl went off to find a hair-dryer in the changing rooms. 'Who's she kidding?'

'Was Miss Gates really as polite as all that?' wondered Mara.

'Yes, she was probably stunned,' said Sue.

Rebecca said nothing, for she was experiencing a deep pang of bitterness. If only she and Roberta could change places! Life just wasn't fair.

The others looked at her and knew exactly what she must be thinking.

'Come on, the rain's easing off a bit,' said Elf. 'Let's dash back to Juniper. Looks as though it's going to be wet all afternoon.'

They ran back to the junior boarding house and went along to the Hobbies' Room.

'Let's start to think what we're going to put in the Farewell Issue of the *J.J.*,' said Tish. 'We'll get hold of Susannah.'

'We haven't solved the mystery then,' sighed Mara.

'It's sickening!' Rebecca burst out. 'We've tried so hard. It's sickening to think of the £30 lining somebody's pockets when it could be helping those animals.'

'Miss Morgan said the person would own up before the end of term,' remembered Elf. 'Well, they'd better get a move on, they've only got till Thursday.'

'That's right,' said Rebecca, thinking how upset Miss Morgan had been. 'She said a guilty conscience's a terrible burden to carry around! Well, at this rate, the person concerned's going to have a ton weight on their shoulders all the summer holidays – for the rest of their life, maybe!'

'Got it!' exclaimed Tish. 'The *J.J.*!'

'The *J.J.*?'

'*That's* what we must do. One last appeal to the guilty person. Not just a couple of lines, like we did before. We'll make it the main story, pulling no punches, a full-blooded appeal, saying just what £30 can do for an animal that's ill and in pain –'

'Rebecca must write it!' said Sue, clapping her hands. 'You remember, Rebecca, that marvellous piece you wrote before Charity Week –'

'Who else!' said Tish. Her black curls were full of bounce, she was waving her arms around like the editor of an important daily newspaper instead of a 5p news-sheet. 'Just supposing it works – what a scoop for the *J.J.*! We'll go out on a high! *Will* you write it, Rebeck?'

'I'll try!' said Rebecca eagerly.

'Don't let's ask the guilty person to own up,' said Mara realistically. 'That would be hoping for too much. Let's appeal to them to return the cash box, with the £30 in it, anonymously.'

'Good idea!'

'Where can we ask them to leave it?'

'The church!' said Rebecca. 'Just outside in the porch. No-one goes there much during the week. The girl who took the money – she can sneak over there, through the trees – no-one will see her. We'll tell her she can leave it there, any time, and we'll check every morning before breakfast to see if it's come back.'

'Tell her she's only got till Thursday! Tell her time is running out!' said Margot.

'I think I'll go to the library right now,' said Rebecca, 'and scribble down a few sentences.' There was an intent look in her eyes. 'It's taking shape, what to say. Thanks, Margot, I think I can see how it should go . . .'

'Go on then!' Tish pushed Rebecca towards the door, excitedly. 'Quick, before you lose your inspiration! Try and make it the best thing you've ever written.'

'You bet!' thought Rebecca. 'I want to go out on a high, too.'

The piece that Rebecca wrote won much praise. Tish gave it a simple, direct headline: *Please Get Rid of Your Guilty Conscience, Whoever You Are. This is Your Last Chance*. The words that followed were also simple and direct – and very moving.

The *J.J.* sold round the school on Monday rather faster

than usual. When Miss Morgan delivered the regular order of twenty-four copies to the Staff Room, she did so with pride.

'I've had my ups and downs with them,' she told Mrs Dalzeil, 'but on the whole I think this is the best lot of Second Years I've ever had.'

Rebecca and Co. kept wondering on Monday if the *J.J.* would have any effect on the thief.

'Just think,' said Elf, 'the cash box might be there in the morning.'

'I don't think so,' said Sue. 'That would be too soon. The person needs time to think about it. But as Thursday gets nearer – and it's their last chance to do something before the summer holidays – then maybe it'll really hit them hard. What Rebecca's written.'

'I don't think anything'll happen for a day or two,' agreed Tish.

But they were both wrong.

Late on Monday evening, in the long shadows, a figure dodged through the trees until the church came in sight. St Mary's looked silent and deserted. The only movement came from a bat, swooping down and round in the still night air, making a series of configurations before it darted back into the bell tower.

The figure waited and waited until, convinced that the coast was clear, it crept forward through the little wicket gate and up the path to the church. The huge oak door into the dark porch swung open easily to the touch. The figure entered, took the metal cash box out of a carrier bag and deposited it carefully on the porch seat. Then the person backed out, pulled the porch door shut, turned and walked away up the path.

'Stop!' said a voice.

The culprit stood stock still, then slowly turned.

The porch door had opened again and a sepulchral grey-haired figure stood there, holding the cash box. Miss Gates had been sitting inside the church since sunset, waiting and listening.

'I telephoned Greencourt this morning,' she said in hollow tones, her voice echoing in the porch. 'I suggest we leave the cash box here overnight, so the girls can find it in the morning. I shall make an appointment for us both to see Miss Welbeck after assembly, if that's convenient.'

'Damn,' said Max.

TWELVE

SORTING OUT MAX

The six crept out of the dormitory early, while Jenny and Joanna were still fast asleep, and ran across the school grounds to St Mary's church.

Tish was the first to open the door.

'It's there!' she shrieked.

They all crowded into the porch, blinking in the darkness as they came in from the early morning sun. They stared at the cash box in disbelief. Then they pushed Rebecca forward.

'Go on, Rebecca! You open it!'

Her fingers were shaking as she opened the lid and took out thirty pound coins and counted them. There was a square of paper lying at the bottom of the box. The others crushed round her as she took it out.

'What's it say?'

There was just one word written on the slip of paper, in block capitals:

SORRY

'Oh,' gasped Rebecca. 'Isn't it marvellous?'

She'd sent out a message to somebody unknown, written from the heart – and the message had got through! The person had responded! Responded at once! It was a very special moment for Rebecca.

They ran all the way back to school with the cash box, jubilant.

'I wonder who it was?' said Margot.

'I don't suppose we'll ever know,' said Sue.

'Who cares!' said Rebecca, in awe. 'We've got the money back. We can send it to the Fund now. They've given the money back – and they're sorry! That's all that matters!'

The news spread round the school. By the time Rebecca and Co. went into the dining hall at breakfast time, just about everybody knew. They were greeted by cheers and banging cutlery. Miss Morgan, on duty, hurried over to them as they took their places.

'Well done, all of you!' she said. 'Especially you, Rebecca.'

First lesson was maths and Max didn't turn up. Jacquinda Meredith, the senior prefect, came into the form room to keep order until he arrived.

'How long will he be?' asked Roberta.

'Not very long, now,' replied Jacquinda. 'He had to go and see Miss Welbeck and Miss Gates. They asked to see your exam papers, so he's had to go home and fetch them, but he won't be long.'

A faint stir of interest ran through the room, but Rebecca wasn't even listening. Before the lesson began she'd started reading a P. G. Wodehouse under the desk and was now deeply engrossed.

Roberta Jones nudged Debbie Rickard, hard. Margot had changed places with Roberta some time ago, so that those two could sit next to each other in class.

'I bet it's to do with me!' Roberta whispered. 'I said Miss Gates was going to take a special interest in my case.'

For once she was right.

What was taking place in the principal's study had quite a lot to do with Roberta, though not exactly in the way she imagined, and Miss Gates had indeed taken a special interest in her case.

After catching Max at the church the night before, she'd gone over to Miss Welbeck's house and had a word with her. So when Max entered the principal's study, immediately after morning assembly, there was an icy reception waiting for him. Both women were seated, with their arms folded, not looking in the least friendly.

'Sit down, Dennis,' said Miss Welbeck, nodding towards a chair.

Max threw himself down in the chair, looking rather hangdog. He crossed his knees and flicked some dust off his elegant trousers. Then he smoothed down his dark hair nervously.

'I'm afraid I'm hopeless with money,' he launched forth. 'I was in a dreadful hole that Friday evening when I shoved the cash box in my brief case. I was supposed to be taking some terribly smart friends of Katie's out for a meal, and I'd spent my last quids buying some flowers for Bobbie Jones and having a bit of a party for the rest of the kids . . .'

'I'm sure a member of staff could have given you a loan,' said Miss Welbeck coldly. 'Did that not occur to you?'

'I couldn't find anybody – and Katie was in a furious temper because we were late and –' Max spread his hands out. 'What else could I do? Of course, I had every intention of paying it back. I was going to send an anonymous donation to those animal people in London.'

'And did you?' inquired Miss Gates.

'Well, no. I was just getting round to thinking about it, when I saw what those kids had written in the news-sheet yesterday. I'd no idea they were still brooding about it! So I thought I'd give them a nice surprise. Do what they suggested and take the money over to the church. I didn't think anyone would be spying on me!' he added, quite indignantly.

There was silence for a few moments. It was broken by Miss Welbeck.

'It was a pity there was nobody to jog your memory in similar fashion at Greencourt. Were you going to pay back the money there? The money for the school trip to France, that had been entrusted to your care? And if you were, why did you say it had been stolen from your flat when in fact you'd spent it on a new car?'

Max looked at Miss Welbeck from under his dark lashes and then flicked some more dust from his trouser leg. He was not deeply disturbed.

'I did pay it back, in time. Of course, it was rather a large sum. But I found some way of paying it back. I had the most deadly run of bad luck at Greencourt. I crashed the car and it wasn't insured and I had to have some transport in a hurry – I only borrowed the money.'

'You were very lucky not to go to prison,' said Miss Gates, who had telephoned the headmistress of Greencourt first thing on Monday morning and got the full story from her. 'It was all hushed up.'

'Was it? I wasn't sure. I left the district rather soon after that.'

'Neither the children nor their parents were ever told why you left Greencourt so suddenly. That includes Roberta Jones and her family. The Governors stumped up for the trip to France and the truth never came out. As a matter of fact I talked to Roberta on Saturday about Greencourt and it's quite obvious that she hasn't the slightest inkling.'

'She hasn't?' For the first time Max showed some emotion. A delighted smile lit up his bronzed face. 'Nor her parents? Really?'

'Yes, really,' said Miss Gates, drily. 'So all your efforts this term have, in fact, been a complete waste of time. You have showed her rather special consideration, haven't you? Just in case something might click in her memory? And you really had no need to bother.'

'Hey, that's an unkind thing to say!' Max suddenly looked angry.

'Unkind or not,' broke in Miss Welbeck, 'this brings us to the question of the maths exam. We were both very impressed with the mark that Roberta achieved. I'm afraid it will be necessary for us to check through all the papers.'

'There's nothing peculiar about those!' exclaimed Max. 'If that's what you're thinking.'

'We'd like to check them, all the same,' insisted Miss Welbeck. 'Where are they?'

'They're back at the cottage,' said Max sulkily. 'And Katie's out today in the car, so she can't come and fetch me and beside –' he looked at his watch, 'I'm due to take II Alpha in five minutes.'

Miss Welbeck picked up the internal phone and dialled.

'I'll ask Hodkin to drive you to your cottage so that you can pick up the exam papers. It won't take long,' she said pleasantly. 'Before you leave, I suggest you find a prefect to go and sit in on your class for the time being.'

Fifteen minutes later, Max re-entered the principal's study with II Alpha's maths exam papers rolled up in a bundle under his arm. He plonked them down on Miss Welbeck's leather-topped desk, almost jauntily.

'Here they are. They're all in order.'

He threw himself back in the chair while the two women sorted through the rather dog-eared papers. Miss Gates withdrew two of them and held them up between forefinger and thumb, looking quite shocked.

'Whatever happened to these? They look as though they've been in a washing machine.'

'They blew away into the sea, while I was marking them,' said Max nonchalantly. 'Luckily, I got 'em back and they soon dried out in the sun. The top one's Bobbie's – I mean, Roberta's.'

Miss Gates picked up a pencil and checked through it carefully.

'Hmmmm,' she said at the end. She was a little put out. 'Yes, I make it 61%. Very smudged in places, but that's not her fault. Quite a good paper in fact.'

'I'm glad you agree,' said Max. 'The other one's Rebecca Mason's – hopeless.'

'Let me see both papers,' said Miss Welbeck suddenly.

She examined them, holding each one up in turn, looking to where each girl had written her name, at the top of the first page.

'How do you know which is Roberta's and which is Rebecca's?' she asked.

'Well, their names –' began Max.

'But both names are badly smudged!' observed Miss Welbeck. 'I can make out that they both begin with R and are both the same length, but that's all. And as both girls have very similar handwriting, why are you so sure which is which?'

'Well,' said Max, 'I suppose I just took an inspired guess. If you compare the marks they've had in term, then there's no question –'

'I had the impression that Rebecca had been doing rather better lately,' said Miss Gates. 'I think Pippa –'

'Yes, Pippa Fellowes-Walker has been helping her,' said Max. 'Doing her homework for her too, I expect, so I haven't taken that very seriously.'

'How seriously do you take Roberta's marks through the

term then?' inquired Miss Gates. 'Haven't you been giving *her* a great deal of help?'

'I'm sure Bobbie's done much better than 28%!' said Max, quite heatedly. 'I'm sure I've got the papers the right way round!'

'You *wanted* her to do well. You made up your mind in advance that hers was the good paper and Rebecca's was the bad one,' said Miss Welbeck sharply. 'You may be right. You may be wrong. But you didn't even bother to check! This is disgraceful. Worse than Greencourt. A lot depends on it, as it happens. It's quite essential that we find out which paper is which.'

The principal rose to her feet, her lips set in a hard line.

'Go back to II Alpha and take your maths class, Dennis. Ask Rebecca Mason to come to my study at once and to bring her maths exercise book. Carry on teaching here until Thursday morning, when your contract expires. As far as I'm concerned, that won't be a moment too soon.'

After Max had gone, Miss Gates looked at her watch.

'I have to take a tutorial,' she said.

'Then run along, Evelyn,' said the principal. 'I'll see to Rebecca. By studying her handwriting carefully, I'll soon be able to establish which paper is hers. I wonder which one it is? I must confess, I am going to find this very interesting.'

THIRTEEN

TERM'S END

Rebecca didn't hear Max coming back to the form room. She was well into her book. Since Saturday she'd been buoyed up by the feeling that they were doing something to get the charity money back. That buoyant feeling had come to a head early this morning when the six of them had carried the cash box back to school in triumph. But now the excitement was over, a dull heavy ache had settled back inside her. Term was nearly over now. Next term, all the changes would come. Much better to escape into a book than think about unpleasant things. At the moment, the world of Blandings Castle seemed infinitely preferable to real life.

Roberta, on the other hand, heard Max's footsteps at once.

'He's coming!' she whispered to Debbie. 'I'll be summoned to see the Head now! I wonder what they've decided?'

'Let's cross fingers,' said Debbie, as the door opened.

Max stood framed in the doorway, but didn't come in. To Roberta's annoyance he didn't even look at her. He peered round the door and called to Rebecca, sitting at the back of the class.

'Rebecca Mason. Come out here in the corridor – and bring your maths workbook with you.'

Sue gave her a hard nudge.

Guiltily, Rebecca shoved Wodehouse inside her desk, got her exercise book and went out to join Max in the corridor. She couldn't imagine why he'd called her out there.

The senior prefect gathered together some work she'd been doing and waited for Max to come in and take over. But first he hustled Rebecca along the corridor to the top of the stairs, where they couldn't be seen from the form room.

'Miss Welbeck wants you to go straight to her study,' he said, 'and take that book with you.'

He hesitated, as though he wanted to say something else. Rebecca noticed that he looked rather agitated and she waited expectantly.

'Look, Rebecca,' he glanced around, almost furtively. 'There's only a few minutes of the lesson left now. I don't want you to come back here. When you've seen Miss Welbeck I want you to go straight to the library and sit there and wait for me. And you're to tell *no one* about anything, until we've had a talk. Promise me!'

'The library?' Rebecca was amazed. But she nodded. 'All right then.'

What on earth was going on?

When she entered the study and Miss Welbeck showed her the two exam papers, all withered and smudged, Rebecca stared at them in shock.

'Whatever happened to them?' she blurted out.

'An accident,' Miss Welbeck said hastily. 'The point is, Rebecca, the names are smudged. Which one is yours?'

'That one!' said Rebecca promptly, pointing.

'Let's make quite sure, shall we?' said Miss Welbeck,

holding out her hand for Rebecca's workbook. She took it and opened it at random, then checked it carefully against the two exam papers on her desk. 'Yes, you are quite right.'

She closed Rebecca's exercise book and handed it back. She was smiling.

'You achieved 61% in the maths exam. Well done.'

'61%!' gasped Rebecca. 'But –'

'The 28% belongs to Roberta Jones, I'm afraid. There's been a mix-up. These things happen.'

'Then –' A feeling of great joy was welling up inside Rebecca. 'Does that mean I might go up into III Alpha after all – into Court House like the others?'

'Without question,' nodded the principal. 'Run back to your lesson now. Don't say anything to Roberta Jones, yet. I'll arrange for Miss Gates to break the news to her as soon as possible.'

Break the news! As she left the study, Rebecca wanted to laugh, hysterically. Roberta wasn't exactly going to be upset! But even her happiness wouldn't possibly match Rebecca's at that moment. She was delirious.

She wanted to run back up the stairs, whooping for joy, and rush straight into the form room and whisper the good news to Tish and Sue and Margot and Elf! And then find Mara!

But she steadied herself. The library! She'd promised Max. She had to get a grip on herself and go and sit quietly in the library and wait for him.

'He wants to apologize!' thought Rebecca as she sat in the big window seat, waiting. She should have felt furious with him, but she didn't. She felt quite light-hearted with happiness. 'He let the sea get on the exam papers! He must have been down on that rock again, when he marked them! Isn't that just typical! Oh, I can't wait to tell Tish and Sue, they'll see the funny side . . .'

She started to smile to herself and she was still smiling when Max walked into the library. One look at her face told him the truth.

'So I *did* get the papers the wrong way round, after all!' he groaned, covering his face with his hands in mock shame and then sitting down next to her. 'Did I?'

'Yes!' said Rebecca happily.

'I want to apologize –' he began.

'No, it's all right!' said Rebecca, starting to get to her feet. She didn't want to listen to Max's apologies. She'd spare him that! She wanted to find her friends – *now*. Before biology started! 'I'm glad it's been sorted out.'

'No, wait.' He grabbed her arm, urgently, and pulled her back down on to the seat. 'Don't go. It's not only that I want to apologize, though I do, of course. It's Roberta.'

Rebecca stared at him in surprise. He seemed very agitated.

'I expect Miss Welbeck's told you that it was me who pinched your charity money and that I got the sack from Greencourt, but –'

Rebecca's head began to spin dizzily. *Max* – the charity money! Greencourt! That was the school that Roberta used to go to! She remembered her happy cry, on the very first morning of term: *'I remember! You were at Greencourt!'* And suddenly Rebecca had a vivid mental picture of Max, his back to the class, chalking up a number then freezing – freezing at Roberta's words! Of course. Why had she never, never suspected anything?

Although Rebecca's face portrayed her astonishment, Max just went rattling on. Gradually his words began to untangle in her brain.

'I soon realized that Bobbie didn't remember any scandal,' he was saying, 'but I could never be sure that something might not stir in her memory, especially if she found she didn't like me. So I set out to pretend that I liked her a lot and hoped it would make her like *me* a lot.'

'It did,' said Rebecca. 'And she still does.'

'I realize that. But you needn't look so disgusted. I started off only pretending that I liked Bobbie, but after a while I found to my amazement that I really *did* like her. I still do. I like her very much.'

He looked Rebecca straight in the eye and she knew that he was speaking the truth. Now she knew why he was agitated.

'She'd never believe you if she knew all this, would she?' murmured Rebecca.

'No,' said Max. 'I think it would be desperately sad if Bobbie found out about what happened at Greencourt.'

'So do I,' said Rebecca.

'It would make her think everything was a sham,' said Max. 'Which it wasn't. Can you keep it from everybody?'

'I can't keep all this from my two best friends,' said Rebecca. Her mind was feeling rather numb. 'That would be just too much to ask. But – we – the three of us, we'll make sure that Roberta never, ever finds out.'

'You will?' They both stood up. Max looked tremendously relieved. 'And Miss Welbeck or Gatesy wouldn't ever say anything to her, would they?'

'Of course not!' said Rebecca. She wanted to add: *Whatever made you think that they'd told me?* But she didn't.

Roberta had to go and see Miss Gates during the biology lesson and she came back, smiling, just in time for morning break.

'You'll be getting some good news very soon, Rebecca,' she said. 'I've already had mine. I'm going into III Beta after all, because of my maths – so I'll be in Norris House with

Debbie and the twins! What's more, you can have my place in Court House and in III Alpha as well.'

Rebecca, Tish and Sue all nodded and smiled and said nothing.

'Of course, Gatesy would never have agreed to it in a million years. It was Max. He knew how much I wanted to be with my friends and so he wangled it somehow. Told them some fantastic story about our marks getting mixed up. D'you think that could possibly be true?'

'Well, I suppose it's possible,' said Rebecca.

'No,' Roberta shook her head. She looked animated, almost pretty. She never ever wore her hair in those lumpy plaits these days. 'I think he did it for me. Well, you as well,' she added hastily.

There was a faraway look in her eyes.

'I can hardly believe that the term's almost over and he'll be going. I'll never forget Max, as long as I live. He really is a very wonderful person.'

'One of the best,' said Tish.

As Debbie came up and bore Roberta away, Rebecca and her two closest friends exchanged looks. Soon, very soon now, Max was just going to be a beautiful memory for Roberta. They would never do anything to spoil it.

Tish and Sue each took Rebecca by the hand.

'Come on, let's find the other three,' said Sue.

'Mara's got a cake –' said Tish. 'It's covered in chocolate icing and little sweets – it's been hidden away in Miss Morgan's office since Saturday morning!'

'Why?' asked Rebecca.

'Her father sent it for an end-of-term celebration. We just didn't know what to do with it. We haven't felt like a celebration, any of us.'

'Until now!' said Sue. She laughed and flicked back a

strand of sandy-coloured hair from her forehead. 'We know exactly what to do with it now!'

'You bet!' cried Rebecca in delight – and off they ran.

Term's end was full of goodbyes.

Goodbye to Juniper House and dormitory number six with its primrose-coloured walls and big windows and its view of the sea. Goodbye to Miss Morgan, the junior House Mistress. They would never be juniors again! Goodbye to the *J.J.* which had given them so much fun and plenty of drama, too. Susannah Skelhorn would be its editor next term.

Goodbye to Audrey Maxwell, who had produced a brilliant issue of the *Trebizon Journal* in her last term, with the juniors well represented in it. And to Jacquinda Meredith and Joanne Hissup, who were both going up to Oxford, and all the rest of the Upper Sixth. Goodbye to their form-mistress, Miss Heath, and the funny little II Alpha form room stuck up high in old building.

Rebecca's first year at Trebizon was over.

As well as the goodbyes, she said a special thank-you to Pippa for helping her with her maths.

'In a way, though you don't know it, you've helped *me*,' said Pippa.

'I have?' asked Rebecca in surprise.

Pippa, who would be going into the Upper Sixth next term, had been voted in as next year's editor of the *Trebizon Journal*.

'It was neck and neck,' said Pippa, 'and I think the thing that really decided it was the illustrations I did for your essay, *A Winter's Morning*, remember?'

Rebecca was never likely to forget her prize-winning essay in the school magazine the previous term. For her, it had been a high point of the year.

'The drawings were beautiful!' she exclaimed. 'That snowman – and the birds. And the poor little squirrel, frozen in the ice.'

'But it was what you'd written that sparked them off! So you see, Rebecca, I've got something to thank *you* for. I've always wanted to be editor of the *Trebizon* one day.' She looked very happy at that moment. 'I never, ever thought I would be!'

Rebecca wasn't really convinced that she'd had very much to do with it, but she felt a surge of pleasure, all the same.

Then something else happened, on the last morning of term, that brought even greater pleasure – it was so totally unexpected.

'I'm sorry you won't be coming to the County Sports with us this afternoon, Rebecca,' said Miss Willis.

Rebecca was silent, as all the old disappointment over that returned with a dull thud. Her parents were back home in London now, just back. How different things might have been! They might have been coming down to the west country today, to see her run this afternoon, as Tish's family were.

'But I've got some good news for you on a different front,' continued the blonde games mistress. 'You can count yourself lucky that you were born in this county –'

Rebecca wondered what was coming next. It was true that, by some fluke, Mr Mason had been working in the west country when Rebecca was born, although they'd returned to London when she was three months old.

Suddenly Rebecca realized what *might* be coming next and a thrill of shock ran down her spine. That tall lady who'd been walking round the tennis courts with Miss Willis recently, watching some of them play – the county tennis scout, someone had said!

'That's right, Rebecca,' said Sara Willis, reading her face. 'You've been "spotted" as having special promise. You've been selected for a new county scheme for junior players – indoor training in the winter months. Your parents will be getting a letter, giving all the details.'

'Me?' Rebecca felt dizzy with excitement. 'But I've only just started –' Something else to thank Pippa for!

'It's the promise that counts.' The teacher laughed. 'I can see us losing you from athletics again next summer. But, am I right? I think you prefer tennis.'

'Well –' Rebecca was still feeling rather stunned. She'd never thought about it deeply until this moment. 'Why, yes . . . maybe I do.'

Tish and Sue hugged her when they heard the news. They went for a last exhilarating surf-ride together before they packed. The bay looked at its most glorious. Later, just before dinner, they joined up with the other three and went and had a look at Court House from the outside. It was a lovely, rambling old place covered in Virginia creeper, on the far side of the Hilary.

'And that's where we'll be living for the next three years,' sighed Mara, a peaceful expression on her face.

'They share studies in threes,' said Elf. 'We must bag two right next door to each other.'

'Studies!' said Margot.

They continued to gaze at Court House.

'Not bad, is it?' said Tish.

'Not bad at all!' agreed Rebecca.

After dinner, everything broke up. Max was the first to go. The familiar red sports car drew up in the main forecourt to collect him. He came jauntily down the steps for the last time. A small gaggle of admirers waited to see him off, with Roberta Jones in the forefront.

He gave them all a wave, hesitated, then walked across to

Roberta and kissed her gently on the cheek – 'Goodbye, Bobbie!' – before climbing into the car.

Roberta waved and waved until the car was out of sight and then linked arms with Debbie Rickard.

Upstairs, in the panelled study, Miss Welbeck and Miss Gates had been standing by the window and had watched his departure.

'I made a mistake with that young man,' murmured the principal.

'He was a dead loss,' said Miss Gates.

Miss Welbeck gazed out through the window at Roberta Jones and Debbie Rickard, walking arm in arm, past the big cedar tree which was an oasis of dappled shade in the strong July sunlight. Their heads were close together and Debbie, no doubt, was comforting Roberta.

'No, Evelyn,' she said at last, with the merest hint of a smile. 'His presence here was not all loss. Not entirely.'

Even Rebecca would have agreed with that.

Also by Anne Digby

ME, JILL ROBINSON AND THE TELEVISION QUIZ

Moving to Haven is full of unexpected excitements for the Robinson family. But for Jill, making friends with the high-spirited daughter of the town's mayor makes it all worth while.

However, Melinda isn't everyone's favourite person, least of all her father's. So when she gets the chance to compete in a television quiz, she really hopes that at last he will be proud of her. But it isn't that simple.

ME, JILL ROBINSON AND THE SEASIDE MYSTERY

Keeping an eye on her younger brother, Tony, certainly makes the Robinsons' seaside holiday an exciting one for Jill. Why does he keep disappearing on his own, and who is his new friend, Sam? Dad gets more and more angry with Tony, so Jill and her best friend Lindy try to solve the mystery, only to find themselves in real trouble!

ME, JILL ROBINSON AND THE CHRISTMAS PANTOMIME

Jill's sister, Sarah, is helping Roy Brewster produce the Youth Club's Christmas panto and Jill is dying for a leading role. It looks set to be great fun for Jill and Lindy, until the Runcorn boys get involved and spoil it for everyone. But Jill discovers that their leader, Big Harry, isn't as tough as he makes out.

ME, JILL ROBINSON AND THE SCHOOL CAMP ADVENTURE

When Jill and Lindy start looking after a stray dog at the school camp on a remote Scottish island, the scheming Rita is determined to get them into trouble and Miss Rawlings threatens to take Cu away from them. But when Rita goes missing on the mysterious island it is only Cu who can find her.

ME, JILL ROBINSON AND THE PERDOU PAINTING

Jill is really excited when Polly Pudham invites her home for tea because 'Pud' lives in the most expensive road in Haven. But why is Jill so interested in the painting Polly's father has just bought? And what happens when Jill's sister goes to the Pudhams' cocktail party to see the painting – what is she *supposed* to have done?

ME, JILL ROBINSON AND THE STEPPING STONES MYSTERY

Feelings in Haven Youth Club run high when it is decided how to spend its hard-earned money. Not everyone is in favour of Roy Brewster's cracking idea to transform the river at the stepping stones bend . . . Then the bridge-building project is sabotaged! But who could have done it? Sir Harry, the local landowner, Jill's brother, Tony, or perhaps someone from the club? Jill and Lindy are determined to find out.